The River by Starlight

The River
by Starlight

A NOVEL

Ellen Notbohm

SHE WRITES PRESS

Published TK
Printed in the United States of America
Print ISBN: 978-1-63152-335-9
E-ISBN: 978-1-63152-336-6
Library of Congress Control Number: 2017957716

For information, address:
She Writes Press
1563 Solano Ave #546
Berkeley, CA 94707

Interior design by Tabitha Lahr

She Writes Press is a division of SparkPoint Studio, LLC.

For my once-in-two-lifetimes man

Part One

The evening star, multiplied by undulating water, is like bright sparks of fire continually ascending.

—"The River by Starlight," from the journal of Henry David Thoreau, June 15, 1852

1

Of all the heartless things Annie's mother has done in twenty-six years, this might be the corker. She did it in a manner most unusual for her, did it without raising her chapped hand or equally chapped voice. Did it with silent duplicity undiscovered until this morning by her youngest child, who should know better than to allow it to shock her.

The unread letter sizzles in Annie's fingers, as if it's her fault she hasn't read it yet. Her brother Cal intended it for her alone. Her name, Analiese Rushton, sprawls across the full width of the envelope, the ink-splotch dot of the *i* sailing high as a jackdaw over the scrawl. Cal's rogue humor leers up at her from where he penned the address, *Cherry Pit, Iowa*, crossed out *Pit*, and block printed *Hill*. She wouldn't have found the letter had not she wanted to settle the doctor's bill before he leaves, had she not had to lift the iron cashbox out of the drawer of Pa's desk to jimmy the crotchety latch. The letter's postmark, so bold she can hear the stamp striking the envelope: *January 11, 1911*. At least five months this letter has lain in dark limbo, hidden in the lowest reaches of a desk everyone still tiptoes around.

A single minute is all she would need to separate the message from its envelope and lay eyes upon news Ma found dire enough to keep from Annie in such a devious way. But Doc's step descending the stairs melds with the scrape of the front door. That would be her sister, Jenny, exchanging murmured greetings with the doctor. Annie shoves the letter into her apron pocket and removes two bills from the cashbox.

In the parlor, Annie meets Jenny with a squeeze of hands. It brings a pang of relief that won't last. This day will be but a protraction of the previous one.

Jenny pushes a strand of Annie's hair from her forehead. "You look tired. Bad night?"

Annie nods. A bad night, yes. For their mother, calling brokenly for her dead husband and son. And for Annie, the only one to answer.

To the doctor she says, "Well?"

The doctor places his bag on the parlor table. "Hard to say how much longer. Partly depends on her—we know your ma can be tenacious as tar." He sucks in a long, noisy breath. "Thirty-three years she's hung on, since Teddy's gone," he says, separating each syllable like a spelling lesson.

Yes, a firstborn now dead nearly three times longer than he lived, forever twelve in the mind of a mother who has relentlessly, irrationally tortured her lastborn for it. *Leave,* Annie entreats behind her teeth. *You're no healer.*

But the doctor talks on, turning to Jenny. "You and Cal were this high." He stair-steps a hand at hip level. "Your mother wanted to lie down and go right along with your brother." To Annie he says, "The Lord spared you the sorrow of that day."

Annie seethes, a wave of anger breaking against the chronic heartsickness this man never sees in her. Decades of his fawning over her mother's deforming grief, and he's blind to the never-ending ransom she's demanded of Annie, born seven years after the fact.

"She's ready to join him, and your pa," the doctor continues. He unhooks his tiny spectacles and folds them with an anemic click. "Just keep her as comfortable as you can." He turns to Jenny. "Might I trouble you for a glass of water?"

Jenny disappears into the kitchen in a graceful swish of calico.

"Her discomfort may increase," the doctor says to Annie, lifting from his bag a brown glass bottle. "Laudanum. Mix it with strong tea. This much to ease the pain, as needed." He indicates with a fingertip. "This much if . . ." His finger moves up the bottle. He purses his lips.

Annie clutches the fabric inside her pockets. "You think I would do that?"

That crazy Rushton girl. She doesn't need special powers to read his thoughts or those of a town that loves to talk not-quite-under its breath.

"For pain." The doctor drops his full weight on the word.

"I wouldn't do that." She hands the bills to the doctor. He places the brown bottle on the parlor table and folds the money into a vest pocket as Jenny reappears with a glass of water. The doctor wets his lip and hands the glass back to her. "Please give my best to Seth and your fine boy."

Another wordless glance at Annie and he's gone, leaving her heart pounding. He got the last word with that glance, didn't he? A rebuke it was, but for what? The laudanum, or her own lost husband and child, gone now these six years and forever? The clack of hooves and buggy wheels leaps down the drive, then melts into the distance.

"Don't like that man," Annie says.

"He delivered you." Jenny smiles. "That counts for a lot with me."

The brown bottle squats on the parlor stand. Annie eyes it, thinking, *Whose side are you on?* Purveyor of relief, or guilt? Or both? Perhaps her mother would thank her for speeding her reunion with Teddy and Pa. Or perhaps the remorse of having played God would only add to the deadweight Annie already carries.

Damn that man! Annie shakes her head to clear it. What passed for sleep last night was no more than skimming at the surface of consciousness for a few hours. *Keep her as comfortable as you can.* What does he think she's been doing?

"I wish every day anew that I could be of more help to you," Jenny says. "She was such a different mother to me."

The letter in Annie's pocket threatens to smolder a hole through what remains of her composure, so she says only, "We can wish in one hand and spit in the other and see which fills up first, eh?" She gives her sister a playful thump on the arm. "You can't help more, not without neglecting your own family." Nor can their brother Chase do more, having taken full charge of the farm since Pa died. *Pa died.* How long will it be before Annie can confront those two words without choking?

When the poplar windbreak crowds Jenny's buggy from sight, Annie sinks into Pa's porch chair and takes the letter from her pocket. It feels weightless, as if it still might find a way to comply with Ma's intentions and make itself not exist. The slit across the top of the envelope is as cruel a violation as a paper cut to the skin, a surface injury that brings pain far out of proportion to the wound.

Cal seldom writes to anyone, rarely stays in one place long enough to send home the same postmark twice. But this thickly inked mark—*Caswell, Montana*—is his third in three years. The letter ranges over two pages, his devil-may-care scrawl honking across the paper like geese before the gale.

> Li'l Bit, think seriously about coming out here. My homestead is only 37 acres, but it's mine, with less than two years until I prove up. I work out on the Dunbarton farm a few miles from here, for extra income. My place is cozy (to put it kindly), but you don't take up much room (clobber me when you get here!). Your old bachelor brother could use some help with the things you're good at. What's holding you to Iowa anyway?

Annie tries to swallow. If she nails her feet to the porch, she might keep herself from storming a dying widow's bedroom and throttling an explanation out of her. Concealing this letter amounts to yet another act of war in a lifelong conflict. Annie's fault, everything always her fault. The beans tasting off because her five-year-old fingers shelled them imperfectly. Ma being unable to enjoy the hymns at church because Annie sat too far back in the pew, still as a dressmaker's form. Annie's fault, the blood staining her socks where she jammed them between her legs when her first monthly came, Ma snorting at Jenny's reprimand: she couldn't have known Annie's time was close, didn't think to prepare her. To Annie it's been death by a thousand cuts, except that she's managed to deflect the thousandth cut a thousand times. Why would Ma hold back this letter? Five months ago, before her illness, when Pa was still alive, this should have been her gold-plated opportunity to rid herself of her unwelcome daughter. Her lifelong refrain, telling Annie how Teddy played "Amazing Grace" on his mouth organ before every blessed Sunday dinner. "That's why I named you Analiese. It's German for 'grace,'" she'd announce, every time as if it were news, and always adding, "Not that you have any."

Standing now in the doorway of her parents' bedroom, Annie can't find her voice. The letter suddenly outweighs her. She needs both hands to hold it up, letting it speak for itself.

"So." Ma's spidery hair encloses her withered neck. Whether she's unable or unwilling to say more, Annie can't tell.

"'So'? That's it? 'So'? Why did you keep this from me? It's your chance to be rid of me. Your heart's desire. If you weren't going to give it to me, why didn't you destroy it?" It's just like Ma to play dead, unmoved and unmoving. Annie strides to the foot of the bed. "Ma, you've always had tongue enough for ten rows of teeth when it comes to me. You owe me an explanation. I'm sure it's ugly. Let's have it now before I—"

"All right." Ma still has the power to halt conversation.

Annie clenches the letter against her waist.

"I knew I was ill. For some time before I let on. There was nothing Doc could do." The words come as unapologetic wind over a dry streambed. "With Pa gone, if you left, it would do Chase in. His hands are full running the place. He postponed his wedding. He—" Ma's hand twitches on the coverlet, the purple map of veins pulsing in obstinacy. "I meant for you to find the letter after I'd gone. I didn't see where another year would make a difference to you."

How much more, Annie wonders, can this woman exact from her? That Annie's days are so meaningless as to justify conscription, that the role of servile divorcee is her only place? "How dare you?" she breathes behind unmoving lips.

And yet. How must it be for Ma, to die as consumed by a bitter heart as by cancer. To be dependent upon the mercy of one she has so spurned. Annie suddenly realizes she has neither the stomach nor the stamina to continue a battle whose end is in sight. She needn't win; she needn't retreat. She need only let the clock run out. Annie slides the letter back into her pocket.

"So be it, Amanda," Annie says. "I am my mother's keeper." As she does every morning, she opens the family Bible to the book of Ecclesiastes, her mother's favorite, and reads aloud:

The thing that hath been, it is that which shall be;
And that which is done is that which shall be done:
And there is no new thing under the sun.

As Annie reads, Amanda drifts into unconsciousness. A tear escapes her right eye and courses a shallow path until stopped by a jutting cheekbone. On the opposite side, a trickle of wetness trails from the corner of her mouth along the deep groove that should have been a laugh line. The two strands of dampness frame Amanda's face, incongruous parentheses. *Here is where I'm supposed to forgive her,* Annie thinks. The fragrance of the violet that clings to the heel that crushes it. It won't happen. Annie stoops under the weightier burden of forgiving herself.

I lost my firstborn too, Ma. Except she's not dead. She lives, calling someone else her mother.

How she prayed, when she felt the flutter of her child deep within her, *Please don't let me be my mother's daughter, oh, anything but that,* never imagining something even worse: a diabolical treachery of her own mind that left her no choice but to forsake husband and child. Forced to come back to this house, the very place she'd left so joyously less than a year before, forced to live again under the thumb of humiliation. Ma, who wielded words like an ice pick, also knew how to wound by withholding them, knew the power of her long months of mocking silence.

To err is human; to forgive, divine.

Not yet. Amanda sleeps, and Annie wonders, *What dreams color such a sleep? What deeds haunt the sunset of one's life?* The secrets Amanda felt justified in keeping, the dreams she kept her daughter from dreaming?

And Pa, did he dream? Or did he, like his daughter, forget how? Annie knew Ma's antagonism troubled him, and that if he'd had more fight in him, he would have given it to Annie gladly. But he'd left it on the battlefield at Bentonville, blacking out when the shrapnel buried itself in his neck. Forevermore, he told her, he would wake each morning with the feeling he was missing something. If his dreams died long before his being did, Annie understands.

To dream again. Cal's letter has touched a match to the wick of her doused dreams. Dream enough it is for her to stroll the length of a town without the abortive glances, the stilted greetings, the wider berth given her on the sidewalk.

Amanda sleeps. Annie tucks the Bible, open to Ecclesiastes, under her mother's loosening hand, whispering, "To every thing there is a season, and a time to every purpose under heaven."

Annie dreams, in the arms of her father's porch chair, gazing west across their tiny corner of Iowa.

Amanda clung to life until the July morning of Annie's birthday, when she opened her eyes for the space of four weakening heartbeats. "Analiese?" she murmured. "Grace." Annie rested her hand over her mother's. The last word between them would be hers. She wished only for enough grace to lend it sincerity.

"Peace."

It lasted as long as the moment in which it was needed. It wasn't forgiveness, but it was as close as she could come.

Annie takes the arm Chase offers for the walk to the grave site. "My marriage won't change anything," Chase tells Annie. "Lavinia agrees, you stay on the farm for as long as you want. It will always be as much your home as mine."

The gash in the ground looks deeper than six feet, but Annie doesn't step close enough to see the bottom. Portal to heaven or hell, she has no curiosity.

"The wisdom of the world comes to but four words," intones the minister. "Words that caution us in our hour of pride and elation, and comfort us during times of trial. Four words that make a sad man happy, and a happy man sad: 'This too shall pass.'"

And four more words, Annie thinks. *I'm going to Montana.*

A week following the funeral seems enough time. Over glasses of lemonade on Jenny's porch swing, Annie reaches into her pocket. Sweaty finger marks dot the edges of Cal's letter where she's opened and refolded it a hundred times, fuzzy slits forming in the creases.

Jenny reads the letter without expression. A hot breeze whooshes through, making the screen door cough on its hinges. Annie follows Jenny's eye to the bottom of the page, preempting any reaction Jenny might attempt with "I'm going to accept Cal's offer. I'll write to him tonight."

"Are you sure?" Jenny's calm surprises Annie. Did she already know? "No one is running you out of here."

No one is running her out. And no one, not even Jenny, would beg her to stay. In this town, she will always be a woman apart.

For six years, her husband has maintained silence on the

subject of their divorce. Thomas Day remarried within the year, a girl from Nebraska who'd come to town to visit family. Annie understood his haste. A baby needs a mother. He rented a farm two townships west; there would be no awkward chance meetings on the streets of Cherry Hill.

"Yes, I'm sure," Annie says, just as calm as Jenny, feeling the distance opening between them already. They could be discussing butter and eggs.

"I've never pried, have I?" Jenny asks, sounding as far off as the back of the hayloft. "Forgive me for what I still don't understand. How could you leave your husband, your baby? How have you survived that?"

Even Jenny. Six years. Annie tosses her lemonade over the porch rail and watches it soak into the ground. Moments ago it swirled prettily in a ruby tumbler, and now it's nothing but a darkened splotch, the color of a lost cause. After a while Annie says, "You know the answer to both those questions. I had to."

From the moment Annie consented to marry Thomas Day, she considered her job as his wife as much a covenant with herself as with him. The full moon over their wedding supper had not yet waned before Annie was pregnant, and before anyone else could see the evidence, she had sewn, knitted, and quilted a year's layette. Her lush vegetable garden surged across the yard; she managed meals effortlessly, tending teams of pots and bowls with practiced motion, pausing to turn the pages of a book, a slim volume of Emily Dickinson, on the counter. *Were I with thee, / Wild nights should be / Our luxury!* She handled money like a banker, tended their chickens and livestock with deft respect. She saw Thomas off to the fields each day, both of them reveling in the rhythm of life unfolding as it should in their little corner of Iowa.

Then the baby came.

A heavy curtain dropped on their brief happiness. The Annie who rose from childbed was a creature neither of them knew, rocking maniacally in her chair and wishing it would go over backward and finish the charade.

She could not understand the rages that engulfed her, dropping out of the sky like the cyclone three years before that tossed their barn, cows and all, into the northeast forty. But she understood enough to be scared, for herself and for the bundle of suffocating obligation that was her newborn daughter.

Instead of moving on, as cyclones always do, this twister of the soul remained in place, spinning and roaring and draining her of everything she knew to be Annie. Nineteen years of becoming, undone and gone. In creating a new life, she'd been robbed of hers. Her sweet, forbearing Thomas. She tried to tell him that the baby was a tourniquet, squeezing until her sensibilities spilled from her ears. *It's sucking the life right out of me.* She must have uttered it aloud that night. Thomas materialized at her side, bending over the rocker where she nursed. "*She,*" he said, "not *it.* Cynthia is a *she.*" Her arms went slack around the baby, who pulled herself into a ball of clenched limbs, anxious mouth searching for the breast that should have still been there. The whimpers escalated to wails. Annie yanked the blanket tighter. Swaddling was supposed to quiet babies, but not this one, not this howling lump of never enough, this potato with lungs.

Annie, who also used to be a she, not an it, leaned her dead weight back in the new rocking chair Thomas had insisted upon, the one with the stout caning stretched across the lower back and seat. Cooler, Thomas had said, for a mother nursing a late-summer baby. Cooler, was it? Heaving to and fro in the chair, Annie couldn't remember a time when the sensation of being on fire wasn't her omnipresent warden.

But outside, almost four interminable months later, it was cooler, oh yes. The frozen branches of the poplars flailed in the dry wind. When the bough breaks, the cradle will fall.

I wouldn't be that lucky.

Annie hated her own thoughts as they wormed their maggoty way through her. For weeks upon weeks, Thomas refused to believe what she tried to tell him, that she must give the baby up, that she yearned to be free of her torment. He said it was the voice of exhaustion speaking, nothing more. She felt herself ebbing away by the day, and his feeble explanations and pleas couldn't dam the slide. She avoided his eyes when he came in at sundown each night, as he swallowed his cold suppers without comment, stroked her sweat-soaked hair, and gave no voice to what she knew he must have been wondering, the question under which she cowered every minute of each eternity of a day. How much longer would they have to hang on to ride out the inexplicable possession of the woman who used to be Annie?

At 2:00 a.m. on a bitter December night, she lay rigid in their bed, grinding her teeth until her jaw spasmed. Somewhere beyond the bedroom door, their infernal cows set to bawling again. What blight on their boring bovine existence could have started them up in the dead of night? Beside her, Thomas stirred. "Baby's hungry." It came to her as an apology. From someplace remote, a voice eerily like hers snapped their life in two.

"I don't give a damn." All of a sudden the picture came into focus. She saw right through him, into a vast world beyond this tiresome corner of Iowa. She saw the kindness and decency in her husband's soul and heard the fear in his voice. *This is his doing,* she thought, and watched a disembodied fist smash into his face. The crack of the cheekbone under her blow felt good. *I told him the baby was too much for me, but did he listen?*

Then the disembodied fist flew on disembodied feet down the hallway, where it joined up with the disembodied voice, screeching as she rifled the kitchen cabinets, crocks of relish and jam crashing to the floor, "Where, oh where, do we keep the rat poison?"

Down the hall, Thomas secured the door of the nursery, muffling the squalling baby, and stood there, rooted and mute as an elm, arms crossed, feet apart, a blackening contusion spreading under his eye.

The remaining scraps of Annie fought their way to the surface and died on contact with the horror she had created. What little of her was left could still walk, must walk, across the house, out the front door, and who knew, who cared where. The baby sobbed for all of them, louder at first. But a mother's most sacred duty is to protect her baby, no matter the cost.

So Annie stumbled on, until the cries quieted under a blanket of distance.

Who could fault Thomas for understanding less about women's rages that drop from the sky than she did herself, and for coming to a swift decision based on what he did understand?

She can still feel the paper in her hands, igniting her fingers, her eyes, her guts.

This Plaintiff states that because of the actions and threats made by this Defendant, his life and the life of his daughter are imperiled. Plaintiff hereby prays that he may be granted an absolute Decree of Divorce from this Defendant and that he may be awarded the custody of his daughter.

She spent the first night buried in Ma and Pa's hayloft, hoping to suffocate or die of rat bite, knowing that Ma would turn her away in the morning. And she did. Annie was halfway to Jenny's place when Pa caught up with her.

Three more months the formless demons stalked her, stealing her sleep, drawing it out of her like a rope of pearls, snapping the string, sending the gems bounding. She pulled the shades and barricaded the doors, begging Pa to install locks on a house that had never known them. She dressed in light colors that matched the day—blue, gray, dull yellow—frantically changing to dark colors come dusk, hoping to blend in, to escape the vindictive sentinels. Winter, indifferent as ever, encrusted her misery with its extravagant monotony.

On a morning a few days shy of the vernal equinox, she awoke to the sun pouring into a silent house. She fancied herself dead, but as she moved barefoot down the hall, she realized that it was Sunday; her family had gone to church. At the top of the stairs, she clutched the post and wept with a strange joy, still chained by anguish but pulling the links apart one by one. The face in the hallway mirror was her own; the spacious expanse of her thoughts was once again her own.

That night she sat on the leather hassock, resting her head in her father's lap. She told him it was over; the maggots were gone. He held her close and said sadly, "No one understands this."

To this day, no one ever has, though one almost did.

She couldn't afford an attorney. Kindly, retired Judge Owen was the only person she felt she could ask. In the book-lined parlor of his home, she tried to explain: "I was ill. I was scared. I've recovered. I want my daughter." The judge listened contemplatively. No point in fighting it, he advised Annie. She'd done what she'd done and no court would side with her. "The law is meted out by men," he added in a minor key. At the door the judge said, "My sister heard the demons after her boy was born."

Annie closes her eyes. If he said more, she can't recollect it.

She'll bid her beloved sister goodbye without telling her that Cal slyly planted the idea of Montana a year ago, when he sent her an odd little thimble. A red band with raised lettering encircled it: FOR DRY GOODS GO TO COFFEEN'S. Annie rolled the strange, shiny thing about in her hand, appreciating his thought but feeling at the time that pricking her finger and falling asleep for a hundred years sounded appealing. She kept the thimble anyway, as proof, however crude, that someone far away cared about her enough to spare a postage stamp.

The touch of Jenny's palm cupping her cheek brings her back to the present. "Annie, I'll miss you terribly. But I won't insult you by trying to change your mind."

"Thank you for that." Annie picks up her bonnet and leaves, blurry-eyed, without looking back.

That evening, she writes to Cal. *This Thursday's child has far to go. Can you meet me at the evening train on August 5?*

She pulls Pa's pebbled leather satchel from under the bed, the warm, faded brown grain so like the arms that used to circle her in his lap, reading aloud the newspaper's "Daddy's Hour" story.

Pa.

Recollection and loss gather in her throat. The loose joints of the bag fall open, releasing wafts of brilliantine, licorice drops, charcoal-ironed shirts. This is how she'll take Pa with her.

The familiar smells and the open satchel buoy her. She's been too long without hope, and now it's hers for the price of a train ticket. She and Cal will be a family. The homestead will bloom and flourish. In time she may consider filing on a homestead of her own. A resplendent thought indeed. To be mistress of her own land and life. Oh, the delicious liberty of the thought. The pursuit of happiness.

The satchel will hold her aspirations. She's taking little else. *Travel light,* Cal's letter warned. *Whatever I don't have, there's no space for.*

A few clothes, her ivory knitting needles, her grandmother's rose glass jar. At the linen trunk at the foot of her bed, she hesitates. She cracks the lid, then slips a hand past the sheets and slipcases. She extracts a book from the bottom.

She can't say why she finds comfort in the poetry of Emily Dickinson, even less why she would consider taking this book with her, this knife in the wound perpetually salted.

To fight aloud is very brave,
But gallanter, I know,
Who charge within the bosom,
The cavalry of woe.

It's just a book of poetry, she tells herself. The problem is the inscription: *Birthday wishes for my Analiese, with everlasting love, Thomas.* Who would have thought that everlasting love would die within months, that this book would be the sole gift he would ever give her? Pressing her thumb against the binding, she rips out the inscription page and crushes it into a marble-sized ball. She slides the book to the bottom of the satchel. Perhaps she, like Dickinson, will spend her life unmarried. She'll have this slim book to hold when those rare moments strike, when she relives the luxury of being held and recalls that someone desired her, however fleetingly.

Atop the satchel she lays her train ticket. At the end of the train ride waits a clean slate. For dry goods she'll go to Coffeen's. Everything else she intends to find within herself.

2

The Prairie Dog Saloon, Caswell's hoariest, simmers with its usual stew of Friday-night leftovers. Clots of railroad workers jabber in rapid-fire Chinese, Italian, Japanese. The commercial travelers loosen their ties, their tongues, and their manners, killing time until the 5:24 a.m. train, which will carry them back to wherever they came from with their sample cases and catalogues.

Tumbleweeds, Adam Fielding thinks as he shoulders open the door of the saloon. Not a collegial way to characterize his associates, the necessary nomads of his profession, but he's not a particularly collegial fellow. The juniper smell of gin rushes to greet him, melding with the low-hanging fumes of beer-stoked braying and belching, inhibitions of all kinds checked at the sidewalk. He maneuvers through the crowd of ranch hands and day laborers who either eye his clothes or ignore him. He claims the last vacant table.

Adam sweeps a half-dozen empties aside and wipes his hands on a coat lying abandoned on the chair behind him. He surveys the house impatiently. He agreed to meet the leather-goods fellow here, damn generous by Adam's standards considering that his store's fully stocked and he's not given to spending time with folks who can't do anything for him. But the poor devil is a downright pitiful greenhorn. The call he paid to Adam's establishment earlier in the day embarrassed both of them, the young man chanting a veritable textbook on how to break the rules of wholesale selling. Adam surmised that the lad's starchy stance and breathless presentation betrayed the trial-by-fire week he'd had, ending up here, lonely and worn out in an amber bead of a town along a peculiar-colored river at the northeast edge of Montana. In a measure of Adam's growing boredom with his own job, he told the fellow to stick around and, between customers, spent a couple of hours setting the kid straight.

Courage, courtesy, and confidence, he told him. More sales are made on the fifth call than the first. "Don't shove your whole line at me at once. How will you know what I need if you do all the talking? Breaking the ice should have been enough for you today."

"But . . . but . . ."

"Don't contradict your customer. I'm carrying your competitors' goods. If you knock them, you're questioning my judgment. Don't put me on the defensive. Convince me that your goods will make me more money."

The young buck scribbled frenetically in a pasteboard notebook, the part in his hair blazing white, wetness gathering in the creases of his eyelids. Before leaving, he prostrated himself, begging to buy Adam a few rounds of drinks. What with being new on the route, he hankered for "a taste of Caswell."

It looks like he's found it, without the expense of buying his magnanimous mentor a thing. Adam tips back on two legs of his chair, the better to see around a post near the rear of the room. Isn't that his supposed host playing foot hockey with Fancy Nancy? She's in fine form for him, petticoat creeping up a comely leg sheathed in the latest black lisle hosiery with the silk embroidery. There go yesterday's commissions, assuming the fellow had better luck in the next town over.

Adam lets the chair drop to the floor, feeling for his wallet. He doesn't need the table, but that's no reason to pass on the drink. He makes his way to the bar, sidestepping a suspicious-looking amber puddle.

At the bar, the two brothers who run the Milk River ferry run their jaws in an *Oh yeah? Says you!* rhubarb that climbs a notch with each boozy breath.

"Take it outside, fellas," booms the bartender. Adam bets himself: *A count of four.* He's right. No man dares goad Sprat Douglass into throwing his weight around. An inch shorter, by Adam's estimation, and he'd be round. The boys taunt and shoulder each other on out the door.

Adam steps into the open space. "Just beer," he tells Sprat, and turns to face the room. Two glasses slam onto the bar behind him. Next stool over, a lanky man in earth-stained trousers grabs one and raises it to no one in particular. "And here we are, the farmers in the dell, drinking deeply to these last apprehensive hours before another spring." He aims a pair of snapping dark eyes at Adam. "Heigh-ho, the dairy-o. Will the price of wheat go up? Will the price of wheat go down?" A long, musical slurp empties half the glass. "Sometimes I think it's the most tedious line of work under heaven."

"Sorry to hear that," Adam offers, as no one else pays any mind. Despite the man's shabby clothes, his face reflects neither age nor worry. Adam decides to toss a pop fly and see if the man catches it. "Maybe it's because this whole area is underproducing."

"Is that a fact." The farmer fields the remark, unfazed. "Tell me more, Perfesser."

"Don't need to be a teacher man to see that dry farming can be a long sight more productive than I've seen here. It's just a matter of math, and common sense."

"Common sense?" The farmer tips his hat and laughs, an infectious chuckle. "I've yet to see that come in on the boxcar. And some folks think the weather has something to do with it."

"I've seen the last few years' rainfall records. The area will support more than wheat and potatoes."

The man's tar-colored hair scatters across his leathery forehead as he jerks his head toward Sprat, calling for another round. "You're a dapper one," he says. "Seen you around town, what, the last year or so? The gents' shop? Yours?"

"No. Just the manager. Company's first Montana store. I let them convince me to come out here and run the place for a cut."

"How's business?"

"The head office is happy."

Happy, if baffled. Adam met with the Big Guy in Chicago before he agreed to the job. "I don't get it, Fielding. How many stores have you opened for us? The kind of results you get, I'm damned if I can see how. Frankly, I don't find you very personable." The district manager perched on the edge of the Big Guy's desk, swinging one leg at the knee. "This man moves goods," he told the boss, drumming a cigarette on the back of his hand. "Picks up local buying trends like this." A firecracker snap of the fingers three inches from the Big Guy's nose. "It's as simple as that. He knows how to sell to men because he is one, and he draws women like germs to the bottom of a shoe."

"I don't sell people what they don't need," Adam told them coolly. "It's as simple as that."

They said to pick a town, any town along the Great Northern, west of Williston. Adam chose Caswell as much for what it lacked as for what it had—plentiful entrepreneurial opportunities in a burg yet without any number of essential businesses, in a state that was about to boom. In a year, he calculated, he'd be able to break with his employer and have what he'd craved for years: a comma after his name, and a title that meant he answered to no one. Adam Fielding, Proprietor. Sole Proprietor.

The farmer drains his glass in a single pull and bangs it on the bar. "Another round on me," he says, lifting Adam's glass from his hand and throwing back the suds. "My friend, I smell some experience under your belt. Your hands have too many miles on 'em to have been buttoned up in that suit your whole life."

True. The family had a quarter section in North Dakota, took a stab at farming. Five years, a good solid try. In that unforgiving climate, it could do no more than pad the modest income from his father's ministry. Adam had charge of the spread for a while, learned all he could as fast as he could, but it was a game of make-believe. He stayed until they proved up, owned the place free and clear.

Two saloon honeys rustle by, cutting a channel of violent crimson and turquoise through the gray-brown throng. The girl in red, a new face, slows to look Adam over, as the new ones always do.

"Not that one, sugar." The gal in turquoise glowers at Adam. "Ice don't melt in his mouth." With a mouthed indecency and a pointed look at the farmer, she steers her protégée away.

The farmer crosses his arms over his chest in amusement and cocks his head toward Adam, a black brow shooting up like an arrowhead.

"Not my type." Adam shrugs. "I like a little more for my money. And a lot less." He flaps fingers against thumb. *"Plura loquitur."*

"Ah. The gentleman prefers native delights. Few words, many talents?"

Adam puts his untouched beer on the bar. This conversation is headed where it's nobody's affair but his. A last glance across the room tells him his leather-goods colleague is about to lose his own belt and wallet. Fancy Nancy's got her fingers under his lapels and heading south. Time to wrap this evening up.

"My father sold the property soon after I left, for two hundred

dollars an acre," Adam says with finality. "I think of it as my parting gift." He straightens up, again feeling for his wallet. "Thanks
for the—"

The farmer whistles through his teeth, a low, melodic, and
startling sound. "Two hundred dollars an acre for my humble
dominion would make me a kind of glad I doubt I'd survive. Tell
me more, Mister. Let's hear what you call 'common sense.'"

The discussion is pointless and growing irksome. Adam
didn't come to a saloon to talk to a stranger about a life he couldn't
wait to escape. But the man seems serious. Adam decides he can
spare the one-minute version. "Break ground early spring, put in
crops that can tolerate cool soil, get two rotations out of a season.
Break to six inches, not four. Don't bring in more livestock than
you can grow—not buy—feed for."

The farmer has grown quiet. His hand waggles in a *c'mon,
keep talking* gesture.

"For sections along the river," Adam continues, "garden vegetables are the answer to raising a money crop on only a hundred
sixty acres. They call it truck farming where I come from. There's
enough local market here that both import and export would be
unnecessary. No need to be at the mercy of the railroads and their
unconscionable rates." He traces a section of track along the side
of his glass. "Railroad could be a good customer. Someone has to
feed those crews."

"Just common sense. Whew." The man tips his glass and
again guzzles what's left in a throat-bulging swallow. "You gonna
drink that?" He motions at Adam's untouched beer.

"Go ahead."

"Thanks. Cal Rushton, by the way."

"Adam Fielding."

"I take it you don't got a woman with you here, Adam Fielding. That by choice or luck?"

"Would it be good luck or bad luck? Or just dumb luck?"

"Ha. You know what? I like you. No dames on my property
either, although I've asked my baby sister to come out and join me.
One of us needs rescuing. Not sure if it's her or me, although she's
taking her sweet time answering. Now you," Cal continues, "I'd
like to see what you can do outside a damn store." He dribbles a
splatter of beer onto the bar and draws a lumpy finger through it,

forming snaky bends. "I have thirty-seven acres south of town. It's a thumb sticking into a bend in the river that didn't fit into a four-cornered section." He taps a dry pocket in the curves of beer. "I've got thirty of it in wheat, and in a very good year it might support a peasant bachelor like me. I keep my head above water working for Reuben Dunbarton, a few miles downriver. Have you met him? Probably not. I doubt he shops your store."

Adam's kangaroo-leather oxford taps the floor. Cal Rushton is several beers ahead of him, and it's making his conversation lazy. *Get to the point. If there is one.*

"Dun has talked about truck farming, my friend. Thinks it could work, but he started a construction business, and that's where his time goes. I'm part of a crew that keeps his grain crops going, but I'm not the foreman type. You have grander abilities. And if you're the gambling sort, willing to forego your safe, cozy haber-dasher salary, it might not be a waste of your time to talk to him."

The whole evening's been a waste of time. Adam snaps, "Didn't I just say that my farming days are over? Didn't you just call it 'the most tedious line of work under heaven'?"

Cal smiles and folds his arms on the bar. "I meant no offense, Perfesser. As for tedious work, I may have to change my mind on that. What do you see when you look up, down, and sideways in that store?"

On anyone else, Adam would consider Cal's furled features to be a smirk. Might be worth seeing if Farmer Rushton could keep smiling with a fist in his mouth. But that would be bad for business. And there's a small but irresistible chance the man is touching a nerve Adam thought long dead. "Farmer in the dell," he says slowly, "let's hear three more sentences about Dunbarton."

For a stiff half minute, Cal doesn't answer, panning the room as if picking up inaudible telegraphy. Adam's tenuous patience gives out. He slides off the stool and thumbs the center button of his jacket through the buttonhole.

Cal says, "Dun is a good man to work for, but his wife will test your powers of discretion. She don't cotton to her hired hands drinking and carousing. An excellent cook, runs an admirable house, but it ain't free."

"What is?" Adam sighs.

"Nothing." Cal stands abruptly and hitches up trousers

that promptly fall low again on his gangly frame. The woman in turquoise leans over the end of the bar to Sprat Douglass, speaking behind a cupped hand strangled by silver bracelets. Cal winks at Adam. "I'm looking forward to hearing what you did to earn her disfavor. Hope it doesn't involve money. She's got some noble friends who don't use the front door here. Friends with badges. Friends with swank offices." He nods in her direction. "And other friends."

"Hell." Adam stifles a yawn. "If I'm going to have something on my conscience, it'll be plenty more than stiffing a two-dollar whore. You one of those other friends?"

"Let's say we're well acquainted. And now if you'll excuse me." Cal clumps his way through the crowd, smacking the door open just before he looks about to go right through it. The woman in turquoise breaks off her conversation with the bartender and disappears out the back.

The grating squeak of dishcloth on glass catches Adam's attention. Sprat Douglass ambles over and eyes him amiably.

"He didn't pay, right?" The bartender nods. Adam drops some coins on the bar. A half-dollar lands on its edge and careens off the side.

3

The first step up to the train is knee-high. Annie grabs the railing to boost herself to it. When she turns to take her satchel from Chase on the platform below, she is looking down at him for the first time in her life.

"Safe travels, Annie!" he calls when she raises the window by her seat, and she calls back, "Nothing but!" The train pitches forward and the whistle blares. Its shrill seems to last beyond the usual short blasts, echoing the wail of a child left behind. *Goodbye* . . .

She's never been on a train, and she gives in to the rhythmic rattling, swaying along in her seat, finding it soothing rather than grating. The sweep of Iowa framed in the window takes on the patina of a still-life painting. Annie gives her birthplace a last, unsentimental look. The town, then the countryside slide on by in a manner that doesn't seem momentous. Annie hasn't peppered Cal with questions. Caswell is a speck on a railroad map to her now, but before the following day is out, it will meet with her feet. Then it will be real.

The August heat grows stickier by the hour. A string of newsboys rotate through, badgering her to buy papers, candy, fruit. One seems more raggedy and melancholy than the others, his need for her nickel more urgent. She buys an orange from him. It looks and tastes the same as the oranges that have occasionally appeared in her Christmas stocking. It smells delicious, but the juice stings the corners of her mouth, the membranes are tough, the pith crawls under her fingernails. A fine clarity rushes through her. *Don't like oranges. Never have.* She needn't ever again eat an orange. Cal mentioned an orchard and wild berries; she loves berries, their mellow sweetness, the wild tangles where they grow. She walks to the back platform and sends what's left of the orange zinging over the prairie.

Crossing into Minnesota, she leaves the boundaries of Iowa for the first time, but there is little to affirm it. The clouds and the sun cross the border with her. The towns strewn every ten miles along the line look like first cousins of Cherry Hill; the people who board the train could be her neighbors. Only the mighty Mississippi River has changed, so much smaller here, moseying through the center of Minneapolis. Some things, it seems, grow larger and more powerful the farther they travel from their source.

Between trains she stays the night in a modest hotel. "Will you feel frightened?" Jenny asked. Now, lying in bed, reading by the light of a dangling bulb, Annie absorbs the sounds of people through walls as insubstantial as curtains. No, it doesn't frighten her; in her first day untethered, she's learned that most traveling folks are not much different from her, and she falls asleep filled with peace, and perhaps a grain of smug.

Through a dewy morning and another kiln of an afternoon, the train hurtles across North Dakota. Annie marvels at the endless miles of sunflowers, taller than she is, but the passenger next to her sighs. His kin sunk their souls into trying to homestead this prairie. It wasn't the winters or the droughts that did them in, he says. It was the damnable, incessant wind. Drove them away just minutes ahead of driving them crazy. "How sad," Annie murmurs. What more could she say?

An hour later the train pulls into Caswell, crawling up to the shoe-box depot in a town that from Annie's window looks to be no more than a few blocks deep. Beyond it, browned-butter stands of waving wheat ripple to the horizon.

The engine pants to a stop. Annie pauses on the bottom step of the train, looking for Cal, a short search with so few people on the platform. Did he forget? She again grabs the railing, this time in reverse, and lowers herself to the platform, noting the clack of her boots on the boards, her first contact with Montana. More clattering, and here comes Cal at a gallop, dodging a trunk-toting porter and an elderly couple propped on canes. The eight years since she's seen him have thinned and grayed him around the edges, but not slowed his stride or softened his tongue, not one bit.

"Li'l Sisser!" he crows, arms wide.

"Big Brudder!" She hugs him tight, breathing in his never-quite-clean, bachelor-farmer smell.

He tosses her satchel into the back of a one-horse wagon hitched to a gelding that resembles him: shaggy, long-lipped, with a devil-take-it stance. "And now, for the chariot tour of Caswell on our way to the *domus*."

"The *domus*? Do I need to brush up on my Latin to live in frontier Montana?"

"Nah. My new boss spouts Latin. It's forced me to pick up a word or two."

The wagon creaks down First Street. "Got most of 'The Twelve Days of Christmas' here," Cal says. "Ten lawyers braying, nine houses boarding, eight docs and dentists, seven savory saloons . . ." He ticks off stores, blacksmith and barber shops, banks and real estate firms, and, rising from the dust at the edge of town, a brand-new hospital. "Over yon, two houses of questionable repute. And speaking of questionable repute . . ." He points to a lavishly lettered storefront sign: THE CASWELL CHRONICLE-TIMES. "The *Gaswell Comical Times*! All our fits they print as news!"

"And is there an actual Caswell in all of this?" Annie asks as they pass city hall.

"Oh yes. See the mercantile over there?"

"Melton's?"

"Yep. Complete with Her Imperial Proprietress, Elise *Caswell* Melton, self-anointed clearinghouse for all information concerned citizens need to know. You know the type." Her father, he goes on, was the railroad foreman who got to name this particular siding, and what better namesake than himself? He stayed, and Elise has evermore considered herself the Countess of Caswell. "Go beyond small talk at your own risk," Cal snickers. "This town's most efficient mode of communication isn't telephone. It's tell-Elise."

"Okay, then. So where is Coffeen's?"

"Coffeen's?" He looks genuinely puzzled. "Coffee beans?"

"You sent me a thimble. 'For dry goods go to Coffeen's.'"

"I did? Oh yes, that sweet little thing. Well, there's no Coffeen's here. I got it from a lass traveling through. Her family's place, I think."

A *"sweet little thing." The thimble or the girl?* Annie wonders. "Why did you send it to me?"

His lower lip pushes the upper one toward his nose. "I don't know," he says, and she can see that it's true.

A few more blocks and they've left the town behind. A mile and a half on, they pass a turnoff leading to an immaculate farmhouse. "Our closest neighbors, the Eulenbergs," says Cal. "We're invited for supper as soon as you're settled."

Around two more bends in the road, a shack comes into view. From an adjacent shed, a preternatural howl and a slam against the door give Annie a start.

"What the deuce was that?" asks Annie.

"Squatter," says Cal, "in the canine form. Settler of prior claim to this property. But I thought I'd give you a chance to get your footing before you meet the resident cur."

"Why? What is he, some kind of swamp bogey?"

"Gosh, that's possible." With that, Cal reins up in front of the shack and falls silent, watching for her reaction. Annie climbs down and takes a long first look. It's about as she expected. It's bigger than an outhouse, isn't it? She laughs, somehow delighted. Cal steps in front of her and opens the door. "Madam—your manor house."

Like most homesteaders, Cal is no carpenter. He nailed the shack together in a day or two. Inside, Annie sees two rooms, every inch tightly purposed. The whole affair measures about twelve feet by twenty. A canvas stretched tight under the roof serves as the ceiling. Bare tar paper lines the walls. Off the main room, a doorless alcove contains a rope-frame bed topped by a hay mattress and a simple quilt. At the opposite end of the house, a ladder leans against a loft just the width of the narrower hay mattress it holds. A sink and counter hang from the back wall, shelves above. A fancy woodstove dominates the main room, an unlikely bachelor furnishing with its patterned exterior, nickel-plated fittings, and porcelain-lined reservoir. "Got that beaut for twelve dollars, overstock." Cal beams. "I'm looking forward to your getting my money's worth out of it."

Her first look takes less than a minute, the second even less. She laughs again and removes her bonnet. "Be it ever so humble!"

Brother and sister embrace again, laugh some more. Cal puts her satchel in the alcove while she moves the three steps to the kitchen. Through its window, the late-afternoon sun hangs over the wheat like a rosy penny. The image lingers on the back of her eyelids when she closes her eyes, and she suddenly realizes how long it's been since she could look forward to a carefree night's sleep.

Next day she awakes in the simple bed in the alcove in a place without a single familiar landmark. "I love it!" she declares out loud, to which Cal hollers back from the loft that he'd love some breakfast. After seeing him off to work—he can't miss a day at the height of summer, so he bays, "Don't leave town!" and leaves with his ragtag dog straggling after him—she steps outside to explore. Over the next few hours, she falls even more in love. Never has she seen a prettier, more promising piece of land, flat and fertile, ringed by cottonwoods and the opaque Milk River, with its curious lightened-tea tint. A luxuriant thicket of blackberries ranges near the bank. Overcome by the joyous freedom of being watched by no one, she pulls down handfuls of berries, tipping her head back and funneling the fruit into her mouth. Even after washing her hands in the river, they glow lavender. "I love it," she announces again. Coming up the bank, she notices an open space tucked into the brambles and ducks under an arch of vines to find herself in a small, clover-carpeted clearing. How odd, she thinks, that the brambles halt and protect the privacy of this spot. She sits, then lies down. *Mine.*

On the other side of the property, she lingers along an orchard of eight apple and eight pear trees stirring the air with heady fragrance.

When Cal comes home for supper, she plies him with blackberry crumble and a request. Keeping the "manor house" clean and its master bachelor fed isn't going to occupy much time. What would he think of staking her to a few chickens so she can start an egg business? "Fowl? How foul!" he cries. "Why not?"

The sun sets on her first full day, deep-pink sky marbled with nimbus. From her bedroom window, Annie watches a lightning storm afar. The bolts break behind the cottonwoods on the opposite side of the river, making them appear to rush toward her. For an illuminated instant, when she reaches out to touch them, a few large, warm drops of rain walk across her arms. She knows already. She's made the right decision.

The next afternoon, Cal escorts Annie to the Eulenbergs'. "I'll keep the introductions short," he says. "Karl, Annie. Annie, Margrethe. Oh, and I'm Cal."

"Don't we know it!" laughs Margrethe. "*Willkommen,* Annie."

In the living room of the frame farmhouse they built last year, Margrethe pours cider while Karl tells Annie how Cal's high-spirited humor got them and their three children through the toughest work they had ever done. "We had to dig out rocks the size of our cow—just the tip showing above the ground like an iceberg."

"Yes!" Margrethe chimes in. "And Cal here, he say, 'First things first.' We were new here, from Bavaria, and Cal tell us that in America long names must be shortened. 'Now, Maggie, dear,' he say. 'Or is it Greta? Oh, what us Yanks will do to that name. You must choose a poison before someone choose for you. Will you be Meg, Madge, or Peggy?'"

Annie toes Cal's shin. "I can just hear that."

"We love Cal," Margrethe laughs. "But those names I hate. I keep the name I am born with. Good enough for my grandmother, good enough for me."

The Eulenbergs remind Annie of salt and pepper shakers. Margrethe is the pepper, with her zest for conversation and her freckly complexion that tattles on a girl who forgot her sunbonnet too many times. Karl is the salt, shaken out in crystals to enhance things. He has yet to say much tonight, but Annie senses in him a quiet fortitude.

"Did you notice the flagpole outside?" Margrethe asks. "And that your place has one too? Karl think that up. Crazy stuff happen out here, need six hands for. You run a white towel up the pole if you need help, and Cal or Karl or I come running."

"That's one kind of surrender I can accept," Annie says with a smile.

On Saturday, Cal drives her into town. She doesn't expect he'll ferry her around making introductions, and sure enough, he pulls up at First Street and asks if she has any money. She does, a little. "Don't spend it all in one place," he chortles, adding that he'll pick her up in an hour, "give or take." She watches him rattle down the street, certain he's off to disregard his own advice.

At the bank she opens an account, watching the clerk's face as she lays down two dollars. The clerk writes it up as if it were a hundred. "Welcome to Caswell, Miss Rushton. We appreciate your business."

At the post office she buys a stamp for her letter to Jenny. The postmistress, too, welcomes her warmly, noting her likeness to Cal. "He says, 'You can always tell a Rushton! But you can't tell them much.'"

"Might be about the size of it." Annie smiles. Lots of smiling and nodding today, more than she's used to.

At the cash grocery, the proprietor tilts a bushel basket of leafy apples to greet customers. "G'morning, ma'am," he says with a nod, and Annie responds in kind. As she surveys the shelves, he asks, "New here?" and she nods yet again. The proprietor plucks the largest apple from the basket and hands it to her. "Me too. Welcome. Neil Muir. Been open a month now."

"Annie Rushton. Cal's sister." *Calssister. My new name.* "May I ask where you get your eggs?"

"I could sure use a better supplier, if that's what you mean."

"Then I hope to see you again soon."

Their conversation hasn't been private. A few minutes after entering, Annie became aware of a silent figure shadowing her. She has moved through the store, gathering coffee and sugar and flour, the shadow hanging back behind the baked goods or stooping to blend in with the cans stacked along the wall. Annie isn't alarmed. When she lays her purchases on the counter, the shadow revealed itself to be a little girl, now emboldened by curiosity that moves her on tiptoe bare feet to clutch the end of the counter and stare while Annie pays her bill.

On the sidewalk Annie turns with a swish of skirts.

"You're following me," she says lightly.

"No, ma'am." The girl studies her stubby toes.

"That's a pretty hair ribbon," Annie says. Her thoughts spiral back through the years of *not pretty, not graceful, not charming*; no embellishments could change that, so she didn't have any.

The child now stares fixedly at Annie's hair and blurts, "Your hair sure is black. Are you an Indian?"

"No. I'm an Iowan." And the instant the words clear her lips, a strange sensation darts through her; the truth of the words starts to drain.

"An Eye-what?" The child looks dubious.

She's around six, not quite filling her cheap gingham shift. For all Annie knows, this child could be her daughter. That's her cross to bear, the inescapable possibility that any six-year-old she meets could be her daughter and neither of them would know. Moving to Montana lessens that possibility, but she'll never be able to squelch it.

"An Iowan," she repeats. "I'm from Iowa. A state far from here. A thousand miles."

"Why are you here?"

Why indeed?

Thomas Day could have his pick of girls, her mother had said. "What does he want with a girl like you, plain as a post and—"

"He wants a wife, Ma." Annie cut her off. "Someone to work alongside him and dream and love him and make him more than he is now. A partner. Do you know what that word means?" Amanda's arm reared back, but Annie raised her hand firmly in front of it.

"That doesn't work with me anymore. I'm going to be happy, Ma. Something that up until now I've only heard about."

"You are stepping out of your place, Analiese. The Lord punishes those who step out of place."

Why are you here? The child's face suggests she's asked the most logical question in the world. Annie stoops and reaches her hand out, and the girl inches forward and lays her fingers in Annie's. So small and tender. Annie hasn't held a child's hand since . . .

"Child, be off with ye!" A stout man in a boxy black suit stops on the walk beside them. His whitish bow tie blends with his whitish shirt under a yellowish walrus mustache that all but covers the lower half of his face and looks like it will fall off if he sneezes. "Miss Rushton? Cal's sister? I'm Sheriff Blandish. I'm sorry this child is bothering you. Her ma works over yonder edge of town." He tips his head to indicate and gives Annie a pointed look. "Part of town you'll not be visiting."

"Pleasure to meet you, sir," Annie says. "And thank you for your concern, but the child isn't bothering me. We're having a nice chat."

The sheriff raises a brow and glowers at the child. "Don't be askin' too many questions, girl."

"Good advice for all," Annie agrees cheerily.

The sheriff raises the other brow, his shoulders leaning back slightly. After a moment he nods. "Good day, ma'am."

She smiles back. "Good day to you too, sir."

The child watches him go, then asks, "Where are your children?"

Annie wavers. In this moment, when she can write her story any way she wants, how does she answer? She can't deny her daughter by saying she has no children. "I have a daughter who lives away," she says.

"Why?"

"Because I am here and she is there."

The child takes Annie's answer as an invitation to a game. Her nowhere-brown eyes glint as she launches every nosy question Annie thinks adults likely long to ask her but won't. Did you have a husband? Is he dead? Was he mean? Did he drink? Annie's heart goes out to the child, who so obviously speaks from the observations of her short life, her mother's profession. The questions go on. Was he a bore? A scofflaw? A deadbeat?

The child's questions free Annie. She doesn't have a husband, but her child has a father. He's not dead or mean, not a drunk, a scofflaw, or a loafer. With each *no* she becomes more settled. Her daughter is safe, loved, provided for. It will always hurt, always be wrong that Annie cannot be the one to keep her that way, but now she's prepared for whatever comes her way in her new life. She places a penny in the child's hand and folds her fingers over it. "Buy yourself a peppermint stick," she says. "If your mama won't get mad."

The child blinks in surprise. "Thank you, ma'am." Clutching the penny, she asks again, "But why are you here?"

"I've stepped into my place." Annie squeezes the child's hand. "I've come here to live."

4

The conversation with Cal Rushton wandered around Adam's head for days, trying to find its way out. Why he would even consider leaving the store, and by extension the plans for his own store, made no sense.

On an unseasonably warm April day, when no one needed club ties or half hose or Dakota-style Stetson hats, he stared at the door, which hadn't opened once since he had unlocked it and walked through himself, and it finally registered. It wasn't the farming from which he had desperately wanted to distance himself. It was his father, the fruitlessness of part-time farming, and the knowing that working for his father meant he would never accumulate enough money to have something of his own.

When he called on Reuben Dunbarton, the man seemed to be expecting him. "Just in time," he boomed, chestnut eyes bobbing beneath shafts of chestnut hair. Adam asked the salary he was offering. Dunbarton named a fair number, and Adam, somehow needing to give himself a last out, said he had a higher number in mind—say, half again more. Dunbarton laughed, clapped him on the shoulder, and said, "Go to it, lad."

In the months since, running the business of the Dunbarton farm from a desk and a phone in a niche by the back door of the farmhouse has brought Adam deep and startling contentment. Coaxing living products from the dark beneath the soil thrills him in a primeval way he doesn't try to understand.

It's been some weeks since he last came by Cal's place. This late of a September afternoon, deep shade veils the riverside path beside the swaying rows of wheat. From his wagon, Adam notes the new chicken corral. He pulls his horse up, scanning the fields for the rangy Cal's distinctive gait. A woman emerges on the path, her tread so light that he isn't aware of her until she's almost upon him. She resembles Cal, although more than a foot shorter. And while Cal's step carries the impression of perpetual inebriation, this woman's stride is all business. A blue dragonfly hovers over her shoulder like an escort, zooming away when she waves it off and stops a cautious distance from Adam.

He jumps down and tips his hat. "You must be Cal's sister. I'm Adam Fielding."

"Charmed, I'm sure." She seems about to offer her hand but instead slides it into a fold of her skirt. "Analiese Rushton. Cal speaks fondly of you. The 'taskmaster,' yes?" Unlike Cal, she delivers the handle with a straight face.

"He's fond of telling me that I can't fire him; slaves have to be sold."

She nods knowingly. "What can I do for you? Cal had to go to Havre. He accidentally plugged a gopher hole with his foot. The doctor wanted it examined with an X-ray machine."

"I'm sorry to hear that. It sounds painful." And costly. He's concerned for his friend, surely. But now his crew is down a man, and there are no extras to be had this time of year.

"It was. You won't soon see a fatter salami."

Adam holds the reins of his champagne palomino loosely at his side. "Cal said he couldn't afford a threshing crew and aimed to winnow the crop by hand with an old Confederate flag. I couldn't tell if he was joking, and when he didn't show for work today, I thought perhaps he wasn't."

"True, we're going to winnow by hand. But I'll be coming up with a less wieldy fan than a Confederate flag."

"No need, Miss Rushton. I came to tell Cal that I've arranged for our threshing crew to do it. If he's hobbled, he won't be able to refuse, will he?"

"How very kind of you. And thanks for coming out. I'm trying to convince him to put in a telephone. To save important folk"—this too she declares with a poker face—"the trip."

"Obliged." Adam touches the brim of his hat again. The telephone at Dunbarton's is indeed where he's headed. He faces an afternoon of calling across the countryside trying to scare up an extra hand for the threshing.

An explosion of leaves and snapping branches erupts from the trees along the river, and a blur of fur hurtles toward the chicken corral. *Wolf!* Adam registers like a shot from the rifle he doesn't have with him today. A bold daytime offensive in full view of people means the animal is wild with hunger. Adam gropes under the seat of the wagon, hoping he's wrong about the rifle, astounded that the Rushton girl shows no concern, barely glancing at the animal. She's apparently too new here to recognize what she should fear.

The blur of fur sails over the side of the corral. The squawking fowl seem to scold rather than flee, the scene almost comical as the wolf catches a hind foot on the coop's fencing and crashes into its center, careening bum over teakettle to regain its footing and vaulting the opposite side, paying no heed to dozens of captive meals. It shoots past Adam, between the legs of his palomino. The horse shrieks and bucks, catching the wolf in the rear quarter and sending it into the road, where it lands in a heap for a second time. The Rushton girl, who must be mad, trots toward it, tossing her head and clucking something that sounds like, "Oh, Dio." Before she can come close enough for the mauling Adam is sure will follow, the wolf leaps to its feet and throws itself into a whirling dervish, mistaking its own tail for an object of pursuit.

Adam grabs for the harness of his spooked horse, but it twists to get away and the cart fishtails, knocking his legs out from under him. The reins whiplash the air and wrap themselves around Adam's middle like a frightened child. His back smacks the shaft on the way down, snatching the wind from his lungs. Voiceless, laid out flat, with a wolf on the loose and his friend's sister directly in its path, he's about to see a woman be eaten alive. Like a bad dime novel. If only it were.

But the Rushton girl bellows, "Blasted varmint" and "Stay there, Mr. Fielding." She marches right up to the animal and backs it into a ditch on the side of the road. The beast hunkers down, feral eyes fixed on her, tail swishing while she commands, "Duo, you moronic menace. You stay your sorry carcass right there until I tell you otherwise!"

Adam, pulling himself up, sees now that the animal is no wolf, but a mongrel dog of incomparable homeliness. Its eyes don't match, one brown and one gray with a rusty ring and cocked outward. His mangy coat furrows across his spine; he doesn't fit in his own skin. Inches of pink tongue dangle from his muzzle, too long for his mouth. Miss Rushton glowers at the mutt, starts to turn to Adam. The mutt skulks a tentative step out of the ditch.

Cal's sister whirls on him, snapping, "Try it!" and the hound tries no more. Bloodshot eyes blink meekly over the rim of the ditch. "Sawdust where most critters have brains," she grouses. "Mr. Fielding!" She hurries across the road. "Are you hurt?"

Adam regains his footing, but his palomino is still stamping and prancing. Adam grasps the bridle's cheekpieces and pulls the horse's head to his level. Whispering in Michif—"*Tapitow* . . . steady . . ."—he strokes the palomino's neck, then brings his face near the nose, breathing in and out along with the animal, calming both of them. He pulls a pouch of oats from a pocket. The feel of the horse's velvet muzzle in his hand diffuses some of Adam's own agitation. When the horse quiets, Adam lets its head up for a cautious look around.

He probes the sore area of his lower back. It's throbbing, but not as dire as he feared. The Rushton girl asks again if he's hurt. He's not about to tell her that the wound to his pride stings worse than the one to his flesh. His gaze goes to the cur in the ditch. "Duo?"

Miss Rushton rolls her eyes. "Cal's idea of a joke. 'Dog of Unknown Origin.' You haven't met? He came with the property." She throws a barbed frown at the ditch. The dog lays his head on the ground, looking sorry and resigned. The girl shrugs. "They love each other."

"What in tarnation was he chasing?"

"Who knows? Dog dreams? I truly am sorry, Mr. Fielding. Can I get you some coffee?"

He's trying to work a thumb into loosening a knot of leather in the tangle of reins. "No, I don't want any damn coffee," he mutters.

"Something stronger?" she asks, unruffled.

For the first time, he eyes her closely. She's not much to look at. Absurdly small. She disappeared a minute ago when she darted behind the horse to grab the other rein, momentarily confusing him. Maybe five foot tall on tiptoe, he judges. A child-sized woman who melts in and out of view.

Her face seems unfinished, as if the artist started work on it and grew bored, packed up the brushes and chisels and paint pots and moved on to more inspiring material. From a distance he might have called her plain, but this close she radiates an uncanny energy. Her hands, too large for the rest of her body, glow two shades darker than the wheat behind her, as do her arms, up to the elbow because—oh, woman after his own heart!—her sleeves are rolled up. Most unlady-like. Most attractive. His eye drifts to her lightweight skirt. With her back to the sun, he can see the silhouette of a slender thigh. Sweet jumpin' joey, the woman isn't wearing undergarments? He forces his attention to her face. He's not seen black eyes like those since his horse-trading days. Dark and bright at once, that magnetic pull, slivers of white at corners, and—

Yes, he could use a drink.

"I wouldn't mind." Then, testing her, though he's not sure why, he adds, "Would you join me?"

"Sure." She starts toward the house.

He can't believe it. "You're going to drink with me?"

"Put you under the table, big fella."

Adam isn't a particularly big fella, and she's downright puny. He can't tell if she's being insolent, if she's calling his bluff, or if she's just damn interesting. Does it matter?

"Where do you get the stuff?"

"Homemade, what else?"

"You have a still?"

"I have a grain barrel and a Ford radiator. Does your horse have a name, Mr. Fielding?"

"Tipsy."

She laughs, an enchanting chuckle from such a plain face, the breezy retort of a butterfly flirting with a falcon. "Better put Tipsy in the pasture. You look thirsty."

Before he turns the palomino out, he scouts the pasture, wading into the grass halfway to the woods. A flash of gray tail in the trees tells Adam that Duo is in retreat.

At the open door of the shack, he knocks politely.

Two chairs huddle under a plank table where Annie has set out an amber bottle and two glasses. Light enters the cabin through two windows, one tall and narrow over the sink, facing the river, the other square across the front of the shack with a long view up the road. Rich blue damask framing the front window suggests a tablecloth has been conscripted as draperies. She waves him in. "Would you like ice? I have plenty in the cellar."

"Straight up, thanks. No ice."

"I meant for your back."

He lowers himself into the chair without comment. He'll have to pay attention if he's to stay a step ahead of her. Why can't he take his eyes off her?

"No? Suit yourself." She uncaps the bottle, and the glug of whiskey splashing against glass fills his ears. "Bottoms up, big fella."

"And the fourth deadly sin is sloth, according to my father, the Reverend Fielding." When he tips the bottle against his glass, nothing comes out, and his watch has slipped a gear and advanced two hours in the space of a few minutes. It doesn't usually take him this long to impress a girl out of her bloomers, and this one may not even be wearing any. Not that he's trying to. Not her. Not his type. "In Latin, *acedia*—how about that?"

"This isn't sloth," she tells him, somehow stone sober. "It's convalescence."

"Convalescence?"

"You were hurting and now you're not, am I right?" She gets up without waiting for his answer. "You look as if you have taken root in that chair. Are you staying for supper?"

Is that some sort of convoluted invitation? She's an impudent girl, even if she is his friend's sister. From gracious to audacious and back again in the same minute. And she's wrong about the chair. He could get up if he wanted to. But what the heck, why not play along a while more? Sure, he'll stay.

The food clears his head enough to recover some decorum. "Splendid supper, Miss Rushton." Another reason to envy Cal: being permitted to eat without enduring Fiona Dunbarton's incantation of grace in three languages. "Do you have a special name for this?"

Annie nods solemnly. "I call it chicken. The round green things, I call them peas."

"Charming, aren't you?" So much for decorum. "And where did the lady learn to drink like that?"

She settles back in her chair. "The red slices, I call them tomatoes."

"Cal?" Adam cocks a cupped hand to his lips, tipping an invisible glass.

"I'm not going to tell you. I don't know you well enough."

Adam, not a man who laughs readily, can barely keep his lips together. A smoke would be the thing right about now. She won't object; she's no temperance lady. Reaching inside his jacket for his pouch of Prince Albert, he asks, "Would you mind if I were to have a smoke, ma'am?"

"If you do, I'll assume you're on fire and douse you with the bucket I keep under the sink for such occasions." She indicates with a finger over her shoulder. "I can't promise that Duo hasn't sampled it."

He holds a hand up. "No offense intended, Miss Rushton. May I call you Analiese?"

"Could I stop you?"

"Do you want to?"

"I couldn't care less what you call me. I may or may not answer to it. Whatever you come up with, I've been called worse, and by my own relations."

Is that a dare? Baiting him to press her for more, so she can dodge again? He must remember to ask Cal if this is her nature, or peculiar to the situation.

"You too? At least your name isn't a profanity with a vowel in front of it. My uncle used to swear when he was exasperated with me: 'Aaaaa-*damn!*' Then I would remind him of the biblical origin of the name."

"Ah, the sacred and the profane, conjoined. I can see how that would be exasperating. Courtesy of Reverend Fielding, I take it?"

"His father. I'm named for my grandfather."

She props her elbows on the table, her hands together under her chin. "This grandfather, does he, too, consider you to be profanity preceded by a vowel?"

"No. I was a boy when he passed, but the old gent liked me. He and my mother. As for the rest of the gospel-breathing, Bible-thumping Fielding clan . . ."

His voice trails off. Too much work to finish the thought. He can feel the girl searching the blankness of his face, looking for a chink in the surface that will tell her something. She won't find one.

"The rest of the gospel-breathing, Bible-thumping Fielding clan," she finishes for him, "deem that such a well-reared, industrious, good-looking gent should have settled down by now. Don't tell me—firstborn, right?" He doesn't answer. "Roaming the prairie, back and forth over the border a thousand times. Heaven forbid, consorting with the natives your father tries to convert."

Bold little wench, isn't she? "I didn't say—"

"You didn't have to." She gets up to clear the table. "If that has earned you the reputation of a profanity with a vowel in front of it"—she raises the empty whiskey bottle—"the hell with 'em."

He tips back on two legs of his chair. How does she know these things? Four guesses and she's batting a thousand. "What about you, what's your story? Cal doesn't talk about his family."

She turns her back and hefts a pot of water onto the stove. Into the pot she scrapes the chicken bones and potato leavings, an onion still in its papery skin, the tomato cores, some carrot tops. He half expects her to toss in a stone. She's avoiding and provoking him, and that's a conundrum. With women, the decision to avoid or provoke has always been his. The food has soaked up some of the sway of her moonshine but left a gap he must close to regain his accustomed upper hand.

He hooks his thumbs into his belt and feels the watch in his pocket tick against his hip. She grinds pepper into the pot and chops a handful of parsley. She seems to have forgotten his presence. He draws in a deeper breath, as if he could pull her head around.

Just when he thinks she's sidestepped his question entirely, she dries her hands on her apron and returns to the table. Her words have a minuet recital quality. "Cal became a firstborn by default when our brother died, seven years before I was born. In our mother's eyes, those were shoes no one could fill. Her very words. Cal left home about twenty years ago. Our sister married. She's still in Iowa. Our other brother took over the farm when our parents died. I'm . . . lastborn." She turns to the window, speaking to the river. "I was five when Cal left, and it broke my heart. He rarely came home. His last visit, our ma was particularly hard on me, and Cal told her that ours was 'the very house where glad comes to die.' He left the next day. That was eight years ago, and I didn't see him again until I stepped off the train here. But I hold that memory dear—the rare occasion when someone shocked our mother into silence." She tugs her apron off and tosses it on the table. "Is that a good enough story for you, Mr. Fielding?"

"No," he says, more sharply than he intended. She gives him the slightest of shrugs. "You left eight years out. But I bet I'd have to put a ring on that finger to get the rest of it, eh?"

There, he's thrown down a gauntlet. If she's anything like Cal, she won't be able to refuse picking it up.

"Aren't you the brash one." She slings a dish towel over her shoulder and crosses her arms, one hand beating a tom-tom rhythm against her elbow. "A bet assumes that you have something I want, Mr. Fielding. Tricky business, assuming. How drunk are you? For all you know, the rest of my story includes Cal teaching me bare-knuckles boxing and a nasty left uppercut."

Her look could melt the stripe from a skunk. Now he does laugh. She is, oh yes, she is a worthy sparring partner. "Ladyfriend, I'm left-handed. I could stop your uppercut cold. Might even break your sturdy little arm."

"My, you are terrifying. After I finish washing up the dishes here, I'll consider fainting."

"Analiese—if I may call you that—you are something."

"You are something too, Mr. Fielding."

"Adam."

He might be drunk, but he can still count. Eight long beats and she doesn't blink. On the ninth beat, he wins.

"Adam."

5

When Cal returned from Havre, his foot wrapped like a cigar, Annie tossed him the empty whiskey bottle and said, "I met your boss." Cal dropped into a chair and laughed until he was quite helpless, pounding his crutch on the floor and gasping, "Who won?" It's been two weeks, but Cal went back to work this morning, heading down to Dunbarton's after dropping Annie in town. Behind the counter at the cash grocery, Neil Muir holds up one finger when she enters the store with her first two weeks' worth of eggs. She hangs back along the shelves, making mental notes on the prices of canned goods while he deals with another woman selling eggs. His brow arches in irritation at the grimy eggs piled in a bucket, a jumble of sizes and colors. He discards at least half the lot.

The cowbell above the door jangles, and from the corner of her eye, Annie catches the entrance of a man, moving with purposeful momentum but braking three steps in. His clothing straddles the line between business and farming: neat gray-striped duck pants and a dove-colored flannel shirt with a dark vest hanging open—hardworking furnishings, but not a loose thread anywhere.

Adam Fielding.

She's not the superstitious type, but how is it that whenever she comes to town, he's there? When they meet on a busy street, it's "Good afternoon, Miss Rushton." If no one's within hearing, it's "Hello, Analiese."

She moves toward the back of the store. Did he follow her here? She can't fathom his fascination with her, which he seems to pursue and resist at once. The uninvited familiarity, often bordering on rude, the questions about where she's headed and why, so serious, does the man ever smile when he's not drunk? When they talk, it's as if he's trying to get her to say something he needs to hear. She hasn't an inkling what. No matter. She didn't come to Caswell to be someone's conquest, and there's no shortage of ladies vying for that job. Blind kittens couldn't miss the fawning of his admirers, even interrupting their conversations on the street. "Soooo sorry to intrude, Miss, is it Rushton? Trudy Durant. From the millinery. Do come see me. Now, I must ask if Mr. Fielding will be attending the basket social?"

Annie cranes around a table stacked high with jarred asparagus spears in gaudy green labels. She could duck out and return in half an hour, except that the ubiquitous Mr. Fielding has parked himself a step inside the store, one foot against the wall, penciling notes in an account book steadied against his thigh. She drags a hand across her cheek to wipe away the embarrassing blush that leaps up her neck. Following her, indeed. What was she thinking? Mr. Muir is his customer too.

"Six cents a dozen," the proprietor offers the woman at the counter. Annie waits until she's left, then steps forward, hoisting two cloth bags with large flaps protecting her cargo.

"Good morning, Mr. Muir," she says. "Do you still need eggs?"

"Neil, please." He pushes the previous seller's box aside. "Yes, I do."

Annie unpacks her stash, clean and nested in cartons of a dozen according to size and color. Stored in straw in the root cellar, they are still fresh and cool to the touch.

"Twelve cents a dozen," Mr. Muir declares. "These are the best to come through that door yet. Is this everything you've got?"

He's dialing the phone before she's out of earshot. "Hello, ma'am. I have just the eggs you were asking for."

Annie sails past Adam without a look. "You're staring, Mr. Fielding."

Twelve cents, she calculates, is a top wholesale price when the going retail is fifteen. Sidestepping two sleeping bulldogs inhaling each other's snores in front of the barbershop, she decides she'll invest half of her take today in more laying hens. They'll pay for themselves within a few months. The boardwalk under her vibrates; someone behind her is in a hurry. When she moves aside, Adam Fielding catches up to her, touching the brim of his hat.

"That was some smooth business, Miss Rushton. Those eggs have sold already. There are a few dozen omelets in someone's future tonight."

Annie eyes him sideways and keeps her pace. "You can't be sure about that. One can't make an omelet without cracking eggs, but it's possible to crack a great many eggs without producing an omelet."

They've reached his parked cart. She has no intention of stopping, but his champagne palomino tosses its head as she passes and captures her attention. Such lovely deep eyes. She reaches out to run her fingers through the pale mane.

"They say you see something of yourself when you look into a horse's eyes." He leans on the post, arms crossed. "What do you see?"

"I see he's missing something," she says, and kicks herself for falling into yet another prickly conversation with him. Stuck now, like a hair in a biscuit. Stepping around the horse, she inches away with "I trust you're keeping busy, Mr. Fielding."

He pushes his hat back on his head, his crystalline eyes glistering at her evasion. Though younger than Cal, he's long past youth, but his eyes are still those of a child, large and round, and never the same blue twice. Slightly close-set, they give Annie the sense of being studied through binoculars. She stops and waits, her face daring him to push her on her evasion of his question, but after a charged pause he hooks a thumb in his vest pocket and says, "Yes, ma'am. Business is good. You too, I see. Cal didn't used to keep chickens."

"He staked me to ten layers, and I bought ten more." She has to have something of her own, though it's doubtful Mr. Fielding would understand.

"Hope you're not keeping the profits in a sock under the mattress."

"Thank you, Preacher Fielding," she says, with all the hosanna she can muster. One thing she doesn't cotton to is being scolded about money.

But her sarcasm gives him no pause. Keeping cash at home is foolhardy, he tells her. Prairie fires work faster than any bucket brigade ever assembled. Houses, crops, whole blocks of town, leveled in minutes. "Being near the river creates a false sense of security," he warns.

She needs to get home and start canning the thirty pounds of tomatoes an unnamed "good friend" bestowed on Cal yesterday. But not until she evens the score. "Being near a bank can create a false sense of security," Annie advises Adam. She once rescued her father's life savings from a bank president who didn't notice her at the teller window when he told his vice president that the bank was headed for serious cash problems after approving loans to a large family of newcomers who'd then skipped town. "When he tried to tell me I had no authority to withdraw my father's funds, I told him I had the authority to go home and tell said father—and the neighbors—what I'd heard. He couldn't count that cash out fast enough. Darn right it sat in a sock under the mattress that night."

There, that ought to cork him.

But no, he almost smiles. "May I drive you home, Analiese?"

The faster to get to those tomatoes, she reasons. Jouncing along beside him, she listens without comment while he tells her that Dunbarton has given him free rein with his market garden. "It's my conviction and it's true," he says without a trace of levity. "Farms on the river can produce a combination of irrigated and non-irrigated crops. The quality will be superior to imports and the cost less."

He's quite wound up, and Annie finds it entertaining to follow his line of thinking. She must admit, he does make sense. He points out that with underground cold storage, he can offer fresh produce all the year round. What the area needs, he says, is a county fair for folks like him to show what they can do. "Most people don't see a business opportunity unless it's bobbing in front of their face like the nether end of an antelope," he says. He's been a player from an early age. "Darndest thing, people moved out to those remote North Dakota homesteads. They'd bring their dogs, horses, and livestock, but no one brought a cat. Didn't cross their thoughts until they had a house or granary crawling with mice. I watched them turn themselves inside out trying to get a cat, and there just weren't any." Twelve years old he was when he hopped a train up to Winnipeg. Alleys crawling with cats. Boxed up a pair and strolled in the door before his mother could miss him for supper. *Look what I hunted up, Ma.*

"I did a brisk business. The kittens sold for a dollar fifty each for females, a dollar for males."

"You're a born salesman, Mr. Fielding." Annie smiles, unable to hold her tongue any longer. His earnestness is too tempting a target. "How fortunate for you, that everything in life is a sell."

Under his breath he exhales a soft "Ho!" then leans to talk to the horse, quiet words in a lyrical native dialect. The horse listens, holding its head at an odd incline. To Annie he says, "How so?"

"Goods and services, obviously. Then we must endure the politicians, hawking plans and promises. Teachers sell students on the importance of education. Parents sell children on their chosen code of conduct. Then it's to each to determine how much of it is snake oil."

"My father is a ticket seller," he reflects. "Entry to heaven."

"And are you buying?"

"Would you?"

"Not yet. I bought a ticket to Montana and haven't begun to see my money's worth out of it."

The homestead comes into view, and with it a couplet of relief and regret. "We don't have a cat. Cal is afraid it would scare Duo away. Won't you come in? I'm sure he would be glad to see you."

"The wagon is gone. He's not here."

"I meant Duo." The cart rocks to a halt. She steps down and touches the brim of her bonnet, aping his usual greeting. "Thank you for the ride."

"Let me know if you ever need a cat," he retorts.

"If I do, I'll call you. We have a phone now," she tosses over her shoulder. She stamps down three gopher hills pocking the path; she's never seen so many of the garden-destroying varmints as there are here. Maybe she should tell Cal they're getting a cat.

She closes the door behind her, stores her egg carriers under the counter, hoists the canning kettle onto the stove, then hesitates. It's barely midmorning and the house is already stifling. Suddenly the thought of lighting the stove seems beyond endurance. It's hot enough in the shack to cook fruit without striking a match. But the choice is air or insects. Would a screen door be such a luxury? Today air wins out over pests. She throws the kitchen window up and opens the door.

He's still there. He stands with an arm over the palomino's neck, watching the river. His weight settles on one leg, the other casually bent as though he doesn't need it. He wears his shirt sleeves rolled up, folded twice, smoothed to just shy of a crease. His hair, lush as a hayfield, is so close to white it should make him look old. Instead it gives off the vibration of lightning. The horse nudges his master's face, bringing forth a hint of a smile. Heaven help her, she understands why he withholds the full-strength version. It would melt a glacier. It might even strike flint in her carefully flameproofed heart and work faster than any bucket brigade ever assembled.

She eases the door closed and stands over the sink, fanning herself with last week's *Caswell Chronicle-Times*. Air, she needs air, and there isn't enough for both of them. On this prairie that pulls down the entire sky, he's drawing hers away.

He's courting her.

Now what? She pleats the paper into a crude glider and heaves it out the window. Ah! A minute later she follows it, first tossing a wicker basket ahead of her. The sod barn stays cooler than the house, and Cal doesn't own a sock that doesn't need darning. She'll sit on a hay bale and make a dent in this hummock of mending.

Courting, good heavens. The only time it happened to her, she was barely out of girlhood. That particular Fourth of July, Thomas Day was the center of attention, cranking ice cream under a spreading oak at the town picnic.

She took no note of it, thereby snaring him without the slightest intent, by refusing what the others were clamoring for. "No, thanks. I don't care for ice cream."

What a sweet summer that had been, right up until Thomas came to ask for her hand. Her mother had waited a whole day—it must have nigh unto killed her—before unleashing her horrible prophecy: *The Lord punishes those who step out of place.*

A stinging pain pierces the tip of her finger, and a spot of blood appears under the sock she holds. Stabbing herself with a dull darning needle, that takes some doing. She couldn't be more annoyed with herself for letting her thoughts stray backward, something she strives never to do and now has, compliments of the disquieting Mr. Fielding. He must be gone by now; it's been at least an hour. He should have learned something today, that one way or another, she can outlast him.

She tucks the socks and needle into the basket and steps out of the barn.

Her grip on the basket tightens when she sees his horse still idling about the pasture. She approaches the shack cautiously, bracing herself at the doorway with a hand against the frame. He's pacing in front of the table, an unopened bottle of her moonshine sitting between two glasses.

"It's a little early for that, isn't it?" She manages to keep her voice mild as May.

"Where have you been? How did you leave? I was standing right there."

"Do I owe you an answer, Mr. Fielding?"

"No." He comes close enough to press her back against the doorjamb, holding her in place with a knee grazing her thigh. Close enough for his essence to fill her head and force her to breathe through her skin, close enough to turn the humming in her ears to thunder. "Tell me how you knew about my horse. You said he's missing something. Tell me. *Annie.*"

She closes her eyes against the accusation in his. "I can't," she manages. "Please go now."

His lips touch just below her ear. "I can't."

There's so much more to him than just minutes ago, in her head and against his body, thoughts coming undone, flesh and fears and desires rising in tangled tandem. *Not now, not him, not here. And yet . . .*

"Please . . ." She raises her hand to his cheek, intending only a gesture of gentle pause, but her internal flailing carries to her fingertips, and the smack of her palm causes both of them to recoil. He rears back, eyes spitting sparks, clawing her hand and crushing it against the flat of muscle under his rib cage.

Her eyes spread so wide and dry she fears she may never blink again. "I won't ask again," she whispers. *I can't.*

"You won't need to." He flings her hand away, jamming his thumbs into his pockets, fingers splayed over the tops, *see?* "It appears I'm missing something too."

The next instant he's gone, striding across the pasture, whistling for his horse in a piercing pitch that slices the thin skin over her breastbone, exposing what lies within to the sun.

6

"Miss Rushton."

"Mr. Fielding."

And so it goes as September yields to autumn, because they can't avoid each other in town. Annie's chagrin at being on touchy terms with anyone so soon after her arrival feels like a boil that needs to be lanced. Maddeningly to her, they owe each other an apology. He overstepped; she overreacted.

And so it goes, he tipping his hat with exaggerated slowness only she would notice, she tilting her head with acknowledgment of a degree only he would notice, until one afternoon when a gaggle of unmannerly ranch hands crowd the sidewalk and Annie's hand brushes Adam's as they pass and Adam answers her "Pardon me, Mr. Fielding" with an almost inaudible "Adam" and she slows her step for a bare second and whispers "Annie" before hastening on.

The days descend into the approaching autumn, stealing an extra evening hour from the sun. Supper at the homestead becomes less hurried. Annie accepts it as a compliment, Cal using the last of the brown bread to wipe his bowl clean. "Frontier bachelor manners," he grins. "If you weren't here, I'd just put it back on the shelf." Annie ducks as he winds up and throws his balled napkin at her. "Missed!" she jeers to his cry of "Dang!"

"It couldn't have been that good," she notes. "You're wearing half of it on your shirt."

"Young'un, don't tease me. I'm forty-two and feeling every day of it. It happened while I wasn't paying attention."

"I've noticed how restless you are." He's like spit in a hot skillet. It's forced her to admit that, despite their blood ties, she doesn't know him well. Has he always been this way, his easygoing daytime demeanor giving way to pacing, wandering, disappearing as the night rolls in? His restiveness fills their close quarters.

She conks him lightly on the head with the frontier-clean bowl and kisses his scruffy cheek. She owes him for this new life and freedom. Whatever his need may be, she'll figure out how to put it right.

"Tell me what's wrong, Cal."

"Don't know," he says, the tone of his denial leaving Annie little doubt that he well knows. "Been here a while. It's closing in on me. Town this size, a cat can't sneeze without gagging on its own fur."

"Then it's fortunate we don't have a cat, isn't it?" she smiles.

"Per'aps." He yanks the laces of his boots undone. "I saw you talking to Adam Fielding outside the bank. Again."

"Oh, crikey. Am I being watched? I came out here to get away from that."

"It's hard not to notice you two when you're together. You're like piano keys. Do you fancy him?"

"Well, let's see. He's about as warm as New Year's Day. He has a short temper, doesn't suffer fools long enough to draw their next breath, and doesn't trust anyone much."

"Do tell. Do you fancy him?"

"Haven't seen mention of it in the *Comical Times*."

"That's an Annie sort of answer." He steps out of his boots, holding one down with the heel of the other, wiggling his toes in their freshly mended socks and whimpering, "Where's my favorite hole? The piggies cain't breathe."

Annie takes up her work at the sink, ducking Cal as he reaches over her for the can of tooth powder on the lowest shelf. He wraps a coarse linen rag around his finger, dunks it in water, then in the powder. "'e to'd me how you met, by t'e way," he says, mouth full of paste and cloth and finger. "So I 'ave bot' sides of t'e story. Soun'ed 'ike a fair fight to me. An' since then you've—"

"Good night, Caleb." She wraps the dish towel around his neck.

"Don't 'orget to 'ay yo' pwayers, Ana'iese."

Across the supper table where last week they talked of manners and cats, Cal delivers his curveball with no more heft than another wadded napkin. At first she thinks it's his typical buffoonery. But when he sits there smiling, twiddling his thumbs in stop-and-go motion, cold horror taps at the hollow of her throat. This talk of proving up and selling out—he means it. He even has a buyer in mind.

"No, Cal! This is the worst sort of matchmaking. Dangling a homestead in front of us? That's not a reason to marry. We don't even like each other."

"I think it is, and I think you do."

"Tell me you haven't already talked to him about this." She leaps to her feet, knocking over the cream pitcher. A thick puddle creeps toward Cal.

"You two have more in common than you'll admit, little sister. Hardheaded as you are hardworking, both of you. I have a year to go to prove up. Then I'm selling. A hundred dollars an acre to any starry-eyed homesteader stepping off any train that pulls in. Fifty dollars an acre to you two. What I'm doing is giving you first shot at something very, very good."

"What you're doing is making me very, very angry. Luring me out here to make a fresh start just in time to tell me you're leaving." She smacks the spilled cream with a rag, sending white flecks across Cal's face and hair.

"Pardon me for thinking you deserved something more than a pigeonhole behind Chase's kitchen in a town that won't forgive you." He wipes his face with a sleeve. "Don't give me that look. Why do you think I've kept my distance from Cheery Hell?"

"Then sell me the homestead. I can handle it alone. Why is Adam Fielding part of the conversation? He's no settler. He's a businessman, a salesman, an opportunist. Want to know the longest he's ever stayed in one place?"

She learned the answer to that after Adam drove her to the gooseberry patch upriver, a truce offering she thought it best to accept after their contretemps. She filled three gallon buckets and got the whole story. He had done his father's bidding, worked the farm and attended the normal school, taking away from it a mastery of Latin and the conviction that his future lay not in teaching, but in opening the frontier to business. He incensed his father and stupefied the faculty with his cogent commencement address explaining that it would be a long time, if ever, before eastern North Dakotans were anything more than a colony of

Minneapolis, hostage to the racketeering of bankers and rail-roads. The morning after that provocative farewell, he was already out, comfortable as a house cat in his window seat on a train headed west. Dakota was young but growing fast. People bought land, lumber for homesteads, and the goods to furnish both, sometimes right off the trains. Adam sold it all, working for the Danforth-Bryant Company as it expanded across North Dakota. Larimore, Grafton, Rugby . . .

"Minot, Wallace, Williston. The man is no more a settler than I'm a princess, Cal."

Cal smashes the shortcake biscuit on his plate into crumbs and stirs it around the crushed blackberries. "Let's skip the geography lecture and talk arithmetic. One plus one is two, but the whole is more than the sum of its parts. The know-how you two have together is enviable. Farming, selling." He shoves berries into his mouth, spoon clenched in a toddler's overhand grip. "You think you don't like each other. Force yourself. You might be surprised."

"What I feel like forcing is my fist down your smug throat."

Cal chuckles. "Annie, I like him. He has an earnestness about him that I think you like too. And the ladies sure think he's easy to look at, if I may be so shallow."

"You may not!" His merriment only fans her fury. "Easy to look at, just what I need. The last one worked out swell." Out of the shack she stomps, toward the riverbank, picking up stones and firing them in every direction. *Sprack!* into a tree trunk. How dare he? *Skik-skik-skik-skik,* a handful of gravel into the path. Some letter to Jenny she'll write. *Plonk-plonk* into the river. *Did you know our brother is a conniving low-down coyote?*

A collective squawk rends the henhouse as she smashes a high, fast pitch into the side. She thinks she hears him laughing, the rotter. She'd stay out all night if she'd thought to grab her coat. Her ire keeps her warm long enough to think up choice words for her dear brother, but when she throws open the door of the shack, he's tucked into the loft, giving off mellifluous kazoo snores.

The eggs quiver on the plate she slams in front of him in the morning. With a straight face, he tells her she'd make a crackerjack pitcher. No one could steal home on her.

At forty bushels to the acre, it's Cal's best year yet. In his small wagon, the crop will require a dozen forays to the elevator. But Dunbarton's wagon could do it in half the time, and they can't afford to decline Adam's offer of assistance.

Adam extends a hand to help Annie up to the seat of the wagon. A flick of the reins and the ground starts to move under them.

"It's kind of you to do this for us," she says.

October in Montana might become her favorite month. Could there be a more pleasant day? Summer's oven-dry heat has retreated. Colder, dewy nights have painted the cottonwoods dazzling gold. Cal has said nothing more about the future of the homestead since their squabble. She half closes her eyes and allows the swaying of the wagon to lull her into a few moments of indolence.

"Cal tells me he wants to sell."

Adam's voice jolts her to attention so violently, he jumps. "He didn't," she snaps.

"He did."

"He dies." The wagon rolls along at a swift clip, but she grabs the rein nearest her, yanking with all her might and sliding to the edge of the seat.

"Analiese!" He reins up with one hand and grabs for her with the other, but the sudden stop allows her to jump down. Before she's backtracked five paces, she's mentally packed Pa's old satchel. She's heard there are jobs in Great Falls. Heck, why stop there, why not break completely with life as she's known it and head north? "Where are you going?" her meddling, scheming turncoat of a brother will ask. "To *Cal*gary," she'll retort. She can get her own homestead. She can—

"Annie!" Adam has tied the wagon to a tree and caught up to her on foot. She marches on, not about to look at him.

"I know I'm not your favorite person."

It's enough to stop her. She's not being fair. It's Cal, not Adam, who's infuriated her.

"But I don't think I'm so bad." He pauses. "That you would throw yourself off a moving wagon."

A laugh escapes her clenched thoughts. She thinks, *You're not my favorite person. But who is?* In the absence of other candidates, he might be in the running. He came after her, didn't he?

She told him she would think it over. She'll never be able to say she didn't give it enough thought. She's thoroughly memorized the ceiling over her bed these past weeks.

Cal is right. She and Adam together have the makings of a successful venture. She can't deny the promise of the land, or the earnestness about Adam that draws her, though she suspects it hides something. In this they are alike. But are they contemplating a marriage or a business arrangement?

On one hand, she has reason to doubt her fitness for marriage. On the other hand, Adam never even took that chance. And on the other hand . . .

On the other hand, she tells her exasperated self, *I have five more fingers.*

Five more fingers. On a tiny hand the size of a quarter, fairy fingers that would curl around hers. She's forced herself to admit it. She longs for a baby. The cleanest of slates. Someone who will look up at her and know nothing except what happens from that hour forward. A baby with corn-silk hair, blindingly blond, the image of him. Maybe another little girl, with a champagne-palomino mane.

The image tears the bedding from her legs and hurls her out of bed. She throws open the window. The night air rushes in to ravish her, touching every inch save what she protects between clamped thighs. Another baby. It's not the birthing that would be agonizing; it's the trusting. Trusting Adam Fielding as a husband and father would be a pale challenge beside the charge of trusting herself again.

A moth flits around her shoulder, its wings whirring against the darkness. She lifts her chest to the night and feels the gooseflesh rise on her breasts. To be a wife and mother again. She's put a thousand miles and six torturous years between herself and a disaster that's defined her life. Is it enough? She folds her hands together in the closest thing she can come to prayer and presses them to her face. *Cynthia, I am sorry. So sorry.*

The moth settles into a corner of the ceiling, safe from owls and frogs and other villains of the night. In the loft, Cal snores in his singsong rumble. Annie lowers the window. The gooseflesh melts; her skin settles back into its place.

The hay mattress sighs as she crawls into bed. She tries to picture Adam Fielding asleep in his bunk at Dunbarton's. Before she can picture herself asleep next to him, she has to tell him. She must be fair. To him, and to the someday little girl with the fairy fingers and champagne-palomino mane.

In his solitary room off the end of the Dunbarton stables, Adam waits. Every glint outside his window catches his eye, each only a star pricking a clear sky, but any day now white flecks of light will signal the first snows and should be his cue to move to town for the winter. It was supposed to be that simple. Wouldn't his father be pleased to know that the mystery of the Lord's way has at long last impressed itself upon the impervious Adam Fielding? How else to explain it, a woman taking until the End of Days to consider his proposal of marriage, an offer he's withheld against the strenuous efforts of so many for so long?

She's giving it the full measure of thought, that she is. But no less than he did in those weeks following Cal's bumptious proposal.

"Why not?" Cal jeered when Adam met the proposition without reaction. They'd hiked four miles upriver, wading into a pocket where bass and walleye gathered. "She's not that ugly."

The water around Cal's thighs rippled with his stifled laughter. Adam cast his line with a vicious snap of the wrist, the minnow lure catching Cal in the shoulder. A swift tug brought him down, and when he surfaced, sputtering, Adam tightened the line. "Your sister isn't ugly, but you are."

Cal shook his shaggy head, flinging droplets in a pinwheel. A dog in a man's body, Adam decided.

"Guess you're not the businessman I thought you were," Cal laughed, with that taunting edge of his.

"Business, hell. Annie isn't a piece of property."

"Oh, it's *Annie* now? Ha. I was right. Hey, did you make this lure? See-through hook, that's clever. Thanks." He plucked the wooden fish with its ogling glass eyes from his shirt, tied it to his line, and didn't raise the subject again. Every few days, though, he raised that arrowhead brow of his. *Well?*

That was five weeks ago, when Adam still fell into bed as he always had, asleep on contact. Not tonight, again. Three weeks since he asked her. He swings his legs off the fold-down bed and lights the oil lamp. The shadows jigger up the wall, dancing over the calendar his aunt sent last Christmas. Scenes from the New Hampshire countryside. *Remember any of this?* she wrote in her feisty hand. Adam takes a block of wood from a shelf and nicks the corners with the penknife that belonged to the grandfather who taught him to whittle when life got knotty.

It surely distressed his parents and a string of disappointed ladies, his reticence to step up to the commitment of family. His father can look for blame in the mirror. Eight generations of Fieldings had rooted themselves in New Hampshire, but that changed the day the reverend announced they were headed west. Dakota needed supply ministers, and under the Homestead Act, they could be landowners.

But the free land exacted its price. Dakota was hard country. Jonas Fielding presided over funerals for the young, for it was the young who came to settle the unprotected prairie. They produced the next generation of young, many of whom couldn't survive the harsh world awaiting them. The young whom Reverend Fielding buried included his own.

Twenty-one years it's been, but Adam can't thresh the images from his head. That first winter. His mother laboring through a century storm to bring forth a baby who did not live to see a blue sky. The howling blizzard that buried their house in drifts, his mother's soundless weeping, the silence of the infant in her arms, the stifled sobs of Adam's three younger sisters. Digging a passage from the back door to the barn. Nailing together a box wherein the babe lay in icy repose for days until a warm wind swept through and they could make their way to the town cemetery to chisel out a tiny tomb. The graveyard only a few years old, but the farthest corner already filling with undersized markers. Our Mary. Baby Irene. Beloved Gilbert.

To this day, when a woman takes his arm, he feels the weight of his mother, leaning on him on that march to the cruel miniature grave while his father strode ahead, leaning on his Bible.

They would make that unthinkable journey again in but months. Another winter, another storm, another soul born only to die. That time, neither he nor his father could keep his mother on her feet. The indelible sight of her, on her knees in the snow, her hands spread over two small graves under a single stone.

The last baby, a sturdy brother named Malcolm, came along a few days before Adam's eighteenth birthday. Though Malcolm thrived and bestowed his infant adoration on his brother, Adam's thoughts on parenthood were sealed: it was a lottery fraught with vulnerability and grief. The randomness of it all both scared him and hardened his resolve not to be part of it. Like the cattle spreading over the grasslands, everyone was expected to come in from the free range, enter the corral, and play their role in populating the prairie. If that role involved devastating loss and sacrifice, that was God's will. Well, no one, God or human, was going to funnel Adam into that chute.

But Annie's capable, no-nonsense ways and the vision of the bountiful truck farm they could create have somehow become a believable notion. He knows Annie isn't in love with him. But she is smart, fearless, and devoted. Knowing this, he's allowed himself to admit what he never has before: he wants to be a father. He's ready to take that risk. The evidence is in his hands, where his grandfather's knife whittles away at what was supposed to be a fishing lure. But the tail became a baby sacque and the gill marks curved into sweet coiled ears. If he can carve a doll without knowing it, it's time. And he can carve his own path; he can be his own kind of father, not a sanctimonious, hidebound douser of dreams.

To be a father. The thought follows him everywhere, like a child itself. And though a man is expected to want a son, when he closes his eyes, he sees a little girl with a cloud of crow's-wing hair. Born with just enough to curl over his finger when he holds her for the first time.

The last signature of fall autographs the countryside where they sit on an uprooted cottonwood on the riverbank by the farm. Annie says, "What has Cal told you about me?"

"He said his baby sister was coming out to live with him."

"It's not what you might think."

"You're not a spinster."

"No."

"And not a widow."

"No."

"I see."

"Do you? I'm what my mother called used merchandise."

"I'm thirty-five years old, Annie. I haven't spent that time in a birdcage."

"Then here it is. Married in January. Baby in September. It was over before our first anniversary."

"That sounds traumatic. May I ask why you divorced him?"

"He divorced me. I was very ill after the baby came. We couldn't cope."

Adam exhales soundlessly. So there's the root of her reticence. She chose poorly. No doubt a smooth-talking cad who needed a workhorse wife and thought her lucky he lowered himself to ask. Got his heir apparent and tossed aside a wife barely risen from childbed. Good Christ, it won't be much of a challenge to do better.

"And the baby?" he asks.

"With him."

"Do you ever see—"

"With him."

"Does it bother you?"

"What do you think?"

He thinks she's either very brave, being so forthright with him, or she's trying to get him to renege. He thinks of all the women who have tried the opposite. None ever seriously tempted him. Why now?

What does he think? He thinks that sometimes he thinks too much.

"It's only fair," he says, "that you too ask me about my life. Is there anything you want to know?"

She is silent for so long, her skirt bunched between her hands, that he fears she may be working up a list. Her hair smolders in the stippled light, absolute black, no red or blue reaching from its depths, piled toward the top of her head like a cut bank of coal. The minute she says yes he's going to sink his hands in to his wrist. Agitation stirs inside him. Is she going to force him to ask again? Finally she speaks.

"No. Nothing."

Her simple demurral stuns him. How the hell can she have no questions, be above what so many woman seem possessed to wrest from him, the everlasting questions; it was like being pecked to death by ducks. That Annie has no questions—he could love her for this alone.

"My marriage and divorce are public record," she says, hands clasped around her knees now. "I prefer you hear it from me, and if it's something you can't live with, let's face it now."

The ground is damp. He watches a tea-colored stain seep along the hem of her skirt, darkening to a thin scallop.

How does he know if he can live with it? If she asks him nothing, isn't he beholden to her for the same? She doesn't fear what she doesn't know about him. She's lobbed the decision to where it started, in his hands.

"That is fair." *But is it possible?* "Are you certain there's nothing you want to ask me?"

"I trust that you'll tell me anything that's important for me to know. If I have to pry it out of you, it belongs to you in a way that's too private to be shared with me."

She reaches across his lap to hold his hands between hers, a gesture of unexpected tenderness, the most affectionate touch that has yet passed between them. It hums, low and warm, a train approaching but still distant.

"I don't care about what came before, Adam. I get out of bed every day determined to keep my sights forward. Who doesn't harbor an unhappy thing that we would undo if we could? What we're talking about today is whether we can be together and not punish each other with our pasts. I can. I can give you that."

No one has ever held his hands, or his attention, as she does. "I don't know what to say."

"I like that about you. You don't ramble on when you don't have anything to say. I have as much respect for what you don't say as for what you do."

"You are the most generous woman I have ever met."

"I hope I never do anything to change your mind."

He wonders how she does it, a flame that throws off such heat but remains cool.

"I dreamed of doing this alone," she says, indicating with her chin the homestead behind them. "You are . . . unexpected."

"I can say the same." He pulls her hands, still around his, to his chest. She doesn't resist. "There's one more thing that I need to know."

"That can be arranged," she says, smiling, as the dance of time descends into the auburn evening. For the rest of his life he'll remember the wind whispering around them, *you can, you can,* and the leaves rustling their reply, *you will, you will,* and that she tasted of promise and possibility, and that in stepping off this bluff together, they would defy both history and gravity. They would rise.

Darkness creeps in as they start for the house, her hand lying still in his. "Will you tell me now how you knew about Tipsy?" he asks. "'Missing something.'"

"I didn't. Is he?"

"Deaf in one ear and blind in one eye. The one you were looking into."

"Poor dear. How did it happen?"

"Maltreatment. I bought him from a sharper who was about to sell him to the knacker." At this she stops, waiting for more. "I've always had an affinity with horses," he says. "It was my way out."

On the days the trains streamed in with their carloads of horses, he tells her, everyone came to town. People clogged the streets, jabbering. He stood against the fence adjacent to the livery barns, watching and listening as the buyers trotted the beasts up and down the street, examined teeth for age, palpated joints. Then buyer and seller set to haggling. Adam silently observed this cauldron of trade. He parsed the exchanges and followed the pantomime of the sale. In time he could single out any transaction and write the script.

He was fifteen but could pass for twelve.

A pounding rain had swamped the streets and thinned the crowds one afternoon when a discouraged buyer happened to glance Adam's way and bark, "Whatta you lookin' at, kid?"

"He was looking at a Percheron," Adam says to Annie. "I told him the horse had a lemon up his nose. He was, of course, incredulous. The fellow was a member of my father's church. Said he hadn't taken me for a comedian."

Annie cocks her head in agreement. "Nor had anyone else, I'll bet."

The trader steered the buyer away with a jovial remark about needing someone to strap some respect into that boy. But the buyer knew Adam enough to shrug the trader off. Adam, hands in pockets, knocked elbows with the trader as he passed.

He spoke a few words of Michif into the horse's ear and took a crow feather from his chest pocket, drawing it back and forth across the horse's nostrils.

The trader tugged on his chin. The horse bobbed its head and sneezed. A shriveled lemon bathed in mucus dropped at its feet.

"Sharpers commonly use lemons to plug a roarer," Adam says as Annie puts a hand to her mouth. "That horse put up some hair-raising snorting. The buyer was apoplectic. 'Kid, how did you know that?' He gave me two bucks to shadow him for the day."

A strawberry roan with a bright black mane got the buyer's twice-over. *What do you think, kid?* The horse's hoofs had been varnished, he told the man. Laminitis. The trader was trying to hide it by rasping away the ridges and painting over the rasp marks. Next, a marvelous mare with a long, braided tail.

What do you think, kid?

"And?" Annie breathes.

"Undo the braid and you'll always find a switcher. Tail like a bullwhip." Adam gestures, flogging the air right and left. "A sharper will try to tell you it's only an annoyance. It is, until your marvelous mare starts throwing urine."

It went this way for more than a year; he must have met thirty trainloads. He heard the mutterings of buyers and sellers as he passed: *There's that preacher's kid who sees through every trick in the book.* It amazed him, how low some people would sink to make a sale, and how seemingly intelligent people would fall for it. No business college could have ever given him a keener crash course in the art and science of selling.

Annie chuckles. He certainly took it a step up from his kitten business, didn't he?

Another year trickled by. He made allies and enemies. It came to an end the day the church sexton overheard the growling of two sharpers after Adam averted a sale. Repeated the conversation to the Reverend and Mrs. Fielding in their parlor that night. "'I've got a mind to kill that kid, preacher's boy or no,'" the sexton quoted, squinting to avoid Adam's gaze. "He says, 'I seen plenty of accidents the good Lord been too busy to thwart.'"

By then Adam had accumulated enough dollars to take him wherever he might choose to go, stowed in a place undisturbed by fire, flood, critter, or parent.

Annie smiles and exhales. "That's a tale for the grand-children. Am I not lucky those two were all hat and no horse?"

"Those kind usually are." They come to a clearing in the cottonwoods. Adam nods toward the sky. "Do you recognize Pegasus there? Most people don't, because he's upside down."

"And missing his hind legs." Annie's finger traces the constel-lation: the square of the body, the head, the front legs. "Goodness but it's a bright night. The stars almost cut shadows." She stops and takes three steps toward the river. "Ever read Thoreau?"

"Oh, yes. 'Civil Disobedience.' Brilliant. Terrified a genera-tion of politicians."

"I was thinking of his journals. He described a summer night on the river, by starlight. It was just like this. The low light from the north and the occasional shooting star. The evening star, mirrored in the water like a stream of sparks thrown up to the sky. Just like this. He captured it in words. If I could . . . in my own way . . ." She reaches out, palm upturned to the stars, and closes her hand around the night air.

7

They wait a week to tell Cal. When they've worn the idea long enough to know it fits, Adam comes to supper at the homestead and, holding Annie's hand, breaks the news.

"A wedding? You two?" Cal warbles. "Mercy, why didn't I think of that? When is this splendid event, and where the heck is the whiskey?"

Six weeks, Adam tells him. January 1. Nice clean start.

Out comes the whiskey bottle; glasses clink.

"To you." Cal downs the drink and pours a refill. "And to whoever conceived this brilliant idea." Their talk jumps ahead to spring. Adam should start the conversion to truck farming as he sees fit. *Hear, hear!* They'll have a full-year planning cycle before Cal's prove-up date; then he'll sell to them. *Cheers!* Adam will continue with Dunbarton until then. *Your health!* Finally Cal unfolds himself from his chair. "Goodness me, I'll bet you kids would like to be alone." He bends to Annie's ear, the weedy tang of the whiskey fighting the aroma of the harness-oil stains on his jacket cuffs. "The blushing bride. Very fetching, my dear."

The door bangs. Cal's footsteps die away. The fire crackles.

Adam tips his glass to Annie. "To us." He tells her he sees no need for the fuss and expense of a formal wedding, does she? They can accomplish the deed with a stop at the Valley County courthouse for a license and a trip to the parsonage for the vows. Does this make sense to her? Annie nods her agreement. She'll write their good news to Jenny tonight.

On the bright, cold Monday after Thanksgiving, Adam's cart clatters to a stop midway along Main Street and Annie hops down, dodging Clotilda Sandifer as she scuttles by in a rush of nattering taffeta. "I won't be long," Annie tells Adam. "Please give Mr. Barrett my best."

At the door of Melton's Mercantile, she finds Mrs. Sandifer hovering, a gloved hand on the knob. She greets Annie with stiff gaiety. "Why, hello, Miss Rushton. I couldn't help overhearing you. Mr. Barrett is my brother. Is Mr. Fielding thinking of renting Mr. Barrett's cottage on Third Street?"

"Oh, I couldn't possibly speak for Mr. Fielding. Are you going in?"

"Surely-y." Mrs. Sandifer hiccups into a garish pink brocade handkerchief. The older woman precedes Annie into the store, trotting toward the counter where Elise Melton is arranging a display of holiday candles. Annie veers to the wall where bolts of colorful fabric line the shelves. With luck, Mrs. Sandifer will keep Mrs. Melton engaged for a while.

But no, here comes the mistress of the store, accompanied by an overpowering cloud of Le Muguet, her hands clasped at the waist as she trills her phony soprano greeting: "Good moooorning, Miss Rushton!" Absorbed in examining fabrics, consulting a sketch in her hand, Annie at first doesn't respond, then answers Mrs. Melton's delicate "heh-hem" with a low "Good morning" and a half smile.

Mrs. Melton clears her throat a second time. "He's a handsome one, Mr. Fielding."

"Indeed," Annie murmurs, pulling a pencil stub from her bag and making a note in the margin of the sketch.

Mrs. Melton's tone tips toward scolding. "We all think highly of Mr. Fielding. He's a reputable businessman and an estimable citizen. But the likes of him won't be waylaid. Many have tried."

Annie murmurs, "I didn't try," under her breath. Her eye travels up the stacks of fabric.

Mrs. Melton's voice rises. "I wouldn't want to see you hurt, dear. You being new to us here and all."

"May I see the bolt of the indigo weave on the upper shelf, Mrs. Melton?"

The woman, not accustomed to having her counsel ignored, stares at Annie as if she might have a hearing problem. "Yes, it's such a rich shade, isn't it?" Mrs. Melton moves behind the counter to face Annie square. "May I cut you a dress length?"

"I'm not making a dress. It's for a quilt." Her eyes dart across the rows of cloth.

"Log Cabin? Bear Paw?" Mrs. Melton strains to see the sketch.

"No."

"Bow Tie?"

"No."

"Not a crazy quilt?"

Annie taps her pencil on the counter. Crazy quilts have fallen from fashion. Does Mrs. Melton think Annie wouldn't know this? "It's my design," she says equably.

"May I see?" Mrs. Melton reaches for the sketch. Annie sighs inwardly and lays the paper on the counter.

Mrs. Melton takes in the sketch only to pull back, pale fingers with satiny buffed nails worrying the cameo at her throat.

"Well" is all she can manage.

"A deep subject," Annie declares, "as my grandfather used to say." She's deeply pleased with her design, wrought during a week of evenings by the river with paper and pencil and a timorous knuckle of flame from a kerosene lantern.

Unlike any quilt pattern in any book, Annie's *The River by Starlight* paints a celestial tableau unrestrained by symmetry or the usual ordered repetition of shapes. The background is a series of blocks of changing lengths, widths, and shading. A wide swath of twilight spreads across the bottom, narrowing into smaller blocks of night darkness that seem to float at the top. A waxing crescent moon glows amid a shower of stars that starts at the upper left corner and opens into a spray down the opposite side. Halfway to the horizon, the Great Square of Pegasus: the horse's outstretched neck and legs gallop toward morning. A river curves its way across the foot of the sketch, disappearing into the night before it reaches the edge.

Mrs. Melton pigeon-blinks, as if she fears the paper might burst into flame. "It's certainly . . . original. You do break with tradition."

"I do," Annie agrees gravely. Back and forth she swivels from the sketch on the counter to the bolts on the shelves. This black with the chrome-yellow stars is perfect. The dark sapphire with the concentric swirl of white dots is just right for the middle ground, with the cadet-blue weave shot with an occasional white thread for the lower third. For the river, a faded green with faint triplet arcs of off-white. For the moon she chooses a bolt of blazing chrome orange. She gives polite to-the-inch orders to Mrs. Melton, whose locked jaw belies the difficulty with which she holds her tongue as her scissors slice the fabric. Annie counts out bills and coins while the proprietress measures the batting under narrowed eyes. At last, with everything bundled and parting pleasantries exchanged, Annie moves toward the door.

Mrs. Melton hurries from behind the counter and chirps, "That's a mighty unusual pattern. Is it for yourself?"

"Not exactly," Annie says over her shoulder. "It's a groom's quilt. A wedding gift, from me to Mr. Fielding."

She doesn't wait for the response that won't come. *Congratulations* is no doubt too long a word for someone whose tongue lies vise-clamped by the cat freed from the proverbial bag. Annie pushes out into the brilliant afternoon. She must remember to tell her intended he can expect some reaction.

Jenny's reply comes as a parcel. The brown paper falls away, and Annie's fingers tremble as she lifts an indigo wool gown trimmed in crystal beading.

> Congratulations, dear Annie. You've gladdened all our hearts with your unexpected news. I know you admired my wedding dress, and thought you might like to wear it for your special day. Do you remember helping me sew on the beading? Whether you wear it or not—be happy. Oh, do be that.

Annie slips her arms into the sleeves of the gown, holding it to her body with an arm at her waist. It settles in a cloud around her, beads sparkling in every direction. She remembers Jenny's wedding as if it were yesterday. Annie was only twelve years old, and more than anything she prayed she would grow to be like Jenny, kind and loving and making practicality seem so classy. Jenny, her face framed by the gown's timeless wide lace, looked like a brilliant-cut sapphire. Annie watched Jenny move among her guests, the bodice of her gown forming a gentle V over the skirt, its bright beaded edges pointing insistently downward to that place of womanhood, itself a gentle V. It seemed to tell Annie there was no escaping their fate as females. And while she wished nothing but the best for her sister, she also feared for her, feared that marriage would somehow stamp the fizz out of Jenny, leaving her as flat and pallid as their mother.

Like the quilt Jenny's girlfriends made for her. Annie made the appropriate noises about the lovely workmanship, such even stitches. "I love the colors," she gushed, hating the blank white border, the pieced pyramids and lifeless rectangles in gray-blue, brown, and green, meant to suggest the trees around the newlyweds' home. All of it impeccably symmetrical. Annie already knew life wasn't like that.

But the gown! She shakes the memories from her head and decides she'll wear it. She will remember only Jenny's radiance on her wedding day, how her husband cleaved to her, and how they reveled in their years together.

Annie holds the gown to her shoulders, wrapping her arm around at the waist. She'll have to take it in and raise the hem. She steps to the window to try to catch a reflection of the length of it, and sees Adam coming up the path. He knocks, opening the door at the same time. Part gentleman caller, part family. The sight of Annie with such an elegant dress stops him short.

"Close the door," she says, feeling almost naked behind the gown. "Are you trying to heat the whole farm?"

"What is this?" he asks. "I had three sisters. Are you playing dress-up?"

"It's Jenny's wedding dress. She thought I might like to wear it. Unless you dislike it."

"Why would I? It's a dress. Wear it if you want. If you don't, then don't." He comes closer. "You know, I like this color. You'll look beautiful. That reminds me. See over there?" He gestures out the window across the road. "I want to put plum trees in there, with the apples and pears."

Beautiful. He called her beautiful. "I'll wear this." She pulls the dress tighter to her waist. "I can kill three birds with one stone. The dress is something old, borrowed, and blue."

He leans against the unpainted window casing. "Ever the practical one, aren't you? What will you have for something new?"

"Why, you. And that's enough quaint wedding claptrap."

"Glad you feel that way. Being that I've now seen your wedding dress, and isn't there some claptrap about that being bad luck?"

"Such twaddle." She arranges the gown on the needlepoint hanger Jenny included. "We're going to the parsonage together. I don't plan to wrap myself in the draperies until it's time to say 'I do.'"

Now she needs him to leave. She has a quilt to piece and a dress to alter. As if he's read her mind, he says he can't stay; he only stopped by to tell her that he's given the first month's rent on the Third Street house to Mr. Barrett. Another cat is out of the bag, racing with the prairie wind through the streets of Caswell.

On the way out, he notices the slim book she left on the footstool last night.

"Poems of Emily Dickinson? Where'd you get it?"

"A gift."

"From?"

"Thomas."

"Why'd you keep it?" His voices rises with a chill edge.

"I like Emily Dickinson," she says carefully.

"Did he write in it?"

"Why don't you look for yourself?" She picks it up and offers it over.

He looks at it without moving. "Why must you keep it?"

"Why should I get rid of it? Oh, Adam. I don't want to play Twenty Questions. How about Animal, Vegetable, Mineral? Books are paper and paper is trees, so it's a vegetable, on a farm. That's all it is." She makes sure she's still talking as she squeezes into the bedroom alcove and shoves it to the back of her drawer of underthings.

Then she sees him to the door. He runs a finger under her chin and with a quarter smile whispers, "Animal."

She watches his cart recede down the road. "Green-eyed monster," she says, matching his quarter smile.

"She cheats!" Cal yells.

Annie fans out four aces, a trio of jacks, and a straight of clubs. "You shuffled. You dealt. You're keeping score. Want to blindfold me too?"

"Make her push her sleeves up." Adam frowns over his T-square and blueprint paper.

"Her sleeves are always pushed up. Horn spoons!" Cal grabs a fork from the sink and attacks half a pear pie still in the pan.

"Everyone loves a sore loser," Annie tuts, collecting the cards. "At a penny a point, Cal, I may be able to buy the homestead out-right—with your money—by the time you're ready to sell." She shows Adam the scorecard.

"Nice hieroglyphs," he grunts. With his papers and tools cov-ering half the kitchen table of the Third Street house, he thinks for the sixty-seventh time what a damn long December it's been. Waiting and watching. Waiting because the January 1 wedding date was his fool idea. Watching the woman with whom he has chosen to join forces. She's a force, all right. She has yet to succumb to what he believed inevitable. The history exam. The questions about what came before. He's beginning to understand, uneasily, that he's not her equal in this. That she belonged to someone else, however passingly, gnashes at him. He must get hold of himself. She's caught him stewing about it, although she didn't know it. *I love how your eyes change color with your mood, big fella. They're almost green right now. Penny for your thoughts?*

"Mmm, that blunts the edge of my humiliation." Cal sends the pie tin clanging into the sink. "Needs more cinnamon, though. Didn't quite singe my uvula. Have the great perfesser over there figure out how to grow cinnamon in Montana."

Annie folds her arms. "He could do it." She makes it sound enough like fact that Adam scribbles *cinnamon? greenhouse?* in the margin of his tablet. She bends over his shoulder, warming the air around his neck. "Show me," she says, and he begins to walk her through their farm, in acre-by-acre diagrams. Cabbages here, onions here—red, white, pickling. Potatoes here, Early Rose and Irish Cob-bler, varieties that mature early. Corn, large and small varieties.

"Let's grow popcorn," she suggests. "Cal used to build a campfire behind the farmhouse for Chase and me. We'd pop the corn in an open pot and try to catch the kernels before they hit the dirt. Remember, Cal?"

Cal nods. Adam conjures a picture of Annie at four. Black eyes. Brown bare feet. Gray dress. She runs on reedy legs across dusty roads, through fields of faded hay, wan wheat, and pale corn. The picture is fuzzy. Where's the color? Child Annie reaches for the white blossoms of popcorn. . . .

"And what we didn't catch," she finishes, "we ate with a bit of dirt rather than waste it."

"Damn straight," Cal avows. "It's not dirty if you get it within five seconds."

Adam brackets off four rows.

On to the roots: turnips, parsnips, beets, carrots. Then the expenses: seed, stock, workers, a typewriter, a truck. A farmer friend of Dunbarton's has one for sale, not a year old, says the two of them just don't get along. The truck has everything a wagon doesn't: headlamps, covered cab, windshield, horn. Four hundred dollars is serious money, but they could swing it if they plan carefully.

"Careful planning, how dismal." Cal yawns. "This is where I take my leave, folks. Annie, are you coming?"

Annie glances at Adam, at the kitchen table papered with their future.

"Tipsy's still hitched. I'll drive her home, Cal."

"I bet you will."

Annie sees her brother out, raising a V of fingers in front of her face. Two weeks.

At the table, she rests an arm on Adam's shoulder while he takes her through more diagrams. Construction of a twenty-five-foot vegetable cellar, expansion of the poultry business, of which she'll take charge. How about adding turkeys, ducks? He wonders aloud if Duo comes with the deal, a wolf that actually does guard the henhouse.

She adds a log to the stove and settles into the chair across the table from his. Her face reflects the amber light as she knits from a ball of cream-colored wool without looking at her needles. A lacy garment flows into her lap.

"How do you do it?" he asks.

"Knitting? It's just a series of interconnected loops."

"Not that."

"I know. Do what?"

"Turn your back on the past. Live without regret."

"Who said I live without regret? But to carry it around like a millstone?" She settles deeper into her chair. "'God pity them both! and pity us all, / Who vainly the dreams of youth recall; / For of all sad words of tongue or pen / The saddest are these: "It might have been."' John Greenleaf Whittier."

"Have you ever written poetry?"

"Heavens, no. I barely finished my sixth-level reader."

"You never know. If you've never tried."

Her needles tick in measure with the clock on the shelf above the stove.

"How about if I write you a limerick about what a twit Mrs. Melton is? 'Merchant madam from eastern Montana, speckled skin like the peel of banana—'"

"Oh no. Annie, no. Did you tangle with her again?"

"I bought some yarn. For a bridal shawl." She holds up her needles. "She took exception to my pattern."

"Again? Why on earth?"

"It seems the pattern I call 'Jenny's four-row repeat' is something she calls Spider's Web. It seems that a pattern with that name is unseemly for a bridal wrap. It seems she thinks I have ensnared you in my sticky web. It seems I'm not her first choice of a wife for you."

"She said this?"

"Of course not. One perceives. By the way, I'm not offended by her characterization of me as a spider. I am offended that she equates you to a fly."

"The old battle-ax," he mutters, one temple starting to thud. "I shudder to ask, but did you slay her in your usual manner? Direct hit?"

"Poetically. I told her, 'The bird a nest, the spider a web.' William Blake. I thanked her for her warm wishes for our new home."

Both temples thumping now. Maybe they shouldn't wait out December. He needs to corral her. Brand her for all to see; sear his mark into her flesh. The sooner she becomes Mrs. Adam Fielding, the sooner she can begin to behave accordingly.

"Analiese, you need to be careful with her."

"Pah." Annie winds another buttery snowball of yarn, draping the skein over the back of the chair.

"Because you're correct," he says.

The whipping of the yarn stops. She meets his gaze, but her face is blank.

"You're not her first choice of a wife for me. That distinction goes to her niece. A deeply boring damsel whose idea of fun at a social is flapping her eyelashes at all the foods a lady dasn't eat in front of a man, then packing away enough ice cream to freeze hell. She tried to get me to propose during a canoe float. Unfortunately, there was a bit of an accident. I—"

"Adam, I don't want to know this."

The fire in the stove crumbles to hissing embers. He pushes his chair back, a reptilian scrape grating the floorboards.

"And I don't want you shopping at Melton's, ladyfriend. Take your business elsewhere."

"Don't be silly. I wasn't born on a farm to be scared by a goat."

He reaches over the table and grabs her wrist, feels the heat shooting from his fingertips into her flesh. The ball of yarn hops from her lap and lights out across the floor, freckling with bits of bark and wood dust.

"Are you scared of snakes? You don't know what she's capable of. I said take your business elsewhere. Understand?"

8

On the Saturday before Christmas, Annie takes Adam down the road to meet the Eulenbergs. She points out the tall pole at their house that matches the one at Cal's shack. "Before we had our phone, Margrethe and I would run a white towel up the pole when we needed help. I used ours twice during my first few weeks here, once when Cal hurt his foot, and again when Duo made friends with a porcupine and I needed someone to hold him while I yanked out the quills."

Until tonight, Adam has known the Eulenbergs as nodding acquaintances in town. Now he grasps the hand Karl offers, his palm meeting a warmth that goes beyond welcome, the mild shock of spirits melding, as invisible to the eye as the line where the land that will soon be his meets this neighbor's. Adam has never tried to put a name to the spur that drives him to believe he can tame the land, that intricate work of nature that for time immemorial knew no border, no cultivation, no dictator. Challenge, gamble, defiance, ambition? Arrogance? All those things drive him, but now, in Karl's handclasp, he sees it's something higher. Hope. *Spes et futurum.* Something he's never courted consciously. Like the river, it surges to its own level, obscuring everything jagged and perilous that lies below.

Margrethe brings a steaming tureen of potato soup and two loaves of dark bread to the table. The children—two boys, eleven and thirteen, and a girl of seven—appear at Margrethe's call of *"Abendessen!"* The oldest boy tugs her apron string undone as he lopes by with "You mean 'sup-per.'"

"Yes, Lukas. Sup-per." Margrethe elbows her son and winks at Annie. "Kids! They know more than their parents."

"Does he know what to do about Viveka?" Karl sighs.

"Sorry, Dad," the boy apologizes, while the girl sighs, "Poor Viveka."

"Tell Adam about Viveka," Annie says.

"Viveka," Karl begins, "is one of the best, and one of the stupidest thing I've ever done. When we arrived here, I needed a saddle horse, and I didn't like what came in on the train." He pauses to push his bowl toward the soup tureen. Margrethe ladles out a helping. "I mean the people. Not the horses."

Under the table, Annie pats Adam's thigh.

"I hiked out into the range and found a herd of broncs. I knew as much about them as they knew about me. But I spotted a mare who carried herself as one who'd be nobody's fool. I threw a loop around her nose, jumped on, and held on until she ran herself out. Brought her home, fed her, sheltered her. She's been an ideal animal."

"Yes, that horse would do anything for Karl," Margrethe says reverently. "But she won't let anyone else near."

"And now there's a problem?" Adam asks.

Karl smiles with worried eyes. "She shows no trouble in the pasture, but the last two weeks, she's been going down in the stall and has a dreadful time getting up."

"Adam is magical with horses," says Annie. "You must let him have a look."

"Oh, please, Mr. Fielding, would you?" the little girl implores.

"I'm not a vet—"

Karl passes a napkin over his lips and pushes away from the table.

"Okay." Adam rises, laying a hand on Annie's shoulder as he leaves.

As Karl pulls the kitchen door closed behind them, they hear Margrethe say to Annie, "That horse like a second wife to him."

Karl adjusts the flame on the kerosene lamp and chuckles. "The loyalty of a courageous female is not to be taken lightly."

A ring of reddish clouds circles the moon as they follow a path along the picket fence surrounding Margrethe's dormant vegetable patch. The barn looms out of the dark, warm inside with the breath and stirrings of horses in their stalls, a trio of cows chewing and swaying, and half a dozen spotted hogs asleep in a bristly pile, smelling of tails and all that befalls a tail. The mare lies on her side in the center stall, legs outstretched, stiff as rakes.

Adam sweeps an eye around the stall, digs a toe into the straw, overturning it. Squatting at the mare's head, he whispers in dialect. Her head comes up to meet his, limbs twitching. Adam works fingers gently along each leg. "No breaks," he murmurs, then sets to brisk rubbing with handfuls of straw. In minutes the mare heaves to her feet, stamping gingerly.

"*Mein Gott,*" Karl breathes.

"This a different stall for her?" Adam asks.

Karl nods. "Moved her here two weeks ago."

Adam points to the front boards of the stall, which stop two feet above the floor. "You need to extend these boards all the way down. She's catching her feet in that open space when she kicks at mice or just moves about. Tonight her legs went numb, but it's only a matter of time until she breaks a leg, or her neck, when she goes down."

"You," declares Karl, "have done some doctoring."

"No, none."

"Raised on a ranch?"

"Raised in a parsonage. Many parsonages."

"I grew up living over my father's butcher shop. Knowing something about dead animals hasn't helped me with live ones."

"For a spell, I was probably the Dakota territory's youngest horse-trade advisor." Adam thinks that should be answer enough, but the mare bobs her head against his hand. *Tell him,* she seems to be saying.

Karl lowers himself to a hay bale, his eyes bright and interested. Adam strokes the mare's neck. This is a part of his story never shared.

"I was fifteen," he begins.

People called the grizzled pioneer Old Timer, an intentional garbling of his Norwegian name, Aalthaammer. He had worked the wild-horse roundups on the plains of Oklahoma and Texas.

"He said I'd never in my life see anything free and brave as those horses," Adam says, and Karl nods. "Thundering herds, uncountable thousands, spilling off the edges of what the eye could take in." All of them, powerful wonders. Their speed, their stamina, their spirit.

The trapping of the horses sickened Old Timer, his telling of it sickened Adam, and now Adam sees the effect of his retelling on Karl, who sits with arms crossed, one hand in a loose fist with the back of his thumb against his mouth. Adam describes the huge corrals, mesquite poles bound with rawhide, mustangs driven through a chute built to face the wind, blinding them with dust clouds of their own making. Their shrieks of fury and terror.

The ones whose panic cost them their footing perished first, trampled by their brethren's wild search for escape, magnificent animals dying as though they were nothing more than mosquitoes. Others stamped and spun until exhaustion and apoplexy wrung the life from them.

"Old Timer could see it in their eyes: 'Better dead than penned.'" Adam shuts his eyes and he's there again, sitting on the upended coffee crate in Old Timer's dugout, the day he heard the story for the first time and realized that men were not superior to animals by virtue of their supposed morality.

Karl listens without moving a muscle. Adam scoops a handful of oats from a bin and offers them to the mare. Her flannel lips knead his palm.

One day, a small buckskin mare caught Old Timer's eye. She exuded iron determination, her mane beating like a crow wing around her face, her tail sweeping up bursts of dust as she reared. When her eye met his, he swore he heard her thoughts: *I will not go quietly.* Then she plunged into the mass and he lost her. She had no chance.

She broke Old Timer as surely as he had broken thousands of her kin. He turned his own horse and sprinted away, barely slowing until he got to Dakota, where any hunting he did ended up on a dinner plate. "And when you sup with me," he told Adam, "you'll say grace for the life of that creature."

Karl nods. "As it should be." A swell of sibilant grunts wrinkles the air above the sleeping pig pile. *Amen.*

"I never thought I'd marry," Adam finishes, feeling unburdened in a way Cal's companionship hasn't provided.

"Roping a wild one is always dangerous," Karl says, folding his hands over a knee. "Often foolish. But sometimes necessary. There's more than one way for a wild one to be content."

"Do you think Annie is a wild one?"

"Was I talking about Annie?"

When Adam asks Annie if she'd like to attend the annual firemen's masquerade ball on New Year's Eve, she hesitates. What is the right answer?

If it's all the same to her, he tells her, some of the fellows are insisting on buying him drinks at the Prairie Dog that night, what with Adam really ringing out the old and ringing in the new, they say. His tone makes it clear he wants her reaction but isn't asking her permission.

"Go right ahead," she says. "You've gotten this far in life without my advice and consent."

"Not to worry," he assures her. "There won't be any funny business."

"Not to worry," she replies. "There won't be any questions."

In the first light of December 31, she puts the final stitch in the quilt, marrying the captivating top to the plain backing. She'll bring it to the house on Third Street today but leave it wrapped in a sheet under the bed. He'll see it for the first time when they return to the house as man and wife.

He's not there when she arrives in the afternoon. Just as well—she doesn't intend to linger. But she grows mesmerized with the subtle transformation of the house as she places pieces of her life alongside his. Her clothes touching his in the cabinet, her combs next to his shaving cup. She makes three trips to the woodpile, stacking the log cubby to overflowing. A few flakes of snow coast on a dove-colored sky. She should start for the homestead soon if she wants to arrive before dark, but hauling wood in the cold has sapped her more than she realized. She'll take just a few minutes' rest, counting the lacy flakes drifting by the front window, then be on her way.

The party's for him but Adam observes from the sidelines. The toasts and the backslapping faded an hour ago, and now it's just New Year's Eve. He's somewhere short of pie-eyed, although closer to it than he planned. He can feel the whiskey creeping from his pores. Enough with the jollity. He leans over the bar to ask Sprat Douglass, "Where's the back door?"

"Sneaking out on your own party?"

"I'm already happier than a baby in a barrel of titties. The door?"

Sprat ambles to the end of the bar and indicates a narrow hallway that cuts a sharp corner around a staircase. "Congratulations, Adam," he says. "Guess we'll be seeing less of you."

Adam claps a hand to Sprat's shoulder. "Her rotgut beats yours, my friend."

The cold slaps him a notch toward sober, but the walk to the house isn't enough to finish the job. He's slow to register the low light in the front room and the shadow of a figure asleep on the settee.

"I didn't want to startle you, so I left the lamp burning," she says, sitting up, her voice coming to him downy and warm.

Those obsidian eyes, tossing the low glow of the lamp about her head like Salome's seven veils. He'll make it a point that no one but he ever sees her this way.

"To what do I owe this unexpected pleasure?" He shrugs out of his sheep-lined coat. "Another quaint tradition, the wedding night, about to be discarded?"

"I brought some things over this afternoon, did some chores. I dropped off in the chair, and when I woke up, it was too dark to start back." She pauses. "I called Cal. He's laughing himself sick."

"My lascivious ladyfriend, how lucky can we get? Most of the town is at the firemen's ball and oblivious to your sleeping arrangements. Shall we?" He starts for the bedroom.

"We can wait one more night, given your—"

"What if I don't want to? Is it 'forcing my attentions on you' if we're within twenty-four hours of being married?"

"Given your condition, I would say it's a question of . . ."

The end of her sentence dissipates into the walls. She tucks herself under his shoulder and guides him to the bedroom.

"You make me drool," he breathes into her hair, just before he hits the bed. Her charming chuckle tickles his cheek as she pulls blankets over him and whispers, "See you next year." She lingers, fingertips on his. *Oh promise me.*

She wakes to a house warm but silent. The room comes into focus, furnishings that came with the house and the only piece that's

Adam's, the Massachusetts desk that belonged to his grandfather. In the kitchen, the stove simmers but the coffeepot is clean and cold. In the bedroom, the bed lies rumpled like an abandoned nest.

The morning crackles around her. Thirty below, she judges, dropping Adam's saloon-stinking clothes on the back porch, resisting the impulse to draw them to her nose lest she detect something floral, more exotic than booze and smoke. *No questions.* As she puts the bedroom right, she tries to fend off subtle fears about his whereabouts. If he's fled, she can retreat to Cal's, as disregarded as ever, and never come to town. Plenty of homestead women don't make it into town for years, and—

A sharp knock brings a gasp and a rush to answer. Where she half expects to see the sheriff, there stands Mr. Magruder from the bakery with a covered cake, redolent of sugar and lemon. "Congratulations, ma'am. May you live to hold your children's children, and may the saddest day of your future be no worse than the happiest day of your past."

Behind Mr. Magruder comes Mr. Alquist, carrying cold roast chicken from his café, and a messenger from the hotel with two bottles of champagne. The Seviers from next door bring hot cross buns, and Margrethe blows in with soup and a winter fruit compote.

"He said he didn't want any fuss," Annie says faintly. "I took him at his word."

Margrethe just laughs. "Do you have everything you need, dear?"

"I do," Annie says humbly. "Everything except a groom."

"How many do you need?" Adam stands in the doorway as if he has strolled in from the next room.

"*Ja*, there he is," Margrethe says, "rousting folks on the holiday they least want to see the sunrise."

"For no better cause," he says, "though it looks like we may have a storm whipping up. Shall I drive you home now, and hope we can gather later?"

Annie covets Margrethe's confidence, her telling Adam that her buggy will make it if she leaves without tarrying, and of course they will meet later. A little snow can't hold off the first wedding of the new year. Annie stands at the front window until Margrethe is out of sight. Outside, nothing is moving save a soft snow starting to fall. Annie throws a blanket over the settee and motions Adam to sit with her. She lies back in his arms, wishing they'd scheduled the wedding for earlier in the day.

"We should have scheduled the wedding for earlier in the day," he says. "By now, we could be done and on with it."

"Shhhh." She pats his hands, crossed over her waist.

Adam shifts and pulls her closer. His hands travel up her bodice, close under her breasts. "You're awfully calm. Maybe because you've done this before and I haven't?"

His breath on her neck has a cold edge to it. Should she tell him that her calm is outward only, that she has no more surety of the outcome of "this" than he? He knows enough that she shouldn't have to tell him. Unless she hasn't told him enough. Unless.

"If you're having second thoughts, let's have them now," she says. "There's still time to call it off."

His hands move over her breasts and linger before sliding the length of her and slipping between her legs. "I don't want to call it off. I want you."

Two hours, she thinks. *It will go by quickly.* She rolls over to face him. Her knees pressing against his waist are a perfect fit.

The temperature rises to minus ten in honor of their wedding hour. When they open the door to leave for the parsonage, a bullying snow-laced blast shoves them back into the house.

"Sure you want to go?" Adam asks.

"Poo," she replies. "So it's breezy."

"Then let's do this, ladyfriend."

"Into the fray, big fella."

He opens the door again. Slowly, magically, the wind lays itself at their feet. The air sparkles with the cold, a toast to their resolve. The silver beading at the throat of the indigo gown twinkles back.

9

Cal wintered over in the Blackfoot Valley before landing in Caswell, and to hear him tell it to the newly joined Mr. and Mrs. Adam Fielding, spring on the Rocky Mountain Front was some kind of Eden. April, he rhapsodized, descended like a fairy godmother, sweeping a sparkling swath across streams and meadows: yellow clover, wild roses, and chokecherry bushes bursting forth, reaching for the sunbeams glinting off gurgling creeks rowdy with the spring thaw.

Seven hundred miles downstream, this spring paints a different picture. Frigid air hangs in the valley around Caswell. Ice crystals frost the fields broken for spring planting but still too hard to absorb moisture. There's no stopping the coursing torrent of melted snow when it hits the ice jams in the Milk River, jumping the banks and invading the land at a crazy tilt.

At his desk in the Dunbarton farmhouse, a primal roaring not of any animal pulls Adam's head up from his work. He smells the water's metallic tang before he sees it; then it comes into view, scrambling over the fields, erasing them with surging gray gesso. The tectonic boom crescendos as the ice jams in the river give way.

Adam has heard tales of flooding in the region. With the fleeting thought that thanks to luck they haven't planted yet, he sprints for the barn, where Dun and two hired hands drag sandbags from underneath.

"This is what we keep them for," he indicates to Adam, although it's clear that the water will win this race.

"I don't know where my wife is." He would never have believed it of himself, this new shade of fear, overriding the familiar primacy of work. He should stay with the man who pays his salary, the men who take their directions from him on a daily basis. More is at stake here than at his three-room house in town. If that's where she is. At three in the afternoon, she might well be at Cal's, only yards from the river, where she could be tossed like a rag doll across the fields or, worse, swept downstream in a petrifying glacial instant. He may already be too late, may have already failed her.

He shoulders past the hired hands to the tall cabinet inside the barn. "Lend me your river boots?" he asks Dun, already pulling them from the shelf and unlacing his plow shoes.

"You're heading out?" one of the hands asks. "You're daft. You don't know——"

"My wife is alone."

"She'll go to the neighbors'."

Dun ignores the man and points Adam at a tool rack. "Take that shepherd's crook. You're going to need it."

The water rises to knee-deep before he's put Dunbarton's half a mile behind. The invading river has become a dangerous obstacle course of debris hurtling by. A milk can careens off Adam's thighs. A section of fence slams sideways into a huge elm, and a dog, paddling like mad, clambers up the posts into the tree. The vision of Annie moves him along, one combative step at a time. Where, where is she?

He snags a piece of barn siding floating by and poles along with the shepherd's crook. The roar of the water dulls along with the landscape, layering over him a dubious sense of peace, which lasts until a chunk of ice the size of their cellar rams the raft, splitting it in two. Adam scrambles to the larger half. He struggles to keep his weight centered, all feeling gone below the knee, and prays for his precarious craft to hold together. Praying, that's a good one, isn't it? He doesn't have any favors coming in that department.

At last the grain elevators of Caswell rear up on the horizon. The sun drops over his shoulder; the current bears him along, careening into town, all of it still as a stage set. Pushing off a submerged auto, he picks up enough speed to propel him the last yards up to his house.

"Annie!" He pounds the door with raw hands, maneuvering himself off the raft and shoving it away, knees buckling as they find solid ground three feet down. The door resists opening against the water, but he is more determined than the elements. He shunts his way in and slumps against the wall, all parts of him screaming in choral abuse.

And there she is, bedraggled but safe, the hem of her skirt tucked into the waistband, her bare legs beet red just above the black water. She throws herself into his arms, her relief written bold across her face. It brings him up short to realize that no woman has ever looked at him that way, and the relief in his heart is no less. Three months after their wedding, he finally knows it's real—he is a married man.

She tells him she hasn't been afraid for herself. But the hours of waiting for him, working against the frigid water to haul their belongings into the attic, stopping every few minutes to climb the ladder and slap the circulation back into her legs . . .

The blackened ladder and the scene in the attic paint the full picture of her last four hours. The first thing up was the most irreplaceable thing in the house, their wedding quilt, *The River by Starlight*. Clothing, food, matches, and the kerosene lantern, along with tools, linens, and utensils hunker under the rafters. "A regular little dry-goods store," he tells her. He wouldn't have been surprised if she'd managed to tow the furniture up there.

They can do nothing more but wait out the water. Without words they peel the icy clothes from each other. Numb fingers drop the garments into the black water below. They crawl between layers of blankets and the quilt and close exhausted eyes.

The evening star, multiplied by undulating water, is like bright sparks of fire continually ascending.

The water slaps at the ladder below, but it can't douse the bright sparks of fire, its namesake quilt. The world beneath it warms quickly.

Three days the river loiters, but at last it retreats to its banks, leaving behind a layer of silky mud. Annie lights the stove as soon as the water drops below the door, sloshing her way out to the woodpile, finding toeholds in the blackened logs to climb to the dry pieces.

The walls and floors are drying, but the furnishings are a loss. Fingers of filth stroke the chairs and the settee, their legs bent or split. Mr. Barrett has said he will come by to pick up the ruined furniture but has mentioned nothing about replacing it.

She had hauled the contents of Adam's desk to the attic, removing the drawers intact, in the hope of saving his beloved heirloom. Today the stout mahogany secretary appears to be the lone thing in the house worth salvaging, its finish destroyed but lordly legs unbowed.

"Mother Nature does let folks know who's boss," Annie observes. "An Irish neighbor once advised us never to move into a house without inspecting the treetops. If you see clothes hanging from the high limbs, you're on a floodplain."

Adam snorts, "*Natura nihil frustra facit.* Nature does nothing in vain? We'll see. What's that?" He peers at the floor.

"What's what?"

"That." A wink of something shiny pierces the mud, halfway under a floorboard. He works his fingers around the object and pulls out a metal thimble with red lettering: FOR DRY GOODS GO TO COFFEEN'S.

"This is the thimble Cal sent you, isn't it?"

"It is. I needed it yesterday and couldn't find it."

Rinsing the mud away, they see it has buckled, leaving a sharp edge inside. "You can't use it," Adam says. "I'm sorry. I know it meant something to you."

He's wrong about that. "It was a lure, and I was willing bait," she says. "Some lucky charm, eh?" He pockets the thimble as she turns away.

Several days later, the subject closed and forgotten, Annie startles at the sight of a silver thimble standing on a china saucer at the foot of the bed. Heavy and elegant, carved with a riot of daisies that seem to be moving, it has beauty uncommonly commanding for an object so small. The maker stamped a mark into the bottom band, three tiny thimble shapes in a triangle. When she places it on her forefinger, her insides tremble, the same flutter she felt when he slipped on her wedding band.

Will she ever get used to the fishbowl feeling that comes with living in town? Annie misses what she's always taken for granted, being able to sit in front of her bedroom window on a summer evening like this one, letting the breeze blow the shirt off her shoulders, tease her midriff. On the farm in Iowa and on Cal's homestead, the only eyes upon her belonged to passing critters. But from every window of the house on Third Street, her eye meets a neighbor's window.

Even when she draws the curtains, she feels spied upon. Sometimes the spy is her own husband. Now and again she's nudged awake when the meter of his sleep-deepened breathing stops and he pulls away. A channel of cool air crawls between them, and she feels his eyes on her. He wants to penetrate her dreams. She wishes he would. It would calm his jealous heart; he would see that her sole dream is that this marriage thrive. She must be patient with this impatient, possessive man, that in time he'll see it is so. Then they can stop having conversations over supper such as the one this evening.

"Adam, I picked up coffee at the cash grocery today, and Neil seemed surprised to see me. He said he misses my eggs. I thought you were delivering them with the rest of your orders."

"I do deliver them with the rest of my orders. To the hotel."

"Why would you do that?" She laid her fork down. "Neil was my first customer. How could you cut him off?"

Adam pushed away his plate and parked both elbows on the table. "Neil Muir," he said, pouncing on each word, "is a bachelor. He's had too many friendly conversations with my wife. The hotel is delighted with your eggs. You keep doing whatever your hen sorcery is out there and leave the selling to me."

She managed to hold her wifely tongue as he went on to tell her that he'd heard the farm-to-city postal service was coming to Caswell, which would give them a toehold into exporting.

"Imagine," she murmured.

"Oh, I'll be doing more than imagining," he assured her, and went out to stable Tipsy for the night, his sun-colored hair glowing against the twilight.

Adam knows there's nothing interesting about the way a woman pegs laundry on a line. So why does he find himself watching?

Annie reaches on tiptoes to secure the pegs on the line. A scorching draft of puckish wind swoops in and lifts her skirt above her knees, then drops it coyly, like the curtain on a burlesque show. She doesn't see him when she picks up her basket and moves away from the sheets spanking at her in the wind. As she rounds the corner, his arm, outstretched to the house, catches her shoulders.

"Adam! You startled me. I didn't know you were home."

"Oh, I'm home. And I happened to notice that you aren't wearing proper undergarments, Mrs. Fielding." On his way across the country to the haberdashery in Montana, he worked in enough department stores and undressed enough women to know that appropriate ladies' undergarments number no fewer than four, and here's his wife, barefoot, with no petticoat, lacking who knows what else. A state of affairs that requires immediate investigation.

"I skipped the petticoat and the stockings today. It's too hot."

"It's about to get hotter, ladyfriend. Tomorrow's my birthday. I feel like starting the celebration early." He backs her up against the house and gathers a handful of her skirt.

"Yes, about that. If I don't have to light the oven to bake a cake . . . how about just ice cream, without the cake?"

He needs both hands to work up her skirt. It's hot today, all right. Her neck glistens with sweat, and he has to press his lips into her, right there. "No," he breathes against her skin. "I don't like ice cream."

She gasps, melting under his touch. "You don't like ice cream," she repeats.

"No. I don't like things that slip through my fingers when they warm up." He's worked his way to that provocative little bottom of hers that fits in his hands just so when she squirms smoothly into place like that. She weighs next to nothing; he could lift her up with one hand. She grinds her knees into him.

"Not here, big fella," she whispers. "The Seviers are home. I heard them in their kitchen."

"They've heard squealing before." His voice drops; he needs to breathe every few words. "They know we're moving to the farm soon." He fumbles for her drawers. Please let them be the kind with the open seam. "They'll think we have a new . . . pink . . . piglet." Let her squeal. Please. He has no objection to his neighbors knowing exactly what belongs to him.

She digs her knees deeper into his sides. With one arm hooked around his neck, she could haul off with the other and slug him for his insolence. But she won't. He knows it. That would be a waste of a good romp.

Sure enough, she raises her hips to meet him, wrapping her legs around his waist and arching until the tips of her breasts brush his chest. Her fingers slip under his hair, trailing across the back of his head; the slightest guidance from her and his mouth slides down her neck, below her shoulders to where she's already opened her shirtwaist in the heat. He guessed right— no chemise.

"I don't care for ice cream either," she says, her voice rising as he tongues her nipple.

"Why?" he asks, because he has to know these things, but she only laughs and begins to sing a birthday tune in ragged gasps, her breath hot beneath his ear.

His rumble of frustration interrupts her song. Grappling with her drawers, he's made an unpleasant discovery.

"Closed? Closed? Woman, don't you always wear open?"

"Not always, big fella." She picks up the pace of the dance, matches her undulations to his uneven breathing. "Not when I don't fancy visits from flying pests and blowing dirt. Is this a problem?"

He's practically foaming. It's blue-blazes hot today.

"That depends." His fingers work the fabric between her thighs. Summer-weight, well-worn. Good. Damp underneath. Even better. "How much for muslin drawers these days?"

"About twenty-five cents."

"Worth it." A swift yank, then her honeyed dare: "We'll see who squeals first!" The house groans at her back and the earth lists under his feet. She clamps a hand over his mouth and presses her own over her fingers. From far away, an astral tap on the shoulder warns him that he is not in control.

He doesn't care.

When the house ceases its groaning, when she's lifted her hand from his mouth, when he can breathe normally again, he kisses her in the gently roughneck way she provokes.

"It is," he allows, "fiendishly hot today."

"Hinges of hell," she agrees. "Had enough birthday yet?"

This woman, his wife, is a shameless tease.

She won't release her leg lock around his waist, so he leans in to the house and eases her down the side. Her birthday banter is cut short by a yelp of pain as a splinter pierces her exposed bottom. She skids the rest of the way to the ground, laughing, dragging him with her.

"Oh my, look at this," she laughs, rubbing the splinter. "I used to ditch my chores to sit and bang my feet on the fence by the barn and watch for hawks. My mother declared me the only child in the world who could come home from a simple chore like feeding chickens with splinters in her backside. 'Lord A'mighty, Analiese, how did you manage that?' Here I did it again—and all I did was peg out the wash."

He can't explain why this inflames him anew, but why ask why? He's not a man to question his extraordinary fortune, not when he's spent half a lifetime in saloons listening to men talk about wives who "lay there like a shot doe." As he sinks into her again, he tells her, "I can say one good thing about your mother."

"That's one more than I can. What might it be?"

"I didn't ever have to meet her."

"And will I ever meet yours?"

Her hair in his hands slips from its pins, puddling around her shoulders; she smells of grass and laundry soap, and of him. "Not today, Mrs. Fielding," he breathes. *His* Mrs. Fielding. "Not today."

It's so hot. The sheets on the line flutter like harem fans, not enough to cool the torrid air, only enough to throw a whitewash illusion of privacy around them.

An hour later he's easing himself into the tin bathtub, water unheated, and even that might not lower the internal mercury. Annie tops the tub with a last pot of water and folds a towel for him to lean against.

"Look at that—he's relaxing," she marvels, and he bestows upon her the full-strength, Cheshire cat smile that knocks her knees out from under her.

He watches her wobble out to unpeg the wash. Through the kitchen window he can see the top of her head, a sable exclamation point against the white linen and pale sky. When the sheets drop from the line, she comes face-to-face with Mrs. Sevier doing the same in her yard. She's taller than Annie; he can see a ginger fringe of tiny curls under a panama sunbonnet, and nutmeg brows arched high on her forehead in amusement.

"Hot enough for you today?" she asks Annie.

"Yes, indeed. Perhaps we'll get a break tomorrow."

"Perhaps." She pauses to snap a pillow slip. "Will you give Mr. Fielding our best wishes for his birthday?"

Two days after Thanksgiving finds Annie staring at Cal across the plank table at the homestead while Adam pours coffee as if nothing of importance is happening today.

"Mmm, my favorite traveling breakfast," Cal purrs, ladling cold gravy over turkey and the last slice of pumpkin pie. His fork clangs around the tin, scraping out flakes of crust. Then he gets to his feet and shrouds himself in a dark mackintosh and black leather gloves. Adam holds the door open, and the three of them leave the shack and walk a piece up the road.

"I expect big things from you," Cal intones. "Take care of each other." Dry leaves skitter around their ankles as he bends to hug Annie. "On second thought," he warns Adam, "take care of yourself, or she'll take care of you!"

Their handshake is long and slow. Cal lays his free hand atop their clasp. "I don't want to get too soggy, but take care of Duo, too, if he'll let you. I said my goodbyes yesterday, and I know he understood. Tailed off into the woods and I haven't seen him since."

Annie pulls Cal's hand from Adam's and hangs on. The same hand she watched scrawl across the deed that placed the homestead in her hands, hers and Adam's. The same hand that waved her goodbye as a child, now about to do it again. She wonders, *How many years this time?* "Are you sure you won't let us drive you to town?"

"Nah. I'm gonna do the long last look. Five years here. It may be the longest I ever stay in one place." He winks. "But if I'd been out of here sooner, where would you be?"

"Let us hear from you. Where you go and what you do."

"When have I ever been good at that?" With two fingers off the brow, he starts down the pebbled road. A sharp draft of wind off the river blows a tear across Annie's cheek, drying it instantly. Adam's arm circles her shoulder and they walk back to the house. On the stoop, he sweeps her off her feet, saying, "I forgot to carry you over the threshold."

She laughs, "But haven't I seen you here before?"

"You have," he says. "And now I'm going to make you see stars you didn't know existed."

These three weeks of solitude on the farm have enfolded them, been their belated honeymoon. How could he not resent this letter's request, reasonable though it may be? He stares out the window, tapping the envelope against his thigh.

"News from the folks?" Annie asks.

"They want to meet you. Been asking all year. Now it's 'come for Christmas.'"

So they board a series of trains to a Minnesota town with a mystical native name, his father's latest parish. It's been so long between visits, Adam barely knows his brother and sisters. But the discomfort is all his. Annie pitches in with meals, plays with his nieces and nephews, lets his parents win at rummy, lavishes them with handmade gifts. He doesn't have to say much, a blessing, as he can't seem to find a subject of common interest with his father, and his mother seems grateful to simply gaze at him and smile. After five days he ends the visit, citing "business concerns," which no one questions or, he suspects, believes.

The train carrying them back to Montana groans heavily along. Adam feels sure he could trot home faster. He wedges his elbow into the window track, two fingers pressing into a stabbing pain behind his temple. Across from him, Annie knits a sock and asks if there's anything special he'd like to do for their upcoming first anniversary. When he doesn't answer, she glances up from her needles. How shocked she must be to see the flint sparks in his eyes.

"You hit quite the home run with my family, didn't you?"

"Your mother's a lovely woman. I can't understand why you neglect her so."

"You like my brother, don't you?"

"Of course. A charming young man."

"No. You like him." His tone frightens himself. She freezes mid-stitch. "You two were out in the stable for a long time. 'Visiting the pony.'"

She has her own stash of flint. Her voice comes low and with deliberate patience. Yes, Malcolm told her the pony's story. He saved it from the knacker. An evil brute had tried to hold the poor beast still in the shoeing shop by putting a twitch on its tongue. The pony fought it and tore half its tongue away. It couldn't eat or drink. Malcolm retrained the pony by mixing its oats with water in a deep bucket, and the pony learned to suck up the feed. A sweet and gentle animal, now that it has a sweet and gentle owner.

The train slows. The whistle shrills. Another faceless, graceless, utilitarian prairie town. "Malcolm," she continues evenly, "talked quite a bit about your legendary horse-trading acumen. How he would have loved to be there with you. Very admiring of his big brother. Very."

Adam's fingers stab back at the pain behind his temple.

"You *like* him."

Those opaque black eyes. She could win a staring contest with the *Mona Lisa*. She incontestably wins this one with him.

"No, Adam. I don't like him. I do not like your brother." Her work spills to the floor when she rises, and there it stays, a pile of reproach. She disappears down the aisle, her absence outlasting his headache and the dread that stays awake with him through the night, filling her empty seat. When the train pulls into Caswell, there she stands on the platform, calm as if she'd disembarked alongside him.

"Headache better?" she asks, and he can't see anything but sincerity in her face.

Oh, to ravish her here right on the platform. The two miles to the house suddenly seem an ocean. "You're a headache," he says, hoping she can tell whether he's joking, because he can't. "But, my dear, you are never a bore."

In the station he calls Karl for a ride, as arranged. They'll be home soon. Then everything will be as it should be, just the two of them. He can't make Karl's horse go faster, but he can lean in close to his wife and whisper, "Ready for some stargazing?"

10

Annie is no screamer, not like that. Her terror shatters the spring morning. Adam, from the far edge of the property, is on the way before the first cry has faded, leaving the team and plow where they stand. The newly broken ground slows his run in a manner that seems willful. The shack jumps around in the crosshairs of his vision, a moving target in the mottled early light. The scene that confronts him when he throws open the door sends his stomach into his mouth.

Bright red rivulets studded with dark clots course down her legs. She's trying to staunch the flow with a bedsheet, but it's saturated in seconds. He knows instantly what's happening, what's lost, and that there's more to lose.

"Annie, we need to get to the hospital."

"No!" she screams. "No!" She seizes another sheet and wads it between her legs, as if she could stuff the baby back in. "I can stop this," she weeps. What frightens him more than the blood is that he has never seen his plucky, practical wife like this—utterly beyond reason.

"You can't stop it. We have to go to the hospital. I'm going to carry you to the truck."

She wheels around and backhands him into the wall with force he's only seen in a boxing ring. He fights every instinct not to slam her back. Wonders whether hitting her might subdue her enough to get her out of here. Instead he circles behind her, pinions her arms, and half hoists, half drags her out to the truck, leaving a dark red trail of finality. Clutching the sheet with fingers that look about to snap, she lapses into earthquake sobs.

"I want this baby, Adam. I *need* this baby!" Too many words; they leave her gasping. "The baby is leaving me! I can be a good mother. I can, I swear! *I want this baby!*"

"I want the baby too, honey." How can the distance to town have doubled overnight? "Hold on for the doctor, just a couple of minutes."

The truck barrels across the outskirts of town, scattering citizens and dogs, buggies and carts. For once he disregards the horses he's terrifying. Beside him, Annie slips from hysteria into unearthly keening, the sound of a human turning herself inside out. Valley County Hospital looms six blocks ahead, all of them mud. Against sweet reason, he floors the gas pedal. The truck fishtails a broad fan in the muck before the rear wheels sink and spin. *Dolt!* Downshift, breathe, swear. The truck lurches forward and plunges down Caswell's busiest street, turning heads, drawing gasps of disbelief.

Everyone will know. So be it.

The truck careens to a stop in front of the hospital. He lays his full weight on the horn and vaults out. A nurse appears at the door.

"Get the doctor!" he shouts, gathering up a wife who is changing color before his eyes. His grip on her tightens; he fears she'll slip through his arms, slick as she is, bathed in every fluid a body can ooze, blood, bile, sweat, amniotic fluid, and the slaughterhouse smell of it. "Get the goddamn doctor!"

The nurse disappears into the building without a word. In seconds, a gurney and two more nurses materialize, whisking Annie through the entrance toward a pair of heavy matching doors. "Adam!" she screams. "I want this baby!" The doors part and the nurse raises a hand. *Sorry, Mr. Fielding.* "I want my husband!" is the last thing they allow her to say before the cloth covers her nose and mouth and the double doors rip husband and wife asunder.

It's not Annie who wakes up that evening. It's a statue, sitting in bed so white and still that Adam wonders what they did to her behind those doors. The doctor talks in a sympathetic but factual way.

"It's nature's way of saying something was wrong this time. There's no reason there won't be many more little ones in due course. She's already carried a child to term—"

"How do you know that?" Adam snaps.

The doctor's lips flatten to a stiff line. "Scarring around the perineum. As I said, there's no reason—"

"Yes, you did say. What happens now?"

"It's important that you wait awhile. Let her heal. She's suffered some internal tearing. A rather dramatic injury."

Around midnight Annie slides into sleep, having uttered not a word. A dying-lightbulb moon broods over Adam as he makes his way home. At the shack, he veers away. He can't go in there tonight, can't face the scene of the struggle, the empty bed. He heads for the barn, where, bless Karl, the team and plow are safe and seen to. He splits a bale of hay with a stroke of the pitchfork more savage than necessary and spreads it in a thick mat. Sleep arrives before he's finished rolling himself into the heavy blanket that smells like Tipsy, as in days not so long gone by.

In the morning, he tries to put the house right. He scrubs the stains from the floor and shovels over the blood in the dirt, folds the gory sheets and buries them among the cottonwoods behind the house. He marks the spot with a stone, rounded like a sleeping cat that will be comfortable remaining in place for a long, long time. He'll never tell Annie what lies under the stone, but it doesn't seem right that something that would have been their child could dissipate in the space of a few minutes and leave nothing behind.

He didn't know he had it in him to feel these things.

The sun is waning when he brings his breathing statue of a wife home. She hesitates at the door. Then she goes into the bedroom alcove and lies down with her back to him. The crying comes low and primal. He lowers himself to their bed, presses himself against her, and lays his cheek on her hair. "We'll have more children, you know that, right?" Weak, shallow sobs are her only response.

By morning she hasn't moved, but the farm demands his attention. Before he leaves, he looks in on her. The slightest rise and fall of her shoulder above the quilt tells him she's still among the living. When he checks in on her at noon, she is crying. When he comes in at twilight, she is crying, and as he drops into an uneasy sleep beside her, she is crying. In the night, she seems to choke on her own breath, trying to whisper something that sounds like *Cynthiaaaaa.*

Spring turns to summer and still she cries, her back turned to him, to the world. He never sees her eat, rarely sees her sleep. He begins to deflect his fear with anger, and his anger with fear. After weeks of making excuses to Margrethe—no, Annie isn't up to visitors—he heads up the road to ask his neighbor, *What the hell is going on with my wife and when is it going to end?* At the property line, he leans his back against a fence post, suddenly exhausted at the thought of asking, feeling the weight of his plight swell beyond words.

The strain of running the farm without her mounts. One sultry dawn he storms through the henhouse, trying to gather up days' worth of uncollected eggs. The unlucky oak by the privy bears the brunt of his frustration. *Walter Johnson on the mound.* He fires a pitch that rewards him with a satisfying crack and splat of tawny yolk oozing down the bark. He's got enough eggs to go the distance. *The Big Train racks up another shutout. "You can't hit what you can't see."* The respite lasts all of five minutes.

Fifty-three eggs on a tree, now that is some disgusting mess. Adam hates mess, and he's got mess now, in spades. Someone has to be to blame. Who? It's hard to see how Annie is. Maybe he himself? Hard to see that, too. God. Now there's a possibility. God is to blame. Or him, that shadow in her life before, the one who scarred her. Yeah, that's it. He's to blame.

"Is that supposed to be art?"

She stands in the center of the road, washed and dressed and smiling with basket in hand, taking in the befouled oak. "I've been looking for you. Where have you been?"

Exactly the question he wants to ask her.

Where have you been?

11

nnie makes a show of turning the calendar over each month, tearing off the old page, folding it into a glider, and sending it through the open stove door. August is three days in the past but its page is intact, and good luck to her trying to find it. Her husband has every inch of reachable wall surface and half the floor papered in plans for his display at the county's first fair, two weeks away. He's planning a show of superlative quality and abundance no one will dare ignore. "Be coming home with more ribbons than a Bolivian general," he told her.

Midafternoon, she takes a bottle of cider down to the river, where he's assembling a pump. A few yards down the bank, a can catches her eye. She's accustomed to finding strange river debris around the farm: a tiny animal skull, a rifle barrel, a quirt missing its frills. The can, an unopened quart of paint, lies tucked into the exposed roots of a cottonwood, looking exhausted.

Adam agrees it's a choicer find than the usual junk, but a quart of paint won't go far.

"It already has," she says. "Great Falls Hardware. I wonder how it ended up in the river. What shall we do with it?"

"Don't care." Adam turns back to the pump he's assembling. "Not my department."

Coming from him, who has an opinion on everything, this amuses her. He gives the wrench a two-fisted yank. "You want to know where it came from, Mrs. Fielding? See the color there. Cardinal? A wife hurled it at her husband and missed his head by an inch. 'I said rose, *rose*, not red,'" he barks in falsetto. "'This isn't a bordello, Horace!' I worked a hardware counter in Bismarck for a year and can tell you: that paint could be liquid gold, but if it's not the color the wife had in mind, the discussion is over. So don't tell me what you're going to do with it. I'll find out soon enough."

The walk back to the house is all the time she needs to figure out why the can of cardinal paint came to her. She runs a finger around the bare-wood kitchen window frame and smiles.

The casing soaks up the paint like a thirsty sailor. She steps back to get the full effect. The window, now kissed in red, showcases to the south a lush carpet of wild grass. To the north, the corn sways; the squash vines twine in leafy elegance; cauliflower and cabbages squat solid and resolute, outer leaves parting for the sun. Through the window, now a portrait frame, she breathes in the sheer beauty of their farm.

She's at the sink washing up, blouse removed and hair unfastened, when he comes through the door and stops in his tracks.

"Welcome to the bordello," she says.

The first three buttons of his shirt come undone before the clack of the door latch fades. "Quite the exclusive joint you have here. Clientele of one."

He sleeps through the supper hour, his nakedness outlined under the sheet. Around eight o'clock, a rustling from the alcove brings her head up from her knitting. He crosses the room in three strides, trousers and shirt hanging unbuttoned.

"You," he points accusingly, "wore me out."

He slaps a tablet of paper and several pencils on the table, straddles a chair, and for a half hour utters not a word. Then he pivots his pad of paper for her to see.

He can make the case to the bank. With a two-story poultry house they can both expand and protect the business from flooding. More eggs. Turkeys.

Turkeys, no, she shakes her head. The dozen she had at Cal's last year convinced her. "They can't be counted upon to take themselves up that ramp when the water rises. They're so stupid, they drown if they look up while it's raining."

"Everyone raved about your turkeys," he says.

"It's a miracle any survived to make it to the table. Every darn train-whistle blast, they pile themselves up in a corner. Every darn time, I had to go out there and break them up before they smothered each other. No more turkeys."

"Forty instead of fifty."

"Some of the chicks almost starved to death while walking all over their food. I had to put it directly onto their beaks. And they draw rats. They try to befriend them."

"I'll elevate the pen a couple of feet."

"No."

"Thirty-five and that's my final offer."

She exhales a soft "eccchhhh," but he's already on to the next thing. "The hotel wants some of your 'heavenly' jam, too. What's that about?"

Her jam, an almost no-cost product. Made from their wild blackberries, cooked up with the peelings left over after she put up pie filling and applesauce. She gave away a few crocks of the jam, to the nurses at the hospital who'd cared for her, to Margrethe's cousin who's a housekeeper at the hotel, and to the Finnish couple who own the drugstore and soda fountain, with the suggestion they serve it as an ice cream sundae topping. Not everyone likes chocolate.

"Not everyone likes ice cr—" Then: "Hey . . ." The spark of another idea sends his pencil skipping across the paper. His free hand moves over the table and finds hers, playing with her fingers, though he seems unaware of it. "Blacklecream," he mutters. "Blap-plesauce. Heavenberry."

"Beg pardon?"

"Mrs. Fielding's Heavenly Blackberry-Apple Ice Cream Sauce," he says. "People who eat ice cream at soda fountains like that sort of catchy shorthand."

"Black Heaven. Crabby Pal. Blearycream. We have only eight trees. That's not enough to produce a significant quantity."

He waves her off. Limited quantity makes it a specialty product, drives the price up. They'll roll out the sauce as the newest thing for Christmas or Easter.

"Whoa, big fella." Her hands cover the tidy columns of figures. "This started off as a discussion about an outbuilding. How did we get to ice cream?"

In the yellow glow of the cut-glass oil lamp, their heads bend over his sketchpad, their banter animated and spiked with merriment, until the crickets pause and his voice carries in the evening stillness: "Is there anything you can't do?" The last two words are muffled against her face.

She's glad for that. He won't see the pain behind her lowered eyes. Packed away in a trunk in the darkest corner of the shed, a never-used layette bears tacit witness to what she hasn't been able to do.

But surely it will be different this time? Should she tell him this soon? While he's dreaming up two-story poultry palaces and high-priced specialty products? She'll dream too, that this baby may yet drink from a silver cup.

She places his hand on her belly.

He doesn't remember finding the bloodied nightdress. Doesn't remember following its trail to the river, where he finds his wife with a towel twisted between her teeth, standing in the strongest part of the current, her eyes fixed on the night sky. Doesn't remember driving to the hospital.

She didn't cry this time, didn't wail or fight. The nurse says she's resting "peacefully." He and the doctor walk without speaking until the hallway ends at a weather-pocked window. "I have to be honest with you, Adam. I was sure we were going to lose her this time. A tiny body like hers can't withstand that kind of hemorrhaging. It would have killed most women. Your wife—she really wants to live."

Adam says, "May I see her now?"

She's the only patient in the ward today, lying there gathered in on herself. Her face grazes the edge of the bed.

He kneels on the cold floor so that when she opens her eyes, they'll meet his. "Hello, ladyfriend." He hopes the brave smile works. "Hello, big fella," she whispers through the morphine twilight sleep. "So I didn't die. Again."

"No, not you. You're such a tough one."

"Mmmm. 'Don't tread on me.'"

It's the morphine talking. She's gone backward in time, to a simpler place, an Iowa schoolhouse. He says. "I never took you for a history buff."

"'I regret that I have but one life to lose for my marriage.'"

There is still some mercy in the world. She's drifted into a narcotic cloud and doesn't see him bury his face in the antiseptic sheets. The nurses will find them damp and never know the tears aren't hers.

Three weeks have gone by when she insists she's strong enough to walk to town. He lets her go, hoping that air, exercise, and human contact will invigorate her. The morning is still dewy as he sees her around the bend in the road before heading off behind the orchard to determine where he might be able to construct another vegetable cellar. Three hours later he's on the phone ordering the lumber for the ridgepoles and roof. His hand hasn't left the phone in its cradle before it rings again.

"Mr. Fielding? Sheriff Blandish here. Can you come pick up your wife? She's walking west on the train tracks. Says she's going home. Couldn't get her to come with me."

Adam catches up with her three miles past the grain elevator. He leaves the truck running as he jumps out.

"Annie, what are you doing?"

She seems surprised to see him. "Why, walking home."

"Home is that way." His thumb shoots over his shoulder. "When you said you were going to walk home, I thought you meant to our house, not into the arms of Jesus."

"I hardly think he's waiting for me."

She comes home without a fight, and now she stands there kneading bread as if nothing has happened. He wonders if she knows how he sorrows for their lost babies too, but the world keeps revolving, and sometimes her mercurial behavior is too exasperating. His fingers go to his forehead and work his temple with a rhythmic motion that mimics hers.

"I can't imagine a man alive," he says to her back, "who would be happy about getting a call from the sheriff like that one."

"I'm sorry," she says, with no emotion. "I'm trying. Truly I am."

"Oh, that you are. You are *very* trying." He knows the futility of letting his frustration get the best of him, but he's only a man. "If this is your way of getting my attention, it strikes me as extremely underhanded."

At first her only response is the metered folding and punching of the dough. The heel of her hand sinks into the yeasty bubble, and it burps sharply. Fold and punch. Fold and punch. Then, so quickly he couldn't have seen it coming, she pinches off a handful and fires it at his head. It's a high, fast one. It misses his eye—she wasn't aiming for his eye—and catches him alongside the brow with enough force to turn his head.

"Underhanded? How dare you. Underhand is for the *bush* leagues."

The ball of dough bubbles around his heel as he mashes it into the floor. Who *is* this woman?

She goes on kneading her bread like a windup toy.

The house is smaller than an unmucked stall at times like this. Retreating to his desk, he's still within the circle of that eerie vibration of hers; turning his back doesn't lessen it. For a quarter hour he pours over next spring's planting schematics, tapping his pencil end over end, half-aware that it's keeping time with her kneading.

His trance shatters when he reaches into the drawer where they keep their money. At the bank yesterday he withdrew funds with the intent of ordering seed and supplies today. Before all this. He could still get it done today. Except that the fat envelope of cash isn't there.

The empty space gapes at him, jarring his entrails loose. He rifles the drawer, then the two others. It makes no sense. He must have put the envelope elsewhere.

He knows he didn't.

His head falls back; the ceiling hangs lower than it did a minute ago. He dare not turn around. "Annie," he says, as casually as he can muster, "did you happen to do something with the planting money?"

"You know, I believe I did."

"And where is it?"

Fold, burp. Fold, burp.

"You know, I can't remember."

He reaches her in three strides, churning with fury and cold fear, grabbing her by both shoulders. She doesn't balk.

"This is our livelihood at stake!" he shouts, lowering his face level with hers. "You have to think. You have to tell me where it is."

"I don't know."

"You don't know. You don't know. Annie, I can't print money. We can't handle another penny of debt. Where's the money, *Analiese*? Where is the *money*?"

"I don't know." She searches his face pensively. "You're angry."

"Yes, I'm angry! Do you understand what's at stake?"

"Yes."

"And?"

She watches with nothing more than curiosity while he draws three painfully deep breaths. His fingers cut into her arms where he clutches them, slender as iris stems, his thumb meeting his fingers. It's so odd: This woman looks like his wife and sounds like his wife. But her eyes are backlit and he can't see in, can't tell if she's there.

"Let's think this through," he coaxes her. "When do you last remember having the money in your hands? Is it still in the house? Did you go outside? Give it to someone? Destroy it?"

"It wasn't safe. I put it somewhere safe. I don't remember where."

Wild panic detonates inside him. She tries to shrug herself out of his grasp, twisting sharply to get away. In a horrifying split-second scuffle, he grabs again for her shoulder and misses, his hand closing instead around her throat.

A moment, a month. He doesn't know how long they stand there, frozen. Her pulse under his grip never so much as flutters; she doesn't even have the sense to be afraid! Goddamn it, maybe he should try to squeeze it out of her. The thought isn't complete before he hates himself. She's making him crazy too; he mustn't allow it.

A moment, a month. She is first to speak, her voice as lifeless as the baby they just lost. But she's read his eyes.

"Do it, Adam. Then neither one of us will ever have to worry about this again."

"Not on your life." His hand jerks away. "Jail and hell are two places I am not willing to go for you." He shouldn't leave her alone when she's like this, but he can't be with her. Something bad will happen if he remains in the room.

The bread has cooled on the shelf and his supper congealed on the stove by the time he returns. She sits in the rocker with her book of poetry and an air of calm.

Too calm, she is. With that book. That damn book.

"Must you?" He almost bites his own flesh as he bites off the words.

The creak of the rocker saws the air. *Let him stand there and glower if he hasn't anything better to do.* So she took a roundabout walk on a sunny day and didn't feel like riding home with the law. Sheriff Blowfish, now there's a man she wouldn't look at if she were going blind tomorrow.

Is it asking so much to be left alone to read? He's becoming irksome, his jealous-husband obsession lurking under every inch of ground she treads, every man she talks to, even a blasted inanimate object like a book.

"Dickinson settles me." She closes the book in her lap. "So what?"

"So what? You hide a book from an old lover at the bottom of a drawer in my house." He glares at the book as if he can make it ignite. "What was it about him? He put his pants on some way other than one leg at a time? Or was it the way he took them off?"

"What is it about you, Adam?" She throws her shoulders against the spindles of the chair, hard enough to make it scoot several inches. What a foolhardy mistake, telling him where the book came from. "I keep a book in a drawer, and I take it out to read it once in a while. I scarcely call that hiding."

Her jaw clenches as he leans over her, mouth pushing against the soft helix of hair draped above her neck. "You are my wife now. I need all of you here, with me. *All* of you."

"How can I be more with you than I am? You live between my legs."

He snaps to full height and cracks the back of his hand across her face. "*Do not* talk to me that way."

"How should I talk to you?" She springs to her feet, too angry to be afraid. He's crossed an ominous line. "What answer can I give you for which you haven't already damned me? I can't read a book if it came before you? I thought we covered this before we married. I can't undo what's done. Nor can you, and are you spotless?" He doesn't answer, breathing hard and staring past her shoulder. "You married Iowa stubborn, not Iowa stupid. I have enough imagination to know how a young man whiles away his free time on 'business jaunts' to Winnipeg. Cal spent plenty of time there. I quote: 'Nothing to do but bars and brothels.'"

Fwee-foofoofoo! a meadowlark outside intercedes.

Her voice steadies. "I have never asked you anything. I took you as you came."

Adam spreads his fingers to cover his face. "I'm not a bad man." It comes out half as a question. "I'm just not . . ."

Not a trusting man. He can't say it. But she knows. *Who did this to you?* is a question she'll never ask him. For now, she can't be in the room with him. She pushes past him to the door, down the bank to her cloistered blackberry spot, ugly and bare though it will be this time of year. The withered clover is stiff and cold under her backside as she hugs her knees, pulls her shawl tighter. She left behind both book and husband, and one will surely see to the demise of the other. She thumbs her wedding ring, watching the ivy motif revolve. *I cling to thee.* How has she managed to get cornered in the circle of her marriage? Is it because, rather than having no corners, a circle has infinite corners?

She lays her forehead on her knees. Adam is a watch spring, tightly wound. Sometimes she senses him trying to uncoil, one tick at a time, but something always draws his hand to the stem, to rewind and start over again. He's a hundred tiny parts working in meticulous interaction and yet he loses fragments of equilibrium each day. She can understand that, even as he pushes her into a too-familiar, lonely place. Ironic it is, because he too, in joining with her, gave in to a loneliness he would never admit. Like magnets, they draw close and cling, but for those changeling moments when the polarity of one will reverse and repel. Undeniable, though, that whatever holds them apart melts at a certain heat.

And here he stands to prove it. Her book hangs from his outstretched hand. "Yours," he says quietly, and when she makes no move to take it, he lays it in her lap.

The private space behind the blackberries becomes theirs, not hers. Adam and Analiese, husband and wife, for better or worse, mend the wounds of words with a language that has none. Once again, Annie and this man to whom she is joined by law and under heaven astonish each other.

Miss Dickinson may have been a female poet unrivaled since Sappho, but perhaps not such a favorable influence after all, Annie thinks, skirt bunched in sweaty hands.

And, once again, he's stirred everything in her until what he needs comes to the surface. "I remember now," she breathes. "The money. I buried it. In the orchard. It wasn't safe. I had to protect you."

The Eulenberg boys appear at the door on an early spring evening. Could Mr. Fielding spare a few minutes to explain baseball to them?

"Dad's not a sportsman," Lukas says, his brother nodding beside him. "But he bought us these mitts at the secondhand store and hoped you could teach us to handle the ball."

Annie follows their game of catch from a stump at the edge of the pasture. Ten minutes ago, Adam pushed his plate away, too bushed to finish supper, and now he looks like he'll go until dark.

"Let the ball come to you," he calls. "Hold your glove up and squeeze when you feel it."

His precision thrills her as he puts toss after toss into the boys' waiting gloves, then catches their awkward lobs bare-handed. As the boys catch on, he varies the throws. "This is a pop fly . . . a line drive . . . a hopper . . . a grounder . . ." The boys dart around the pasture. Adam shakes his arm from time to time but keeps on throwing. A long one arcs into the woods and the boys, in hushed awe, watch it go.

"After it!" Adam shouts. "You can stop the runner at third!" The boys tail off and Adam throws Annie a smile so endearing she loses reason.

This man needs a son.

When they can no longer see the ball in the deepening dusk, when Adam announces "game called on account of darkness" and shoos the boys home, when she's brought him pie and warm milk, when the newspaper he's reading slips to the floor, she pulls up a footstool to sit, arms resting across his knees.

"Adam, I've been thinking."

"Well, that's dangerous."

"Could be," she says, then takes a breath. "Honey, we both hope there'll be another baby soon."

A faint wash of light undercut with a pip of alarm skips across his face. "Are you telling me something?"

"Not yet. But before it happens, hear me. We have to be practical. I am, as you say in baseball, oh for two."

"Maybe it will be different next time."

"Maybe it won't."

"What are you saying?"

"I'm saying that we already have hospital bills that will take years to pay off. You've put your all into this place. If things go badly for me again, I don't want you to lose yet more. I want to buy a life insurance policy. On me."

The tensing of his belly, the recoil of his head. He says, "A superstitious person might say that's buying trouble."

"Do you think me a superstitious person?"

"No." His laugh rings bitter. After a while he says, "Life insurance." He's trying out the words, seeing if he can make them fit. "It feels ghoulish."

"It's not ghoulish. To not do it would be foolish. If I beat the odds and live to be a cranky old matron of forty-four, we'd have a paid-up policy." She draws a newspaper clipping from her apron pocket, a narrow ad with bold lettering: MUTUAL OF THE NORTH-WEST. "After fifteen years, we could take lump-sum cash with a small monthly annuity for life, a smaller dividend with a larger one per annum, or a fat monthly annuity for life." She gives him time to consider the numbers. There's no denying the logic. "I want you protected. Both of you. If there comes a baby and I don't make it."

His fingers drum his forehead. She can feel the pounding of his head in her own and knows what he's thinking.

"I hate it too," she says. "But that doesn't change it." She hands him the ad.

"Well, then. Is there anything else to tell me?"

Annie reaches for his hand. It's not easy to lie to him. But it's not a real lie, just a temporary economy of truth. He'll know as soon as she's sure, and she won't let herself be sure until the policy is tucked into the strongbox in his desk.

"Not yet."

12

ecember 24 dawns bright and cold, a dare for them to count the handful of days remaining until the baby's predicted arrival. Annie grips the side of the poultry house and surrenders her breakfast, bracing herself arm's length to keep from splattering herself. Twenty-three turkeys to slaughter and dress; it might as well be a thousand. She can't spend the day extinguishing life when she's this close to bringing a new one into the world.

She'd already strung up the first bird when the biliousness hit. The hen hangs, flapping and shrieking, and agitating the rest of the flock into an earsplitting din.

Maybe they'll all die of apoplexy and I won't have to—

"Annie!"

She can hardly hear Adam over the ruckus. Every wolf and coyote within miles must be on the way.

"What the— Are you . . . ?" Adam hoists her away from the wall, wiping her face with her apron.

"No." She waves a hand weakly. "It's not the baby. But I don't seem to be able to . . ." She can't finish the apology for the burning in her throat.

He carries her to the house with ease. "Still not much bigger than a barley sack," he tells her, depositing her in the rocking chair.

"What will we do about the birds?"

But he's already out the door.

She falls into a half doze, rousing when the patter of voices at the poultry house draws her to the front window. Adam waves her away. Margrethe bustles about the pen with her visiting sister-in-law.

Annie has to do something. She can't just sit there like a . . . a turkey. Leaning against the kitchen counter, she turns apples in her hand, the peel spiraling away in a continuous strip. Pumpkins roast in the oven. Wafts of cinnamon rise from an open tin. The fragrances calm her.

Annie knows Margrethe won't accept payment for the work. "Is nothing!" Margrethe declares. "Is everything," Annie insists. The least she can do is fill the Eulenberg Christmas dinner table. She sends Margrethe home with pies, brussels sprouts and potatoes, jam, egg bread, whiskey, and limitless gratitude.

The next day passes quietly. As twilight spreads its cloak over the holiday, Adam puts his book aside and Annie lays out a simple Christmas supper. The aroma of chicken and dumplings and pumpkin pudding fills the room as a savage wind wipes the last light from the sky, rattles the red window, and tries to wriggle in under the door. Adam folds a horse blanket over the crack to block the draft.

From the space behind the armoire Annie lifts a parcel wrapped in brown paper and cream-colored yarn. "I hope this is something you'll like."

"I got you something too." He opens the top drawer of his desk and brings out a leather box embossed with roses. Their hands brush as she accepts it in a way that strikes him as shy.

"You first," she urges him.

He slips the yarn bow off. When the brown paper comes away, he sits back in his chair in astonished delight.

"A Staunton chess set. Holy Mary, just like my grandfather's. How could you have known that?"

"I didn't. But when I saw this in the window of the second-hand shop, it called me. You can teach me. I'll be the ebony pieces and you'll be the blond ones."

"Boxwood, they're made of." He studies each piece before placing it on the board. The dark queen lingers in his hand, his fingers tracing the curves. "Granddad taught me to play before I even started school." He hands Annie the black knight. "These horses are called knights. Granddad always warned, 'Don't try to stare this fellow down. You will lose every time.'"

Annie laughs, "That'll be the day, when I break gaze with a thumb-sized carving." But holding the horse in her palm, she admits its eyes smolder, feral and challenging; its powerful chiseled head ends in haughty nostrils; its mane seems to lift on a wind created by its own movement. She can almost feel the damp heat of its breath.

Adam tells her the names of the other pieces, stepping them around the board, demonstrating how the pieces move in prescribed ways. Over her ebony head, he catches the blur of a peregrine streaking by the front window, screeching a warning. The insistent wind picks up.

Annie contemplates the board. The queen can move about unrestricted; the king, one space at a time. Did she get that right? The queen is more powerful than the king?

"Yes, but no," Adam says. "If you capture your opponent's queen, you have weakened him, but the game isn't won until you corner the king."

Annie chuckles. "Who invented these rules? A man or a woman? Let's have at it, big fella."

He leads with one center pawn, then the other. She follows his first move, then moves her bishop out on the second play. He counters with his bishop; she steps out a second pawn. He's got her king in check with two more moves. She blocks with a pawn, loses it to his pawn. She moves out her knight; his pawn advances to clear the path for his bishop to move in for the checkmate.

She laughs. "Is it usually over that quickly?"

"No," he assures her. "Games can go on for hours. You'll improve."

He sets up the board again, then spies the rose-embossed leather box, forgotten, tucked behind her in the chair. He apologizes for having been carried away by her sublime gift. She must open his.

Annie lifts the top of the box to reveal an arc-shaped, mantilla-style tortoiseshell comb, a sweeping six inches across. Long, graceful prongs curve along the bottom under a fan of reticulation as fine as lace.

Her lips move in a silent *oh my*; fingers hover over her heart. "This is magnificent. It takes my breath away."

"You deserve it. Put it in. I want to see it."

Standing in front of the mirror, she pulls the pins from her hair, and it cascades to her waist. *Damn*, he thinks, *from the back you can't tell she's pregnant, and wouldn't I love to—*

She swoons against the wall with a soft "oh!" At first he thinks she's jabbed herself with the comb. But her hands slide under her belly and a gush of fluid splatters the floor. The pains come on without fanfare, their ferocity apace with the mounting storm outside. The bare cottonwoods crack in the wind, and the house shudders as a branch half the size of the roof slams into the kitchen wall. Snow whizzes by, horizontal as the stream from a fire hose, piling up against the house, obscuring everything beyond the windows.

Adam grabs the phone from the hook, but he already knows the lines are dead. He starts layering on heavy clothes. "I'm going for help," he tells her.

"You won't make it to the road." Annie tries to pant through the contraction. "It's Christmas night in the middle of a blizzard. You're the help. Now start boiling water."

O Holy Nightmare. "Annie, I'm no midwife." *My mother lost two babies this way.* "We are not going to lose this baby."

She twists into herself as the pain looks to snap her in two. She makes her way to the bedroom, lies heavily on her pillow, motioning him to bring her dry towels. When he does, she lays her hand to his face.

"I know how to lose babies, Adam. I don't know how to lose you. You're not going anywhere." The wind plows into the wall of the front room, bowing it inward.

He's as close to panic as he's ever let anyone see him. "Tell me what to do," he pleads, and she tells him in breaths and gasps.

He boils water, sterilizes the scissors. Mops her face, gives her his hands to grip until the backs are bruised. Warms more towels and spreads them under her. Watches her bite off her screams and knows it's for his sake.

"What can I get you?" he keeps asking.

"A gun," she gasps, her face contorting into an expression he can't read.

He chokes out a smile. "To use on yourself, or me?"

She bears down but rumbles through her teeth, "That's for me to know and you to wonder." The contraction ends with a burst of her musical laughter. He wants to cry. She is helping *him* through this.

She pulls on his arms, hauling herself up. She wants to walk, to relieve the pressure crushing her lower back. Her full weight leaning on him feels so slight. Why didn't he realize it before? That scar! She's too small to birth this baby. What has he done? He curses the weather with every particle of his considerable power to curse. No one, no one on the planet wants a baby more than they want this one.

The clock creeps past midnight and she creeps into their bed again as the pains pile each upon the last. At 12:26 Annie rises to her elbows and pushes with all her mettle, pushes the blizzard of the century into insignificance. Adam catches their daughter, who squalls a greeting mightier than any force of nature. He swaddles her in the blanket he's warmed, the first fatherly thing he does for her. She's a slippery, blood-flecked mess, and she's the most beautiful girl in the world. His hand goes to her head. She has just enough black hair to curl over his finger.

We have a girl. It's only four words, but a surge of tears overcomes his voice. In those first moments, he knows more about their child than Annie does.

How long has she let him sit on the edge of their bed, rocking and weeping, before she touches his arm? "Are you going to introduce me?"

He looks at her, for the first time through a father's eyes that have watched the events of half a lifespan and now behold a miracle. "We haven't discussed a name."

"Anything you like." She lays her hand on his.

He buries his face in the warm folds of his daughter's neck, whispering something unintelligible even to him. Her squalls subside into tiny sighs and hiccups. Before he surrenders the baby to Annie, he has to lean over and kiss her, lingering on her mouth.

"Thank you," she says against his face, "for letting me be the one."

He eases their daughter into her arms. "This is Julia. Julia Ellen Fielding."

The baby latches to the breast, knowing exactly what to do. Tranquility, in quiet triumph, settles over the house. The storm battering their home is a million miles away. The soft *nuk-nuk-nuk* of Julia's nursing is the only sound in the room. The afterbirth slides out. Adam cuts the cord and ties off the stub. Eventually the baby's rosebud mouth slackens into slumber.

Annie sinks lower into her pillows. Her eyes fix on Adam but soon flutter and droop. Adam shucks his clothes and climbs into bed with his little women. He has more than enough room in his arms for both of them.

Throughout the night, Adam wakes when the baby does, asking if everything is all right. Annie changes the towels beneath her and tells him not to worry, that a certain amount of bleeding is normal after a birth. But by morning he can tell something is amiss.

"It should be tapering off. It's not, is it?" he demands.

She struggles to keep her voice noncommittal. "Why don't you get me some ice chips and let's see if that works."

By afternoon the growing pile of bloody rags by the bed stands in accusation. "We're going into town," he tells her, gathering coats and cloaks and blankets. "You need a doctor."

"Can we get through?"

"I'll carry you if I have to."

He stamps out to assess the main road. A stroke of fortune: it looks like the storm hit their section with more wind than snow. The going will be slow, but with Tipsy and the sleigh, they can get through.

Annie allows Adam to help her into the sleigh. She didn't put up an argument, and that confirms his fears. Julia, bundled to triple size, lies blessedly asleep in Annie's arms.

At the hospital they're received with a flurry of congratulations and fussing over the baby, followed by consternation when Annie relates her condition. The staff sends an urgent summons for the doctor and hurries Annie to an examination room.

"Keep an eye on Papa," Annie coos under Julia's dime-sized ear.

The doctor arrives, exclaims over the baby, and disappears into the examination room. Minutes later he waves Adam in.

Annie won't look at him. The doctor says, "We have a surgical emergency here. It appears that there has been a rupture of the uterus, perhaps a result of fetal extrusion. I can't tell without going in. We're looking at tremendous risk of infection. The uterus must be repaired immediately." He addresses Annie. "Or removed."

"I said no."

The doctor glances at Adam. "Mrs. Fielding, given your history of pre- and postnatal trauma, the odds are—"

"I've beaten the odds, and the results are right in front of you."

"You can say no to the hysterectomy, although I strongly

recommend you have it, but you can't say no to repairing the rupture, not without endangering your life. Your baby can be cared for by hospital staff while you're incapacitated. We will bring her to you as soon as it's safe for her to nurse again."

"I would like to be alone with my husband, please."

The doctor nods and leaves.

"It never ends, does it?" she says.

"Don't lose heart, ladyfriend. Things are shifting our way. Julia is perfect. I'll be with her every minute. You'll come through this like you have everything else."

Annie tosses in her bed. She envisioned their first days as a family at home, not in a hospital. Meanwhile, Adam has exhibited more patience than she knew him capable of. Julia is in his arms every minute the nurses allow. One comes in to change Annie's dressings, chuckling. "Your husband's reading the football scores to your daughter. Fussing up a storm for us, but she calmed right down for him." Later, while Julia sleeps in the nursery, he sits with Annie and writes to his own mother the glad news of the arrival of her namesake granddaughter.

> Julia has a lush head of black Rushton hair, but her nose and mouth are pure Fielding. We can't tell about her eyes yet. They appear to be black like Annie's but have a definite blue overcast. And you should hear this little miss sing for her supper!

Annie agitates incessantly for release. "I don't like Julia being here. Please get me discharged," she begs Adam. They can manage at home. She promises to obey the doctor's orders.

It takes her five days to wear the doctor down. It's against his better judgment, he says, but they send her off with explicit instructions for her convalescence.

With their long-awaited baby home and her husband happier than she's ever seen, Annie can withdraw from the world and let her broken body mend in peace. She waits for the melancholy, the disorientation, the frightening fits of temper. She's afraid to say anything to Adam but wants to plead with him to protect Julia at all costs, even from her. Although a few blue clouds darken a day or two, they miraculously blow over, and Annie dares to hope that a horrible spell has been broken. Surely they have earned this joy-filled ever after.

Adam scans the *Chronicle-Times*, glad of his family's homebound isolation, and grimly determined to keep it so.

```
    Bordetella   pertussis,   vile   thief   of
childhoods, is among us, traveling its sneaky,
lethal path unseen on the infinitesimal droplets
of a simple sneeze. Pertussis—whooping cough—is
easier to catch than a weak pop fly; one need
only be in the room with it. Draw a breath and
you've drawn a losing hand. It will make itself
at home in vibrant pink lung tissue, and it will
be days before anyone will know. As our schools
and churches sit empty and silent, our hospital
staff has set up a quarantine area, and the city
cemetery commission has been alerted to the
sad task of preparing for an imminent public
health crisis. How many will be snatched from
us this time? The real question is, how many can
we save? The answer: not enough. There is no
medicine, no treatment, and too often no hope.
```

Adam twists the paper into a log and shoves it into the stove before Annie can see it.

A few days pass before Julia's lusty voice falters over some phlegmy business in her throat. Just a cold, her parents assure each other, until her dainty cough escalates to twice-hourly paroxysms punctuated by a ghastly whooping sound that renders them wild with fear.

13

"**D**o something. Anything. I don't care how slim the chance. This is a hospital, isn't it?"

"There's nothing more we can do, Adam. I'm sorry." The doctor gestures with a limp hand that holds no power to heal. Not this time. "It's been a God's-dreadful week. She won't be the only one."

"She's the only one who belongs to me," Adam snaps. "How long?"

"Hours. I'm sorry. We'll keep her comfortable as we can in quarantine here."

"I'm taking her home." His hands move to wrap Julia in the pink wool baby robe Annie finished only three days ago.

"Do you think—" the doctor begins.

"Yes, I think. I think she needs to be at home."

"Are you sure you can—"

"You said 'hours.' I'm taking her home." The doctor opens his mouth to speak again, but Adam knifes the exchange to a close. "What's the worst that can happen?"

The doctor backs away a step. "God bless you, sir."

Inside the truck Adam swaddles the baby in a sheepskin lap robe. It makes for a snug fit in the willow Moses basket Karl and Margrethe couldn't wait to give them. No friend or fiend could have dreamed it would carry Julia through her last trip home, on the very heels of her first.

The car should drive itself, Adam thinks furiously; doesn't it owe him that? The coughing of the engine can't cover Julia's wheezing. Unmerciful God, it's the most horrible sound he's ever heard. In the wind singing through the floor, he can hear Annie's lullaby: *Hush-a-bye, don't you cry. Go to sleep, my little baby.* He urges the car over a ridge of ice where the culvert in front of the Eulenbergs' place has overflowed. *When you awake, you shall have cake, and all the pretty little horses.*

The flash of a snowshoe hare cuts across the front of the car, disappearing into the stubble of last year's corn. The next instant, a snowy owl shoots past. Another swooping arbiter of death. Adam jams the brake to the floor, throwing an arm across the basket on the seat. The screaming of the rabbit slices the wind.

Adam hasn't sung to anyone since he faked his way out of the church choir at the age of ten. No ear, his father scoffed, but Adam's ear was keen enough to sing exactly the off notes he wanted. Now he raises his voice above the chaos as he slowly pushes on the gas pedal. "Black and bay, dapple and gray. Coach and six-a little horses."

When he brings Julia in, Annie rests in bed, paging through a book by the light of the oil lamp. She'll be many weeks more recovering from the surgery. Seeing he has the baby with him, she tries to sit up and reach for them.

"You've brought her home! Is she better?"

Her face is so bright and hopeful. And he will be the one to kill it.

"She's . . . No, she's not, sweetheart. But I thought she should be with both of us. She only has a few hours."

Color, texture, and every vestige of life drain from Annie's face. "I hear that freezing is a painless way to go," she says, in a voice as flat as the prairie outside. "You just feel less and less until you don't feel anything, and go to sleep."

Without looking at Adam or their daughter, she hauls herself up the bedpost. Her feet hit the floor like stumps. Her first steps slip sideways and collide with the chamber pot under the bed. The contents slosh over her instep and across the floor. She doesn't feel it but smells it, the acrid odor of uselessness and waste. Julia's hair-raising retching drains the will from her legs, and she must cling to the wall as Adam rushes the baby to the front room and frantically stokes the fire with one hand. "Shhh, shhh," she hears him crooning, the clang of a pot hitting the stove. Water for steam, it might help, but will the watched pot ever, ever boil?

Annie feels for the red slash below her navel. Another scar. She doesn't care.

She makes it to the front room, where Adam rocks Julia by the fire. Feeling her way along as if blind, she brushes past him. At the door she remarks, "It's cold outside." Cold enough that she'll just feel less and less . . .

With the baby in his arms, Adam throws himself against the door, trapping her against the jamb. "Annie, don't do this. Our daughter is dying. For the love of heaven, come back here. For her. For *her*."

"How much more, Adam?" she screams, shoving the door open with supernatural strength. How much more can she lose and continue to exist? Around the side of the house, out of his sight, she slumps halfway to the ground under the narrow eaves that won't protect her from anything.

It's so cold she can see it, seeping into the buttonholes of her thick flannel nightdress, pushing out the hope that arrived with her the first day she set foot on Montana soil. *She who lives on hope shall die fasting.* There's no more hope here than there are dry goods at Coffeen's.

Inside, Julia struggles. Adam's hand on the basket, swaying on the curved rocking stand, helps him if not her. "Black is the color of my true love's hair." He sings with his eyes closed, barely above a croak. "Her face is like some roses fair." Does Julia hear him? Now the croupy cough-cough-cough until her lungs are empty. Now the soul-curdling gasps, *whoooop, whoooop.* Now flailing against the pink quilt with the tiny roses; now limp with the exhaustion of staying alive. He wipes the vomitus from her pixie face and hands.

Back and forth, through the night, Adam moves between daughter and wife. Annie will not come in. He drags her as far as the door; she escapes with the ferocity of a wolverine. For all her wanting to bear him a child, to create life, she seems now just as determined to die. "'Who ever perished, being innocent?'" The words break against her cracked lips. "'Or where were the righteous cut off?'" The cold is stealing her away.

"The book of Job, Annie. I know. It's a trainload of *shit*. Please come to us. *Please*." Her face in his hands already feels lifeless.

"I have watched the righteous destroyed." She sounds far away. "Sometimes it is I who destroys the righteous. No one can hate oneself more than that." Her hand crawls over her nightdress, wet circles spreading from her breasts.

Adam tries to tuck a coat around her but she pushes his hands away. "No one hates you, Annie. Julia and I need you. This is *insane*." In one sharp move, he slides his arms around her waist and heaves her over his shoulder. If this is the only way he can get her in—

She looses the scream of a soul disemboweled. He drops the dead weight of her to the ground, and her eyes warn him not to try again. How much more loss, indeed. He's always known he could lose them both, but he never envisioned it this way.

"I have to go back to Julia, Annie. I hope I . . . I hope you . . ."

He leaves her huddled against the house.

As dawn creeps through the cottonwoods, Annie prays that her daughter will forgive her, that Julia, whose mother was there when she opened her eyes for the first time, will understand that Mama cannot be there at the moment she closes them forever.

Julia spends her final hour in Adam's arms. He sings on brokenly: "The sweetest smile and the gentlest hands . . ." His voice will be the last thing she hears in this world. Nothing has ever mattered more.

A blunted sun creeps over the riverbank, and also dawning on Adam is the understanding of how Annie can cry uncontrollably for days. When the cold can no longer hurt their daughter, he brings her outside to her mother. At last Annie holds their baby, and he holds them both, tears freezing their lips and cheeks to one another, fearing that it may be the last time they will hold anything together.

So it isn't true. Annie can barely believe it. Another lie about what her body is supposed to do. She's just spent an eternity of dark hours outside, listening to the howling wind around and within her. What others call the bitter, gripping cold called to her with charity, sweet wintry friend whose grip would help her feel less and less until . . .

But it didn't. Instead she'll feel more and more. She'll endure the searing pain of frostbitten fingers and toes screaming back to life.

Yet again she steps over the threshold of their home as a childless mother. Inside, the wreckage of a family fighting a losing battle, two of them bravely, one not.

Adam kicks a chair closer to the stove and shoves her into it. Julia lies like a stone in her arms. *Yes, stone,* Annie thinks. Julia has turned to stone, a work of art, exquisitely carved white marble. In all the world and through all time, there will never be another so perfectly sculpted.

Adam covers Annie with a quilt she made for Cal, a no-nonsense patchwork of duck cloth, corduroy, and denim. When Cal left, he wanted to travel light. His quilt stayed, to weigh her down, to keep her in her place when she might otherwise slide from the chair and melt into the pile of stinking linens and dirty footprints and scatterings of bark and ash around the stove.

Her fingers begin to swell and sting. Adam lifts her feet into a basin of warm water. He puts a warm, wet hand to her face and kisses her unresponsive lips. He lifts Julia's body from her arms and takes the motionless bundle into the bedroom. When he returns, the baby is clean and white in her pink sacque and bonnet, and his face is streaked.

She sees him lower their daughter into the Moses basket. She sees him cover it with the pink wool blanket. She doesn't want to see what happens next.

She comes to with the sense that she hasn't been asleep long. Still morning, she guesses, judging by the sun not yet past the window. The parlor holds its pose, still as a photograph. The Moses basket is gone. Adam lies asleep against her legs in the clothes she last saw him in, breathing in a jagged cadence she's never before heard.

The fire has gone out.

Day into night into day again, as if it matters.

Over, knit 1, over, narrow, knit 1, over, narrow. She knits for hours.

Adam wakes more haggard than before the sleep. He runs a hand over the length of his face, etched in disbelief. About what, she doesn't wonder. It could be so many unbelievable things.

Over, knit 3, over, slip 1, narrow, pass slipped stitch over. Halfway done.

A glance at his watch tells Adam he's slept around the clock. Jesus H., no wonder he's exhausted. And there she sits, propped up beside him, knitting. Those ivory needles and their hellish clicking, with the precision of a military dress parade. Up, up. He must get up and stop her.

If he hasn't washed in a day, it's doubtful she has either. A sheen of frost covers everything in the front room. Without speaking or looking at her, he moves as briskly as he can to reload the stove and, when it's roaring, heat several pots of water.

He folds the pine stand that rocked the Moses basket and puts it outside. Into the fire he feeds the sacque and diaper in which Julia died and the eyelet-edged cloth he used to clean her for the last time. He recalls Annie making the baby bath set, the washcloth and its matching mitt and hooded towel. They skipped the Halloween ball. Annie sat by the fire with her black hair undone, the definition of bewitching, her needles tapping out their mystical meter, as she's doing now.

Finally the water warms enough to bring him up to clean, although not shaven. He hates his unshaven appearance, like he's been dipped in sawdust, but today the effort seems insurmountable. He leaves a pan warming on the stove for her.

In the bedroom, he sits, crowding her away from the edge of the bed, forcing her to move to make room for him. Her needles tick on without pause.

"That's lovely."

"Thank you."

"But you have to stop." He covers her hands with his and the clicking ceases. "Julia's gone. She's gone."

"I know. This is a shroud." She tries to slip her hands from under his but he tightens his hold. "Please let go of me. I must finish this before the funeral."

He gathers the shroud and the needles and the ball of yarn in both hands and, with all the authority he can summon, commands, "Give this to me."

Fresh dread clouds her eyes as she surrenders the unfinished work. He puts it out of her reach and wraps her in his arms, pressing her head to his shoulder; he can't bear to see her face when he tells her.

"She's been buried."

She holds her breath for so long, he starts taking slow, deep breaths, as if his own could get her going again. Then comes the trembling in her chest, delicate as butterfly wings but growing until it pushes both of them over: dry, quaking grief beyond tears.

"How?" she gasps. "The ground is frozen. Were you there?"

"With pickaxes. 'Whatever it takes,' they told me. Communicable disease. It had to happen fast. The city handled it. I was here with you."

"No one with her to see her into the ground?"

"I was here with you. We'll go to her together when you're able to."

Day into night into day into night again. He's fallen asleep with his hand on her belly, as he did each night less than a month ago. Where tiny toes or elbows or knees within her batted at his palm, now only an unforgiving scar remains. She wonders, do the departed visit the departed? She needs an answer, for although she alone knows it, she is as dead as Julia.

14

Every wedding she's ever attended has ended the same way: "I pronounce you man and wife." And every time, Annie can't help thinking how ludicrous the words would sound if reversed: "I pronounce you husband and woman."

A man is always a man first, but a woman, at marriage, hands her identity over to society. It started the minute two words, "I do," wiped two words, Analiese Rushton, off the page and replaced them with Mrs. Thomas Day, Mrs. Adam Fielding. That's a stunning amount of power embodied in a mere three letters. *I do think so*, Annie reflects, from the grief that has become a freefall. Days without number she's lain in their bed, watching the winter sky crowd her window, weightless but holding her down. Space and time have ceased to hold any point of reference for her. It's the least of what's been taken from her along with Julia.

But Mr. and Mrs. Fielding go on as man and wife, if only because the sun keeps coming up each day. She knows his grief is as bottomless as hers. But he claws his way through it in a manner incomprehensible to her.

Julia's frozen tomb has not yet softened when he tells her he's bought a 160-acre plat south of town, unbroken dry land. He can increase his production by a factor of four within three years. He'll supply the whole damn town—and beyond, since he'll be exporting—with table necessities.

"Everything except coffee and pineapples." His thumb flicks the end of his forefinger, over and over, like trying to strike a wet match. "See the fencing going up along the river? Two hundred Duroc-Jerseys are on the way. You must know something about pigs. I need you on your feet *actutum*. It's three months since your surgery. That's enough time for any incision to heal."

He rattles on, hands flying. He's been paying someone to supervise the poultry business, someone who isn't anywhere near as capable as she. He wants to bump the chicken population to four hundred and the turkeys up to fifty. What are they waiting for?

Her fingers play over *The River by Starlight*, trailing from star to star. One of them might be Julia, woven as she is into the tapestry of her mother's soul, however broken the thread.

"Analiese, are you listening? I want you back to work. Now, or sooner. I want—"

"I heard you. You're putting another forty acres of potatoes and another twenty of vegetables. To export. You're putting in a flower plat, gladiolas and asters. Hundreds more critters." Her eyes rove over the quilt. If she seams her hands together just so, she can stifle the orange moon. What is the color of hope, whose eclipse cannot be averted by man or wife? "You haven't told me where you're putting in the money trees."

"What?" His voice has a wild edge to it.

"To pay for all this. You'll need a great deal of capital." No sooner said than she wishes she could suck the words back in.

"Damn right, I will," he barks. "That's why I need you to—"

She lacks the will or the interest to fight him. "All right, Adam. Your dreams are my dreams." Easy to say when she doesn't have dreams of her own.

"And another thing." His voice is as dispassionate as if reading the phone directory. "I'm building us a house. A real house. A painted house. Yellow. Over there." He indicates fifty yards up the road. "Two bedrooms. Front porch facing the river. Oil-burning stove. Winter laundry room. Lots of windows."

A virgin house, untouched by memories.

She married him admiring his earnestness. Now grief has seeded that earnestness; it has mushroomed to reckless proportion.

But she's forming a plan of her own. Not grandiose like his, and it won't cost a penny. He can build his yellow house, but she won't allow him to tear down the homestead. It's his business if he wants to cold-storage his grief at the bottom of his two-story underground vegetable cache. He can stash his soul at a constant forty-two degrees along with the tons of cabbage and turnips, platoons of celery, subterranean cloud cover of cauliflower heads suspended from the rafters. Her grief will be sublimated to his, as is her name. It may bankrupt them—financially, if he's gone too far too fast, and emotionally, if he thinks that working them both to the edge of collapse will somehow heal the loss of their daughter.

But even if he builds a palace up the road, she needs this ramshackle homestead to remain. She needs to be able to return to this place where Julia lived and died, to see her world through the red window, to remember Julia's warm face at her breast and how in her daughter's eyes she saw infinity, full of exciting possibility. Not as she sees it now, an unscalable abyss. The face near her breast these past months is her husband's, scraping the tender skin raw (he who never used to miss a day's shave) and leaving the blue-black stamp of overwrought lips.

A two-bedroom house. He must still hope. She'll haul herself back to life on that.

He rants on. "The chickens aren't wintering well. I want you to check on the feed, and I'll bet there's a lice problem too. And let me reacquaint you with the phone over there. A modern convenience we use to call the *noise*paper and get up an ad. Find Easter dinner tables for those damn turkeys. Not everyone wants a ham, but by next year, we'll be supplying those, too."

On and on. Doesn't he need to stop for breath? He keeps plowing into her with his cowcatcher plans, hammering down track he expects her to follow. She can start planning for the county fair. He's won everything in sight the last two years and it's time she stepped up. He's financing part of the purchase of the new land with money from fair premiums. That armoire she loves, a fair premium, as is his hand tool set, team harness, corn cultivator. . . .

All she wants to do is close her eyes and shut him out before she drowns in his river of dreams and demands. But all she can do is hold still and let the torrent flow on.

". . . I've had it with your modesty, apathy, whatever the hell you want to call your reasons for never entering the fair. Fed up with seeing everyone else's wives waltz away with prizes that you could win in your sleep."

Sleep? she thinks. *Does he think I sleep?* Yesterday she caught a glimpse of her reflection in the bedroom window, her black eyes like tea brewed too long and left to go cold.

"And why is it you won't enter our quilt? The one that would win first, second, *and* third?" he demands, arms folded across his chest. "I wouldn't mind having that prize, the high-speed washing machine. Less time on the laundry, more time on a line of Mrs. Fielding products. Yeah, a line." His fingers drum the window frame. "You need to come up with something new this year. I want enough output from you to export along with what I'm already—"

"No, Adam. The quilt is for you alone. It stays in our bedroom and our bedroom is not public viewing space." She's up in an instant, cutting a wide berth around him on her way out the door.

"Where are you going?" he demands. "I'm not done—"

"To the poultry house." She snaps her coat off its hook, grazing his face. "You can come with me if you can shut up long enough."

The flock breaks into frantic clucking when she stalks in. She pulls on a pair of battered leather gloves and traverses the yard, scooping up a flailing bird for inspection, then dropping it like a piece of trash. Her voice carries in bursts on the stiff wind, churning with disapproval.

"'Not wintering well.' I don't wonder." She glares at Adam. "What are you feeding them, sand? They're so weak. Couldn't outrun a snail. Missing half their plumes. What's this junk in their eyes? Oh no. Dixie!" She stoops to lift a large hen tottering toward her on gnarled legs.

Annie has no patience with the folly of getting attached to food-producing animals, but for Dixie she made an exception. Dixie came as a wedding gift from their small but stately Third Street neighbor Mrs. Leventhorpe, herself an exception. She had introduced herself as a "Suthanuh," from Alabama, her measured demeanor such that Annie could picture her fanning herself on an antebellum porch fifty years earlier. She brought the Fieldings a chick a week after their wedding. Her hen, a pet that had strayed into her yard from whereabouts unknown, had gone broody shortly before Christmas, mighty unusual. "This gal has a beau," the white-haired belle declared. "Must be a-sneakin' through the fence, the little coquette." Mrs. Leventhorpe thought it took spunk to present themselves at the parsonage on a subzero New Year's Day to be married, and she thought the chick had that sort of spunk, to be born that same week. "Many happy breakfasts, my dear," she told Annie as she handed it over. Annie named the chick Dixie in honor of Mrs. Leventhorpe's origins. That tickled her "like a new paintbrush," she drawled.

The wind riffles Dixie's sparse plumage and sets her rheumy eyes twitching, severing Annie's hopes for saving the flock. More death ahead. Her fault, for letting things go. She lowers Dixie to the ground.

At last Adam has run out of gas. She strides past him into the roost and seizes a notebook and pencil from a shelf by the door. Pages flip back and forth; she squints as she works the mental arithmetic, scratching a series of numbers in the margin of the notepad. Shoving the pencil behind her ear, she marches up to a hand's width away from him.

"Let's talk turkey, big fella. I left you with a flock of a hundred in December, and I'd say you're down at least thirty. I didn't cook 'em for supper, so where are they? Dead of disease, gone home with the help, a dinner party for the coyotes?" She waves the notepad. "This shows less than fifteen hundred eggs collected for each of the last three months. About a hundred and twenty-two dozen, and I had these girls laying about a hundred and eighty-five dozen a month. That's a major drop-off even for winter." She tosses her head in disgust. He offers nothing but a twitch of pale brow.

She holds her notepad up like a summons. "That's over twenty dollars a month we're down. You could buy your darn washing machine with what you've lost on eggs."

He's not the only one who knows how to rant, damn it. She's got plenty more to say, but the stricken look he's allowed to creep onto his face stops her. It's part shock, part anger, and part something like happiness. He has tried to carry on in the best way he knows how—his way, no less painful and inadequate than hers.

"I'm sorry, sweetheart," she says softly. "I keep them laying by replicating summer conditions. Light, warmth, exercise. A simple thing like keeping the roost lit until bedtime might have increased production. I can see that the frost-proofing hasn't been maintained. The worst of it is that many of the girls are sick, but still hobnobbing with the flock. The sick ones should have been isolated at the first sign of illness. Now it's too late. The whole flock has been compromised. We have to do away with the lot and start over."

"You're joking."

"Whoever's been watching after them hasn't raised many chickens. You're right about the parasites—that's why so many are missing feathers, picked out—but your fellow added too much ash to the dust bath. Some is helpful for killing parasites, but too much is toxic. They've got respiratory infection and the ash worsens it. It's too far gone for me to doctor them out of it. Except for Dixie. I'm going to at least try to save her."

Annie scans the yard, making sure she didn't miss any saving-grace factor. "Gonna make a heck of a bonfire." Another gust of wind shoos the flock up against the fence. "It's not the end of the world, Adam. You want to increase to four hundred. Most of these girls are close to three years old, the ones from my original flock going on four. This laying season is their last. Hatchlings are fifteen cents each? What's another sixty dollars in the grand scheme of Adam Fielding?"

He's still simmering, although the wind is starting to cool more than his skin temperature. But she's a stronger person than the one who stalked out of the house half an hour ago. She feels life seeping into her blood. She must find her way back to being the person he knows and needs, the one who aggravates and elevates him. It wasn't fair of him, unleashing his fomented frustration on her. But maybe he did the right thing, rousting her in such brutal fashion.

The effort he makes to gentle his voice pulls her heart into her throat. "Are you up to raising several hundred hatchlings?"

She draws a quivering breath and counts the buttons on her shoes.

"No, but—"

"Then we'll get pullets."

"We can't get away from hatchlings. Four hundred pullets will cost as much as that new house."

He shuffles in a slow half circle. The wind whistles around their heads, working a tendril of her hair loose and blowing it across the hollow of her neck. He faces into the wind, as if hoping it will swallow his painful explanation.

"I can't believe how foolish I was. Assumed all farm women knew about raising chickens." He had hired a local farmer's daughter without asking her experience. "Where was my head?" he wonders. "It's so peculiar. How I can't remember much of the last three months."

The ill-fated flock scatters behind Annie and Adam as they leave. "Let me think on it," she says. He slides an arm around her shoulder, and she lets herself lean in to him. It's months since she's been on her feet this long. "Something new, hmm. Let's see what you've got left in the cellars and go from there," she says, as she closes the gate to the corral and takes in the fencing along the river.

"Yes, we kept hogs," she says. "Don't tell me Cal spared you his favorite joke? A man hiking along the road with a pig under his arm met up with a friend. 'Hey,' said the friend, 'where'd you get him?' The pig said, 'I won him at the fair.'"

It's the closest they've come to sharing a laugh since Julia died. The wind joins in, with a swooping gust that pitches her sideways. She pulls her coat closer and her husband pulls his wife closer.

On tiptoe she can reach to kiss the sandpaper underside of his chin. "You," she says, "could grow pineapples here if you put your mind to it."

"Funny you should mention it. I'm also putting in a hothouse."

"Why stop there? The town needs a flour mill."

They turn their backs on the fencing and the cellars and the henhouse. Under the wind he says, "It's nice to have you back."

What a long day it's been. She drops to the bed and closes her eyes. *Yes, we kept hogs. My mother wouldn't go near them.*

It's a dim memory, Jenny and Cal talking about the hogs and stopping short when they see four-year-old Annie standing there. "Speaking of piglets," Cal exclaimed, scooping her up, making loud hog noises under her chin. "Omp, omp, omp, reeeeeee! Jenny, I dare say Analiese is old enough to help with the slopping. Bet she slings a mean bucket!"

Haze of a memory blowing through the homestead shortly after she arrived in Montana.

"Cal?" she asked. "What was it about Ma and the hogs? Was she afraid of them?"

Cal slid lower in his chair, his long legs seeming to reach across half the room. "I suppose you could say that." His sober tone unnerved her. "The doctors couldn't say what killed Teddy. Thought it might have been trichinae. But they couldn't be sure."

Annie waited, patient as a candle flame, while he seemed to weigh how much more to say. After a while, he cleared his throat.

"One day Jenny and I came home from school and heard

shots coming from the barnyard. Pow! Pow! Pow! One after another. We crouched in Jenny's bedroom window to see what was going on.

"Ma had the rifle and was picking off the hogs." His face had melted, trancelike. "I have never since been more terrified. Pa came running, shouting, 'Amanda, what in purple Jesus are you doing?' She went crazy." He passed a hand through the air. "If you had known Teddy! He was such fun. Jenny and I suffered without a word, for fear of what it would do to Ma if we showed our feelings. Until Chase was born. The pinch hitter. It's like he knew it from the start. Good old *boring* Chase. He was just what Ma needed."

Annie stood up abruptly. "Thank you for telling me, Cal."

In the pallid twilight, she's barely aware of Adam unbuttoning her shoes and tucking their quilt around her, the faded green river curving over her ankles, the stars sprinkling her shoulders.

"I never learned to shoot," she murmurs, at the edge of sleep. "Haven't you ever thought that odd?"

"For a farm girl and a homestead woman, yes. Odd enough that I thought it best not to ask."

"For some reason, my pa refused to teach me."

15

Work is their opiate. It numbs the pain, but requires ever-increasing amounts to sustain the level of relief. Up the road, what first appeared to Annie as a skeleton rising from the grass is fleshing out as a house, bones of pale lumber filling in with limpid windows, smooth siding, and a shaggy coif of shingles. Adam hasn't offered her details and she hasn't asked. Goodness, when would she have time, with all he expects of her? On the new land, ten acres of potato tops bob on a sea of ceaseless wind. The flower plat resembles an army in full dress: row upon row of staunch soldiers, long bayonets of gladiola in fearless red and outsized tufts of aster in gunpowder white. Adam materializes everywhere at once, on the land, in town, at the house raising Cain if a window goes in without his supervision, hauling sample floral arrangements to churches and funeral homes across two counties.

At times Annie feels they're but an audience to their own life, watching it play out on a faraway stage. On a sallow evening when talk eludes them, Adam leans against the kitchen counter, watching her. Her chair rocks; her needle dives into the fabric of the shirt and comes up again. And again. And again. Rocking and stabbing the silver thimble. *Tk . . . tk . . . tk . . .*

"Do you have to do that now?" he asks, his voice too thick.

"These buttons are hanging by a butterfly lash. They're not going to tighten themselves."

He lets five ticks of the needle go by.

"I was thinking of loosening yours."

She lowers the shirt to her lap and gazes out the window. "That is such a bad idea."

"Annie, we're married."

"But we can't keep doing this."

After the Chautauqua lecture on the national parks last year, they picnicked with a group that included several fire rangers. They said, "You can stay ahead of an inferno if you run down the hill, not up."

Adam can't help it. He moves uphill. He runs a finger under her hair at the nape of her neck. The tortoiseshell comb comes away in his hand.

"You have to understand how fire behaves," a ranger declared, thumping Adam's shoulder. "Combustion requires oxygen and fuel. You can squelch a small fire with a shovelful of dirt. You can fight a wildfire by lighting a backfire to destroy the fuel. But respect you must the lightning bolt that strikes at fifty thousand degrees Fahrenheit. Some fires tender only one course of action—get the hell out of the way."

Annie knows she and Adam are playing with fire. Yet they keep striking the match, lighting the backfire that's supposed to stop the larger blaze from incinerating the precarious life they've built together. She didn't factor passion into the equation of this well-thought-out marriage of opportunity. Her resistance clatters to the floor along with the comb.

The nurse at the hospital is a cheery woman with a bosom that could comfort the entire population of the county. But this time it's not comfort she offers Annie. "Honey, I have cared for you tender as I know how these last few years, but it's time for me to say something," she begins. "You gotta think about your own self's health, and know that some of us wasn't meant to be mothers. How many times you gonna do this? You gonna have to get your man to back off of you." Annie finds two tins of prophylactics tucked under the napkin on her lunch tray. PRESS TO OPEN, directs the tin. She takes up her fork, rams it into one tin, then the other. Six rubber sheaths, enough to arrange into a sweet daisy pattern with an olive at the center. When the nurse returns, Annie hands her the tray and says, "We want a baby."

Adam brings her home on a morning overhung with pink feldspar clouds, lifting her from the truck, guiding her to the house with an arm around her waist, taking her coat, as if they are courting. Inside, she sits on her side of the bed, putting her hand down first to brace herself. The bed seems colder for her absence. She feels as if she might never recover.

Adam appears in the doorway. "I'm making coffee. I'll bring you some." She's removed her shoes and shirtwaist and undone her skirt. She unbuttons her chemise but stops at the sight of her breasts swelling through the parting of the fabric. "The nurse gave me some protectives."

He sighs, reaches into an inside pocket of his jacket, and holds up two tins. "Like these? The doctor has the same idea." He sounds depleted. "Maybe we should think about it." The sputtering hiss of coffee boiling over jerks his attention from her. He drops the tins on the foot of the bed.

Maybe they should. She listens to him mopping up the spilled coffee, damp rag sizzling on the stove top. He can sweep away the burned grounds, but the smell will linger like an unwanted guest. Like an unwanted blue tin slashed crossways with white stripes and bold green lettering: ASSUR$_x$ANCE. FOR THE PREVENTION OF DISEASE. AIR TESTED AND GUARANTEED PERFECT.

Her skin has gone cold where her chemise hangs unbuttoned, though her face feels aflame. She crawls under the quilt and pulls the sprinkle of stars up to her chin. The two tins sit in the middle of the green curve of the river near her feet. She slides a hand out from under the quilt and pulls them toward her with the tip of her thumb.

When Adam returns with her coffee, her fingers splay in front of her, gloved in prophylactics. One by one, she tugs them off, each sounding a cap-gun report and sending up a puff of urine-like odor. "He loves me. He loves me not. He loves me." The last one clings to her wedding-ring finger. She snaps it off, looking him straight in the eye. "He loves me not."

The cup in his hand streaks across the room, a dark comet shedding its tail of steam and coffee. The window shatters in a sleet of jagged slivers.

"Goddamn you, woman! Who are you to talk about love? Good Christ, what if my father is right? What if this is the hand of God?" He snatches her blouse from the foot of the bed, ripping it from hem to collar and hurling it to the floor. "You abandoned *his* baby. You even abandoned Julia at the end. If you never have another baby, you can't abandon her!"

"Cynthia. Her name is Cynthia," Annie says slowly. "I always knew you would dig for it."

"I didn't have to dig. You said it yourself: Divorce is public record. It was one letter to the Jones County courthouse." The admission is no sooner out than he recoils from its stink. It curdles the air in the room.

Annie can't summon any outrage. "You got his side of it. Men," she sighs. "You always stick together. Even siding with one you've spent years trying to exorcise."

How long has he known? She clenches shut her chemise, feeling naked although clothed, and that she wants never to be naked in front of him again. She'll miss that. But it will be more effective than any Assurance they can get from a tin.

Why did she goad him? Because somehow she knew? She had hoped for better. That's now out the window he's so savagely opened. But his anger has crept below the floorboards along with the coffee, leaving him slumped against the wall, hand burrowed into his hair, clutching the roots as if trying to hold himself up.

"I'm sorry," he says to the floor. "I should have . . . I never should have . . . Please tell me now. Please."

What's to tell that he hasn't already seen for himself? *I'd just had a baby. Figure it out.* Should she describe in unsparing detail the consumptive fear that she would hurt her baby, the relief that instead she "only" hurt her husband? Should she tell this second-chance husband that she wouldn't even have considered marrying him but that she thought he must have a stain on his soul from somewhere in his past, and that it would somehow balance hers, though she would never know, never want to know, what it is?

Is it too late to touch you, Dear?
We this moment knew—

Emily Dickinson be damned. Suddenly Annie can't fathom why she ever sought comfort in the writings of a woman who neither married nor mothered.

The cold hectors her skin as she slips from the bed. The floor burns, ember and ice, under her feet. She yanks the book from its drawer. The stiff cloth cover disgusts her. *Everlasting love,* it was once inscribed. Everlasting nonsense. She'll have handsome blisters where she wrenches the stove open with bare fingers, but that's the price of what must be done. The book crackles like popcorn when it hits the coals. Annie slams the door, the pages already settled into their cremation.

She sidesteps a speechless Adam, half reaching for her, upturned palm asking *what the . . . ?*

"Who has abandoned whom?" she murmurs, sliding into bed. She turns her face to the draft streaming from the broken window. "I was ill, had no money, couldn't work." Her belly twitches. The anger that left him has crawled into her. "Maybe you're right." She stops short of a snarl but can't stop the words. "Maybe this is God's way of ensuring I'll never bear a son who abandons his mother for no reason. So big of you to write to her when Julia was born. Does she know the rest?"

There is no rest.

Adam thumbs the broken glass from the window, shards tumbling into the grass, until his hand lies on the sill, hashed with tiny cuts. "I love my mother," he says in a voice foreign to Annie. "But I can't abide my father's brand of piety."

She's so tired. Of all of this.

"Maybe you're right. About these." She gathers the protectives in her fist, balled under her chin as she slides deeper under the quilt, down the escape hatch that mimics death but never extinguishes the guilt.

He was right. Bold sun shining on their bright new yellow house. Buttercup tiles in the kitchen with the black-and-white linoleum shot through with daffodil, the goldenrod-upholstered settee in the front room.

"You were right," she says, turning in a slow circle in the room that will be their bedroom. A different view: she'll now go to sleep to the lullaby of their rustling orchard. On summer nights when she misses the coo of the river, she can sleep on the covered porch that shelters the front of the house.

He says, "Karl's coming to help move the furniture on Sunday."

He's not asking her if she's ready, if she likes it. He needed this house, to reign over every inch, every angle, every last nail.

And yet she can see that he kept her close in his thoughts, sees it in the kitchen with its lowered cabinet and sink, its pull-down pantry shelves. In the front room with its graceful candle sconces placed at her height, in the waterfall steps ascending to the porch.

It's her house too.

"Invite him and Margrethe to stay for supper. We'll eat on the porch." She can feel Adam relax.

"How about a christening?" He drops the last syllable, taking her face in his hands and tipping her head to meet his. "Four rooms," he says, lips moving along her neck.

"And the porch?"

"Of course." He's pulled her spoon-tight to him, rising to the moment and lifting her with him. "But this room first."

"Of course."

He shuts the gate of the truck. They linger over the sight of it before he climbs into the cab. Stacks of crates so new the wood still smells alive. Labels so shiny it looks as if the ink is still wet. Indigo sky, orange moon, green river. STARLIGHT RIVER MARKET FARM, CASWELL, MONTANA, the lettering in a bright white that he says will glow silver in indoor light. Melons and onions, squash, spuds, and the first cases of Mrs. Fielding's Cinnamon Plum Ambrosia, headed for Great Falls: they're now in the export business.

She watches the truck around the bend, then crosses the grass to the shed. Amid the implements and instruments, the can is still there, a wire-bound brush alongside it, where she left it half-full years ago. With some coaxing, the lid comes up. She stirs the paint cake-batter smooth with the end of the brush.

Sandpaper roughs up the yellow window casing over the sink, giving it the patina of spoiled mustard. The red paint smothers the yellow, kissing the new kitchen as it did the old with its sultry confidence. But rather than fertile fields, this window frames a study in gray textures both quaint and flamboyant, weathered wood and river rock. Front and center is a two-room shack nailed together by a brother they sometimes wonder if they imagined, so thoroughly has he vanished.

Annie watches from behind the steam rising from her evening tea as Adam reads the newspaper item aloud.

```
Five of our well-known ladies have formed
a committee to see to the beautification of
the cemetery. Recent plantings of trees and
shrubbery now line the paths, and water pipes
ensure their proper care. The committee calls
upon families having loved ones buried in our
Silent City to donate appropriately.
```

Adam closes the newspaper. "More than a year now," he says. "I suppose it's time."

"I suppose it is."

"I want a plain white marble stone. No lamb."

"Agreed."

"Shall I go alone?"

"No. We'll go together."

The cemetery sexton's shack is nothing more than a rectangle of poorly painted lumber with a door gouged into a corner and a single window. Through it Annie hears muted voices and knows she and Adam should not go in there. Her hand in the crook of Adam's elbow tugs a warning, but he mistakes it for reluctance about their sad task, puts a reassuring hand over hers before pulling the door open.

Six heads swivel. One is the sexton, Seamus Kefover, a man whose lifetime of frowning has ironed permanent pleats into his forehead. The other five are the gloved and bonneted ladies of the Caswell Cemetery Beautification Committee.

"We can come another time," Annie says, fingers harrowing deeper into Adam's arm.

"Nonsense," booms a matronly voice. "We're here to help you." Elise Melton steps forward.

"We can come back," Annie whispers to Adam, somewhere between insisting and beseeching.

"*They* can come back," Adam replies, and to Mrs. Melton: "We require a private word with Mr. Kefover." His unblinking ice-blue gaze herds the ladies to the far end of the room, where they take up halting chatter about shrubbery for the front entrance.

The sexton motions them to a corner with a barge of an oak desk flanked by mismatched file cabinets. Two heavy books lie open, surrounded by a posse of scruffy counter stools. Adam ignores the ladies and glances at the books. "We're here to see to our daughter," he says. "We'd like to visit the grave site and order a stone."

"Surely. Deepest condolences for your loss." The caretaker nods toward Annie, a jerky loll that comes off as nervous. "Ma'am."

"Thank you."

"Unfortunately"—the sexton drops his voice and begins closing the tomes on the desk—"we have a bit of a problem."

"And what might that be?" Adam asks, benign as water.

"Might be that . . ." The sexton glances at the committee ladies, then lowers his eyes. "We don't know precisely where she is."

Adam spreads his hands wide across the desk. "What do you mean?"

"I'm sorry, Mr. Fielding. We lost several children the same week as your daughter. They had communicable disease. We had to work fast." He forces a dry cough. "I'm not pleased to say that our records aren't what they should be. We know approximately where your daughter is. It's the potter's field."

The caretaker's jaw contracts as he realizes too late: the explanation with its thoughtless coda goes too far in trying to defend the indefensible. It has lit Adam Fielding's short fuse. Annie can feel him beside her, his every fiber tensed.

Go, she pleads with him silently. *Go. Now.*

He does. The door of the shack screams, hinges wrenched loose under the force of a father's undammed heartache. The door shatters the adjacent window as it rebounds off the side of the shack and sags halfway between open and shut.

Annie hears a choking sound, followed by the roar of ignition and grinding of gears, nerves, what's the difference? Hail of gravel strafing trees and gravestones, down the slope to the main road.

The ladies of the beautification committee stand dumbstruck, all except Elise Melton, who rushes to tut over the damage. "Mercy sakes!" she huffs to Annie. "I can't believe he left you here."

"I told him to." Annie's eyes follow the sound of the truck. He's stopped at the main road. He's waiting for her.

Mrs. Melton preaches on. "There's no call for such behavior. The city acted in kindness. Where else could they put the child? She wasn't baptized, was she? Perhaps if——"

Annie's hand smacks across Elise Melton's face. A choral gasp rises from the ladies of the Caswell Cemetery Beautification Committee.

"Perhaps nothing," Annie says evenly. "Mr. Fielding doesn't require your thoughts on the subject. We aren't of the belief that a baby can be possessed of sins she never got the chance to commit. You, on the other hand . . ." She lets the accusation hang. "If you breathe so much as a syllable of your contemptible thoughts about our daughter in the direction of my husband, I'll baptize you myself. I hope you're a strong swimmer. The river is running at twice its usual volume this year."

"Why, Mrs. Fielding. Is that a threat?"

"Not at all." Annie presents the face of sincerity itself. "It's a promise."

If she walks out at a dignified pace, she can rejoin him in a couple of minutes.

If she runs, she can reach him in moments.

Sheriff Blandish's car pulls up shortly after breakfast the next morning. He sits on the edge of the settee opposite Adam, who doesn't look at Annie when she chooses to remain standing. The sheriff's doggish odor and packaged words drift around the room. Unfortunate incident . . . Mr. Kefover wants to pay for the damage, says his remark was regrettable and added to their grief. But . . . Mrs. Melton wants Mrs. Fielding fined for assault . . . committed in front of five witnesses.

Annie decides that the word *tubby* was invented to describe Sheriff Blandish. Look at him sitting there like a scoop of butter, a fifty-year-old five-year-old, that mustardy mustache running like snot in the deep channels of the marionette lines bracketing his mouth. And she's had enough of him addressing himself to Adam like she isn't there. "Mr. Kefover's remark was indeed regrettable," she interjects, one knee against the back of Adam's chair. "But Mrs. Melton's was deliberately cruel. She slandered our dead baby daughter. In front of five witnesses. She can't pay for that damage."

The lawman opens a hand toward Adam, continuing as if Annie hasn't spoken. He managed to calm Mrs. Melton, he says, by appealing to her Christian compassion for grieving parents. "But consider this a caution, Adam," he says heavily. "I won't be able to protect Mrs. Fielding from the consequences of further rash actions."

After the sheriff leaves, Annie says, "Mrs. Melton has had it in for me since the moment she learned we were marrying. I'm beginning to feel that I may be a proxy for your sins against her niece. Is that close to the truth of it? Just yes or no, please."

He winces and scowls at the same time. "Mrs. Melton asked me to call on the girl not long after I got here. I did, a few times. The dame was all talk. Talk to impress me with her schooling and her 'place' and her opinions on food, farms, folderol . . . and more talk only God could tolerate. Talk, talk, talk, thirteen to the dozen."

"I don't want the details," Annie cuts in. "Just yes or no."

"I'm clearing the air here, Annie," he thunders, sending her back two steps. She turns her head; if she must listen, it will be with only one ear.

"She cajoled me into taking her for a canoe ride around the lagoon," he continues tightly. "That was going to be the end of it for me. She babbled a raft of nonsense about recent weddings in town, about autumn brides being possessive and spring brides being amiable and what did I think? I told her, 'I think we have misunderstood each other,' and I docked the boat—I may have rammed it a bit—and got out. She jumped up, spitting mad. The boat tipped. The newspaper had a field day with my 'providing the lady with an unanticipated bath.'"

"In front of five witnesses?" Annie asks.

"At least," he mutters.

"Well now," Annie says, tapping her thumb against the top of the rocking chair. "What reasonable person would call ramming a dock a rash action? After all, when someone affronts another someone—say, a man—accidents do happen."

"I tried to warn you about Mrs. Melton."

"I tried to warn you about me."

"You don't do anything by halves, do you?" Adam says, creasing the newspaper fold to a razor edge. "Page one, even."

Annie yawns. "You wanted me to make a splash at the fair. You should be more careful what you wish for."

"'Mrs. Fielding's Seven-Cup Cookies were the talk of the opening day.'" He reads with exaggerated breathlessness. "'Rather than entering them in the competition where they would be judged by a single person, Mrs. Fielding presented her talents to the court of public opinion, running a booth with a twist of intrigue.'"

"Oh dear, and everyone has to either wait for next week's paper to untwist the intrigue, or come to my booth. This will stoke business for the weekend, won't it? I should think you'd be thrilled," she says, dumping a jangling current of dimes from her canvas bag into a chipped vase.

"I'll hardly sleep."

A throng of early birds mills around her booth when she arrives on Saturday morning. Ten cents buys a cookie and a chance to win a dozen more if the purchaser can name the seven one-cup ingredients. "There are ten one-cup ingredients," Annie confides to her visitors, "but I'm giving you a head start: butter, sugar, and flour."

A carpet of crumbs settles around the booth as no one comes up with all seven ingredients and many a failed guess provokes the sale of a second or third saucer-sized cookie. Chickadees dart among the thicket of feet.

A boy of about nine with hedgehog hair, pants too short and shirt too long, watches the goings-on, bare toes working the ground like a typewriter. After a dozen failed attempts by fairgoers of all ages, he approaches Annie with a grubby coin.

"You been savin' that dime since Christmas," his companion declares. "You sure this is what you want to spend it on?"

Annie crosses her fingers while the lad chews. "Raisins and walnuts," he says right away. "Chocolate bits. Coconut?"

Annie smiles encouragement. "Yes, that's right."

"Oatmeal. Peanut butter."

"Yes." Annie holds her breath, rooting for him. This boy looks like he hasn't claimed many victories in his life.

As he swallows the last of the cookie, the lump in his throat stays behind. The seventh ingredient remains a mystery. So close and yet so far; Annie knows the feeling. The boy's distress shapes his whole face, his eyes wide as moons lest tears spill, his mouth bending downward in teepee lines traveling to his jaw. Did he envision himself presenting his grand accomplishment, the prize dozen, to his mother? Annie hands him another cookie: "For the best effort I've yet seen."

The boy lights up and fizzes. "Wow! Thank you!" He breaks the cookie in two and hands half to his friend. She watches them gallop away, trophy cookie clutched on high.

Oh, that her own sadness could be assuaged with a cookie.

"'Best collection of vegetables from a single farm.'" Annie hooks the ribbon to Adam's chest pocket and stashes fourteen more ribbons in the glossy elm ice chest—first prize, best bushel of popcorn. "Tell me something I didn't already know."

Adam smiles, patting the pocket where an envelope holds a stiff new fifty-dollar gold certificate. He loads the last of their displays and premiums into the truck, a tight fit. "Yeah, I might get a line in the paper for it. But you . . ." He boosts her up to the seat and takes his time coming around to the driver's side. "They're writing next week's story as we speak," he says. "'Mrs. Adam Fielding stunned the crowd by winning the ladies' baseball toss with a throw equal to that of some of the men's competition. We even heard talk of this unlikely athlete joining the local team, whose pitching efforts of late have been uninteresting.'"

"'Sure,' Mrs. Fielding replied," she quips. "'But they'd have to change the name of the team. I'm not playing with a bunch of Hooligans.'"

The truck putts out of the fairgrounds. Adam imitates the sound in his throat and squeezes her thigh. "'Mrs. Fielding embodies the appellation 'small but mighty.'"

"What a lovely evening," she remarks as they pull into home. "Let's go sit by the river. We can unload tomorrow."

On the path to the river, the rising cantata of the katydids encircles them. Adam scoops up a handful of stones and begins launching them, with a little too much elbow, toward the water.

"Ah," Annie says. "Next year's baseball-toss winner, as long as Walter Johnson doesn't show up."

He snorts, "Any cookies left?"

"Not a crumb."

"The mystery ingredient?"

"Mrs. Fielding's blackberry apple jam. I would have given it to anyone who said fruit jam."

"And the raffle? Are you ready to tell me what that was about?"

Ten cents for a cookie and a guess. Another ten cents for a raffle ticket, the prize being an azure knit-lace baby ensemble. She sold more than two hundred tickets.

"I donated the money to the cemetery beautification committee, along with the five-dollar prize from the baseball toss."

"Annie."

"Adam. It will be Mrs. Melton's duty as chairwoman to write me a proper letter of thanks. I might even read it."

16

She doesn't hear him when he comes in. He watches her as she fingers this unremarkable thing. He tries to see it as she sees it. It is tarnished. It has a key to wind it. It has a closed face. That's all. But she'll make it into more.

His stomach braces. "Hello, Annie."

"Adam. What is this?"

"It's a watch."

"Not your watch. I'm wondering how a watch that isn't yours ended up in our house."

He closes his eyes. Preparation for battle. The malignant breath of war blows through his home as surely as it now blows through Europe.

"Whose watch is this?" Her voice is so flat, she might be asking, *What time is it?*

"It's mine for now. It was Benjamin Davis's."

"For now? Ben Davis is dead. Is he coming back for his watch?" Her voice climbs. "What's going on here?"

He jams his hands in his trouser pockets, sending a knuckle into the hole that opened up last time he rammed his hand through the seam. She mended it. It split again, another wound in their lives that keeps reopening itself.

"What's going on is that Ben Davis is indeed dead—"

"Yes, he drank himself to death."

"His horse kicked him in the head."

"He tried to cross the river dead drunk. Perhaps on that hooch you've got buried out there that I'm not supposed to know about."

Adam stares at her. She dismantled her still after Julia died. "I won't be drinking anymore," she had told him. "Nor will I," he assured her. "But I sure as hell won't be drinking any less."

"Two cases of pints! One shotgun blast and I could make the prettiest pepper pattern in those bottles." She smiles sweetly. "But Ben Davis would still be dead."

"Ben would still be dead, but his wife and children aren't. You know how badly she wants to hang on to their place and what a miracle that's going to take. I ran into her at the hotel last week. She's taken a housekeeping job there for the winter. I was done for the day and I gave her what I had left in the truck."

"And the watch followed you home?"

"Jesus, Annie." From the inner pocket of his jacket he yanks papers and a pouch of Bull Durham. Hell, if a man wants to smoke in his own house, he should damn well be able to. He creases the paper over and over. "I gave her a ride home. She was distraught that she couldn't pay me. I insisted it wasn't necessary, and she insisted on giving me the watch. It was a lopsided trade, so I put it away until I can think of a way to give it back to her."

"My, people are insistent these days. It's not such a problem, is it? You can give it back during your next tryst. Then she can insist that you keep it and you'll be all set for another go."

"Tryst? *Tryst?*" He remembers he's out of matches. He shoves the tobacco pouch into his pocket and crushes the paper. "That's hooey and you know it."

"How do I know it? How do I know she doesn't have a watch too, and—my gracious!—it's synchronized to this one. So you need never waste a minute of your time together."

"Goddamn it, stop this. Where do you get this rot? I have never given you a particle of reason to think—"

"Where do I get it? It's contagious. I get it from living with someone who's jealous of the way my very shadow touches me." There, she's struck the flint over the tinder. It explodes on contact. "At least I was married to the object of your disaffection. You don't have the capacity to know how sick I am of your hanging Thomas over us like a specter that you won't let pass into the next life. Oh dear, did I say his name out loud? We don't like that, do we? Well, Thomas, Thomas, Thomas, Thomas!" Her fists hammer the air, physical punctuation. "How about this? Chase wrote last month that Thomas and his wife have new twins. That's five children. What helpful leftovers have you got for them, Adam? *Everyone has children except us!*"

"Damn Chase! We can live very well without that kind of information."

"Don't you dare presume to tell me what I can and can't live with." The watch dangles from her fingers, exuding a faint aura of fear.

She's a runaway train. He wants desperately to get her under control but can't deny that she's articulated an ugly truth, about him and his part in creating the twister that has spawned her mistrust. And he knows what lurks unsaid between them, that the real specter in the house is the threat of failure.

"I'm looking you straight in the eye and telling you this. Would I be able to do that and lie? I did a kindness for a neighbor. The watch is a token of thanks. That's all it is."

She flicks the watch over in her fingers, then lets it drop to the floor. It lies there, abject, as she brings the full force of her heel down on it.

"Now it's junk."

No, it never gets any easier, navigating the landscape of her thoughts, where the things he loves, her pragmatism and her magnetism, become entangled with the more enigmatic workings of her mind.

The sad pile of crushed glass and sprung springs cowers between them. He can't let that be the metaphor for their last stand. "A desperate disease requires a dangerous remedy," his grandfather used to quote. Well, he is nigh unto desperate, and what he's about to do is quite dangerous.

"Analiese," he says, coming closer, "you need to realize that we have nothing between us."

Her anger boils over, sucking the air from the room. "Nothing between us? You are hateful. To go through what we have and say that it is *nothing*." Her eyes blaze feral.

"I didn't say what we've been through is nothing. I said we have nothing between us."

He's taking a chance, coming close to her. In her state of mind she's capable of hurting him.

"May I?" He runs his hand up her arm. It's not his style to ask permission. She'll find that mystifying and his timing despicable. But all he wants is to press her close, as close as he dares without breaking her. There are so many ways he could break her. He must be careful.

She fits under his chin with room to spare. If it rains, she sometimes jokes, she would not even get wet. "This is what I mean," he says. "See? Nothing between us but what we put there ourselves. We hear what we want to hear, believe the worst. But see, there is nothing between us." The last words he buries in that mass of black hair.

She, the immovable object, and he, the irresistible force, press yet closer. Enough minutes go by that the sun deserts the window. When the last ray stubs itself out, she says, "You're wrong."

Then we're finished, he thinks. *I can't—*

"There are a couple of old shirts between us."

As if a couple of old shirts would be an obstacle for they, who have cheated death so many times and who draw purpose from their desperation. Their knees give as they sink where they stand; he refuses to calculate the worsening odds they're playing against. What matters is that they have, one more time, thwarted failure, averted the implosion of their tenuous partnership. One more time, she holds nothing back, straddling him right there in the front room, her hair falling past her waist, clinging like ivy everywhere their need is revealed in dampness. When her rocking and gasping subsides into shivering and sobs, he grabs the nearest garment and wraps it around her, still atop him.

"Have I hurt you?" he asks, knowing the answer. Her hair falls across her face in breakers, one upon another faster than he can brush them away, while she struggles to slip her arms into his shirt. Her weeping raises the hackles on his neck, guttural, as if she were being strangled from the inside.

"Yes." Her forehead drops to his chest; she might be trying to flatten the breath out of him. "Please, please," she implores. "Let Thomas go. He was no saint. He sold every last thing we owned before he filed for divorce, so he wouldn't have to pay a settlement. I was sick—you *know* how sick. I had no choice but to crawl back to my parents. I tried to send a note for my baby's birthday. It came back unopened and marked, 'Mrs. Day requests you not try to contact her daughter.' Let him go! It can't be harder for you than it was for me."

"Annie." He has to stop her shaking, before she falls apart, pieces of her everywhere. Gently, he guides her off him and carries her, swaddled in his shirt, to the bedroom, where they will start again under *The River by Starlight*. What can he say? He can't choose between knowing he'll hurt her again and making a promise he fears he won't be able to keep.

But in the hour before daybreak, he decides the time has come. Propped half-sitting on their pillows, he pulls her hands from beneath the quilt, holding them as he did the night they married.

"I promise you," he says, "that I will never invoke a certain person from your past again."

In the silence that follows, he thinks, what did he expect her to say?

"You took as much a chance on me as I did on you," he continues. "I don't want you thinking you sold out to the wrong party."

The quilt falls from her shoulders as she reaches to twine her arms around his neck.

"I didn't sell out," she says, tenderly kissing the hollow behind his ear. "I traded up."

When he opens his eyes, the room leaps at him with uncharacteristic intensity. A knot in the wall pouts at him only a body's width from the bed. The third floorboard from the window is warped, looking like it's been pried up. Beyond their bedroom, clothing lies strewn around the front room, her pink shirt crumpled on top of his dark trousers, its rosy arm looking almost alive, loving and protective. Sudden apprehension shakes him fully awake.

It's midmorning; he's never stayed abed this late in the day, never seen the room underscored by full daylight from flat on his back. But it's not what he sees that's disconcerting. It's what he hears.

What he doesn't hear.

Normally she would be up before him. He would hear her moving around the kitchen; he would smell coffee and ham and oatmeal. The silence in the kitchen and the disarray in the front room tells him she's not up. She weighs barely enough to dent the bed, but now he's aware that she's still beside him. As usual, she faces the edge of the bed. But it's her stone stillness that alarms him.

He can't detect her breathing. Suddenly he hears everything around him: the breeze whistling around the window, the nattering gossip of poultry in the yard, the river slapping the rocks as it careens by, the voices of the field hands, who, astonishingly, haven't come knocking yet, or have they? Out of bed, dash for those blasted trousers before he's caught, literally, with his pants down. He catches his thumb in the fly, swears loudly. She doesn't move. Her arm hangs over the side of the bed, the cuff of his shirt obscuring all but her fingertips. Motionless as a painting. Good God. They outlived the night, withstood their polarity. The reconciliation, hours longer than the row that precipitated it. But not a first. Adam sometimes wonders if they lose their way on purpose because the homecoming is worth it.

A memorable night. But why now so still, so very still?

He slips her hand between his two, swaying with relief to find that it is cool in the morning air, but not cold.

"Ladyfriend." He pats the hand in his. "Rise and shine."

He's intent on her face, any less concentration and he wouldn't see the slight quiver around her eyes. She speaks from a depthless place. No muscle moves.

"See . . . Jamie."

See Jamie? She can't mean it. Jamie is Hayes Jamieson. Hayes Jamieson is an attorney.

"No. We don't need to see Jamie. Stick with me a little longer. I know what to do now."

"Jamie."

"Why, Annie? Why?"

17

It defies comprehension, but she already knows. The ageless molecular miracle is already underway, thousands of cells dividing under their own ardent motivation. She doesn't need the aching breasts, the fingers of nausea reaching up her throat, and the missed monthly to confirm it.

And she already knows another thing. This promising bud of life will end as all the others. The monthly bleed will cease, but after a hopeful wait will come the expulsion, the swell of new life canceled. Again.

How long will fate toy with them this time? Will the end come early on, confining her to bed for a few days before she'll be expected to get up and get on? Will it come later, when she must endure the laboring and give birth to a doll-sized child, perfect in every way except that it will never breathe? Or will they again be punished in the cruelest manner, rejoicing in their child for a fleeting space of time before the babe is snatched away to join its sister?

Again they'll be forced to bear the unbearable, but first will come the desperate rush to the hospital, followed by the staggering bill to add to the pile of biblical proportion that keeps replenishing itself. Here's something she does know: there will be no tears this time. She's going to will herself out of that if it kills her. She owes Adam that. He carries too much inside. She carries the physical scars, but he bears the weight of what her illness has done to the financial health of the farm, their home, the reason they came together in the first place—wounded it as gravely as the string of failed pregnancies has ravaged her insides.

The farm is everything he said it would be, a glorious, prize-winning jewel of the community. But she reads both the newspapers and the sky. Tougher times loom ahead. The mortgage they took on the dry land was a gamble, and this year they lost, hail leveling their wheat stands and flower plat in five minutes flat.

Her hand lies in his like lead. Her eyelids feel as heavy, a wall against which the retelling of last month's storm plays out before her. With her eyes closed she can't shut it out: the red window exploding in a rain of hailstones, Adam restraining her, furious and screaming "I told you! I *told* you!" as fifty turkeys stood dumbly in the yard to be flattened into unrecognizable heaps of pulp and feathers. They must not be allowed to forget that they can nurture life for months but it can be annihilated in an instant.

Adam's dark prediction that President Wilson wouldn't be able to stay out of the war has come true. With troops conscripted, farm labor is in short supply. With higher end costs, people are buying less. More people are putting in their own thrift gardens, keeping a few hens. A desolate picture for businesses like the Fieldings'. But without her hospital debt, their position would be substantially different.

Now he's trying to rouse her, but she's too drained to respond. He mustn't be hurt further. She must think. She can only think of one thing.

"See . . . Jamie."

She hears him saying no, they don't need to see Jamie. He wants her to stick with him a little longer.

He misunderstands. They don't need Jamie to negotiate a separation.

"Why, Annie? Why?"

He's holding her hand between his. Once more she pushes past her desolation and summons what she needs. She folds her fingers into his, lacing them together. He has to bring his face closer to hers to hear.

"Get my name off the deed."

"Mr. Fielding, you're probably not familiar with the term 'pseudopregnancy.'"

The doctor's office is a regular museum. Books, antique instruments, diplomas. And this medicine man has called him Adam for years; now he's Mr. Fielding?

"I know what *pseudo* means, but I don't see how it applies to pregnancy."

"It is as it sounds. False pregnancy. A woman experiences the symptoms of pregnancy: the missed menses, the swelling of the abdomen and breasts, weight gain, sensations of fetal movement. But there's no fetus."

On this hundred-degree day, Adam feels himself hardening to ice. The doctor continues in careful textbook timbre: "Psychosomatic illness has always been with us. False pregnancy is recorded as far back as Hippocrates. It's well documented although difficult to explain."

"Try."

"The human mind is complex, and sometimes it seems to have power over the physiological workings of the body. We think false pregnancy is the result of a woman's acute desire for a baby, which can trigger the pituitary gland to secrete hormones that simulate the ones released during pregnancy." The doctor pauses, as if this explanation should be enough.

It isn't. "Go on," Adam orders.

The doctor gathers his words guardedly. "The desire may be a woman's own, or may be a reflection of her husband's. She may believe a baby will fill a void, compensate for a loss, or be her redemption for a guilty deed. Given your wife's history of failed pregnancies and infant mortality—"

Adam springs from the chair. "False pregnancy? My wife is lying in a hospital bed three-quarters dead of hemorrhaging. She stopped breathing in my arms. That wasn't pseudo blood, sir. I saw it; I felt it; I even tasted it."

Library-perfect rows of tomes form regal lines on the oiled oak shelves of the office. Adam drags *Principles and Practice of Gynecology* from its place. Eight hundred and six pages. He slams it on the doctor's desk.

"I do not understand," he says, forcing his voice low. "Show me in this book where it explains how a woman who wants a child so badly can will herself into pregnancy, without my contribution. How that pregnancy can be readily observable in every aspect, and then, against all logic, she can will herself to nearly die giving up this imagined circumstance. I want to know more, a lot more. Show me." Adam shoves the book toward the doctor, whose smooth, pale hands lie half curled in his lap. Hands, Adam knows, that have touched his wife in places no man but he should have the right to. "Show me *now*."

The doctor retreats farther into his chair. "I'm afraid this book doesn't address pseudopregnancy. It's considered more psychiatric than gynecological."

"What about these other books? Nothing in any of these books?"

The doctor tilts his head. Or did he? Was that a *no*, or did he not move at all? Is it the heat that makes everything in the room seem to undulate?

"Not this one? Not this one?" Adam sends a row of books flying from the shelf. They land in splayed heaps of bent spines and crushed pages. "Imagine that." He kicks the inert offenders out of his path on his way out.

Outside, the searing sun berates him. *Nice going, Fielding. Shoot the messenger.* He sits in the truck until sweat has crept the length of his back and thighs, pooling under his knees, braising him in his own misery.

Yes, he shot the messenger. Now he can't go back and ask the most agonizing question of all.

Does Annie know?

Three hours it takes to compose himself enough to go see her. Three seconds, standing at the foot of her bed, answers his question.

She knows.

The nurses avoid him. The floor under him is the color of mud and feels about as solid. Annie pulls the sheet up to her chin when he appears. She looks as if she might vanish, wants to vanish. He should take her in his arms. They should share whatever nameless, poisonous emotions suffuse them. But there are too many people around. They are done with *should*, anyway. *Should*: ought to, not necessarily will. Life has denied them some very basic shoulds.

What they will do is hold each other with their eyes for a long time. Then he'll leave and she will continue to study the empty space where he stood. He was there. She didn't imagine it.

For weeks they circle like wooden figures atop a music box, moving along slender grooves, turning and turning, now toward each other, now away, in a slow-motion, silent gavotte.

Except at night, those starless nights when she can hold her hand up before her eyes, palm grazing her face, and still not see it. On these nights, when their faces can't betray unutterable feelings, she allows herself to reach for him, and they find their way to the surface with the words *yes* and *more* and *again*.

When she's thought about it all a person can think, she knows the time has come. Behind the blackberries, a river of tears burns her face and neck. She wraps her arms around herself, squeezing the last of it out. When she returns to the house, washes her face, repins her hair, she sees that her eyes are not red. She is Analiese Rushton. She always has been. She will do what needs to be done. She always does.

When he comes in, she doesn't need to lay eyes on him to see the depletion in his stance, his movements, his face. A growing sense of decomposition permeates the house. She can smell it. They are dying. She, in both body and spirit. He, of grief and of a failure he can't think, build, fight, buy, or sell his way out of.

She hears the flicking of bootlaces and a soft bump as he parks his boots under the pine bench. Muslin rustling as the buttons of his shirt come undone and he pulls the tails out of his trousers. When he moves toward the washbasin in the kitchen, the shirt will slip off his shoulders, baring his back as he shrugs free of the rolled-up sleeves. She grabs her hands under her apron to keep from running to him and pressing her cheek into that familiar back. She loves his back: the valley of his spine and the knolls and dales of muscle that spread out from it, impossibly symmetrical, eerily unmarked for a man his age. Except for the scar, the ghostly welt that cuts six inches of a puckered seam downward from his left shoulder. How many times, washing his back, did she wonder, conjecture. Just once, she couldn't resist running her finger over its length, taut as if someone zipped him up, hiding his most private parts. He tensed that disfigured shoulder, waiting for the question that never came. Quiet as smoke, he said, "You don't want to know."

Without seeing, she'll be able to tell by the way the air moves around her that he's gone into the bedroom for a clean shirt. He'll run his hands through his damp hair several times, but he won't comb it. When they're alone, he knows she prefers him a little mussed. He'll come out of the bedroom, and she'll lay her hand on that scarred shoulder and guide him into his chair. Then she'll go to stand at the window, and though the dark of evening descends upon them, she will see past the poultry and the pigs, past the fallow fields where next year the corn will again wave on high and the potatoes will again burrow warm in the soil. She'll take in the marvelous apples and pears and Tipsy and the team horses grazing in the pasture; she will gaze past all of it, into the featureless future, for as long as she needs to before she speaks.

"It's time to see Jamie."

It's one of those pitch-black nights, a night of a thousand assents and refusals.

He wants to fight it, though he knows he can't and shouldn't. He's killing her.

"No," she tells him. "Mighty as you are, you can't dictate or control my health. I will be the ruination of you. Deep down, you must want to be rid of the craziness and the strife. It's all right to feel that way, Adam. Let me let you go. While you're still young enough to pull the farm out of debt and make another life."

"Make another life?" he cries bitterly. "Could you twist the knife harder? Haven't we spent these last years hell-bent on making another life, and haven't we failed and failed, and isn't that why you are rejecting—"

"Hush." She covers his mouth with her own, lets her fingers find their way around his face so she will have a way to remember it when she can no longer look upon it. "It's a selfish thing on my part. I can't live with the guilt of what I'm doing to you. I'm not rejecting you. I'm releasing you."

The sun slams its forehead against the east windows. Annie attends to the morning chores as would any wide-eyed sleepwalker. Adam lingers over his eggs, asks for more coffee. His eyes rake her face, her hands, and everything that falls under her touch, his movements mechanical and corroded by disbelief he can't voice. He needn't. She can hear it through her skin.

Before he leaves, he asks, "When?" but his back is turned and she can't answer. At the top step of the porch, he veers and strides to her, ensnaring her with his left arm around her waist and lifting her, just enough to take solid ground from beneath her feet. He'll always have the power to disorient her. His lips sink into the soft quicksand of her neck beneath her jaw, the spot he plies when he wants to make her moan. Her hands go to his face; she mustn't let him go further. If he kisses her mouth, she'll never leave.

Something should die when they break contact, shouldn't it? But the sun mocks the yellow of their home, blanching it colorless as the air around them. This time he doesn't look back.

Did he leave the door open to defy the one she's closed? So still is the morning she can hear his footfall long after he's crossed the road, passed the orchard, the piggery, the vegetable caches. Into the south fields he's walking, although they're nothing but stubble, toward the river, although he said he had business in town. She lets the image of his pain draw her outside, to the end of the porch, where she must raise a hand against the sun to see him. His head, too blond, hatless: within five steps, he blends into the light and vanishes.

Inside, she sits at the edge of a bed in which she will never again sleep. She didn't intend to leave today, thought they could be civil and make sensible plans, but now she sees the folly of such thought. To live another night and another morning like this, his heart under the guillotine of her decision. She can't put him through it.

Under the bed, Pa's satchel has collected a powder coating. She wipes it clean with the underside of her apron, fighting the feelings it stirs. Her mother's prediction of failure has followed her and caught her by the ankles. *You're stepping out of your place, Analiese. The Lord punishes those who step out of place.*

From what ordained, inviolable design did she step in marrying Adam? He is just a man. A man both blessed and ill-starred, by turns devoted and detached, a man of valor and vulnerability, a man who dares more than doubts. Just a man, but for a while, her man.

By no measure has he earned the heartache, craziness, and ruin she's wrought around them. She must do whatever necessary to take it from him. *The Lord punishes those who step out of place.* She need no longer fear stepping out of place, accepting now that she has none. She'll make peace with placelessness.

Sheaves of sorrow beat her to the floor, where she clutches hand-fuls of *The River by Starlight* against her face and steeps its quilted waters in the runoff of her mourning. When she's racked herself hollow, serenity settles in. The pebbled leather satchel waits at her side with Saint Bernard patience. She tugs smooth the darkened corner of the quilt. It will dry without any trace of disturbance. Adam, too, will be what he always has been, the personification of industry and facility and self-reliance. In time their years together will be but a tempestu-ous mirage rising only when he imbibes to excess.

Leaving the bedroom, she sees the front door standing open as he left it. Half a dozen fat flies gambol about on the windowsill, their goggle eyes spangling in the sun. Their spastic crawling and jigging and their pestilent droning enrages her. The nearest weapon is yesterday's *Chronicle-Times*, rolled into a cudgel, which she brings down on the invaders over and over, each blow spiked with grunts of anger and anguish at her powerlessness. When she runs out of rage, nothing remains of the flies but a gray smear on the sill.

The front door swings shut with a shove of her foot; she can't bear to touch it. The newspaper, bespeckled with fly viscera, she drops into the stove, closing that door too. The clang of metal on metal swallows its own echo. The house can say no more.

To go without knowing where to go will be an act of rash resolve, and the first test of the constitution that must carry her, alone, to the close of her days.

She hefts the brown satchel and leaves by the back door.

Full circle, and then what? Annie thinks.

"You're doing me a favor," Mrs. Leventhorpe says, refilling Annie's tea cup. "I'm off to visit my daughter in Mobile. A long visit. Likely permanent."

"Oh no!" Annie cries. "When you said 'keep house for me,' I thought you meant . . . No, no. Is it . . . ?"

"It is inevitable, my dear. Now, none of that. You can't go out to work for now. That settles the discussion."

"How can I thank you?"

"By not giving up, dear."

And so Annie again sits in a clapboard house on Third Street, a curio piece, surrounded by the spyglass windows of neighbors.

Hayes Jamieson shows her to a chair facing his charmingly unpolished desk. Reserved and formal, he apologizes for causing her a trip to his office.

"No apologies," she assures him. "I know what this meeting's about."

"Yes, your husband has been to see me. As I told him, I'm sorry that your state of affairs has brought you to this. To get right to the point, I can't represent both sides in a separation. I'd like to assist you in securing representation for yourself."

"You mean pay a second lawyer? That's not necessary. Keep it simple, Jamie. No legal histrionics."

"Let me be more plain. Adam has retained me to represent him. It's not advisable for you to proceed unrepresented. Property is involved and—"

"Jamie, let me be more plain with you. What are you thinking, divide the farm like Solomon's baby so that neither of us can forge a living? He can't cash me out and he can't borrow more. You think I would force him to sell? Give him all the property and all the debt. Give me enough money to get somewhere and start over. That's it. Have I represented myself adequately?"

When she sits across from Jamie two weeks later, it's to sign two pages of paper that will undo the two she and Adam signed almost six years earlier:

> This agreement, made and entered into between Adam W. Fielding and Analiese R. Fielding, husband and wife, witnesseth, whereas the marital relations of said husband and wife have become such that it is necessary for their health and happiness that they separate and live apart; it is hereby agreed as follows.

He recites the terms of the document without embellishment. "You agree to live apart and incur no further joint debts. Neither of you has any say over the trade or business the other may pursue. At your request, you're quitclaiming the property to your husband." He indicates the second page. "Your husband agrees to a cash payment to you upon signing, and monthly payments for six years.

We acknowledge that the payments are small. There are cash-flow problems with the export business and—"

Annie stops him with a look that leaves him pink around the ears.

"Again, I must ask you if you wish to seek representation before you sign these documents."

"Again, I thank you for your concern. What is this paragraph, please?"

"You agree not to initiate divorce proceedings against your husband. He wanted that in here."

She shifts closer to the desk. "Continue."

"You remain legally married unless and until further action is taken. Everything in this agreement is nullified should you return to cohabitation. If you're the slightest bit uncomfortable with any of this, I urge you to seek—"

Annie snatches the pen from Jamie's hand and scrawls *Analiese R. Fielding* across the bottom of the two pages. She's feeling ill, something she didn't anticipate. Her exit is swift, the ink still slick on the page. She'll leave with her dignity, and little else.

18

A nurse from the county hospital comes to check on her each Thursday. Annie is always clean, dressed, buttoned up, pinned up, and dry-eyed when she arrives. She tells Annie that everything is as it should be.

Everything within and nothing without. Annie is gossip fodder; Elise Melton has seen to that. Powerless to do anything about it, Annie doesn't try. She conserves her energy for a higher purpose. She seldom leaves the house. When she must, she swathes herself in a black bouclé cape left behind by Mrs. Leventhorpe. Under the cape, she always wears the same skirt, the same shoes, and the same expression. She might be someone's forgotten doll, tucked away in the closet, in clothing and countenance that never change.

Today she sits in front of the stove, considering whether to drop Jenny's letter in. She won't need to read it again to remember it.

> Your news is too distressing. Adam is the age my own dear Seth was when he passed. You can't imagine how the emptiness of these years has withered the woman-liness in me. I used to miss it terribly, but now I can barely remember it. Your letter triggered dreadful memories. How our esteemed neighbors, those flag-poles of Christian compassion, gossiped wickedly about Seth after his accident, that he had been seen drunk in town that afternoon. It's been five years but I can't shake it. Annie, I am leaving here. Cal works for a rail-road. I plan to join him and sign on as a cook, and

Annie stops reading. So Cal writes to Jenny but not to her. And Jenny's letter offers no comfort, barely an acknowledgement. Annie senses her connection to Jenny straining, fraying. Perhaps Jenny doesn't understand why Annie has done what she has, what she must. Annie fingers the envelope that bears no return address, and feels sick. Perhaps Jenny doesn't understand because she doesn't want to.

The letter isn't the only thing going up in smoke.

Winter is waning and she knows she should have paid Adam a call sooner. She shouldn't call on him unannounced. Her fingers fumble and her lips tremble, but she forces herself to sound calm and casual as she gives the operator the exchange: "147-B, please."

A cricket chirp comes on the line. "Starlight River Market Farm and Mr. Fielding's residence . . . Hello? Hello?"

Say it. "Mrs. Fielding calling." Say it.

The phone swings by its cord and Annie barely makes it to the basin.

She waits for a day when the weather promises to be fair and she feels strong enough to walk the distance. She times her arrival for the hour he always comes in to take lunch and make calls. Four months are gone since she last saw her home, and though she had fair warning, it stops her cold to see a woman moving in and out of the frame of the window. The rushing in her head turns her away, listing in a half-slump against the poultry house.

"Annie?"

He's seen her before she can recover and retreat. He comes closer, his face a palette of mixed emotion. "What brings you . . . ? Would you like to . . . ?" He gestures at the house.

"No." Her voice is so steady, she surprises herself. "You have company."

"She's a cook. You know I have to feed the crew."

Annie starts down the bank toward their blackberry spot. He follows at several paces, enough to be able to see the slight change in her gait. When they reach the clearing, she turns to face him. The reason for her visit is plain. She never could hide it past the third month, and this must be twice that.

"Oh my God. Why didn't you tell me sooner?"

Her explanation makes his breastbone ache. She hasn't been well, she says. If this one went the way of the others, she couldn't see telling him at all. "Now the doctors think we have a keeper. It was time for you to know."

What to do with this knowledge? He can't think. "You must have known what a shock this would be. Have you thought about what to do?"

"I'm going to have a baby. That's what I'm going to do. I can't tell you what you're going to do. I never could do that."

"I'll raise you one on that." An ant dragging a seed three times its size hurries by. A mere insect knows what it's going to do. "Maybe you should come home. To me."

He didn't mean for it to sound so tentative. But he's been betrayed by his deep ambivalence. To be a father, a family, finally. If only he knew this would be the outcome and that it would cure his wife of her demons. But if not?

To fail again, to have to relive these past months. The dead quiet of the house, the empty bed. The many parts of him that have fallen into disuse. The sterile day-in, day-out operation of the farm without his partner, his muse, his sounding board, his conscience. His lover, his recharger, his reason to come home at the end of the day. The remnants of her presence hovered everywhere. The dipped bayberry candles, the embroidered pillow slips, the argyle socks. A cellar full of preserved goods, every mouthful having passed through her hands.

Seeing her now like this, his thoughts race: How has she passed the time, with whom, doing what? Worst for him was Christmas; he spent it alone, sleeping into the afternoon, then heating and reheating the same pan of soup, watching the steam writhe and vanish until the broth boiled away, leaving potato and leek clinging to the pan in a barnacle crust. After the sun buried itself in the snow, he set up the chessboard and stared at it for a long time. He even stared down the black horse. He played hard against himself, but the ebony pieces kept winning. He got mad. It took two hours, past midnight and into the next day, before the boxwood queen checkmated the ebony king.

He resolved to drink his way through January 1. *Should auld acquaintance be forgot, and never brought to mind? Better believe it should,* he thought, uncorking a full bottle. The first swig about-faced well short of his back teeth. The first resolution of the new year, already broken.

It was as bleak a January as he'd ever seen. Adam knew all there was to know about keeping a house warm in winter, but this January, no amount of coal or wood, no oven-heated stone at the foot of a bed, could warm the spaces once occupied by another living being. Some nights he let the fire go out, waking up in the morning to shake the frost from his hair.

Groundhog Day is six weeks past; his crew is starting to break ground. The onions brought huge prices last year. He'll put in more this year. More beets. There always seems to be a sugar shortage. He'll break twenty more acres in the dry section.

He's made it to where his old analgesic, work, can take over.

Now, just as he's crossing the line, he also realizes that for all he misses, there's much he doesn't. The malevolent moods, the melancholy. The blood, the fear. The grief, the anger. The doctors, the hospital, the *insanity*. God forgive him, he's getting used to life without that—sorry, sorry, sorry, but he is. *Deep down, you must want to be rid of the craziness and the strife. It's all right to feel that way, Adam.*

So when he says maybe she should come home, it doesn't ring of open arms. He wants to do the right thing. But he doesn't know what that thing might be.

"You need to think on it," she says, backing away. "It appears that I've already been replaced."

Replacing her, what a ridiculous thought, but he's still too stunned to mount a denial. "Well, she's easier to get on with. Does as I tell her. No back talk." Humor was never his strength, and it backfires catastrophically.

"Damn you!" she spits. "At your own insistence, you are still a married man. Taking up with the cook. I wouldn't have dreamed you could be so common. With any luck, your child will never know. Goodbye, Adam."

His child. Nothing should be more important than that. He gathers himself to call after her, but he's hobbled by his own urgency. He gropes for words of affirmation, but what comes instead is a horrifying question.

"It is my child, isn't it?"

She pulls up, lassoed, whirls on him. He knows that black gaze, knows he deserves whatever is coming. She doesn't need a gun to send buckshot ripping through his heart.

"Not anymore."

Mrs. Leventhorpe's letter urges Annie to forestall permanent decisions.

> I never told you how I ended up alone in a speck of a town at the top of Montana. It is rarely wise to burn bridges. This man is your child's father. Even if you are to be a mother alone, you and he will always be connected. Make no further sudden moves, my dear. He is a proud man who instinctively attacks when cornered.

The days trickle by. Annie smarts with the memory of her meeting with Adam. Who now is too proud, too cornered? Adam's ambivalence stings because she shares it. She misses the purpose and sense of accomplishment her work with Adam brought her. She misses engaging him, challenging him, giving in to him. Yet she's filled with an unexpected, not unpleasant ease without his jealousy, his intensity permeating the house, her thoughts, her existence. In time she comes to see that the wounds to their marriage were not inflicted solely by her.

With a fortress of pillows surrounding her, Annie sleeps more than she ever has, sleeps and dreams about her baby. They float in warm light. The baby enfolds and shelters her, a reversal of nature. It raises its left arm on high, casting glow like a lantern; its chubby right arm moves in a beckoning arc. *This way, Mama. This way.* The baby is neither boy nor girl. It is a creature of the light. *Follow me, Mama. Follow me.*

On an April morning she wakes with unaccustomed clarity. Pride—in Latin *superbia*—the seventh deadly sin. It shouldn't be their baby's birthright.

Adam treads for a moment on the suspense of wondering who would call this late.

She sounds as if she's pulling forth carefully rehearsed lines. "It's Analiese. You are well, yes?"

His answer is tentative. "Yes. And you?"

"I am well," she assures him.

That's not what his cook tells him, coming out from town each day, although she's a conscienceless thing, trying her damnedest to light more than his oven burner. She drops hints that would make a woman with twice her experience blush. "Thanks," he snarled one day, "but I already sleep with a heated brick." She didn't even take umbrage, just changed tack. "Your wife is crazy," she informed him with an air of authority. "Did you hear what Mrs. Melton—"

"Did I ask?" he snapped.

The girl tsked, sounding like a baby banging a spoon on its tray. "Your loony wife and those heinie neighbors of yours. You should think about—"

"I will say this once," he hissed, cursing for the thousandth time the cursed war that brought about the cursed shortage of farm labor that cursedly stuck him with her. "Karl Eulenberg and his family are American citizens. He's bought more war bonds than you know numbers to count. His oldest boy is serving in the United States Army. *Verstehen Sie, dummes Mädchen?*"

Annie's voice over the wire draws him back. "I'm sorry about our last meeting. It was unfair to you. I want you to know that everything is as it should be with the baby. Just a month to go. I wanted to ask you what you might like to name him or her."

His fingers press into his forehead. He may dent his skull this time. "Please give me a minute here. I spoke too soon last time." His voice drops. "But I thank you. For asking." Oh, mercy, why would he cry now, of all the times he should have?

"Sure," she says hastily. "Give it some thought. As much as you need." The tremble in her voice is smothered by the clang of the phone colliding with the hook.

There's no ideal way. They can talk on the phone and risk someone listening in, or they can meet and risk someone seeing. Either way, tongues will flap like snakes on fire. He strains to keep his voice composed, traveling over the line to her. "If it's a boy, I want you to name him. If it's a girl . . . I had a great-aunt. She was a healer, had a large apothecary cabinet of who-knows-what that worked where doctors failed. Passing horses would stop in front of her house. She once ran out of money, signed on with a supply crew going up the Connecticut River, and cleaned them out along the way. A supernatural card sharp." He almost smiles. Some said his aunt had a screw loose. But they had it wrong. Her screws were tighter than everyone else's.

He misses her.

"Her name was Nora Marielle," he finishes. "Originally Maribelle, but she dropped the *b*. Said the world could do with one less ding-dong."

"I like it, Adam."

The line crackles. She seems at a loss for more to say.

"Do you need anything that's here?"

In the farthest corner of the shed, she tells him, is a trunk full of bonnets, bibs, booties, and sacques. Ready, at last, to see the light of day.

He'll get it out tomorrow. Those things have been out there a while. He'll have them laundered for her.

"No!" she screams. "No one touches those things but me!"

"All right, whatever you say. Oh God, please don't . . ." He can hear the sweat pop on his temple. "Please stay calm, please. I'll bring the trunk to you."

No, she cringes to think of yet more chin-wagging. She'll ask Margrethe for help; Margrethe hates rumormongers.

"Good. Then I'll see you soon." He rings off abruptly.

Three days crawl by before she appears at the homestead, alone, and it's clear at once that she has not passed the time in placid thought.

"Adam, who is this woman?"

"She goes by Ermintrude," he says cautiously. "I've told you about her."

"Oh, yes. The cook. The town fryer." Annie peers sideways at the girl. "Erm-intrude."

"It's French for 'wholly beloved,'" chirps the girl, tossing her head with an air of ownership that sets off an alarm in Adam's belly.

"Hmm." Annie's eye travels the length of the girl. "Ermin-trude. Rhymes with vermin, ends with rude. Anything else I need to know?"

"I've explained why she's here, Annie."

A light passes over Annie's eyes, the gray-green scrim that bruises the sky just before a hailstorm. "Ermintrude. Of course. It's Montanan for 'a thorn among roses.' She can explain that to the business end of my diamond-pointed six-prong cultivator." Annie wheels and heads for the shed at an impressive clip given the bulk of a pregnancy approaching its ninth month.

The girl asks fearfully, "What's a diamond-pointed six-prong cultivator?"

He almost laughs. "It's like a hoe except that the end isn't flat; it's an iron claw."

"An iron claw? Goodness, do you think she means it?"

"Yes, I think she means it." A fearsome clatter rattles the shed, and the cultivator comes arcing out like a javelin. More clattering, and Annie strides out, skirts flying, wisps of black hair whipping her face. She hefts the implement without breaking pace.

Adam makes for his truck, motioning to the girl. "Get in!"

Pebbles fly as he cuts the wheel sharply to avoid Annie. Over his shoulder he sees her swing the cultivator with all her might. He hears the splintering of wood, but the truck has rounded the bend and he can't see what she's done.

"Your wife is crazy!" the girl beside him shrieks. "Why won't you do anything about it?"

He pulls up at the edge of town. "Please get out here."

"What will you do?" the girl asks. "When do you want me to come back?"

"I don't want you to. Now, out. Please."

"Your wife is crazy!" Ermintrude screams again, the indictment rebounding off the windshield as he reaches across her to wrench open the door. "She was ready to kill me. If you won't do something about it, I will!"

"Out!"

Unbelievable, he thinks, speeding away from where she stands staring at him from the side of the road. *A silver lining in this abominable mess.* This is the out he needs to be rid of Erm-intrude. Confound Annie and God bless her too, she has again given him what he needs.

The cultivator hangs where she planted it, embedded in the porch railing. He expects to see mass destruction inside, but she's sitting calmly, hands folded on her belly.

"That was some performance, Analiese." He'll get the first word if not the last. "Do you have any idea what you've done?"

She pushes herself to her feet. "Need I remind you that we are still married, Adam? Need I remind you that this is your baby?" Her eyes glisten, and in them he sees both her power and his flicker. He's always had the power to incense her, but she could always give as good as she got. Now he sees their power to hurt each other deeply, irreparably, just as the goal that has so long eluded them comes within reach.

"Did you ever consider," he says, "that it's not what you think, in spite of appearance? You know I can't run the place alone. She cooks—"

"On all burners, I'm sure," Annie cuts in. "It took me a minute, stripped of her frippery, but I know who she is, Adam. My God. Trudy Durant is a *milliner*. She's certainly pulled your hat over your eyes."

Trudy Durant is a pain in the ass. He longs to share the thought with Annie, laugh together at the sheer absurdity of the situation, turn back the clock, or at least turn it forward, or sideways, or anything to escape this moment. "There's a war on," he sighs. "No one's buying hats. Farm girls can't hire out when they're doing double duty on their own places. Trudy was all I could get. Cooks, helps with chores." His voice trails off, but he's determined not to break gaze with her.

Does my other jobs? The question written on her face is too rending to voice. Aloud, she bites off the words. "I'll bet."

"Don't bet it all, Annie. I misjudged you once, and you told me that there was no answer you could give me for which I hadn't already damned you. Now I've lived long enough to know what that feels like."

"And may you live longer still and never have to stand in what was your own home and wonder what I'm wondering today."

"I've stood in my own home every damn day for months and wondered things beyond wondering."

Her eyes grow brighter, and her arm curves under her belly, where, with every minute that ticks by, their child grows.

"Adam." Her voice trembles. "Why is this happening?"

He spreads, then clenches his hands. "Annie, Annie. If I knew that, would we be standing here like this?"

Newspapers report facts, and doesn't the staff of the *Chronicle-Times* rise to this mission like overripe yeast? The words jump at him like buckshot. He knows everyone at the paper. Which so-called journalist, which supposed editor? Such talent and economy, expending only sixty words to repaint both Annie and him in oils that will never fade.

MRS. FIELDING JUDGED INSANE

The case of Mrs. Adam Fielding came before the district court last week. A number of local citizens, including one of our storekeepers, our sheriff, and a young woman said to work for Mr. Fielding, described incidents of Mrs. Fielding's erratic behavior. Physicians testified as to her condition and pronounced her insane. She will be taken to the state hospital.

Trudy wasted no time acting on her hysterical threat. From where he left her, she must have marched her ugly cloth-top lace-ups directly to the justice of the peace. The complaint she filed alleged Annie Fielding to be "disordered in her mind as to endanger persons and property."

Adam crushes the newspaper into a ball, molding it tighter and tighter, his hands darkening to ink black. The wad of paper rotates against his stained palms until he's compressed it to the exact dimensions of a baseball. What a spin he'll put on this pitch, eh?

In forty-one years of life, he's never shirked responsibility. But there will be no son to grow up beside him on their land, no pretty daughter to wrap him around her finger. Instead he's left with the lingering guilt that his wife's empty arms might somehow be the fault of his half of the chemistry, for his part in the transmutation of a woman and wife to a being "disordered in her mind," a danger to herself and others. And he can't live with that.

The newsprint ball grows damp in his hand. Adam kicks the chair out from under him and launches the ball at Annie's red window. The ball bounces off the glass with a weak hiccup and falls to the floor.

What did he expect?

Beyond the window, the cottonwoods show signs of new life. But it doesn't stir his sap as it has in springs past. Any fool farming here knows April to be Creation's most fickle month. Could the weather become part of a person? Could compassion be pounded out of the soul as hail pounds the plums off his trees? Could the floods carry away fidelity, faith, and optimism along with the topsoil? Could a reasonable person's integrity evaporate in the scorching winds?

Let me let you go.

He tosses the paper ball into the stove and watches it flame its goodbye. Then he goes to the bedroom and folds the star-sprinkled quilt in on itself, over by half and again and again, snuffing out the starlight over the river, the last flicker of what might have been.

He can't avoid going to town; that would be a summons for his competition to round up his customers. Stilted conversations, but maybe next time will be easier. And maybe next time he'll accidentally run over Trudy, he thinks, urging the truck past the city limits at a hazardous clip. The shameless minx practically stepped in front of it, in plain sight of everyone on Main Street, a smirk of nauseating expectancy on her face, as if she'd done him a high-minded favor and awaited reward. With difficulty, he swerved wide.

Now he is alone. Home sweet home, where the chickens mince aimlessly around the corral, shitting where they stand. He might have to let that part of the operation go. Limping by with Trudy, he's already seeing a replay of the slide the business took the last time Annie stepped away from it.

Just who is bird-witted? he berates himself. Letting the poultry operation go at this point would be opening his own jugular. No one utters the word *drought* yet, but what else should he call it when last year's rainfall barely reached seven inches? His grain yield fell by two-thirds. The government exhorts, *Plant more land and plow deeper! We are at war. Do your part!*

He'd love to plow deeper, plow every last inch of the fowl business all the way to hell. Then what? "We've got ourselves a *drought!*" he shouts at the chickens. A few look up with flat eyes. Several hundred more pay no heed. *No drought in here, buddy. We're your crop insurance.*

Crop insurance. Another year of drought and the two hundred dollars a month in eggs those bastard birds account for will be a life preserver. Isn't he a lucky man? Between his pusillanimous poultry pals and his few acres of irrigated crops, he won't starve. No, he'll live to numbly plow his dry-land plat deeper, and watch yet more of it blow away on the apathetic wind.

When he opens the door, he finds the house, as it always is now, saturated in silence. For the thousandth time, he thinks what he would give to be able to ask Cal Rushton, *How much did you know about your sister?* They've had no word from Cal in years. He doesn't know all that has befallen the confident couple who took over his homestead. Maybe he wouldn't believe it.

Maybe he would have predicted it.

At least a citizen can still buy a drink in this state, although the bottle Adam's just drained couldn't have been a full pint. Annie should be arriving in Warm Springs right about now. What she's feeling, he can't allow himself to think. For the moment, they are safe. He is safe. She is safe. The baby is safe.

From a shadowed distance, he watched her board the train, the sheriff helping her up. Seeing that four-flusher Blandish touch her, even if only her coat-swathed elbow, nearly drowned him in bile. Adam will be a long time forgetting how the front of that coat splayed over her belly as she vanished into the Pullman. Would it be a son? Or another daughter with a raven curl? Would that change his mind?

Part Two

What old people say you cannot do,
you try and find that you can.

—Henry David Thoreau, *Walden*

19

A nnie reads upside down as the admitting nurse fills in the form with a ponderous unslanted hand.

Montana State Hospital for the Insane
Patient Intake

Name:	Analiese Fielding
Identifying marks:	extended abdomen/ third trimester pregnancy
Possessions:	nothing of value
Appearance:	disheveled
Disposition:	apprehensive, extreme fatigue

What a remarkable grasp of the obvious, Annie thinks with her last ember of verve. Two days on a train headed for deprivation of liberty and all its unknowns. Two days next to her insufferable lawman escort, who deems her dangerous enough to merit nearly a week of his time ensuring she won't return to Valley County any time soon. Two days during which she didn't utter two words to him, although she's sure he'll find a way to punish her silence as surely as he has her words. Two days sitting on a train, and it feels like her entrails have split. Too afraid and depleted. Too depleted to ask for a lavatory, too afraid for what's about to happen if she doesn't.

The nurse seems to understand, gesturing Annie toward a narrow recess in the wall containing a toilet and pedestal. Before Annie can summon a grateful remark, the nurse hands her a bottle.

"Sample, please."

Though Annie begs to be allowed to walk to the ward, the nurse insists on a wheelchair. The wheels whimper along the beige-veined black linoleum. They descend into a tunnel that surfaces in the medical wing, where a chatty nurse puts Annie to bed like a child.

"Have you eaten, Mrs. Fielding? We had cake today. Doctor will see you in the morning."

Annie curls away to the edge of the bed. So far, this is nothing new.

"We have excellent diagnostics here," says the day nurse. "You'll be with us in the medical wing for three days. Then we'll get you settled in a ward and started in therapy."

The three days in bed, Annie decides, are designed to make the inmate eager for whatever therapy and living situation await. Annie tries to walk the length of the ward to get her blood moving, to find sunlight. The nurses swoop down and order her back to bed. "You must be accessible to all clinicians at all times," they insist, and so follows the battery of tests and examinations that spare no surface or recess of her body. The doctors probe, peer, and swab. The nurses observe, record, and chart. The last doctor to see her introduces himself as Dr. Alvord. He has a notebook and pen, instructing Annie to answer his questions as honestly as she possibly can.

"Do you ever hear voices?"

"I hear yours, and all within normal range," Annie answers. They checked her hearing two days ago. It must be in the chart.

"Do you ever see atypical things?"

"No, thank goodness. My mother was nearsighted and color-blind, but my vision is acute." That's in the chart too.

"Do you ever think about dying?"

"I think about giving birth." She steals a look at his notes. *Fetus, eight months. Bladder prolapsed. Uterine rupture repair.* "May I ask you a question?"

"Go ahead."

"How long will I be here?"

"Our examinations and tests are complete," he says, snapping his notebook shut. "We'll make an evaluation and have you moved to a ward by tomorrow."

"No, I mean, how long will I be . . . here?"

"We don't know that yet. But it would be best if we at least see your baby safely into the world. Don't you agree, Mrs. Fielding?"

Crisp words from the night nurse in her crisp white dress and cap.

"This is the women's receiving ward. Ideally, we would find more comfortable accommodations for someone in your condition, but we're terribly overcrowded." She leads Annie to a white-blanketed mattress on a plain metal frame, a bed identical to the other forty-nine beds in the chilly dormitory, spaced so closely as to be almost one. Annie tries to imagine sleeping inches from someone who isn't her husband or sister and cannot. A single pillow, flat as a newspaper, stands against the head of the frame.

"Might I get an extra pillow?" Annie asks. She gestures under her belly.

The nurse laughs. "Sorry, honey. No 'extras' here. Lights out in fifteen minutes, ladies."

"You can have mine," says the woman turning down the bed next to Annie's. "I sleep flat anyway."

"Oh, I couldn't," Annie objects.

"Yes, you could." The woman speaks with a rusty Irish lilt that matches her hair. She extends the pillow to Annie, who holds it to her bosom, the kindness warming her. It lasts but a moment before the clatter of heavy heels rings out and a tall, thin woman with hair as black as Annie's pulls up at the foot of her bed.

"What do we have here?" She takes in Annie's belly with a sneer. "A soiled dove?"

"Leave her alone, Jo," scolds the woman with the Irish lilt.

Jo jangles the bed by the foot rail. "Toffer," she jeers. "Hiding her diddies behind a pillow. Too late for that, wouldn't you say?"

Annie grips her pillow tighter. "No."

Jo's eyebrows climb into haughty arches.

"I'm married," Annie whispers.

"Oh, 'I'm married,'" Jo mocks. "For all the good it did you. Don't wait for your noble knight to ride through here on his white stallion. He's already riding another gullible filly."

"Palomino," Annie whispers again.

"What?"

"Palomino." She finds her voice. "A gelding, not a stallion."

"Jeebus feck, Jo, stop," the Irish woman cuts in. To Annie, she says, "This is Joanne Drake. She rearranged the letters of her name and decided she's Joan d'Arke."

Jo's burned-charcoal eyes trample across Annie's belly. "Married, feh! There's no hiding what you've been up to, is there? You won't get any of that in here, missus. They keep the men far *far* away from us!" With a satisfied cackle—"Slattern!"—she moves away.

"Trollop." Annie's salvo smacks the woman between the shoulder blades. She whirls on Annie, eyes bulging.

"You—"

"Trollop," Annie repeats. "Floozy. Strumpet. Tart. We're done, Jo."

Annie feels the gazes of all in the ward trained on her, telling her she's crossed a line and punishment will follow. But instead, gravity reverses and pulls up the corners of Jo's brittle mouth.

"'Children say that people are hung sometimes for speaking the truth.'"

The inmates exhale as Jo marches away. The Irish woman laughs. "She may be a peasant girl, but she's no saint." She pats Annie's mattress. "Good night, love."

Annie slides under the stiff sheet. The chandeliers dim but the image of the cavernous room burns in the darkness. How will she sleep in this warehouse? The attendants can switch off the lights, but they can't switch off the humanity: the wheezing, the weeping, the muttering in half a dozen foreign tongues, the shifting of bodies in search of comfort, the self-pleasuring, and the unidentifiable noises that defy description.

Annie snakes a finger behind her ear and pulls down a strand of hair. Around and around her finger she twists it, until it's as firm as harness leather. She folds it over on itself several times, runs it across her tongue to slick it down. Then she slips it into her ear. The noises recede. A repeat on the other side, and the sounds in the room die away. The sounds she hears now are even more human, the swishings and pulsings of her own body and the body within her. For the first time, she hears her baby.

The warmth of the glassed-in sun parlor is just the incubator Annie needs. A book on infant care slips down the side of her chair. Her baby sets to hiccupping, tiny jumps that tickle Annie's ribs and make her smile. She watches her belly jump, then runs her hands over what feels like the baby's bottom. The hiccups subside to a sweet bubbly gurgle.

The afternoon sun moves across the farthest glass panel. Annie has no watch, and the room lacks a clock. She wonders idly if time is a man-made concept. Years can fly by in an instant, or there can be an eternity in a single minute. Who defines time?

When she feels a shadow fall over her face, she assumes she's dozed and it must be close to suppertime. She opens her eyes to Jo, staked in front of her.

"You're a scrawny thing."

"I'm just right, Jo."

"You're not properly protected. Your nerves are exposed. You're hurting your baby every time you move."

Annie shifts her bulk in the chair and tries to close her eyes again. "Lucky, then, that I'm so big I can hardly move anymore."

"You're too thin," Jo snaps. She bends over, close enough for Annie to smell an overpowering scent that isn't hospital-issue soap.

"Does this conversation have a point?" Annie knows Jo won't leave until she's unburdened herself of whatever is pressing on her own exposed nerves.

"I could make you an emulsion. To fatten you up. You had better listen to me. Without it, you will sicken and *wither*."

"What's in it?"

Oh! It's the wrong thing to ask. Jo's eyes dart to either side of Annie's head, to the others in the parlor, out the window. "That's proprietary information," she barks. "I'm trying to help you, you *goose*."

"Thanks, Jo. Not today."

Jo recoils as if yanked by a string and draws herself up to her full height, smirking gaze shooting down the plane of her nose.

"They're going to take your baby away from you."

Annie's innards collapse.

"Yes." Jo nods with smug assurance. "That's what they do. You don't think they'd leave a baby with an insane mother, do you? It'll be shipped to the orphans' home, same as all the others." She moves away, wraithlike, sinking a last shaft into Annie. "Don't say you weren't warned!"

Though this is a new definition of unbearable pain, Annie knows she mustn't scream, not here. She mustn't think of all the devastating variations in which she's lost babies, and that it happens there's yet one more way. She mustn't scream. She mustn't . . .

"Now there, Mrs. Fielding, you mustn't upset yourself with the silliness of other inmates." A nurse whisks her by wheelchair to a windowless examination room where yet another doctor reads over her chart. "You have more important things to worry about."

"But that's just it," Annie says. "I'm worried about my baby. Will I be allowed to keep—"

"All mothers worry about their babies." The doctor overrides her question without looking up from the chart. "You were seen last week, and it's unlikely anything has gone awry since then. But let's have a look today and put your mind at ease."

What can she do but submit? Again. Weighed, probed, palpated. The baby has dropped, the head is down, but the cervix is still tight and firm. The doctor says birth is not imminent.

"Everything as it should be," he says. "Except that your fingers have swollen. Very common in late pregnancy. We'll have to cut your ring off." The doctor tells the nurse to fetch a pair of wire cutters.

"No." Annie stands and adjusts her blouse and skirt, throwing her thumb over her wedding band.

The doctor scowls. "What do you mean, no?" His tone allows no mistake: patients don't tell doctors "no" here.

"I mean no, you will not cut my ring off."

"It's going to harm your circulation." His patronizing tone borders on impatience.

"I can still move it. The baby will be here soon. I'll take my chances."

The doctor whispers to the nurse, who leaves and returns straightaway with a tool in her hand and a male attendant behind her. The doctor motions the attendant to restrain Annie's arm.

Annie isn't small and fleet for nothing. Even nine months pregnant, did they think a mere man would be enough to hold her? Her knee shoots up and catches the attendant in the groin. He drops with an agonized groan.

"I said *no*."

The doctor hisses, "Sedative." The nurse prepares a syringe as Annie bolts for the hall.

My ring. *My* baby. *My* life. *My*—

The doctor pinions her with "Where do you think you can get to?"

What more will you try to take from me?

Amid a scuffle of clothing, a needle sinks into her hip. Again and again they force her into a chair. Again and again she breaks through their grasp.

Rage obscures her hearing, their incredulous tones: ". . . gave her as much as we dare . . . enough to down a cougar . . ." Her wrath fuels her, even as the drug overtakes her; this is how the bull must feel, the red flag slicing the air in front of its face. She reaches to claw aside the red flag, but it spreads and lightens to topaz. *This way, Mama.*

She wakes up groggy, in a strange room, alone. The unnatural quiet—this isn't the dorm. Where is this room, when did she come here, and why? She tries to remember what happened before she fell asleep. There'd been a doctor. An edict. A needle.

After that, she's blank. Her sleep was buffeted by vague but turbulent dreams. She has a lingering sense of fighting to escape, that she watched a wild bird beat its wings against the sky, fall to earth, rise and throw itself at the heavens, again and again. In the end, her baby appeared, beckoning her, drawing her into that topaz place where it's warm and light. *This way, Mama.*

Then she hadn't wanted to escape.

When her eyes adjust to the semi-dark, she slides to the edge of the bed and carefully pushes herself upright. Feeling her way along a wall, she makes her way to the window. The chalkboard sky, black but smeary, means it's around 4:00 a.m.

The fading starlight casts a weak beam against the window, enough to guide her to a lamp by the bed, which sputters to life after three tries. Her eyes drift over the room. A marked change from the dorm. Carpeting softens the floor under her swollen feet. Next to the bed is a writing desk and chair, and near the window a leather-seated gliding rocking chair. In the closet, a dresser and several plain dresses hanging. On the shelf over the desk, a mantilla-style tortoiseshell comb and a rose glass jar holding a silver thimble. *Possessions: nothing of value.*

The rocker squeaks as she sways with it, cradling her belly. *Hush, little baby, don't say a word.*

In a half sleep of lingering exhaustion, she rocks fitfully until daylight. Her belly tightens, rocklike. She rouses herself and returns to the window, where she now sees that she's in a corner room on the second floor of a large cottage. Past its deep porch lies a low butte where the hot mineral springs emerge from the ground, the signs warning of danger lettered large enough for her to make out. HOT WATER. KEEP OUT. Greenhouses near the springs overflow with geraniums, hollyhocks, tuberoses, verbenas.

Full light fills the room when her eyes come to rest on the door. Time to find out whether this is a good dream or a bad dream. Her fingers play over the knob before she grasps it and finds, as she half suspected, that it's locked. She holds her breath and raps a knuckle on the door. Almost immediately she hears footsteps and a key.

"Mrs. Fielding, good morning," burbles an attendant. "What a scare you gave us!"

Annie's chin lifts. *How so?*

"You've been asleep for two days. You must be starved. I'll call for a breakfast tray. Doctor will want to see you."

I don't want to see him. "I'd like to wash, please."

"Certainly. Down the hall there."

In the washroom she cups her hands and draws in camel-like drafts of water, violently gargling and spitting every third mouthful. She pushes the rivulets on her face back into her hair, using her fingers as a comb and plaiting it loosely, the end left soft and open.

No one is around when she emerges. She moves stiffly, joints grinding, blood sluggish, but once underway she can't stop. Her body is getting ideas independent of her head. Her belly again tightens, but she doesn't feel hungry.

Clinging to the railing, she descends a wide stairwell to a long, sunny dayroom. A phonograph stands in a corner, a library of magazines and books in another. It's early; she's alone. She'll bear her unbearable pain silently, like an animal. *They're going to take your baby away from you.* She walks the long hours of the morning, back and forth across the floor, pacing herself with long breaths. She nods when the nurse says, "Doctor will see you soon," thinking, *He certainly will,* and ignoring "You really must eat something." Inmates, housekeepers, attendants, nurses come and go. They invite her to join the card group playing Black Maria. Write a letter? Read the new Carl Sandburg book?

Who could sit, read, or write while slowly being turned inside out? Her thighs seem to be crushing her kneecaps, forcing her to pause at the farthest window. She tries to count through the pain, count the rays of the sun, the leaves on the oak, the panes of glass on the greenhouses.

An attendant hurries by with an armload of irises and late jonquils. "Good morning, Susan," she calls to Annie. "Welcome to 2-B."

"I'm not Susan," Annie replies, but the attendant is already across the room, beckoning to several inmates to help her arrange the flowers in metal vases.

"You are to her," says an inmate in a gray pin-tucked dress. "Probably because of your black eyes. She calls everyone by flower names." She points with two fingers, bouncing from head to head around the room. "Heather, Lily, Violet, Holly, Pansy. She calls me Camille. Because I'm French Canadian." She shakes her head. "And they say we're insane. Uh-huh. I'm Anjanette. And yes, welcome to 2-B."

"What is 2-B?" It seems safe to ask Anjanette.

"2-B or not 2-B? That is the question." Anjanette snickers at her joke, and when Annie doesn't respond, adds, "You know, Shakespeare? *Hamlet?*"

"No. Sorry. *Romeo and Juliet* was too much for me." A story about parents behaving so reprehensibly as to drive their children to take their own lives? If that wasn't insane, what is?

Her pain swells again, less than two minutes after the last. She bites the inside of her cheek.

"No, *I'm* sorry. Please don't make such a face," Anjanette apologizes. "2-B—cottage two, second floor—may be the best ward in this whole gothic warren. For people with . . . unusual concerns." She indicates Annie's belly. "I work. In the kitchens. I must be going. Bye-bye . . . Susan." She winks.

"Analiese. Annie." She taps her chest, harder than she meant to. "Goodbye, Camille. Anjanette."

The sun climbs high. *Zenith, such a funny word,* Annie thinks, and, feeling a sudden need to leave the room, heads down a corridor, having no idea where it leads.

"Mrs. Fielding!" An attendant hurries after her. "Where are you going?"

Squat, her body orders her, and she obeys. The attendant crouches alongside and snatches up the front of Annie's skirt. "Honey, where are your drawers—goodness, it's crowning! Why didn't you say something sooner?"

The gurney clatters brash as a freight train, the loudest sound Annie's ever heard. It's jarring her insides loose. It stops in a room suffused in topaz light. People buzz around her, calm but questioning: Why didn't she say something? Was she planning to catch it herself?

Push, her body orders her.

But what if? She resists.

Push!

The pain bursts in a cloud of dirty blue and black, spreading across the expanse below her heart.

They're going to take your baby away from you.

Annie pushes back against the will of her body and its unstoppable mission, to block a truth she needs if she is to go on. What, what brought her to 2-B?

There was a doctor. A nurse.

"We'll have to . . ."

They were holding her down.

She fought it then; she fights it now.

The blue-black pain closes its tentacles around her. Just before it swallows her, a luminous golden mist swells from it and flings her terror to a buried place. Yellow rimmed in violet, spiked with black eyelashes: a Johnny-jump-up, her favorite wildflower, first to flower in the dying breath of winter. A dauntless, tenacious flower.

She can't fight anymore, this primeval force that won't be denied, that decrees when it's time for a new life to enter the world. Her legs part. *Annie, someone most important is here to see you.*

"It's a girl, Mrs. Fielding. A beautiful blond girl. Oh, doesn't she just look like Mary Pickford!"

"Don't wrap her." Annie rips her bodice away and gathers her baby to her, skin to skin, pulling the sheet up over both of them. "Hey, I know you," she murmurs against the shell-pink cheek, and it seems impossible that the wetness on her face was only moments ago deep inside her. After a dozen damp kisses that beg for a thousand more, she manages to whisper, "Hello, Nora."

"Did you say Nora?" The nurse beams. "What a pretty name, for such a pretty little girl."

"Yes. Nora. Nora Marielle Fielding."

20

"You little ferret, you had me worried." Anjanette squints into the shade of the twisted elm. In the folds where the exposed roots have ruched the ground, Annie nurses Nora.

"You're a bloodhound, Anjie." Across the commons, groups from other wards gather around the gardens, the fishing pond, the barns, the walking paths. Annie spots a figure in black and breaks down in a wild river of raw fear.

"Is it true?" she beseeches. "Do they send all babies born here to the orphans' home? Will they take my baby away from her insane mother?"

"Who told you that?" Anjanette's eyes follow Annie's to a group moving across the lawn. "One of those witches?"

"Is it *true*?"

Anjanette places herself where Annie must face away from the commons to see her. "I wish I could say. It's two separate questions, no? The question of whether they will take her away. And the question of whether you or anyone else in here is insane. It depends upon who you ask." She smacks her thigh with sudden vehemence. "What is sane? I made a list, of every word or phrase I could think of that might mean 'insane.' *Crazy, loony, loopy, dotty. Unbalanced, unsound, unstable. Deranged, demented, deluded, disturbed.*" Anjanette's recitation takes on a melodic quality. "*Erratic, fanatic, lunatic. Touched. Mad. Neurotic, psychotic,* and then there's me. *Manic-depressive.*"

"*Non compos mentis,*" Annie says slowly.

"That too," her friend agrees. "Tell me. How many people do you know to whom one of those terms has never applied? None. Being adjudged insane is a random misfortune, dependent upon who you happen to be around when your moment of insanity comes."

The mission of the hospital, Anjanette asserts, isn't to cure people. "It's to keep the pristine public safe from people like us.

We're the reminders of what they could become with but a slight shift in circumstance. So they put us here, with a four-line send-off in the local newspaper. 'Miss Ballamont Adjudged Insane.' Squeezed in above instructions for how to keep a pink shirt from fading in the wash."

Annie can't listen anymore. "Here's something insane. I've heard staff talking about the amount of influenza going around out there this spring. The hospital may be the safest place for my daughter." She hesitates, but a pressure builds behind her voice, and it feels necessary that she trust someone. "I lost my first child to illness—my own illness. There is a hell, Anjie, right here on earth. No one who's never been there believes it. Demonic thoughts that weren't my own, eating my brain. Every slightest movement felt like stepping in front of a runaway horse cart. I'd hold my baby Cynthia and she wasn't a person. She was a thing. Have you ever heard a mother talk about her child that way? I had to leave her before I hurt her."

Anjie grabs Annie's clenched hand. "I believe you." Her voice rings out, then drops to a whisper. "Lots of people here will believe you."

Annie gazes past Anjie and lets her focus blur. "'Puerperal trauma,' they call it now. Thirteen years ago in Iowa they called it just plain crazy. No second chances. I never got the chance to find out what it felt like to love the child in my arms." She pulls her gaze back into focus and thinks she sees her words flying away, free, like feathers from a pillow broken on the wind. Her eyes have dried. "My daughter Julia died of pertussis. Three weeks old." Annie unfurls three fingers in her lap, watching them sway like spring twigs. "Three more babies, gone before they were born. Now I have Nora and *finally* I get to love a child of mine, body and soul. If being here keeps Nora safe, I guess I'm insane."

Anjanette falls quiet. Nora falls asleep.

"But the orphans' home . . ." Annie hides her panic by burying her face in the bunting around Nora's face.

Nora has a father. To look at her is to look at him.

Annie starts writing the letter in her head.

"You did what?" Anjanette is incredulous.

"He has a right to know." Annie settles Nora into an ancient pram that squeaks even when it isn't moving.

"He has a right to *merde*, Annie. He gave that up when he let you come here."

"Do you want to walk with us or not? It wasn't in his hands. We had separated. A third party filed the complaint and it went to the court. If you don't mind, I'd rather not relive it."

What is your testimony, Mrs. Melton?

Mrs. Fielding smacked me across the face, without provocation. The cut to my eye took two weeks to heal.

Your Honor, I most certainly was provoked, and there was no cut. May I speak in my own defense?

You may not, Mrs. Fielding. Hold your tongue or you will be removed. Sheriff Blandish, what is your testimony?

. . . To be clear, Doctor, are you saying that Mrs. Fielding wasn't pregnant but believed herself to be, enough so to bring on life-threatening hemorrhage?

. . . So, Miss Durant, you believed yourself to be in mortal danger?

Annie marches faster, shaking the scene from her head, trying to outpace the humiliation. The carriage clunks along in cornered-rodent squeals. "No one will tell me how long Nora can remain with me, Anjie. I won't allow her to be warehoused. She has a father. He would die at the thought of her being in the orphans' home. What are my choices here? He can fight it from the outside."

"Annie, you have opened an unspeakable can of worms."

"The alternative is worse. I wouldn't want to go on living if they took her away from me."

"You can't talk like that here." Anjanette steps in front of the carriage; the wheel runs up onto her instep. "You can't. It's as good as telling them to take her."

Haltingly, Anjie tells Annie that she's intuitive. She can feel electrical connections to the thoughts and feelings of others. She learned to keep it to herself, to silence her family's jeering that she had a future in the circus. Although she rarely speaks with the voice of her gift, this time the stakes are so high as to move her. She can't bear to see the final crushing of a brave heart that has been riven too many times.

"Annie." Her hand hovers over her breastbone. "He's going to try to take her from you himself."

Dr. Daniel Waterford, Superintendent
Montana State Hospital for the Insane
July 21, 1918

Dear Dr. Waterford,

You have at your institution a patient named Analiese
Fielding. Since her admission earlier this year, a
child has been born to her. The child is my daughter.

I am recently in receipt of a disturbing letter from
Mrs. Fielding. She suggests the baby might be taken
away from her for placement in the orphans' home.

Having not received any information from the
hospital, I would beg your response to the following:
What is Mrs. Fielding's condition? Is she responding
to treatment? What is the prognosis for her release?
Must the child be taken from her mother? How might
this affect the condition of each?

Beg to also state that I am both able and willing
to care for my daughter here. It is an intolerable
thought that my child should be separated from both
parents and under state care when I have a safe and
stable home that meets all her needs.

In anticipation of your reply, I am,

Most sincerely,
Adam Fielding

Under different circumstances, Hannah Madigan and Annie might have been fast friends. They share an unspoken bond: Hannah arrived as house matron the week after Nora was born, a few years older than Annie and from a matrimonial situation undefined, causing Anjanette to remark archly, "There's more than one way to be an inmate."

"I've made your wishes known to the staff," Hannah tells Annie. The October sky beyond Annie's bedroom window flickers both gray and bright.

"Thank you, Hannah. I'm not supposed to know this, but my husband says I have the ears of a bat. Hear through walls," Annie says, rocking with her foot the cradle where Nora sleeps. "I know that even with the quarantine and precautions, people are dying here. A doctor, a nurse, and several dozen patients, some perfectly hale in the morning and dead by suppertime. If I could, I would crawl inside the walls until it's over." Her stomach pulses in time with her heart. She can't read Hannah's tone. Is she here to warn Annie that she's to be put to work, parted from Nora for long days spent in the farm colony, the laundry, the commissary?

Hannah nods. "We understand. I told the staff that you don't wish to leave your room except for outdoor exercise, but that you want to do something productive in confinement with your baby. Under the circumstances, they will give you this time. The sewing room will send you all the work you can handle." Hannah indicates Annie's double-cable slipper socks, lively colors twisting against a black background. "We only need several thousand pairs of socks a year here."

"Is that all?"

Nora coos in her sleep, waves a searching hand. Annie slides her pinkie into Nora's tiny fingers; they close tightly. Hannah slips out. Annie sings.

"Go to sleep, my little baby. When you awake, you shall have cake, and all the pretty little horses."

Dr. Daniel Waterford, Superintendent
Montana State Hospital for the Insane
November 19, 1918

Dear Sir:

In re: my letter of four months ago to which I have
received no response, please advise when I may come
retrieve my child. I'm able to provide her excellent
care here and see no reason for her to continue under
state charge. Your prompt response is appreciated so
that I may make necessary arrangements.

Very truly yours,
Adam Fielding

Annie's commitment record and clinical report sit on the desk of Dr. Alvord, the doctor who interviewed her when she first arrived.

"Mrs. Fielding, your case perplexes me. I'm hoping you can shed some light. In my view, your commitment for manic-depressive insanity doesn't bear out. You have an extensive history of pregnancy and puerperal trauma, but since your recovery from the birth of your baby, you've been sound as an oak."

"What are you suggesting?" she asks.

Dr. Alvord rubs his thigh and shifts in his chair. "Your commitment papers cite your civil condition as married, but you named your brother, not your husband, as next of kin, a brother whose whereabouts you cannot or will not tell us. I explained to you at the time that this was hardly someone who could make decisions on your behalf in time of need, and certainly not someone who could help you should we decide to discharge you."

"And I explained to you," Annie says calmly, "that my husband and I are formally separated. I alone am responsible for my welfare and my debts. What exactly are you getting at, Doctor?"

"Mrs. Fielding, you're not insane. You don't belong here. However, we can hardly release you as a woman of no means, alone with an infant."

"Hardly. That's why, for the moment, this is where my baby and I are safest. She's an infant and winter is coming. As long as she can remain with me, I haven't thought beyond that. She can remain with me here, correct?" She holds her breath for the answer.

The doctor regards her, rolling his pen between thumb and fingers. "We do not take infants from competent mothers," he says, and Annie melts in relief, the rest of the doctor's sentence unheard.

Mr. Adam Fielding
Caswell, Montana
November 29, 1918

Dear Mr. Fielding,

We are in receipt of your letter re: Mrs. Fielding's
baby. As Mrs. Fielding has fully recovered her
physical health and mentality, we would be pleased
to release both your wife and baby to you as soon as
the quarantine here is lifted. In addition, the hospital
would appreciate receiving payment on the bill for
the care of your wife and child, most recent balance
of $330.00.

Yours very truly,
Daniel Waterford, Supt.

It's ironic, in a manner she dare not express even to Anjanette, but confined within the walls of what the world calls an insane asylum, Annie feels unusually free. Free from expectation and failure, free from the woes of disease, weather, and war that are slowly killing those who are truly free. Though incarcerated, she is free to devote herself to Nora in a singular manner that wouldn't be possible were she to leave. Here, she and Nora are clean, warm and fed, and surrounded by doctors. They are here for Annie's being judged insane. Now she's judged herself and her situation and decided she'd be insane to leave.

At her feet, Nora plays with a set of yarn braids, tickling her own baby toes and tickling her mother's knees with her downy laugh. Nora is Annie's everything. Hard to believe it's been nearly a year since Annie cooked a meal, scrubbed a floor, or washed and pressed a shirt. Handled money. Made bread. Made a phone call. Made love to a man.

She jerks too hard on her needle. The wool strains but doesn't break. Annie weaves in the tail of the yarn and turns the sock right side out. Cool white diamonds stand out on stately navy blue, shot with a thread of apple green.

"What do you think, Nora Marielle?" Annie lays the sock in Nora's lap and notes it in her record book. Her hundredth sock. Autumn has passed into winter in a procession of argyle, stripes, and cables.

It's been a soft, selfish time. She's drawn a circle around herself and her daughter. On sprawling grounds, among 1,300 inmates and several hundred employees, she is still alone.

She neither writes nor receives letters, having written only one other than to Adam. In a note devoid of blame or self-pity, she described her situation to Chase. The response she received— silence—served as another judgment against her. Not that she'd ever consider returning to Iowa, the worst of her pitifully few options, but she needed to know the outer limit of just how alone she is.

She has full rights to roam the grounds at will. She's learned the workings of the greenhouses, the mineral hot springs, the dairy, the hennery, the laundry, and the library. She could amble down the main drive and out the ungated entrance, and no one would stop her. No one but Nora.

A tiny hand tugs at her skirt. Nora tries to cram her fist into her drooly mouth, where the first pearly buds of teeth shine. Annie lifts Nora to the window to watch the clouds and marvel at the beauty of the hospital grounds. This is their world, their safe, self-sufficient community.

A sweet O of a yawn from Nora signals nap time. Annie lays her in her cradle, humming until her daughter's pale lashes rest against her cheek. Annie picks up her needles and starts in on sock number 101.

Dr. Daniel Waterford, Superintendent
Montana State Hospital for the Insane
December 11, 1918

Dear Sir:

In re: my child at your institution. Beg to clarify that
my wife and I have a separation agreement that was
in force at the time of her commitment. My attorney
informs me that I have the legal right to the child.

As concerns the bill for the care of my daughter,
I feel certain you are aware that we have been
experiencing drought conditions of a desperate
degree here. My account will be settled in as
expedient a manner as I am able given circumstances
beyond my control. You can avoid incurring further
cost for my daughter's care by kindly informing me
when I may come for her.

Truly yours,
Adam Fielding

Annie raps on the frosted glass. D. WATERFORD, SUPERINTENDENT.

"Knock on the wood, not the glass," the secretary tells her, her words sounding rehearsed. Annie enters an office overlooking the wide, tree-lined walkway leading to a kidney-shaped lake. This summer, the ducklings will nibble at Nora's toes when Annie dips them in the silver-green water. She'll try to catch a fish with her bare hands and—

The doctor's caramel voice intrudes. "Mrs. Fielding. Annie, if I may? I'm Dr. Waterford. I've asked you in because I've taken a personal interest in your rather unusual case. You've been with us almost ten months, I see."

"Yes?" Annie's not sure why her assent comes out as a question.

"I want to ask if you've given any thought to leaving here?"

What was it that Dr. Alvord said? Annie gropes for the conversation. *We can hardly release you as a woman of no means alone with an infant. . . . We do not take infants from competent mothers.*

"I confess, Doctor, not much. Where would I go?"

"You are married. You have a baby. Have you considered a reconciliation with your husband?"

How can she put into words what he can't understand? When her silence begins to feel damning, she says, "We have a formal separation agreement. Of his construct."

The doctor clasps his hands on the desk. "A child is involved now, and we're of the opinion that both parents have a stake in her welfare."

"I've had no contact with my husband in close to a year." A lead pellet of trepidation ricochets around her gut. "Have you?"

More silence. This Dr. Waterford, who has taken a personal interest in her case, isn't going to answer her question. Which means there is only one answer.

Mr. Adam Fielding
Caswell, Montana
January 14, 1919

Dear Sir:

The hospital has neither the legal right nor the desire
to separate a competent mother from her baby. Surely
you understand how detrimental this would be to
the health of your wife. Kindly make immediate
arrangements for the removal of your wife and
daughter from the institution and for the settlement
of your bill, which is in serious arrears.

Yours very truly,
Daniel Waterford, Supt.

On a flirty May morning, Hannah insists Annie and Nora come to the sun porch. They arrive to a room draped with pink streamers and laid with a lovely lunch of petite sandwiches and lemon cake. A dear little birthday party "for our dear little Nora," purr the women of the sewing room. They lay a pink-frocked rag doll with a sweet painted face in Nora's arms. Annie's tongue knots into a lump of gratitude as each tells her, "I spun the hair," "I knitted the anklets," "I tinted her mouth and cheeks."

Annie breathes deeply the affection and camaraderie around her. The asylum, this place of involuntary confinement, may be the most welcoming and loving setting in which she's ever lived. For all she doesn't have here, she and her daughter have community. Is it wrong to want to linger in its safety?

Annie anticipates that Nora's birthday may cue another discussion of her discharge. Once again, she preempts it. After the party she asks Hannah to send word to Superintendent Waterford that she wishes to join the larger workplace. She's ready to show her face again, and Nora will enjoy being with the children in the nursery.

21

The relentless grind of the seasons relieves Adam of any illusion he might have cherished that time would slow itself for him, would hold his daughter in her babyhood while he grapples for a way to knot the fraying strands of his life together. The farm, the most demanding of mistresses, consumes him, day by week by month, the whole year in unremitting peristaltic waves. How can it be that it is November again? All there ever was of November enters the house and lies down upon him: the ever more dissonant call to gratitude, the inevitable death of another year's cycle. But he himself isn't dead yet, so one more time he hammers blackened keys against blanched paper, hard enough to pound winking pinpoints of light above each *i*.

Dr. Daniel Waterford, Superintendent
Montana State Hospital for the Insane
November 30, 1919

Dear Sir:

In numerous previous letters over the past sixteen months, I've made my marital and financial situation as clear to you as the language allows. If I must pursue custody of my child through the courts, I will. Such expense is not in the best interests of either party here, so again I ask that you release my daughter to me at a time of your choosing. Your failure to do so will necessitate further action on my part.

Truly,
Adam Fielding

Adam seals the envelope with a clenched fist. It's a bluff, a slim-to-nothing chance. How would he pay court costs? He can barely pay his mortgage, his suppliers, his crew, his taxes. He can barely pay attention to any of it anymore. And for that he'll pay dearly.

The trees stand stock-still in their subzero January nudity, revealing the approaching car when it's still a half mile away. Adam sits farther back in his chair and picks up the newspaper, reading the same screaming headline for the fifth time. DISCOUNT RATE TIGHTENS, PRICES TUMBLE. FED CALLS HALT TO SPECULATIVE AG LOANS. If bad luck comes in threes, hasn't he surpassed his quota a few times over? Yet this approaching visitor is expected; only the timing has been in question. That the caller comes escorted by the law is an unwelcome twist. When the knock sounds, Adam counts to thirteen before answering.

Sheriff Blandish takes up more than his half of the door entry, alongside a man who looks cut from the same stock colored with a different crayon, a dusky tuft of hair sprouting from one ear, dromedary-humped brows over hooded eyes.

"G'afternoon, Adam," says Blandish. "This here is Deputy Renner from the Child Protection Bureau in Havre. He'd like a word with you."

"I'm sorry for the intrusion, sir," says the deputy.

Adam opens the door wider and steps aside. "You picked a treacherous day for the trip. Coffee?"

"Obliged, thank you. Would you mind if I put my feet in it?" The deputy's weak attempt at humor collides with Adam's back as he heads for the kitchen.

Adam fills two mugs from the pot he keeps perpetually full and places them like chess pieces in the center of the kitchen table, the visitors' only invitation to enter the room and get down to business. The deputy gathers himself and starts in.

"I take it you know why I'm here, Mr. Fielding. In the matter of your wife and child, the hospital has asked me to talk to you. Your wife has long since recovered, and it's the opinion of everyone around her that she'll do well at home. We're wanting to understand why you're reluctant to reunite your family. Particularly in the face of their upkeep expenses, which are mounting as we speak."

"'Upkeep'?"

"An unfortunate choice of word. I apologize." The deputy colors up.

Adam goes to his desk and removes three folders. "You've no doubt gotten several versions of the story, none of which took place behind that door you just walked through. Let's call that one the full story. These files will explain. My wife's medical bills and records. Two surgeries. Five pregnancies. Three midterm miscarriages. The bills include care for the infant daughter we lost. She died but the bill came just the same."

The deputy flinches.

"My wife has a history of erratic behavior associated with pregnancy and its aftermath. She's 'long since recovered' because she hasn't been pregnant. When she's not pregnant or postpartum, there's no one more capable and engaging."

"Well, we all know that the womenfolk can be touchy when they're expecting—"

"How do you characterize 'touchy,' Mr. Renner? Following her last surgery, I had to physically restrain her from picking out her stitches. She was convinced the doctors had 'left something in there.' She read Valley County Hospital as 'Leave Hostile Country' and had to be sedated out of her panic. I got touchy myself hearing her contemplate all the ways she might die following pregnancy, some of them self-imposed, one of which she tried when our daughter was dying."

Adam watches the deputy's growing discomfort scribble tiny red lines across his face. Poor bastard, he came here knowing only what that cartoon cop Blandish told him, and what he's seen on Montana State Hospital letterhead: a few letters from the superintendent, and a column of figures ending in "amount due."

"She's stable now," Adam continues. "Until she's not. Were we to live together again, were there to be another pregnancy and more of the same trauma, this time there would be a child in the house. Sir, that frightens me. We had already separated when we learned our daughter was on the way. My lawyer maintains that our separation agreement is sound, and that I have a right to custody. I've written the hospital repeatedly. They say they have no right to separate mother and child. Apparently they feel they have the right to separate father and child."

The sheriff has retreated into taciturnity, but Adam isn't fooled; this is all being registered for later regurgitation.

"This folder will give you an idea of the costs of running a farm in the midst of a war and a drought. We weren't patriotic if we didn't answer the government's drumbeat to grow more food, break more land, and borrow money at ridiculous rates to do it. I did all that. But you'd have to be blind and deaf not to know that we aren't Europe's breadbasket anymore. And if I'm lucky enough to bring a crop in this year, it'll be worth less than half of what it would have been two years ago." He pushes the folder across the table.

The deputy thumbs the corner of the file. "Mr. Fielding, I don't know the extent to which the hospital has the full picture of your financial situation."

"Is that so?" Adam flips open a third file. "In my first communication, I told them I am able and willing to care for my daughter myself. I also described the drought here and its financial impact on my farm. In these subsequent letters"—he drops them, one at a time, in a deliberate pile at the deputy's fingertips—"I restated the same. The only response I've gotten from them: Pay your bill. Take your wife off our hands."

The deputy leans back and laces his fingers in his lap. Adam doesn't wait long for the response he knows isn't coming. "So here you are, the Child Protection Bureau. How is it that you protect a child by allowing her to be raised in an institution for the insane when she has a father living in a comfortable home in a safe community, who is not only willing to care and provide for her but has been forced to go to reprehensible expense to try to do so? The fact is, it's not my daughter you're protecting. It's my wife. Have the decency to call it what it is. At no point have I been given any consideration as a parent other than as the one who is on the hook for the *money*."

He rises and comes around the table to where the deputy is sitting, subdued into silence. He comes close enough that the deputy must lean his head back to look up at him.

"I didn't create the drought, the war, or my wife's illness. I didn't have a hand in committing her to the state hospital, although I hear the sheriff here did. That true, Blandish?" When the lawman only purses his lips, Adam feels his taut composure begin to waver. "You still waiting for me to thank you, is that why you're here? You have no authority over this matter."

For once, nothing on the rotund sheriff is jiggling. "Suggest you watch your step, Fielding," he says tightly.

Adam turns to the deputy—"He testified at my wife's trial"— and then, shifting his gaze back to Blandish, continues, "and now you want to oversee mine. Maybe you have Elise Melton waiting outside?"

The sheriff hauls his bulk up straighter and growls, "Sug-gest you curb your tongue before you say something you'll re-gret."

The deputy half rises from his chair, palming the air. "Let the man speak, Jasper. I need to hear this."

Was Annie allowed to defend herself at her trial? Why has he never wondered about that? Adam regards the sheriff until the ten-sion crackles. Then he says, "I'm not the only man in this county waiting out adversity. But I am still my daughter's best hope for a decent life."

Adam imagines the deputy is more accustomed to dealing with drunks, outlaws, deadbeats, and bullies. He knows what to do with them. Here instead he faces a volume of fact previously unspoken in a case that's anything but straightforward.

"Mr. Fielding, there's a great deal to consider here. The state wants to effect a solution. Given how you feel about your wife—"

"You don't know what I feel for my wife. I don't have the luxury of allowing what I feel for my wife to enter into this."

Pinpricks of sweat creep from the deputy's temples. *Good,* Adam thinks. "Valley County," he says with a spiked look at the sheriff, "chose to commit my wife to the state hospital, where the only course of treatment they were willing to tell me about is what I call business as usual. They told me how well she's done in so-called occupational therapy, agricultural therapy, and artistic activities. What that translates into is she's a prodigious worker, knows gardening, and is skilled at needlework. As she was here. Nothing has changed except the setting. Nothing to convince me that her illness has been addressed in a manner that would prevent its recurrence. Nothing to negate the reason for an agonizing sep-aration, an excruciating decision to have to arrive at, and frankly, if you've never been in the position, I doubt your ability to understand it."

The deputy coughs twice behind his teeth, shoulders bouncing under his thick shirt. He reaches for his coffee cup and, finding it empty, places it on the table and stares at it.

Adam crosses his arms. "Let's talk about the money, since that's why you came, isn't it? My wife seems to be earning her own keep. So the issue is, as you put it, the 'upkeep' of my daughter. A needless circumstance. Look around you. A safe, comfortable, loving home. What could she need that isn't here?"

The deputy shifts in his chair. "Mr. Fielding, you're correct. I can't imagine what I would . . . You must wonder why—"

"I never wonder why."

"Yes. Well." He moves his hat back and forth between his hands before placing it on his head. "Much to consider." He rises heavily. "I'll be filing my report based on our conversation."

Adam moves to open the door, the muzzled Sheriff Blandish ambling after the deputy like a pull toy. A gust of icy air swoops in. "I'm sorry for your trouble, Mr. Renner."

The deputy stares after the sheriff, who strides to the car without a word. Renner has three inches and forty pounds on Adam, but his voice is considerably smaller when he says, "I believe that should be my line, sir."

When the door is latched and the draperies drawn against the fading afternoon, Adam exhales until his lungs burn. Those were more words than he's spoken to any person since Annie left him.

You must wonder why. Dropping into a chair by the stove, he recalls the spirited schoolmistress who taught him how the same word can have many different meanings. *Wonder*: A sensation of astonishment. A feeling of curiosity. A desire to know. An event not explained by the laws of nature.

I never wonder why.

Still, the deputy's visit wasn't the turn of the screws he expected. There's a slim chance that he's been heard this time. He'll suspend a difficult decision for a while longer.

22

The morning of his birthday marks forty days since the scorching winds began. From the window Adam, numb with resignation, watches his soil spiral a thousand feet into the sky, rush to a horizon he can't see, and plunge over the edge. The winds drive the sandy dust through invisible cracks in his house, piling it in pale dunes in the corners. Though it helps little, he covers his face with a wet washcloth and, breathing deep, thinks about drowning. The wind shovels up the sand and drops it to earth in dervishes that dance mockingly across the road and collapse into shifting humps, carving his land into ever-changing shapes.

The letter from the bank lies on the table where he let it fall last week.

Mr. Adam Fielding
Starlight River Market Farm
Caswell, Montana
July 10, 1920

RE: Demand for Prompt Settlement of Indebtedness

Dear Sir:

Our sustained efforts to resolve your grievously overdue account have proven futile. You are hereby notified that you are in default of your obligation and that failure to respond to this letter with payment in full within thirty days will compel us to initiate foreclosure proceedings on your property.

Kindly conduct yourself accordingly.

Adam squeezes his eyes shut as the last dregs of his pride and confidence disintegrate, burned to cinder at the memory of his first conversation with Cal Rushton, the badinage that wrote the opening act of this disaster.

Dry farming is just a matter of common sense.

Evident, now, that his common sense deserted him when he bought the dry-land plat after Julia's death. Whatever sense he managed to regain dissipated the day Annie boarded the train that severed their bond for good, followed by the event that binds them forever. He should have sold then, when patriotic fever, runaway wheat prices, and blindness to the deepening drought drove land values sky-high. What held him wasn't the relentless government pressure to produce more and more, nor the rumors of the four-dollars-per-bushel wheat price soon to come. No, he abandoned his common sense, sunk his plow deeper, borrowed more seed money, planted more wheat, for that perennial blind spot of the otherwise rational male: for love of a girl. For his belief, not in the land but in the possibility, however remote, that she might come home to him.

The girl is two years old now. The deputy's visit changed nothing, save that the dunning letters from the hospital stopped. It's a sad, defeated silence on both sides. In it, if he empties his head and listens, he can hear his daughter grow.

You are in default of your obligation.

The tap on the front door is Karl, who shows promptly at two o'clock each Sunday with dinner since Adam can no longer bring himself to enter the Eulenberg home. "Must we lose them both?" Margrethe cried to her husband, but Karl's telling Adam this didn't change his mind. He remains at the red window, braced against the sink. The door opens and closes, and Karl's light step brings him to the kitchen. From a metal box he sets on the table dishes of duck breast casserole, roasted cauliflower, and gooseberry pie. He glances at the letter lying at the end of the table. "There's no shortage of irony, is there?" Karl says without pity, because pity would finish the breaking of Adam Fielding. "The banks are failing as fast as the farms."

"Yes." Adam sits in the chair across from Karl and turns over the spoon near his hand. The bowl faces down, like it's awaiting execution. "The bank is in as much trouble as I am. For having been as reckless." He brings his fist down on the end of the spoon handle, and it flips into the air. "Pissed on their own shoes and believed it was raining. The bank may fold before they can foreclose on me."

"A cup of cold comfort, that," Karl says.

They sit for a while in silence, knowing that the proximity of their friendship is about to change. Then Karl continues quietly, "Sometimes when I'm cornered, I try to think, what would be the next best thing?" He turns the spoon between them bowl up. "The farm can be saved. Just not by you."

Their eyes meet. Never, Adam thinks, will he forget those kind eyes and the lifeline they now extend. Karl stands and moves toward the door, laying a hand on Adam's shoulder on the way out. Adam watches him round the bend in the road. In the kitchen he tips the food into the slop bucket. He can't consume what he doesn't deserve. With a linen towel he wipes down the table, his hand moving first in a slow circle, then picking up speed and ferocity. Faster and harder, gripping the cloth so tightly it wells up between his fingers, his knuckles white as ice. The table won't yield under his hand.

It won't yield.

Too many months he's sat at this table, working and reworking the numbers, all but erasing his own fingerprints, rubbed against his forehead in nights spent with the debt he can't pay down and the dreams that didn't add up.

Too late his common sense has returned. Adam hurls the linen cloth against the wall and faces the facts. The war is over. The bottom has dropped out of the world farm-commodities market. The drought is four years on, and this year's wheat burned in the field before the Fourth of July. And the Montana State Hospital will never relent, will never consider him a custodial parent.

Acta est fabula. The play is over.

At the mirror in the front room, he clears a swath through the dust with his hand. He doesn't recognize his reflection. The events of the last three years have done their work. He is no longer blond. But nature has been as indecisive as he. He started to go white alongside his cheekbones and behind his ears. Then the fading slowed and the rest of his head darkened to ash.

"About time," Reuben Dunbarton, himself gone white, ribbed him. "Oldest living towhead, you were." Dun offered Adam his old foreman's job. Diminished though it may be, Dun's farm is still producing. But Adam's conscience is already ravaged. He won't take a job from a fellow burned-out farmer who has a family to feed.

The state of Montana feeds Adam's family.

Still, he's one of the lucky ones. His dry-land plat is lost to him, but Starlight River Market Farm has a buyer. On a citrine September day, Adam crosses the Eulenbergs' threshold for the last time. Margrethe clings to Karl's arm and weeps through a conversation wherein they reach agreement on a price for the thirty-seven acres.

"God go with you, Adam. I still pray that you will find your way back to Annie."

"I sincerely doubt it," he replies hollowly. "On both counts."

Adam packs a single trunk. In its darkest corner he drops a cheap crushed thimble emblazoned in red. F R DR OODS G O COFFEEN'S. He's never understood why he can't bring himself to throw it away, why he didn't just toss it with the rest of the debris from that flood when he replaced it with the silver one. But so what if he hangs on to it? It weighs nothing and takes up no space. See how easily he obliterates it with trousers and shirts and coats and books and a secondhand chess set. When the trunk is full, he snaps the latch and turns the key.

"Never say never!" booms the kindly clerk at Caswell Feed and Implement as Adam closes his account. Adam watched thousands like himself pour in during the last decade, and now they're leaving as swiftly, heading west, heading north, heading back to where they came from. Now it's his turn to be watched. On his way out, a few murmur "sorry" and "good luck." They look scared. Maybe they know they're next.

He stows the trunk at the station and drives back to the homestead for the last time. The truck is part of the sale; he'll leave it at the house and walk into town to catch the train. The sky is brilliantly blank. Inside, the house is tidy, an exhortation to leave before he disturbs it. He takes a last look out the red window. Against his will, he feels proud of Annie, of the grace with which, in the unlikeliest of settings, she's excelled at motherhood, kept their daughter with her, and given no one the slightest reason to think it should be otherwise. Somewhere in the Montana State Hospital, she found the footing that will hold her steady in the years ahead without him. He's never laid eyes on Nora and knows he never will. For this, his parasitic grief may eat him alive, but he's given himself over to it. For now he'll have what he yearns for. To be what he was before there was Annie: an inscrutable, impenetrable automaton.

He's taking little with him. Most of the contents of the house will remain where they lie. But one item torments him. Try as he might to avert his eyes, its pull is magnetic. It's a problem whose moment of truth now closes in on him.

What to do about *The River by Starlight*?

Despite his sorrow and disillusionment, he can't relegate it to a fate less than it deserves. The quilt is the allegory of their life together, what they stood for and strove for. For his eyes alone; she repeatedly made that clear. Without question it's the most loving gift anyone has ever given him, and bestowed by someone who didn't love him. She didn't! She *left* him, didn't she?

He unpacked the quilt only days ago. The spray of stars and the orange moon flirt with him, even when his eyes are closed. He can hear the river in the faded green curve of fabric along the bottom, rushing by just beyond the trees as it has for thousands of years.

He can't take the quilt with him. It has too much power. Giving it to anyone other than her is out of the question. Even in his bitterest thoughts, he can't see cleaving her heart further by returning it to her. He can't consign it to fire or water. Nora should have it. But how to accomplish that? Standing at the red window this last time, he closes his eyes and tries to remember how to pray, at least for a spark of inspiration.

He pulls the door closed behind him. His fingers prickle where he touched the work of her hands a final time. Her wish was that no one but him see the quilt; seeing to that was the least and the last kindness he could do for her.

When he reaches the road, a sharp sense of fate stabs at him. He's taking the same walk Cal did eight years ago, but no sentimentality will turn Adam's head. Not even old Tipsy diverts his eye. The meaty manure smells mock him. Outlasted by a flock of dirt-dumb fowl and hams on the hoof. It doesn't matter now. He's headed north, far north, resolved to a lifetime of never-agains. Never again to live in the country of his birth. Never again to be at nature's mercy for his sustenance. Never again to share his name with another. Never again to entertain the thought of being someone's father.

The conductor passing through the car nods at him knowingly. Adam tips the brim of his hat forward, veiling his eyes. "Are you at peace with God in this?" the Reverend Fielding would have asked, had Adam deigned to share his plans. Adam would have forced his answer, "We're not acquainted." But as the town that was home for the longest stretch of his life dwindles from view, he nurses the humble hope that someone's God might remain behind on a hillside near the unmarked grave of a child whose parents fell off the pendulum of life at opposite ends of its sweep.

The train slows, pulling into the North Dakota town appropriately called Portal. "Name?" the customs agent demands. Where is he coming from? Birthplace? Married, single, divorced, or widowed? State of health? Carrying how much money? Destination? Purpose in coming to Canada?

"To farm," Adam lies. He was warned: Canada wants farmers, not Americans taking Canadian jobs. "In Alberta. North of Red Deer. Do you know the area?"

"No," says the agent, bringing the stamp down: ADMITTED.

Daybreak arrives in Edmonton as he does, the swelling light following him to the boardinghouse on Ninety-Second Street, where the lodgers at the breakfast table glance at Adam with varying degrees of disinterest and mutter greetings, hallo, *bonjour*. The landlady pours coffee. "This is Mr. Fielding," she says to the others at the table. "Just arrived."

The man on his right passes Adam a platter of buckwheat flapjacks.

"American?" he asks.

"Yes."

"Tell 'em you're gonna farm?"

"Yes." Adam smiles, quarter strength.

"Plow deep." The man winks.

Adam bypasses the trolley line stapled to the street a block from the boardinghouse and walks the mile and a quarter to downtown, memorizing the storefronts along the wide boulevard.

Edmonton is larger than the aggregate of all the towns in which he's ever lived. In front of the brick edifice whose address matches the letter in his pocket, it hits him how long it's been since he answered to a boss other than himself. But the ad in the paper answered a prayer he didn't know he had prayed. How a copy of the *Edmonton Journal* found its way to a counter inside the Caswell post office, he'll never know and won't wonder. Folded to page eight, the farm commodities prices straddling the ad: Hudson Bay Company wants commercial travelers for its northern outposts. On the road three out of four weeks. When he saw that, he couldn't get here fast enough. Montana has beaten, blown, and drowned out of him any urge to settle, ever again.

He pushes open the door of the brick edifice. He'll stop moving when they come for him with the big box.

23

"Look, Mama," Nora breathes, cupping a green lacewing in her hands. "You can see right through its wings. Its eyebrows are waving at me!"

That Nora so cherishes life delights and torments Annie. More and more, she squelches her guilt that Nora doesn't live a larger life in the broader world. The hospital, she's reasoned all along, keeps them safe. But Nora is an inquisitive child. Soon she will ask questions that have no simple answers.

There are plenty of those on the outside. It's what's kept Annie here in the safety of the asylum years beyond the dictates of her health. The outside world can't even agree on a definition of the word *asylum*. The tattered dictionary in the hospital library offers contradictory definitions:

> **a-sy'-lum,** n. **1.** An institution for the care of unfortunate persons. **2.** A refuge or retreat; an inviolable shelter from arrest or punishment.

If one has found refuge from punishment in an inviolable shelter, wouldn't one then be fortunate? The asylum is her inviolable shelter; outside is a world of impossible questions that force Annie back into its refuge.

Still, she doesn't hesitate when invited to join an outing to the spring textile fair in Butte. With Nora on her hip, she examines yarns of wool and silk, bolts of flannel and chamois. Nora pets everything with a pensive face. In the livestock barn, Annie sets Nora in front of triplet lambs, their eyes level with hers. It's like throwing a switch. Nora reaches for the lambs, eyes alight, and they nuzzle into her toddler hands as if greeting a long-lost friend. She coos in a baby tongue the lambs seem to understand; they vie for her words and touch.

Annie stands enchanted, oblivious to the stream of onlookers. Comments drift around her until a kind-faced, grandmotherly woman lays a hand on her arm.

"What a darling. Look at those goldilocks! She must be the picture of her daddy."

Annie tenses at the unanticipated directness. "She is," she whispers.

Another onlooker joins in—"You must enter her in the pretty baby contest; she's simply luscious"—while yet another nods and sighs, "Such a natural with those lambs. Does your husband ranch?"

Annie presses her thumb against the inside of her third finger where her wedding ring used to be. This is the way it will be for her if she leaves the asylum, the refuge. Alone but married, she doesn't fit into a convenient category.

She refuses to pass herself off as something she's not, or to be humiliated by what she is. Back in Cherry Hill, "the widow Prentiss" didn't fool anyone. The absence of Mrs. Fielding's husband would remain unexplained. She would be not a person, but an object. Of pity, scorn, mistrust. But the alternative—another man, another partnership?

Unthinkable.

Annie smiles her thanks for the compliments. Then she rejoins the group from the hospital, taking Nora back to the only home she knows. The train leaves them at the wide, ungated entrance. They pass the post office and the fishing pond and the dark brick administration building and the infirmary and the dormitories, over gravel giving way to grass, back to cottage 2, floor B. They find leftover chicken and pineapple upside-down cake in the icebox and eat it in the kitchen. Nora's cheek drops to Annie's shoulder on their way up the stairs. Annie slides her daughter into a threadbare nightdress, wishing she had the money for a length of that royal blue flannel they saw today, with the tiny flower-and-dot print.

That's when she knows.

It's time for them to leave.

Across four hundred miles of mountains and prairie is a man in Caswell who is still her husband and will always be the father of her child. For almost three years, she's tried not to think of how he faces each day, his desperately wanted daughter out of his reach. Now Annie must force herself to think about the way all of them will live in the years to come. Adam has never asked to visit. She understands. He chooses the lesser of two heartbreaks.

But it's time for her to leave, so it's time to talk to Adam. She doesn't know what she'll say, what to suggest, what she can ask. She can't go back to Caswell. They can't live together, but they must try to work something out so they can live with themselves. For Nora's sake.

She's been listening to Dr. Waterford for some minutes. What he's trying to say diplomatically is that it might be difficult to secure employment for a penniless woman with the taint of insanity and a young child besides. "So you see the problem."

What is he hiding behind those little round spectacles? Annie wonders. What would he do if she asked him to remove them so she can see what he's really driving at?

"Yes and no. I'm capable of supporting myself. All I need is a place to start. And I should have a bit of an income, according to the terms of my separation agreement."

The doctor smooths his tie with trout-pink fingers that have never turned sod or mucked a stall. "You have no income. You are completely without resources. Unless you know something you're not telling us."

Patiently, as she would to Nora, Annie explains, "Our separation agreement called for cash payments to me for six years. Hasn't he been paying you that? And, by his choice, the agreement precluded divorce. So mightn't I still have a negotiable stake in the marriage? He wouldn't deny me that. It would be denying Nora."

"He hasn't been paying us."

Annie blinks and feels a chill creeping through her ears.

"And perhaps you've forgotten." The doctor hesitates. "You quitclaimed the property to your husband. You had no stake. If you feel you were coerced, we can speak to an attorney."

"I wasn't coerced. It was my idea. He wouldn't—did you say 'had'?"

"A warranty deed has been recorded. He doesn't own the

property anymore." He pushes a copy of the document across the desk for Annie to see. The recorder's wide, rhythmic script fills the page. At the bottom, the notary seal attests to the signatures of Karl G. Eulenberg, Grantee, and Adam W. Fielding, Grantor.

"We don't know where he is," the doctor says. "We've been trying to locate him for some time."

The toe of her tiny shoe taps the floor with military precision. *Rap rap rap.* Pause. *Rap rap rap.* Pause.

"I see. And you think I may know where he is." *Rap rap rap.* Pause. "How would I know that?"

When the doctor says nothing, she asks, "Where does this leave me?"

"For now, we'd like to put you in a new job. More responsibility and—"

Annie stands, kicking the chair from under her. "Do I need to change my clothes or shall I start now?"

The doctor closes the file on his desk. "Don't you want to know what you'll be doing?"

"Does it matter? You've made your point. I don't have choices. Now, have you told me everything you know?"

His hand on her file judders once. Anyone else would have missed it. Her smirk lets him know she didn't. She turns for the door.

"He's out there somewhere," she says over her shoulder. "Keep looking."

Nora spotted the bedraggled orange kitten in the high grass behind the dairy when she came to share lunch with Annie during her work break. She describes, in her almost-three-year-old way, how she inched toward the kitten, how it staggered away, backing itself into a cellar stairwell. Nora's face shines as she tells how she lifted the kitten to her cheek and felt its heart pounding like hail. Sadness washes over Annie, for both her daughter and the kitten. A kitten won't be allowed in the cottage. Nora has nothing and asks for nothing. Annie's eyes fill; she can't even give her daughter the simple childhood pleasure of a kitten. Casting around for an idea, Annie's eye falls on a ramp to the sagging side door of a dormitory building. Woody vine clutches at it; it hasn't been opened in years.

"Nora, give me your sweater."

"Okay. But why?"

"The kitten likes you, and your sweater smells like you. If we make a bed for her with it, here under this ramp, she may feel like she's still with you. And if we bring her more food, too, she may stay."

Nora peels off her shabby cardigan. "I hope Matron doesn't scold me and think I lost it," she says, frowning.

"You can tell her you gave it to me to mend." Annie twines the arms of the sweater into a kitten-sized nest.

"Why, Mama, that would be a lie."

Annie flushes. "You're right, sweetheart. If Matron asks, you can tell her you gave the sweater to me. That's not a lie."

Nora considers. Annie envies that her daughter's truths can be so simple.

"You don't have to do it, Nora," she says. "It's your choice."

Nora hands the kitten to Annie. "She needs to be safe."

Even a kitten needs the asylum, a place where the unfortunate are cared for.

The kitten stays on, showing up at lunchtime for morsels of cheese and cold chicken. One summer day Nora puzzles over a tiny feather stuck to her pet's face. Annie explains that cats have hunting instincts and that's how they eat and survive if they're wild.

"She ate a bird? Ewwww." Nora shakes the feather at her cat. "No, no, Kitty. You mustn't kill things."

Annie picks Nora up and sits her on her hip. "It's hard to understand, but what she's doing is right. It's the way she's made. Be glad that she can take care of herself now, even if people don't feed her."

"But if she can get her own food, she might run away from us."

"She might. You can't hold on to someone who wants to be somewhere else."

Nora's lip trembles. Annie draws her daughter's sun-warmed head to her shoulder. "It may not happen. You keep being her friend and try not to worry."

Annie leaves the nursery harassed by her own words. *Try not to worry that someone you love may leave you.*

At the dairy, a buzz of commotion flits among the workers. One taps Annie's shoulder as she passes and says, "Boss is looking for you."

"Why?" Annie can't think what she's done.

"Mice," says her colleague.

"So?" Mice in a cellar is hardly surprising, though in a dairy even one can't be tolerated. But why would the facility manager seek her out?

Several of the workers insist that Annie Fielding has a solution, he says. Would she please share her thoughts? Has she built the proverbial better mousetrap?

"I'm afraid not," she tells him. "I'm not sure what they—"

Oh. She glances around gratefully at the coworkers who would not reveal her daughter's secret. "Yes," she tells their boss, "I know what to do."

The workers called her Poos, the Blackfoot word for "cat," patrolling her territory with indisputable authority, retiring to shelter under the delivery ramp. "You're so smart, Mama," Nora says, beaming. "You know how to fix everything."

Dr. Waterford rises from his chair as Annie enters. "Please come in."

He motions to a chair. She sits. She waits. She wilts. She knows that half-averted gaze. Knows it from years of facing doctors who are about to deliver bad news.

"We've been in contact with Mutual of the Northwest," he begins, "trying to find out why you've gotten these nonpayment notices on your life insurance policy. As you told us, your husband has maintained payments. The last one was six months ago."

"You've found him."

"We have."

"Is he dead?" Annie asks sharply. Why is the doctor looking at the paper and not at her?

"No. He left a forwarding address with Mutual of the Northwest."

"He would, as beneficiary. May I see the letter, please?"

"The address is in Edmonton. Canada."

"I know where Edmonton is," Annie snaps.

The doctor stands to come around the desk. "I know this may be a shock."

He says no more, because she's assembled her face into the expressionless façade she watched for six years, the one etched on her heart. She's excised the doctor, this shaman, from her consciousness. *Well done, Annie.* Adam would be proud. Beyond the door with the frosted glass is the rest of her frosted life.

She's moving through the hall under a power beyond her own. Dr. Waterford pulls his jacket on as he hastens after her. "I'll accompany you to the cottage." But her hand flies up as forcefully as a train signal, shunting him onto a siding. His voice, his spectacles, and his intentions recede into the flat, dappled light thrown on the floor by a hazy sun.

Annie feels her insides separating into filaments too thin to shred any further. Canada. To sell the farm is one thing, but to skip the country? She hates him. She misses him. She hates that she misses him. She wants to hurt him. It hurts to want him. What is he doing in Edmonton? He has a new business; he's building a home for them; he's working off the hideous debt she saddled him with so they can start over. He's building a cabinet for Nora, to fill with dolls and books. *The River by Starlight* is on the bed; on the dresser is a tortoiseshell hairbrush in a silver box. He always loved her hair, didn't he? When will he send for her? Why did he leave a forwarding address if he didn't want her to know where he is?

How much can she force herself to believe?

She rushes up the wide stairs of the cottage and on up to the second floor. Somewhere below, a housekeeper sings in a lush alto, her mop swishing across the floorboards. "You made me love you . . . I didn't think you'd do it. I didn't think you'd do it! . . . You made me want you . . . Hm hmm hmm . . ."

Annie braces against the wall. The housekeeper moves on, the song fades. The hall falls quiet and Annie is alone.

She knows now why she is alone. She's weak. She let herself love him.

Alone. She already knew it, so why are her feet disintegrating? Her legs fold in to her chest as she slides down the wall. Through the hall window, she can see the fence around the hot springs, and those moronic signs. DANGER. HOT WATER. KEEP OUT.

Anger brims, fingers of icy vapor seeping between her ribs. *As if words on wood are enough to keep us out of hot water.* Her anger lifts her to her feet and carries her to her room, where, safe inside, she slams the door against every possibility she imagined.

She didn't notice last week when Dr. Waterford revealed Adam's defection, but the windows of this impeccable office are quite dirty. That makes the sky dirty. The air in the room swirls in polluted vortices, dirtied by the exhalations of conspirators doing their dirty jobs, keeping dirty secrets, and carrying out dirty deeds. The threesome sits in front of Annie: Dr. Waterford, Hannah, and Dr. Alvord, who three years ago told her she wasn't insane and didn't belong here. People she thought she knew. Today they are strangers, a jury of apostates. Annie tries to separate the voices, but they've all adopted the same toneless pitch and calculated measure, reciting, taking turns, handing off cues with sideways glances, their voices crackling, surging, and fading, maddening static dancing around a frequency that won't tune in.

". . . not easy for us to tell you . . . your husband . . . outside the reach of American law . . ." ". . . has abandoned you, your daughter, and his obligations . . ." ". . . left no assets in the U.S. . . . egregious debt . . ." ". . . understand the position now inflicted on the hospital and on you. We ourselves are up against the law."

"What are you saying?" Annie's toes clench, looking for anchor to the floor.

". . . so very sorry, but Nora cannot stay here . . . law prohibits us keeping children with their mothers past the age of three . . . cases of divorce where neither parent can provide . . . custody of the orphans' home."

The atrocity they're inflicting ruptures her voice, her spine, her sensibility. "You're taking her away from me. You're taking her away from me? You're taking her away from me!"

"We wish with all our hearts there were another way."

"You're taking her away from me!"

"We've asked the staff at the orphans' home to consider allowing you to work there, as you have here—"

"Stop. Stop! You know there's no chance of that! An asylum inmate working around children?" An overpowering urge to run surges the length of her. Where is Nora, in the nursery? They could run; what if she grabbed Nora and ran and ran . . . "Hannah! How could you keep this from me! What will I tell Nora? What's to become of us?"

"God doesn't give us more than we can handle. Nora needs you to be strong, Annie."

"You're putting this off on God? No, Hannah! Why didn't you tell me?"

"We had hoped—"

"Live on hope, die fasting!" Suddenly Annie sees them for what they are: common laborers paid to do these things to people like her because other, higher people decree it. She turns on Dr. Waterford. "Why didn't you parole me? Nothing out there could be worse than this!"

"Your safety and Nora's are our responsibility." Dr. Waterford's pitch rises as Hannah turns her head from Annie and covers her mouth with trembling fingers. "We pursued what we thought was the best option. It appears we erred in hoping for the reconciliation of your family. We will begin seeking an outside employment situation for you immediately and hope this separation is short."

"Hope, hope. You like that word, don't you? Hope is cheap, isn't it?"

She can't even cry, too deep is her paralysis. Face in hands, bowed over the lap that will now go empty, she gives into keening, something she knows how to do. Do they know how many times a child has been ripped away from her, and that this will be the cruelest severance of all?

They let her lamentation play out; in her powerlessness she's managed to render them momentarily immobile, the infinitesimal price of their incalculable mistake. Hope, hope, she *hopes* it hurts them. When at last she raises her head, it is to ask but one question.

"When?"

"Soon. It can even be today if that's easier for you."

Easier. At least they have the decency to look uneasy. "I want to see her. And then, if you have any mercy, don't tell me when she's gone. I'll know."

Alone in the meadow, Annie cradles her daughter, watching a sprinkling of tiny white moths flit in and out of the grass. "Like snowflakes going backwards!" Nora laughs, and Annie withers inside. Going backward indeed.

Nora's smiles overturn as Annie explains: Nora is a big girl now and cannot live at the hospital anymore. She will live at a big home for big children for a little while, until Mama can find a home for just the two of them.

Nora slips a hand into the folds of Annie's skirt. "I don't want to go away from you, Mama. How will I know what to do?"

"You already know, my dearest. Just keep being Nora. Trust yourself. When you wake up each day, think only about that day, and when you go to bed, think only about the next day. On one of those tomorrows, I'll come for you and we'll be together again. Keep your face forward. Never look back. Okay?" *Protect yourself against the day you realize you no longer trust me.*

"Okay?" Nora echoes. "Mama, did I do something wrong?"

"Oh, no, honey! Never, ever." She can't say more, can't voice how Nora could never be wrong; what's wrong is how life keeps wronging them.

"What if you forget about me?"

What if I forget how to breathe? "Never, ever, ever," Annie whispers, taking Nora's face in her hands, bending so their foreheads touch. "Some things are simply not possible. Ever. Okay?"

"Okay?" Nora repeats. Then the knife: "Will you be okay without me?"

Annie tries for levity, ruffling Nora's hair and tickling behind her ear, making her squeak. "Of course I won't be okay without you. But it won't be for long. I'll write you letters sealed with fourteen— no, twenty-seven—kisses."

On the walk in front of the cottage where they will part without goodbyes, Annie drops to her knees and wraps Nora in her arms, wishing she could knot them. There are no more words, just kisses and more kisses, then valiant smiles and the devastating release of touch. Nora slips from Annie's fingertips, runs toward the cottage. At the bottom of the steps, she stops. Her shoulders rise and fall once. Then she squares herself and dashes up the steps, into the yawning shadows of the veranda, leaving Annie to sink into the quicksand of less: homeless, hopeless, loveless, all but lifeless. True it is, less is more. More than she can bear.

Another day, yet another nurse. They're getting younger, too.

"You must get up, Mrs. Fielding. They're waiting for you in the dairy."

"There is no Mrs. Fielding."

"Of course there is. It's you, right here. Let's—"

"There is no Mr. Fielding. How can there be a Mrs. Fielding?"

It's no match. The nurse, fresh out of school with a limited bag of tricks, versus Annie, an old hand at loss and loneliness. Would anyone have told this aspiring Nightingale that for Annie there can be no lower low? She's been this way for weeks, since they sent Nora to the orphans' home. Since the first horrid hints that Nora could be placed for adoption.

"There is no Mrs. Fielding," Annie repeats. She could say more, had she the strength: how she's learned that when all is said and done, life is something she must do alone. For better or worse—twice she's made that vow to a man. But the cruel truth is that *for better or worse* isn't about marriage. It's about self.

The nurse gives up. The door clicks behind her and Annie sinks under the chalk-colored blanket, gathered in on herself with her cheek at the edge of the bed. She can lie here for hours, listening for signs of life deep inside the mattress. There might be a voice, unheard by everyone else, trying to tell her something. This hinter-world, hovering on the border of sleep's sweet oblivion, is home now, comforting and undemanding, the only place where life is tolerable.

Against the washed-out sheets, her hair swirls around her, a black tornado. She'll be one of the last to bob her hair. It's her signature, isn't it? But she seldom looks at it. She can tend to her locks without a mirror, a hundred strokes for her and another hundred for Nora, seventy miles away in the orphans' home. Without a mirror she needn't acknowledge the first silver threads peeking out of their black surrounds, like the tails of the shooting stars she used to see from her farmhouse window on nights too hot for sleep. Not like now, when sleep is her best friend, her only friend. She dives gratefully into its arms.

The door flies open and bright light streams in.

"Get up, Annie."

She strains to see through the blinding, bevel-edged light that excises her surroundings. That voice, familiar, taut, elusive. Who?

"Get up!"

Most insistent, almost angry. This is no new nurse. The light pulsates. It hurts her eyes. Who is it that would—

"Adam? Is it you?"

"Annie, is that you? You've become your own shadow. Enough. Get out of that bed."

"I'm sorry. This is . . . I never thought . . . Oh my God." Her hands fly to cover her face. She can't let him see her this way. "It's been so hard. I have no reason to—"

"You have the holiest reason of all. You have our daughter."

She tries to find her feet. He's in the room and yet he's not. "Please, no talk of God. The state makes decisions about children of divorce. Nora is at the children's home. They're trying to—"

"There's been no divorce. I need you to listen."

She moves her hands away from her face; her chest rises and falls in ragged disbelief. "I'm listening."

"You aren't the only one this is happening to. You can't know what I live with. That I wasn't able to be what you needed—"

"Oh, Adam. Nor I for you."

That face, that inscrutable face.

"—and that I wasn't able to be what I wanted to be." His chin drops toward his shoulder. "It broke me. I . . . broke. I wear that regret as a second skin."

"I know what you've done," Annie breathes. "You sold the farm. You left the country. The words they use . . . you deserted us. Abandoned us." The words lance her, even now. "But who knows more than I what it's like to feel broken?" She's shaking so hard she can barely form the words. "I can forgive you. You're here now. Are we—"

"I can't face your forgiveness yet." His hands plumb the corners of his jacket pockets. "I did leave. But it was with the conviction that Nora would always be with you. How could you allow her to be put up for adoption? Handed over to strangers? How?"

His anguish rains on her like shattered glass. She bows under the sting, bunching her nightdress in a wad against her stomach.

"So she could have a family. She deserves a family." Her cry is also a plea. "Can't you see how it's killing me?"

"She has a family. A broken one, but still a family. You alone—and I will grieve that forever—have the power to fix part of it."

His hair is longer than she's ever seen, reaching to tender places that need protecting. It stirs in the wind. Slowly, so as not to startle him, she licks a finger and holds it in front of her. No wind. He is the boxwood knight. . . .

"All I've wanted is what is best for our daughter, that she be with one of her parents because being with both isn't possible." When he brings his eyes up, they're not his ethereal blue, but black like hers. "I did every desperate thing I could. Letters, lawyers, pleading, threats. They would not take her away from you."

The air thickens in Annie's throat. She has to push her fingers against her neck to breathe.

"You and I and Nora need the same thing, Analiese. We need you to be a mother. Isn't that what we wanted so desperately that it nearly did kill you, how many times?" His voice breaks. "She can still be with one parent. Be that parent. I beg you."

Adam Fielding never begs.

He's fading. The light seems to filter through his body. She wants to run to him, but she's moving against a current.

"Adam! Can't I—can I touch you? It will have to last me the rest of my life, won't it?"

He is only particles of light, dispersing, dissolving. "Be what you always were: a lover and a fighter. I'm counting on you."

She wills her legs to move, feels herself falling. Her head and hip smack the floor. The sheet entangles with her nightdress, rendering her trussed and struggling. Full daylight hits her; all at once she becomes aware that the door is closed and she is alone, as if no one was ever there. Outside, the hum of midmorning activity fills the cottage. She claws at the bedclothes; it's taking too long to free herself!

Her hair flowing over her bosom, her bare feet raw against the linoleum, she grabs the day attendant in the hall by the arm.

"My husband just left. Did you see him?"

"Mrs. Fielding, are you all right? Men aren't allowed up here. Honey, you look flushed."

"I'm fine. My husband, he was there in my room. He came to talk to me."

The attendant spreads her arms, guiding Annie back to her room. "I'll fetch Mrs. Madigan. Promise me you'll wait here."

"Yes. I will." Hannah is what Annie needs now. A conduit to the top. She dresses quickly, picks up her hairbrush, and begins to count her strokes, an oar through dark water, over and under, pulling her along. At sixty-seven comes the knock she's expecting.

"Annie." Hannah Madigan stands where Adam did minutes ago. "The day girl sent me."

Annie sweeps the brush through one last sleek streak. "Yes. Did she tell you why?"

"She did, but I want to hear it from you."

"My husband was here."

Hannah pulls the desk chair close to where Annie sits on the bed, her feet buried in the pile of sheets on the floor.

"Listen to me. No one here has ever seen your husband. In three years. No visits. Nothing. He would not be allowed to simply walk into your room. Especially not with the frame of mind you've been in lately."

Annie smiles beatifically. "Nevertheless."

"What did he say? I would understand if you wanted to believe he would—"

"Hannah, I have urgent business to discuss with Dr. Waterford. Can you get me in to see him? Today."

"I'll get right to the point, Dr. Waterford. Parole me."

"Parole you?"

"Yes. Release me. Send me off. Turn me out. Whatever it takes."

"'Turn you out'? There's more to parole than escorting you to the train."

"Then, go to it at once. I want to leave."

"You want to leave?"

"Is there an echo in here?"

He chuckles. "Can you tell me what's behind this sudden demand?"

"Certainly. I'm going to get my daughter back."

"You know discussions regarding her adoption are under way."

"Yes, the train is under way. I'm going to derail that train, and I don't care what or who I have to tie to the tracks to do it."

"This is an abrupt change of heart." The doctor removes the round spectacles Annie always assumed were part of his face. Without them, he seems an arm's length closer. "We've had trouble getting you out of bed lately."

"That should be understandable considering what was taken from me. My only child and my hope for the future. It's time for me to take both those things back. You would deny me?"

"Of course not." He squints at his desk. "We will seek outside employment for you. Your long work record speaks well of you, although the right placement may take time. But stopping the adoption may be another story. Two families are interested in Nora."

It's called a three-speed transmission. It's Adam's voice again, from years ago when he taught her to drive the truck. *But one is reverse.* She had to half stand to reach the pedals. Her body remembers, feels that lift now as she pulls herself higher in her seat, the better to bear down on the forward pedals. She's puttered along in first gear long enough. *Increase speed.* He's close behind her shoulder. *You'll shift into high gear. Just hold the wheel steady.*

Annie's foot tenses against the floor. "I am Nora's family. There will never be anyone more interested in her than me. I will not sign consent to an adoption, and if you try to go around me with an involuntary commitment of her, I will fight it, the ugliest fight I can muster, to the last breath in my body." *Keep your foot to the floor to hold your speed.* Three years wandering this enclave and she knows the whereabouts of every pencil, envelope, and telephone. She knows the postmistress, and now, unlike her last time facing a judge, she knows a small army of people who will testify on her behalf.

The doctor doesn't blink. "I believe you."

"Then parole me. Now. Yesterday."

"We will start the process. But these things take time."

"I do not accept that. Did not my husband try repeatedly to get custody of Nora, and did you not repeatedly tell him that you would not take her from her mother?"

A sheen of astonishment spreads across the doctor's face. "How do you know this?"

"Doesn't matter. You told him you would not separate mother and child. So honor that. Parole me. Return my daughter to me."

"Annie, have you been in touch with your husband?"

Annie rises from the cracked leather seat as if weightless and glides to the door.

"Yes, I have."

24

Annie has lived in Montana long enough to know that a prairie summer isn't complete without the artistry of nature adding a few brushstrokes of catastrophe to the landscape. On an ordinary Tuesday when the midday sky deepens to stone, all heads in the dairy swivel to the windows to watch the thunderheads collide in a pig pile of atmospheric irritation.

It's a half-hearted hailstorm by Montana standards, and the damage would have been minimal but for a farewell blast of wind that swoops in even as the sun starts to break through. It blows out a row of windows at the bottling end of the building in a crystal tantrum of glass and ice. Several workers leave for the infirmary, arms and faces mapped in trickling creeks of red. Annie dons heavy gloves and joins a group helping to move some of the larger pieces. The warmth of the building melts the hail into a dirty lake of rubble. "This is going to kill production for the week," the foreman grumbles. It feels familiar to Annie in a distant sort of way. "No use crying over spilled glass," she says, and the foreman grunts.

In her room that evening she watches the sky pinken. On her desk, a red pencil lies atop her calendar, and with it she drives a heavy slash through the square with today's date. She's treading time as she would water, waiting, waiting in place for the sun to rise on the day she will reclaim Nora. Meanwhile, the monotony of her life at the hospital ticks on.

The storm is three days behind them when Annie passes a workman bent over the frames of the blown-out windows. His hammer and chisel clink as he chips out the old glazing putty, catching the remnants of broken glass on an ancient sheet stiffened with splatters. A paint can sits nearby, barber pole-striped with dried drip trails. The paint is red.

The window frames were red. She hadn't noticed. Now she sees her own red window again, exploding under the barrage of hail.

"Quite a mess, isn't it?" The clink of the tools stops and the workman smiles at her.

How long has she been standing here, preoccupied? "Yes, quite." She can't think of anything else to say.

"Part of the job." He shrugs.

"You don't mind?" She didn't mean to say that. It slipped out.

"Mind? What a funny question. Does a cook mind the food? Does a printer mind the ink? Does a farmer mind the dirt?"

"I suppose not."

He laughs. "Is that why you're staring at me? Feeling sorry about the mess I have to tackle? Perhaps your job doesn't involve any mess?"

He's teasing her, for Pete's sake. This impertinent stranger is teasing her. Time to end this unfortunate encounter.

"I wasn't staring at you, Mr.—"

"McCandless. Phil McCandless. And you are . . . ?"

"I wasn't staring at you, Mr. McCandless. I was staring at the window. I used to have a red-framed window in my home. It too was shattered by hail, and seeing this reminded me of it. That's all. Very pleasant to meet y—"

"Did it make a big mess?"

This fellow doesn't quit. If she wants to get away, she'll have to be definite. "Not as big a mess as the fifty dead turkeys, pummeled to pabulum and stinking to high heaven."

"Ah. Precisely why I don't mind this mess. Not a corpse in sight." She nods and walks on.

"Good day, Miss No Name," he calls after her.

Over her shoulder, she fixes a peeved look on him.

"I did ask your name," he says, without reproval. "You do have one, don't you?"

Oh, the dead weight of a simple question. To ask a name is to ask who she is, she of no middle name and too many surnames. Who is she?

She draws a deep breath that lifts her to her full, insignificant height. "Analiese Rushton. Fielding. Annie Fielding. Annie."

Helpless.

Annie feels helpless, sitting with Anjanette in her room, watching her disappear as she picks at the hem of her sleeve. Anjie is sinking again, part of a cycle, a cruel carousel of the spirit that slows down, speeds up, slows down again, but never stops to let her off. Anjanette won't be at work today, tomorrow, longer. They won't let her in the kitchen with the knives when she's like this. Her fellow inmates will know she's down by the absence of her brioche on the breakfast table. Anjie's a master at it. From time to time, someone comments that they must be the only state-hospital inmates in the country eating French pastry every day. "It's not pastry," Anjanette sighs, every time. "It's bread." Sometimes plain, sometimes sweet with fruit, sometimes savory with flecks of left-over bacon or ham. Sometimes, the head cook confided to Annie, Anjanette talks to herself in singsong French. "*Pensez-vous que ceci a besoin de plus de beurre, Grand-mère?*" The cook shrugged. But Annie knows what the cook appears not to, that Grand-mère was ninety-six before she gave in and taught Anjie the jealously guarded secrets of her brioche, on solemn promise that they would never be revealed. So Anjanette Ballamont works alone.

Annie can't help but wonder if Grand-mère shared more than a recipe with her granddaughter. Anjie's is a sad, incorrigible malady. She was here when Annie arrived and she'll be here after Annie leaves. For her own protection, they say. On days like this, she'll sit by the window and write page after page of letters. "I'm a terrible correspondent," she'll scold herself. "I've let this go entirely too long. They must be wondering." Annie doesn't ask who must be wondering about Anjanette, whether the letters ever go out, whether replies ever come. Today Anjanette slides three envelopes into Annie's hand. Would she be kind enough to drop these at the post office on her way to work?

Annie will have to dash to make it to the post office, a low-slung brick building on the edge of the grounds, and still get to work on time. She squeezes Anjie's hand and slips the letters into her pocket. They are thin. Very thin. She wonders if there's anything inside the envelopes. She'll hand them to the postmistress without looking at the addresses.

The morning dawned pastel and indolent, but as Annie nears the post office, the sky darkens and closes in. The first huge drops plop at her heels on the path and give way to the deluge as she ducks in the door. The bloated clouds disgorge a downpour that erases the view a few feet beyond the windows. So much for getting to work on time.

Annie flicks a few drops from her hair and passes Anjanette's letters over the counter to the postmistress, whose face matches the building, squat and ruddy. When she turns to go to the window, she sees that she's not alone. The fellow from the maintenance shop watches the rain with a look of patient abiding. Annie can't remember his name and isn't in the mood for chat.

"We must stop meeting like this," he says.

"Okay," she agrees, without inflection.

"That was a joke. You can smile. You know—mouth curves up?"

"I guess my joking skills are rusty."

"We can work on that. Some cloudburst, eh? Reminds me of home."

"It clears the air."

His eyes follow a squirrel scooting up a tree. He nods but doesn't reply. She feels a pang of remorse for being abrupt with him. He's only being friendly. The rain rakes the brick walls. She prods herself into asking, "Where is home?"

"I misspoke. I've been here the better part of twenty years, so this is home. But I grew up in Oregon. Portland."

"Oregon? May I ask, have you ever seen the ocean?"

"Oh yes. Seen it, heard it, smelled it, felt it."

"What's it like?"

"Wet."

She has to laugh. "I deserved that."

"Noisy, and numbingly cold. You have to keep moving or it'll be less than a minute before you can't feel your feet. But it's grand. The vastness of it. Make a bigger man than me feel small."

Annie brushes her hands on her skirt. "Well. I certainly don't need another thing in this world making me feel small."

He's a little past average height, pushing tall. His comfortable green eyes sit low under brows that have grayed before his ash-blond hair, giving his face an open look not unlike the prairie around them. "Everyone should see it once in their life. I tell my children I sometimes imagined a language in the pounding of the surf. All that noise must be trying to tell us something."

Annie can't think of a response. The storm outside lets up a bit.

"And you?" Phil asks. "Where are you from and what have you seen that I haven't?"

"I'm from Iowa. There's nothing to tell, unless you find corn and cows fascinating."

"On a dinner plate? Very." He doesn't seem to notice that she isn't amused. "Every place has something to recommend it."

Annie leans against the window frame, infused with weariness. Too steep, the arc from Anjanette's despondency to this man's banter. "We had a farm," she sighs. It's too early in the morning to be this weary. "Like everyone else's farm. What's to recommend?"

"You've been away for a while," he says. "When you think of something, I hope you'll tell me."

"I won't."

"Now, that's not fair. I answered your question."

"In my experience, life isn't fair, Mr. McTavish."

"You won't get an argument out of me on that. Guess I'll have to learn about Iowa somewhere else."

The storm has blown by. The sun gets to work drying the mud while the ground competes to soak up what it can. Phil wishes Annie a pleasant day. She waits for him to disappear between the buildings. The postmistress clears her throat and hurls Annie an eloquent look.

"His name is McCandless, not McTavish. Mr. McCandless knows a great deal about how unfair life can be."

From a safe distance Annie watches him apply glazing putty to the four-pane windows, starting with neat triangles in the corners. The red paint glides over the casings in smooth strokes. She might find the rhythm of his work soothing, if she allowed it. She approaches, not an inch closer than she need come to make herself heard.

"I'm sorry I got your name wrong, Mr. McCandless. Why didn't you correct me?"

"I'll correct you now. It's Phil. Please don't worry yourself about it, Annabel."

Like Cal, he is, joshing his way out of any situation.

"That's gracious of you." She forces a smile but can't help backing up a step. "Have your children started back to school?"

She resents how she's always having to small-talk her way around this man but feels she owes him a minute or two of courtesy to make up for her gaffe with his name.

"Yes, ma'am," he says. "They're already looking forward to Thanksgiving. Their favorite holiday. No church, no fancy clothes, no listening to tedious speeches in the park."

"Bravo to them. I dislike church, fancy clothes, and tedious speeches myself." She expects him to register disapproval, but he just smiles with an *oh well* nod.

"They've learned to tolerate Easter. My mother always buys a suit for my son and matching dresses for the girls, because they're twins, but not the look-alike kind. The girls never like the dresses, and the boy's suit always makes me laugh. Double knees and double seat, as if a nine-year-old is going to wear through his britches sitting in church." He brings out his billfold and fishes out a photo. "Here they are last year. Aren't they stoic?"

Annie studies the photo. The twins look to be about six. "No wonder the girls don't like the dresses. There's about twice as much to them as there needs to be." She slaps the photo with the back of her fingers, unable to imagine Nora in such confinement. "These so-called 'fashionable wide collars.' Stiff as a dead cat, all the way to the elbows. It makes them look as if they're about to take flight."

Phil leans on his thigh. "That is exactly what Molly said." He taps one of the girls in the photo. "Threatened to start honking during Mass."

"It's too bad. With some thought, the dresses could be reworked into something they could get some use out of."

"Reworked? How?"

"Hmm." She holds the photo facing him, tracing one of the dresses with her pinkie. "Replace the obnoxious collar with a slim band of fabric around the neck. A white yoke on a child's dress is silly, as if she's never going to eat in it? Then I'd get rid of the soutache braid around the waist." One corner of her mouth ticks up in a sneer. "Three rows, goodness, why not just bind the child with rope?" She's warmed to her task, her voice ringing with annoyance. "Then I'd replace the white cuffs with a fold-back cuff, more comfortable for a child than having all that lace and buttons chewing at her wrist."

"That's marvelous." Phil regards the photo as if seeing it for the first time. "I would never have thought of all that."

"You've never had to wear a ready-made dress. My own daughter taught herself to use a scissors before she was three because she wanted to cut the cuffs off an offending dress. When I saw what she'd done and how she rolled up the sleeves, I all but fainted. My husband wears his sleeves rolled up, exactly this far"— she indicates her forearm—"and pressed, just so."

Phil smiles. "Like father, like daughter?"

"Yes, and it's the strangest thing, because they've never met."

It slipped out before she considered how it might strike him. The curveball, low and inside. She drops the photo of his children into his hand.

"Your children are lovely. You are blessed." The crickets drone like sewing machines as she hurries away.

She has to pass him on her way to work each morning, and she has to admit that there are worse ways to start the day. Phillip McCandless is the most even-tempered person Annie has ever met. He's the seventy-two-degree spring day, the level whose bubble is always right in the middle. Annie pictures his wife as the same, managing the children and the home with effortless charm. Her name would be Rosemary or Mary Rose. Their house would be white clapboard with green shutters and pink cone flowers blooming along the front. A cat on the hearth and grandparents who bring fudge for Christmas. A fortunate family, although a life to which Annie no longer aspires. A vine-encrusted two-room cottage with a few efficient spiders is a picture that settles her soul.

He asks, "How is your daughter? Cut up any clothes lately?"

"Not that I know of," Annie replies. *I haven't seen her in months. Eternity.*

He says he's still smiling about that one, and by the way, how does her daughter feel about hair ribbons? His daughter Jeannie asked him why she has to wear a bow half the size of her head, and Molly wants to know who makes up the rules about what people have to wear.

"Such questions," Annie laughs. "In matters of ladies' fashion, they should ask their mother."

"They can't ask their mother." His ever-genial tone belies the words. His own curveball.

"Oh. I'm truly sorry."

"Thank you."

The day is hot, but a cool, curious peace drapes itself around Annie. She runs a hand up her forearm, breathing in what might have been a strained moment but instead feels companionable. Loss is best understood by those who have lived it.

"Are you as tired as I am," he asks, "of people telling you that things always work out in the end?"

She can barely answer.

"That's a problem I've never had."

The job is done. Rain falls against the shiny new windows. "This is something," Phil remarks. "We're positively soggy here and they say the rest of the state is parched to crumbs." He makes a few notes on a form. "I'm taking the tunnel over to Main. Want to come along?"

Annie is done for the day. Sure, why not.

"What is it about tunnels?" he muses as he packs up his tools. "A purely utilitarian solution to moving things around in inconvenient weather. What could be more mundane than carting laundry between buildings?" But, he rambles on in the careless manner Annie has grown accustomed to, leave it to a schoolyard bully to scare his daughter to death with stories about bodies of murdered groundskeepers and skeletons of patients stashed in the tunnels, chained to the walls. Told her if her daddy ever didn't come home from work, it would be on account of the tunnel goblins who got him and stuffed him into an overhead pipe where he drowned in sewage. He did come home late not long after to find his daughter crying so hard she couldn't breathe, trembling fingers twisting and clawing her stockings to ribbons.

"For the love of heaven," Annie cries. "Did the little monster describe the trolls barricading the entrances?" Tunnels under grounds like this are common. In the hospital library, she's pored over pictures of the orphans' home, trying to imagine how Nora will feel trudging the dank tunnels from dormitory to dining hall come winter.

"It's not completely fanciful," Phil says. "My hometown, Portland, has a system of tunnels running to the basements of hotels and saloons, for unloading and storing goods that come in on the ships. The legend is that underground Portland was a thriving slave trade. Bar owners in cahoots with ship captains. Got their victims liquored up or knocked out, then dropped 'em through trapdoors into holding cells. Sold 'em to ships on the waterfront. Shanghaied, they called it."

"I wonder if there was at least one," Annie says, "who thought that a life at sea was more exciting than what he left. Adventure, ports of call, seeing the world."

"Confinement, seasickness, lousy food, filth. Insufferable, inescapable shipmates."

"Why, Phil, that's the most acerbic talk I've ever heard from you."

"I like my freedom. My grandfather spun vivid enough stories that for a while I believed in tunnel goblins more than I believed in Santa Claus. So I sat up in my squashy ol' chair and let my daughter sleep in my lap that night. This tunnel here"—he snaps his tool case shut—"is just a way to stay out of the rain."

The chill air of the passageway encircles them. A few yards in, Annie's knees buckle and she reaches for the wall. "I can't do this," she breathes.

He reaches for her with "Are you ill?" but she shrinks out of reach.

"No. But this isn't a good idea. For you." *Say it, say it. Already waited too long.* "The appearance of consorting with an inmate. It could hurt you."

"Inmate?" He moves closer and looks her full in the face. She doesn't flinch. "You're an inmate?"

"I'm sorry. I should have told you. The last thing I want to do is endanger your job."

"You're an inmate?" he repeats with a hitch of chuckle. "An inmate! If that's not the personification of irony!" He starts to laugh but it catches on his breath. "If you're 'insane' or 'feebleminded,' I've been breathing turpentine fumes too long. Thank you, Annie. You've validated my long-held belief that the zookeepers here are stranger than the animals."

For starters, he tells her, most of the staff regard workmen like him as part of the scenery. Astonishing, the things he's seen and heard as if he weren't in the room. Attendants who flush toilets with their feet and switch on lights with their elbows for fear of "catching" something. A doctor here has been waiting for years for the letter from Harvard offering him a teaching position. He's sure the mail clerks, all of them, all these years, intercept the letters, under threat from the superintendent, who can't afford to lose him.

As she does many a time in the face of Phil's musings, Annie submits, lets them lap at her edges. But can't he see how distressing it is to her, his freewheeling derision of her safe world?

"But my favorite," he says, with the bravado of a storyteller reaching his climax, "is the housekeeper who counts the supplies over and over. Counts by ones, by twos, by fives, organizing and reorganizing the shelves. Two bedpans went missing once, and she threatened to ferret out the perpetrator who was trying to make her look bad and have her pay docked." His chuckle carries a tinge of pity. "I found one of the missing items myself. An inmate used it to take water to a starving stray dog."

Annie, eyes locked shut, fists pinning her chest to the wall, prays for a tunnel goblin to unlatch a trapdoor and shanghai her away. Did he actually say, "I like my freedom"? Hasn't he noticed that she hasn't moved since he started talking? After an age, he trails off.

She lets her muteness speak for her. Faint voices echo farther down the tunnel. The muscles between her legs tense; her jaw clamps, trapping a sliver of cheek and sending a thread of blood down her throat.

"Annie Fielding," he says, "if you're a lunatic, I'd best sign myself in."

She holds her breath as he moves past her. When his footsteps fade, she blinks, breathes again, and bolts up the stairs into the calmative arms of the afternoon sun.

She's sure that once he's had time to reflect, her revelation will end their odd relationship. It should, if he has any sense. But his demeanor doesn't change. Their exchanges last no more than a few minutes. She's always on her way somewhere when they meet, and never fully stops moving.

He doesn't pry, just slips in a question here and there, so gently phrased she's not sure they're questions. Even this she resists but nevertheless hears herself answer, a sentence or two, handing him jigsaw pieces of her life because he's so unrelievedly congenial, she can't find a way to dodge.

So now he knows. Her daughter isn't here. She's still married, to a husband who is out of the picture. She'll leave on parole in a matter of weeks, as soon as a work arrangement firms up. About the circumstances that brought her here, she gives him three words: "female in nature."

"That's a relief," he says. "So you're not the exiled queen of Persia, surrounded by hidden serfs who will jump to your protection should I overstep my humble place?"

The idea that anyone, even imaginary beings, would offer her protection is so far-fetched, she stops listening. There never will be any such person or people. She has only herself. It should make her sad, but she doesn't have any of that left.

She never asks about his past. It's an old habit she doesn't care to break, and she knows as much as she can bear. Too painful the counterpoint, his motherless children to her years of childless motherhood. The days pass while she waits for her parole, listening to Phil's ramblings about life in Copper Creek. He knows most every business in town, from the merchants, government officials, physicians, and attorneys to the café workers, piano tuners, mechanics, and even the woman who runs a house to care for the children of the red-light district.

Yes, he knows a lot of employers. It must be the reason Annie's heart beats faster when he asks her if she'll meet him in the meadow behind the dairy this coming Saturday morning. There's something he'd like to talk to her about.

25

Annie thought about bringing one of Anjanette's brioches but decided it wouldn't be appropriate for a business meeting. She's certain Phil is coming to discuss work opportunities, and how appreciative she is of that, since the hospital is taking forever and a day to come up with something suitable.

They sit on a burly log at the edge of the meadow. She waits for talk of shops, farms, cafés, offices.

Instead he fixes his sight across the tall grass rustling in the morning breeze, and begins in his usual unhurried way.

"My grandparents left Ireland in 1856 and spent twenty years in Wisconsin. Then a neighbor family moved to Portland and wrote them a glowing letter about the mild climate. My grandmother decided she'd like to live in a place where winter didn't require such a pile of quilts on the bed that she had to wake her husband for help if she wanted to roll over."

"Imagine," Annie returns politely, thinking this an unusual lead-in to an employment opportunity. "And Portland is such a place?"

"Yes indeed. My grandfather and my father were jacks-of-all-trades and had no trouble finding more work than they could handle. Carpenter, painter, glazier, bricklayer. Granddad had lived through the potato famine. He swore before his own mother Mary and whatever saints cared to uncover their ears that in this country, his family would never go to bed hollow."

Annie clasps her hands in her lap and nods sympathetically. "That's one thing about growing up on our farm. Even during hard times, we never went hungry."

"Well, what do you know? You finally told me something about Iowa." He taps the air with his fist, signaling a victory.

Annie shifts her weight on the log and tries for something more than a ship's-figurehead smile. Where on earth is this leading?

"My father called it a two-step of destiny, that my mother's Swiss family took the identical path across the country. When Mom spotted Dad at the Valentine's Day basket dinner, she recognized him as the fellow who'd laid the hearth in their Wisconsin parlor. Am I boring you?"

"Of course not."

"Your hands."

"Oh." They lie in her lap, where she's braided her fingers tightly. "Idle hands, the devil's workshop, you know."

A scuffle of claws and grass and the rising scent of animal fear ambush them from behind. A pheasant shoots from the reeds, streaking across the field with a raggedy coyote on its tail feathers. Startled, Annie slips from the log, driving a hand against the shaggy wood to break the fall. Phil grabs her free hand to help her up. Against her will, her blood races, this first touch in years from a man who isn't a doctor. She rights herself quickly with a firm "Thanks, I'm all right."

The pheasant and the coyote disappear into the sun's glare. "I hardly know who to root for," Phil remarks.

"The pheasant wants to live," Annie says.

"So does the coyote."

"I know," she sighs. "I've killed and eaten a few birds in my time."

"And I killed a swan," he says, the word tipped in black like the bird itself. "Figuratively."

Annie pins the inside of her lower lip between her teeth. Would it be terribly rude to say, *Let's get to why we're here?* Her hand stings where she ground it into the log, and a long splinter has pierced a channel through the ball of her thumb. She yanks it out and presses the skin to bleed the wound. Phil offers a handkerchief. It's clean, she notes, warming with self-reproach that she would think it might be otherwise.

"And now you're here?" she prompts him.

He clears his throat. "Dad had a brother who stayed behind in Butte on the trip out. He invited me to visit. When I landed here, I did bounce a few times, from the shock of the climate and the general unruliness. But my notes home intrigued Dad enough to say, 'What the heck, we'll join you. We could do with a change.' He didn't get the chance to find out if he could have been happy here. Pleurisy, bronchitis, pneumonia. He was dead within a year."

"Oh, Phil." Annie reaches a hand toward him, but drops it to rest on the log between them. "What a shock that must have been. Losing my own father . . . well, it certainly ended a chapter of my life."

"For me, the opposite." His hands hang between his knees in upended prayerfulness. "It started the next chapter." He draws a deep breath as Annie does the same. The air tastes of smoke and lavender. "Mother wanted Dad buried with family," he says. "I took him home to Portland, handled the arrangements and other business, which kept me there through the winter. I wasn't pleased about it. You know what it's like when 'home' doesn't fit anymore."

"I certainly do." Annie sits straighter and smiles invitingly. He's taken donkey's years to weave a story that Adam would have laid out in three minutes. But at long last, it sounds as if he's nearing the point.

"My wife's name was Diana. She was authentic Oregon pioneer stock, and oh, did she hate the stories, especially her grandmother's endless reliving of the Molalla warriors bursting into settlers' homes when the men were out and demanding that the women cook for them. Devouring everything in sight, then leaping onto the table and dancing on the remains."

Dancing on the remains. What in the name of an unholy nightmare, Annie grapples to understand, does Phil's dearly departed wife have to do with this conversation? Her fingers set to trembling like springs.

On he rambles. "Her mother died when she was eight. Her pa parked her and her half brother Jack with an aunt and uncle. Said he was a cowpuncher, not a babysitter."

Annie stands abruptly, throwing one hand over the other like a fire blanket. "Phil. You're scaring me. I don't want to know all this. I know Diana is dead, and I'm terribly sorry for your loss."

His brow twitches, nudging his forehead higher into his hat.

"Diana isn't dead," he says.

Annie looks away from him, listing under the mounting weight of his story.

"Please don't go," he pleads, half rising from the log but sitting down again when she backs a step away. "I do have a reason for telling you."

"Quickly, please?" she begs. She hugs herself with arms crossed at the waist.

He picks a blade of buffalo grass at his feet and draws the sharp edge across his fingertips. "After that, Jack was all she had of her mother, the one to whom she cried out her feelings of desertion. She was ten when he left home. She finished high school, then hightailed it up to Portland, and took a job. I met her at a Valentine's dance."

"What a coincidence," Annie says, feeling like a child expected to recite.

"Quite. I backed into her with a glass of strawberry punch. We left the party and went for a walk along the river."

A walk along the river. Annie closes her eyes and feels for the log again. *The evening star, multiplied by undulating water, is like . . .*

"Bright sparks of fire ascending," she murmurs.

"Say again?"

"Thoreau."

"Haven't read him. Should I?"

"I'm hardly one to hand you any shoulds." Annie brushes a thumb under the hollow of her cheek. Her face has gone stiff.

His thumb traces the air, unconsciously mirroring her motion. "I'd been clear with Diana about returning to Montana. So after our first child was born, I came back and found work in Copper Creek." He gestures toward the hills. "I loved Montana even more once I had a family. I had the kids up on ice skates before their fourth birthdays. The flooding of town commons every year on Thanksgiving is one of our favorite things. In the summers, we'd float down the creek in inner tubes or spelunk through the caves up in the hills.

"We lived comfortably enough, enjoyed decent health and pleasant neighbors. I thought life was good. If Diana seemed quiet, well, she had her hands full, running herd on the children and me. But I had misread her." Annie flinches as his voice downshifts. "She loathed our life here. One winter she remarked that she was waiting for her teeth to shatter. And in the summer, she said, the mosquitoes were large enough to ride out of town.

It came off sounding humorous to me." He shakes his head. "I couldn't believe . . ."

"Montana isn't for everyone," Annie says in a small voice, stepping in front of this freight train of a narrative, knowing it won't stop for her.

He talks faster, shoulders rising and falling. "She detested the town. Half the people are foreigners. She couldn't understand most of them and it made her feel stupid. She started to refuse trips to Butte, where, she said, folks carried guns as commonly as wallets. A few years ago they lynched a union leader, hung him from a bridge. After that she was permanently terrified. Expected to come home and find Indians flattening the food on the kitchen table."

"She told you all this?" Annie interrupts. What sort of man wouldn't take such fears seriously?

"She told me. Not in so many words." The sun hits the side of his face, bronzing his skin to where she can see that he's older than she thought. "I loved my wife. It wasn't fair that she kept the depth of her unhappiness to herself. She left with our baby, Stephen, and her clothes. Jack's letter turned up more than a year later, in a little-used drawer where I was sure to find it, but not right away. He lived alone in a remote cabin outside Laramie. He said, 'We always knew I'm the only person who understands and loves you.'"

Annie, her fingers taut against the base of her throat, fears she may be sick. To leave an infant out of primal fear of self, to answer the temptation of a brother's promise of a second chance, this she's lived and understands. But to leave three children old enough to feel the loss of their mother as a gavel of judgment against them? The plaintive picture show unspools in her head: the children coming home from school to a cold house and a father shocked senseless.

"I'm a churchgoing man who always looked for the good in others," Phil says, "but those dozen words put a silver stake through me."

His crumpled handkerchief has staunched the bleed from Annie's hand. She touches it to her eye, allowing the rim of tears balanced there to rush into the cloth.

Is it for her sake or his that he turns his face away? "The most I could hope for was that word would not get around, or that if it did, folks would be decent enough to hold their tongues for the sake of the children. What I got instead was stark reason to stop believing the best of people." A button on his cuff hangs loose, the tail of the kinked thread dangling. He draws it out, watching it unravel until the button, freed, falls into the grass and disappears. "So that's my story. The truth, the whole truth, and the god-awful truth."

"So help us," Annie says to her shoes.

"Yes, so help us."

Small help it is, but she drives her hand into the grass, her fingers trolling the rough dirt around his feet. Buttons don't vaporize. A half-minute search brings it up. She drops it into his palm and folds his fingers over it.

"Well, that's one less thing lost," he says.

She forces a smile.

"I try not to dwell on how much I've lost," he says, making a fist around the button and resting it on his knee.

Annie looks out across the meadow and sees nothing. Somewhere out there, either a pheasant lies dead or a coyote is hungry. Win. Lose. Life. Death. Right. Wrong. The random duality of it all favors the fatalist. And yet this man beside her, full in the face of loss and wrong, seems the definition of equability.

After a while she asks, "Why did you tell me?"

After a while he answers. "You and I have seen the worst life has to offer. I think we understand each other. I think we would be good together."

And after another while she says, "I'm not often this tongue-tied. But this was not the kind of offer I was expecting."

"What other kind could there have been?"

"Phil, I can't marry you. I don't know if I can love you. That wouldn't be fair to you."

"I think we have both earned the right to define love in any manner we choose. What would be unfair about all of us getting something we need?"

"You seem sure about what you need."

"I am. And I didn't suggest we marry. I don't know that either of us is legally free to marry. I said I thought we would be good together."

So help her, she can't stop her mouth curving upward. She closes her eyes and wonders why she isn't offended. Not in the least. When she sneaks a sideways peek at him, he returns her amused smile.

He stands and offers her a hand up. "Will you walk down this road with me a ways?" He indicates a rutted byway piercing the fields that extend to the horizon on three sides. "I'd like to show you something." When she doesn't move, he slides his hands in his pockets and laughs. "Oh, I get it. I look dangerous. Gonna take advantage of you." He laughs again. "Why do I get the feeling that I'd be the one in peril? I guess that's a chance I'm willing to take."

He's so genuine. After all he's been through. The last thing she wants to do is trust a man again, but how can she do less, when he's been so forthcoming with his trust of her?

"How far?"

"Around the bend, less than half a mile. Scream real loud and they'll hear you in the maintenance shop."

"Where they'll say, 'Ho, Phil McCandless is at it again, out the back road'?"

He toes a crumbling stump in front of them, plants his foot on it. "No, dear, they won't. This will be the first and last time I ask you or any gal. I won't be coming out here after this week. I've taken a job in town with the railroad."

His sincerity stirs something in her, that someone would try to make her feel special again. It's been a long while. It might be all right. It might.

Their first steps are tentative, but they soon fall into an easy gait. The road bends to the right and they pass an abandoned barn with an old bathtub parked in the yard. It might have been white before it slipped into a robe of soft gray grime, molested by oily handprints around the rim. "That," says Phil, "came into the shop to be disposed of, and the guys got to carousing and hauled it out here, aiming to fill it up with moonshine. They thought themselves quite clever. But see the crack near the bottom? Their genius was thwarted."

Annie can't laugh. "These are the guys who will fly to my rescue when I scream real loud?"

"We can go back. This isn't a schoolyard dare."

Annoyance with herself burns pink on her cheeks. She'll have to deal with worse than this man when she leaves the hospital.

"Lead on, Phillip."

They pass through a copse of thornbushes. This isolated corner of the hospital grounds appears exactly like the field behind. Then she notices odd brown creatures poking their heads out of the grass at regular intervals. They cock this way and that, mute and motionless. She gasps when she recognizes the field for what it is. A cemetery. The brown heads are rusted grave markers, smaller than the palm of her hand, knocked askew by years of snowdrifts, critters, wind, and hail. Signposts mark the decades dating back half a century.

She bends to touch a marker. Broken glass covers a card that once bore a name, now only weather-beaten pulp. Here and there, a marble tombstone rises above the grass, a sign that someone held a fond memory of a soul whose life trickled out within the walls of the asylum. But mostly these are avenues of the unremembered.

Standing in this field of the forgotten, Annie can no longer quell memories she's stifled for years, of those who should have been there for her but dissipated into the who-knows-where of their own insular lives. Where is Cal? But for Cal, she would not be in Montana. Jenny, more mother to her than their actual mother was, gone to join Cal and not heard from since. Chase, who said their family farm would always be her home. It's as if, to them, she evaporated. She might be able to bury the pain of that, but she can never forget being forgotten.

Only one person in the whole world, the man who remains at the road as she pushes her way through the knee-high meadow, knows she's here, among the forgotten. She wheels on him, stamps the dead grass as she strides past her dead fellow inmates in the dead quiet that thunders around them.

"Why did you bring me here?" Her arm gestures wildly over the path she's just flattened. What she wants to hurl at him is her white-hot anger, but what comes instead are tears.

"I wanted you to see where you didn't end up," he says. "You walked into this field on your own two feet and you will walk out of here on your own two feet. You could ask for more, but not much would matter more than that. I admire you for all you've survived."

The wind skims across the grass and the whole field waves in agreement.

There's not much that matters more.

Her parole is at hand. Her time is here. She'll do it alone, and the thought doesn't scare her. This time there will be no mistakes, no partnerships. She'll work hard, the one thing she can do that's never been in question, squeeze every nickel until the buffalo shits. She'll reclaim her daughter and both their lives.

It's time to do things she's never done, or at least hasn't done for too long. On her own two feet. She picks up her skirt and runs, right past Phillip McCandless, through the break in the thorn-bushes, and down the road. It feels fantastic.

"Annie," he hollers. "I'm sorry!" He starts after her, but she laughs at the road ahead. He won't catch her, moving as she is at a remarkable pace.

She zips past the abandoned barn and the forlorn bathtub. Before she rounds the last bend in the road, she stops and draws an expansive breath. She wants to make sure he understands she's running to something, not away. "Phil," she calls, flushed with excitement and not the least bit winded. "If I never see you again— thank you."

Around the bend, she runs on, the sight of him lost. But he told her true: voices carry a long way over the unbroken field. His finds her.

"You'll see me again!"

26

When she first lays eyes on Pearson Creamery ranch, the rest of the world retreats. Ten miles up a rough road outside of Butte, it thrives in the able hands of elderly cousins Will and Nels and their corpulent Bengal cat, who meets them as Will's truck rattles to a stop in front of a long shed. "That's William Howard Taft," he tells Annie, scratching the cat's chin with a three-fingered hand. "Our grandmother Francesca always said a beastie will tell you its name if you pay attention. Howie here, he chased a moth into the bathtub and couldn't get out. And here's Nels."

Nels pushes his hat back to smile at her through deep-set eyes. With a fatherly arm hovering but not touching, he guides her up the road toward a cluster of buildings that look as if they've always been there. A tribe of Pearson cousins runs the ranch and creamery operations alongside an ensemble of women parolees from the state hospital. "All are here because of our grandmother," he says. "The fellers you'll work with here are our kin." And Will nods, "Aye. Wish we'd had an opening for you sooner, but you're here now." Annie doesn't ask more.

The women live in a sprawling cottage up the hill from the main house. Nels cracks the front door and shouts, "Man about!" He waits a minute before entering, holding the door for Annie and her beloved brown satchel. A parlor and kitchenette form the front of the house. "Tea and biscuits, that sort of thing," Nels indicates. "Meals at the main house."

The rest of the cottage has been sculpted into a warren of small rooms. Nels leads Annie up a varnished wood staircase. "Not much elbow room, but to many of our ladies, a bit of privacy is more precious than the Hope Diamond." They stop at an oak door at the end of a hall. Nels holds it open for her. "This is yours for as long as you're with us. Trust you'll find it comfortable."

Nothing is more precious than hope, Annie thinks. She steps over the threshold and is greeted by a velour easy chair and quartered-oak book table with glass-ball feet. Behind it is a row of double school-house hooks topped by a long shelf. A cupboard holding towels and bedding hangs over a two-drawer dresser. Annie sets her satchel on the robust iron bed with a quilted coverlet and a gray blanket folded at the foot. She turns to say thank you, but Nels is already slipping out. "Washroom is at the end of the hall. Supper at six," he tells her. "Someone will call for you. You must rest now."

She needs less than the count of fifty to put her things right. A few clothes. A tortoiseshell comb, a silver thimble in a rose glass jar.

The room enfolds her as she lowers herself into the velour chair. She thinks it should smell of something, of cows or grass or the years' worth of stale dust settled into its steel springs, or at least some hint of the women who sat here before her. But the cushions give to her shape and the chair smells as blank as the pages of stationery Anjanette slipped her before she left. *You'll write to me?* Outside the window, the milking barns huddle at the base of a hill. An anise swallowtail butterfly waltzes in languorous swoops toward the horizon. Annie follows its flight until it vanishes. She can see all the way to the Boulder Mountains.

One thing in the room must be changed, though. The quilted coverlet has jarred free a deep-rooted memory, its pattern too like Jenny's bridal quilt. Row upon row of symmetrical trees, motionless, bereft of the life and the sense of family they're supposed to symbolize. The gray blanket will have to do as a bedcover. Annie folds the quilt to the size of the cupboard shelf. Then, in a lower corner, she spots an embroidered square:

Remember me
Lily Stanhope

In the opposite corner, another square:

Barnstable, Massachusetts
1881

Annie sees now that the quilt blocks aren't trees, but lilies. Once-brilliant yellows and greens have faded to browns. Lily's quilt has traveled more than two thousand miles over forty years. How it got here Annie may or may not ask someday, but what she does know is that a woman named Lily, whose last name ends in hope, wants someone to hold her in memory.

She smooths the coverlet over the bed.

A handful of sheep roam the nearby range. "That," Nels tells Annie, "is the Court."

There's a word Annie doesn't like. She bites the inside of her lip.

Nels props elbows on the fence and points. "The ram there is Hizzoner, Oliver Wendell Holmes. The largest ewe there, she's M'Lady. The others are M'Lass, M'Lucky Stars—Stars for short—and M'Goodness! When you get to know her, you'll understand why we added the exclamation point to her name. The others are their offspring. The Court strayed from the ranch over yon some years ago, busted out when the herder drove the flock to winter range. Ever worked around sheep?"

"Not that I can recall," Annie says. How would she have forgotten such a stench, like the morning breath of a long, sickly sleep?

"Sheep need a large amount of range, but these never wander off," Nels continues. "We're not sure how they survive. They seem to eat the same grass over and over again."

One of the sheep is darker than the rest. From the distance, Annie can't tell if it's filthier or if it's a real live proverbial black sheep.

"Our ladies here begged to keep them," Nels continues. "Saw it as a yarn supply dropped from heaven. The sheep are Rambouillets. The wool is so superb even I can tell."

"The horns are lovely," Annie murmurs, holding her hand out to Hizzoner and tracing the translucent spiral.

"We worked it out with the owners. Our gals get their wool, and the rest gets sold for upkeep of the Court. Vet fees, mostly. Some for help with the shearing and the lambing, maintaining the pens. I think we come out even, but we've never paid sharp heed."

The black sheep detaches itself from the flock and trots to within two feet of Annie, inspecting her with all the expression she imagines a sheep can muster. He is an intriguing animal, all of a single color. Wool, skin, eyes, nose, tongue, hooves. This close, she sees that he's not black, but more the color of bittersweet chocolate.

"That's Henry. Henry David Thoreau. Marches to a different drummer."

Annie breaks her silence. "Do you send the wool out for milling?"

"No, I'm afraid not. We have carding tools and a spinning wheel here. It's crude, but I'll bet the dime and the doughnut that you'll catch on fast."

"Has anyone spoken for Henry's wool?"

Nels smiles. "Funny you should ask. He wouldn't let anyone near him with a shears for several years. Got to be the size of Crazy Peak. But this past summer he let us take thirteen pounds of grease wool off of him. Scoured down to half that, but it's still here somewhere. You knit, I take it?"

"You take it," Annie repeats under her breath. Henry grunts, mouth twisting into a toppled question mark. He lumbers off, cutting a brisk path through the flock, tail twitching like a frog on coals. Annie smiles after him.

"Yes, I knit," she says to Nels. "It's something no one's yet managed to take from me."

December 16, 1921

My dearest Nora,

I've been with the Pearsons about two months now, and I like it here. Besides the cows, they also keep a few sheep. I'm learning to spin wool into yarn. That's how I was able to make this sweater for you. The wool is from a sheep named Henry. It's the color of dark chocolate, isn't it? Nora, when you put your arms into the arms of the sweater, think of it as a hug from me, keeping you warm and close to my heart until we can be together again.

So much love,
Mama

February 13, 1922

Dear Mrs. Fielding,

Your daughter Nora is greatly enjoying the handsome sweater you sent. I extend my admiration of your workmanship. The sweater is the envy of many here.

We have a minor problem, however. Nora has taken to the sweater as a second skin. She most obstinately refuses to remove it, even at bedtime, nor will she allow it to be laundered. Nora has always been the most agreeable and cooperative of children. We don't wish to coerce her in this matter, but we do have standards and rules. Might you send a letter suggesting her compliance?

Further, with utmost respect, we have another request. Should you ever find yourself with the time, materials, and inclination, there are many children here whose lives would be cheered in both body and soul by a similar sweater of their own. Your metaphor of the sweater as a loving embrace has touched everyone here, right down to our youngest.

Yours truly,
J. Gideon Rowan
President, State Orphans' Home

February 14, 1922

Nora dear,

You must let the staff wash your sweater. I've made you this light muffler to wear while the sweater is being laundered. It's like a hug too.

So much love,
Mama

February 16, 1922

Dear Mr. Rowan,

I've instructed Nora to allow you to launder the sweater. You will please allow her to sleep with it. In exchange, my colleagues and I here at the Pearson Creamery would be happy to provide the children in your care with sweaters as our time permits.

Yours truly,
Analiese Fielding

Ancient leather portfolios inscribed *Francesca Magruder Pearson* fill a brass-edged wooden shelf, each folder bulging with dozens of knitting patterns covered in notes that sometimes exceed the length of the pattern itself.

The Stonington Shetland shawl fascinates Annie. *Patience! Perseverance!* Francesca has scrawled across the top of the page. *READ the directions. All is—*

The corner of the page is torn away. All is what?

The pattern's exacting mathematical progression captivates Annie. It starts and ends with a single stitch on the needle. The first cast-on stitch increases each row, grows to a triangle, then decreases each row, tapering to a square. A flange sprouts from the corner of the square, another develops by picking up the side stitches of the first one, and so on.

Annie's finger travels the angles along with the directions.

From the original corner, after the completion of the fourth flange, the needles work their way around the whole thing, creating a lace edging that ends with a stitch decrease down to a single stitch, back where it started. *The shawl,* Francesca wrote, the tall letters tailing off like musical notes, *is both graceful and rugged, deceptively delicate but warm as brandy and sturdy as history. So finespun was the yarn, I entertained the children by pulling the completed shawl through my wedding ring.*

With the color and sheen of molasses, Henry's wool reflects light as no ordinary yarn. On the streets of Butte, Annie's Stonington shawl catches the eye of the high-style wife of a local copper king. Annie notices the woman following her after she's left the library, hurrying to meet Nels for the ride back to the dairy. When Annie stops and turns, the woman rushes forward, gloved hands clutched in front of her bosom.

"Your shawl," she exclaims breathlessly, "is the most captivating thing I've seen in years." She has to have it, as a wedding gift for her Boston niece's trousseau. "It will be the talk of the family on the East Coast. They will all want one. Does a hundred dollars sound fair? If not, you can name your price."

A hundred dollars? They will all want one? Annie scans the woman's face to see if it's a mean-spirited joke. She'd happily walk home cold for that amount of money.

Annie offers to wash and wrap the shawl and deliver it when Will or Nels next comes to town.

The woman ("Mrs. Holliday, but you must call me Paula") needs it sooner than that. Her driver will bring her out to the ranch.

"A hundred dollars? Holy Ruth-at-the-well!" The cousins slap each other's shoulders. "Forty years makin' ice cream and we find out we're in the wrong business."

Annie feels that at least half the money is rightfully theirs. Henry is theirs; the wool is theirs.

But the work is hers, they say.

Annie has a proposition. She lays out two sheets of paper covered with figures. "The Stonington shawl takes only a few ounces of wool, if spun finely enough. One fleece would yield more shawls than I could produce in a decade. I spent more than three months making the finespun shawl. But a little more wool, for a heavier yarn, would still yield a glamorous shawl, in much less time." Working diligently, she could produce half a dozen shawls per year. Mrs. Call-Me-Paula Holliday already indicated there would be ample buyers. She'll offer another shawl to Mrs. Holliday at an extremely attractive price in exchange for her agreeing to wear it around town—live advertising.

Annie waits while the cousins look over her numbers. Then, with a deep breath, she puts forth her question. "If I can, in this manner, make the sheep operation pay, might I bring my daughter here to be with me? Nora is a personable and sensible child. She's helpful and uncomplaining." Nels shifts in his chair with thumbs hooked in his pockets while Will works an earlobe. She rushes on, "The staff at the children's home will attest to this. I will do everything in my power to ensure my daughter doesn't interfere with the work of the dairy."

When Will gets up and heads for the door, her heart plummets. She knew it was a bold gamble, and she's lost. She's overreached their abundant generosity and poisoned the most tranquil stretch of life she's ever known.

"Will," Nels calls after him. "Don't be—"

Will turns on him. "You," he thunders, "who saw no point in keeping our grandmother's dolls. Aren't you glad that I did? Oh yes, and remember her hobby horse?"

"Travelin' Jeff Davis? How could I forget?"

"I kept him, too."

Dear Annie,

Upon receiving your letter stating your wish to retrieve your daughter Nora from the orphans' home, Dr. Rowan wrote to ask my view in the matter.

I was pleased to relate to him the current stability of your health and living situation, and to tell him that I can see no impediment to your reuniting with your daughter at the end of your nine months' parole, when, as you know, you will be officially discharged from our oversight.

All here at the hospital wish you continued success and happiness.

With my regards,
Dr. Daniel Waterford, Superintendent
Montana State Hospital for the Insane

Dear Adam,

I trust this letter finds you in good health and spirits. I write to you in the matter of my Mutual of the Northwest life insurance policy.

I'm sure it will come as no surprise to you that I was unable to continue funding this policy after your payments stopped. It has lapsed and will continue in force on term extension until the current value runs out in about two years.

You are still the beneficiary of the policy. Mutual Northwest offered me the opportunity to change this, and after considerable thought, I declined. I am of the conviction that despite how others may judge your actions, you have at your core the deepest wish for Nora's well-being. Were I to make Nora the beneficiary, I would have to name a trustee. By leaving your name intact as beneficiary, I'm handing you my faith that, should dire circumstances transpire, you are the one I can most count upon to act in the best interests of our daughter.

So I ask that for this period until the policy runs out, you keep your address current with Mutual Northwest. There's no need to contact me. Nora and I are safe and well. She is beautiful of both face and soul, and wise beyond her years. Be proud, Adam. She is the validation that we were right to keep trying. Nothing can change that.

Ever yours,
Analiese Rushton Fielding

27

Using the back of her wrist, Annie dislodges a wisp of hair caught in the corner of her mouth. Her hands are slick with lanolin and filthy with anything that will stick to grease wool. Dirt. Grass. Gnats. Manure. Sheep spittle. She's at the shearing pens this morning because Will and Nels thought it the next step in her schooling as a rancher.

"Given your interest in the wool, you know." Will winked as he said this, and Annie smiled back. If Nora could see her now! But Nora will indeed see her soon, as Annie's parole has dwindled to its last few weeks and arrangements with the orphans' home move toward completion.

This morning Annie wielded her first shepherd's crook, snaring M'Goodness! on the first try, learning firsthand how the ewe earned the exclamation point after her name. She thrashes and bawls like hell below water. The shearers ask Annie to "hold the gal's head tight, if you please." They explain that they're paid by the fleece and the less blood, the better.

"Annie," one of the milking crew calls over to the shearing pen, "a gentleman's pulled up in front. He's asking for Mrs. Fielding."

"Thank you, Aileen. Probably someone from the children's home. I'll wash up and be along shortly."

"I don't think he's from the children's home. I think he's from town. And I don't think you should keep him waiting. Ma'am."

The three shearers chuckle. She leaves the pens and slips in the back door of the cottage, removing her mucky shoes and taking the stairs two at a time. What terrible timing this visitor has managed, and who could it be but a surprise inspector from the orphans' home, come to check on her living arrangements and state of health? She washes her hands and face and hastily repins her hair. In the mirror she suddenly sees the silver strands among the black. She touches the deepening lines in her forehead, notices the softening of her neck. She's at least halfway to being a little old lady.

But I made it this far.

Maybe it's time to bob her hair. Get herself a new signature. Feel the wind on her neck and bangs on her brow. Yes, it's time. Tomorrow. For now she sheds her blouse, reaching for the only one she has that's fit to receive a caller. Downstairs, she swipes a rag across her shoes. A peek from behind the draperies at the front window tells her nothing. A dusty Model T sits halfway between the road and the house. A tallish man in a gray suit and matching fedora stands with his back to the house, hands in pockets, taking in the surroundings.

He turns when he hears Annie's footsteps. She barely recognizes him in a suit.

He looks so courtly.

"Phillip McCandless. This is a surprise."

"It shouldn't be. I told you that you would see me again."

"You did. But that was going on a year ago."

When he removes his hat, the breeze pushes a piece of his hair across his forehead, tickling a strawberry birthmark below his temple that she's never noticed before. "Nine months, seventeen days. But who's counting?"

How sweet he looks. How out of place. This is her place.

"If you say so," she says. "How have you been?" That's what she's supposed to say.

"About the same."

She waits for him to say more, and he too seems to be waiting, unperturbed. She can only dent the silence with a limp "It could be worse, right?"

"Yes. It could be worse."

What now? Her manners seem to have deserted her, and, to her shame, she's not sure she wants them back. It's too early for lunch, but she must offer anyway.

"Would you like to picnic? I can't be away long, but we can go up to the rise, and maybe you can shake the dust from your head before you have to drive back."

"Thank you. That would be nice."

The walk to the house buys her time to shore her resolve. She asks after each of the children, in detail. She asks about his job, in detail. She'll ask anything to keep him from asking about her.

In the kitchen she fills a basket with bread and cheese, a bottle of cold tea, a jar of sweet pickles, and last night's lemon pound cake.

"This is rather potluck," she apologizes.

"This is rather wonderful of you to see me on no notice," he says.

They climb over the rise behind the barns. A startled meadowlark bolts for the sky as they pass. Phil stops to admire the setting. To her, it's a view like any day. The cows, grazing and grinding and swaying. The Court, bleating bloody murder at one another. The range, rolling for miles under the patrol of a few sharp-eyed raptors.

Phil remarks that someone should paint this. "Where's Charlie Russell when you need him?"

Such a city boy. Never been close enough to cows to whiff them, their redolent clouds of methane and their muck-streaked behinds; then he wouldn't be as enchanted. But she has to be polite. "How far did you come?" she asks.

"About thirty miles. That last ten, real kidney-shakers."

"How did you find me?"

"It would be romantic to tell you that I had to go to heroic lengths. But I didn't. I know people at the hospital."

"Me too. Too many."

She busies herself setting out the lunch things, spreading a tartan blanket on the ground. When the food and small talk run out and the first of the afternoon shadows tilt their way, he says, "We could sit here all day and you'd never ask me why I came. Am I right?"

"I can't sit here all day, and I know why you came."

"I suppose you do. I can get pound cake in town." When she doesn't respond, he plunges on. "The last time I saw you, you were at a dead sprint. Part of me hopes you found what you were running to, and part of me hopes you didn't."

"I'm happy here. My daughter will be joining me in the next few weeks, and I'm working on a business opportunity. For me, that's a lot."

"It is a lot. It's terrific. I dare to hope it means you might be ready to consider something even better."

She tries to tuck a soiled patch of her skirt hem under her knees, then pulls it back. Why hide it? "Phil, I can't play coy. I remember every word you said. That you think we understand each other. That we would be good together. That we should make our own rules."

"I'm ecstatic that you remember."

She jabs at the space between them with a pinprick of a sigh. She has no kindly way to put it: she doesn't have anything to offer him, certainly not what he deserves. "I'm sorry. I don't have the answer you want. The thought of a partnership makes my blood run colder."

"It chills me to hear you refer to your marriage as if *partnership* is a dirty word. Partnerships can be fulfilling and constructive."

"Oh, constructive, right. Starlight River Market Farm was a constructive partnership. He was the grower. I was the killer."

"That seems an unfairly brutal way of looking at it."

"But that's how it was." Why is he forcing her to remember? "The celebrated Adam Fielding! He won more prizes than anyone at the county fairs, the best-in-show awards at the state fair. Beans, cabbages, cucumbers, pumpkins, melons, horseradish, and a Hubbard squash so immense it scared the birds away. Citrons, blood beets, eggplant." Her voice climbs with each item added to the list. "Kale, chard, celery, and more varieties of onions than you've got fingers."

"I'm not sure what some of those things are," Phil jokes, but she's wound up like an eight-day clock and doesn't hear him.

"Mr. Fielding won so many prizes we had no room for them. Furniture. Farm equipment. Tools. Business letterhead. Fancy harness sets. A rifle and enough ammo to down every critter in the county." She rages on. "Meanwhile, over on the *fowl* end of the very successful Starlight River Market Farm, Mrs. Fielding is the foreman of the poultry business because, boy, does she have a way with birds. Yes, she does, right up to the moment she strings their feet up and holds their heads down—like this—so they won't spray blood, struggling when she cuts their throats."

"Annie—"

"Oh, don't worry, they don't fight for long. Then it's a dunk in boiling water, and the feathers and the bloom slide right off. Then you get to chop off the head and the legs. Then yank out the windpipe, the crop, the guts, the liver, the heart, the gizzard—"

"Okay, stop. What's your point? Are you trying to put me off? It won't work."

The blanket is barely large enough for both of them. When he reaches for her shoulders, she recoils, crablike, onto the grass.

"Don't touch me!"

Too harsh, she berates herself, and before he can react, she rushes on. "I'm sorry, Phil. I do like you. You might be the most likeable person I ever met. But I just can't face another partnership."

"I'm sure your marriage was more than a business partnership."

Doesn't his composure ever falter? He props himself on the blanket with both hands behind him.

"How is it that you are sure of something you know nothing about?" she asks. "He didn't love me. We came together because my brother offered us his homestead. We saw opportunity. He didn't love me."

Phil sits up to protest, but she stops him with an outstretched palm.

"I married the first time, a very nice man, to get away from my mother. I married the second time because 'it made sense.' Now you. Same thing, but rolled into one and without the marriage license. You want to know what's funny?" She laughs, a half-hearted "ha." "The 'living in sin' part is fine with me. It's the partnership I can't step into again. No, not that. No." She pauses for breath, and her shoulders droop. "He didn't love me."

"I think he did. Men will love you if you let them. You don't let them."

Annie lurches to her feet, treading squarely on the pound cake and booting the jar of pickles for emphasis. She leaves the lunch things where they lie and heads over the rise, but he's on his feet in an instant and steps in front of her.

"I came out here because I wanted to see you again, to see if you still made me feel the way I remembered you did. You do. I want you to come live with me. I can give you a hundred reasons."

"A hundred reasons." What an exhausting man he is.

"Yes."

He's given it considerable thought, she'll grant him that. First, he likes her. He'll try hard not to like her more than she can tolerate. He admires her tenacity, her resilience, her stamina. He has a house but misses having a home, and mustn't she miss that too? They each have half a family. The whole is more than the sum of the parts.

"And I'm only on about number thirty-nine. Can we please sit again?" he coaxes. She relents enough to return to the rumpled blanket, toeing the smashed cake into the grass. "Now, where was I?" he continues. She doesn't care for ice cream and he loves it: "double for me." She loves the twilight and he prefers the sunrise: together they've got the whole day covered. And in Sunday's paper he read an article that said the world population of blondes is in decline and brunettes are taking over. He wants to be on her side when that happens.

"That's a reason," Annie chuckles.

"That's number fifty-five: if I try hard, I can get you to laugh. Number fifty-six: I'll teach you to play chess. You'll like it."

"I can whup you at chess."

"Check, mate. Numbers fifty-seven and fifty-eight: you won't have to grow anything, and you certainly won't have to kill anything. Ever. Number fifty-nine: grounds for divorce can be established based on desertion."

Ugly words—why does she have to keep hearing them? She turns away, but he continues in that maddeningly calm, rational manner of his.

"Number sixty: you can leave everything, everything, behind you, except Nora. Number sixty-one: Nora deserves a father, and I promise you I'm up to the job."

"You don't even know her."

"Through you, I know her better than I knew my own kids before I met them."

"Touché." She has to smile, but sadly. How can she make him understand? "But the clean-slate thing doesn't work. I tried that when I left Iowa to come to Montana. We can't get away from ourselves, Phil. The best I'm hoping for is to learn to like myself. It's about time."

"I couldn't agree more. The best way to learn to like yourself is by surrounding yourself with people who already like you. Starting with me."

"Starting with Nora."

"Of course. Forgive me. When will you have her back? Tell me."

Tell me. His face reflects kindness and concern, but his question is a setup. She must resist.

"She'll be here with me soon. I'll be officially discharged by the hospital. Perhaps I'll continue working here; perhaps I'll go somewhere else. I'll work; she'll go to school. We will be enough for each other."

"She'll be enough for you."

"This conversation has gone far enough. I must get back to work and—"

"Yes, she'll be enough for you. For a while. Then she'll be grown and she won't need your permission to make her own life apart from yours. Perhaps she'll think on her childhood of solitude, with a mother who had much to give but chose to give only to her child. Perhaps the responsibility will weigh heavily. Perhaps it will—"

"Stop this, stop this now! It's not worthy of you. Inflicting guilt to make your point—is that supposed to endear you to me?"

"I'm speaking the truth, and you know it. Annie. I have three children at home whose mother is long gone and left them with nothing but gossip fodder. You might give a moment's consideration to how that has reflected on me."

She bristles, "Anyone who knows you would know that it couldn't have been anything you did. Anyone who thinks otherwise would, to me, be a foul ball into the tall corn."

"Thank you for that. As I've said all along, we understand each other. Won't you meet my kids, give them a chance? You put yourself through hell more times than I know of, to become a mother. My kids are going through hell because they don't have one. Am I up to a hundred reasons? It sure feels like it."

She picks a tiny field daisy and plucks the petals off, one at a time. Why has she never noticed that there are two layers of petals on a daisy, that they overlap, and—

"You're not doing that loves-me, loves-me-not thing, are you? I'd be crushed to think that's the only way you could make a decision about me."

She tosses the flower aside. If he understood her as well as he thinks he does, he would know that there's no decision to be made.

"You've been cut to the quick," he says. "Life's been unfair to Nora. My kids are hurting terribly, and I'm a little wounded myself. You're the first woman who's made me feel that I could trust and even love again." Annie's hand flies to cover her face, but he pulls it away. "I didn't think that was possible. So I'm pretty impressed with you, Annie Fielding."

A wave of feeling for him washes through her. It has no name, no color, no texture, nothing to grab on to. What does he do with his leftover paint? she suddenly wants to ask him. The half-empty, half-full cans that by themselves aren't enough for anything. Does he dump them together and come up with a color never before conjured, never to be again? What color is the heart when pigmented with equal parts affection and gratitude and pity and inadequacy and weariness and fear?

"I don't know how else to put this," she says, eyes lowered because she can't look at him while she's closing the door. "I'm the only one who knows how deep the cuts are."

"Yes, you are." For a moment he seems fascinated with the thin clouds hanging torpid on the horizon. Then he picks up his jacket and shrugs into it. "I've said all I can say. I know I'm no prizewinner."

"And I'm no prize."

"That's in the eye of the beholder. I took the day off from work to come out here. I hope that tells you something."

"It tells me you're a fool." She smiles. "I mean that in the best way."

"So be it." He brushes the grass from his pants and replaces the gray fedora on his head. Its charcoal band shades his green eyes and makes them seem deeper. "I'll be going now. Thank you for seeing me."

He moves away, gracious and unbowed, but he can't hide the sadness beneath. She's sorry to have hurt him, but he must have known how slim his chances were. How dear he is, how gallant. Holding her tenacity and resilience up for admiration and not seeing the same in himself. Somebody's white knight. Surely there's someone special enough for him out there. Annie hopes that whoever it is will show up soon.

But how unmannerly of her, to not even say a decent goodbye. She runs after him, catches his arm lightly, and says, "I'll walk you to your car."

When they reach the Model T, she fumbles for the right words. "I can't apologize more sincerely, Phil. But it doesn't serve either of us to not own up to what we feel is right. You've done that for me, and I can't do less for you. A large part of me is saying no because I can't face the possibility of disappointing you."

He opens the car door. "817 Birchwood, Copper Creek. If you change your mind." He kisses her forehead.

She says, "I wish——" but he tips his hat and stops her with, "That's good." A cloud of dust lingers over the road long after he's gone. An eddy kicks up in the middle of the cloud and whirls away, taunting, *Who's the fool?*

A pert Pearson cousin props Annie on a stool in the kitchen and asks, "You sure, now?" and when Annie says yes, the cousin clicks her clippers smartly and quips, "This have anything to do with your gentleman caller yesterday?" She gathers up Annie's mane in one hand, and with four strokes, it's over.

Annie shakes what's left of her hair into a loose fan and squeezes her eyes shut. Oh, the elation of feeling so light-headed when nothing whatsoever is wrong! "What gentleman caller?" she retorts. "I'm joining a hockey team."

What gentleman caller? The one who lingers without being there. How many times a day does she toss her head, trying to oust the proposal couched in terms she can't disregard. *Nora deserves a father, and I promise you I'm up to the job.*

Nora has a father, a broken father, who isn't up to the job. She doesn't deserve that, but neither does he. Nora couldn't choose, and, Annie believes, neither could Adam. What else can she believe when her whole life has been a struggle to mend her own breakage as a parent?

She always thought her hair was straight, but released from its length and weight, it frolics in beguiling waves around her face. She looks years younger, a gentle counterpoint to how her soul feels weighed down by bad luck, flawed choices. Now when she shakes her head, the waves brush her cheeks, as only Nora's father did. It makes no sense, no sense at all, that she wants permission. She closes her eyes and waits until she no longer feels the touch of her hair, and that is her answer.

Nora deserves a father. What does Annie deserve? Does she deserve a good man like Phil? He'll try hard not to like her more than she can tolerate. She could try too. She could try hard to like him as much as he deserves. She flattens her cheek against the cold window, wishing that, for once, there were someone to whom she could turn for caring but clear-eyed advice. In the distance, Nels leaves one of the barns and secures it for the night. In the gloaming, in his stance knocked slightly crooked by his years, in his rubbing the back of his neck and pausing a moment to appreciate the fading sky over the mountains, in his shape and his vintage, she almost mistakes him for her pa.

Perhaps it's no mistake.

The next Friday, Nels steers the truck into the railyard that backs up to the hills at the edge of town. The shift is ending: clots of men in twos and threes move toward the street, headed to homes or speakeasies. Annie tells herself she'll have to talk fast if they're to make it back to the ranch by dark. But she doesn't imagine she'll need many words.

Nels cuts the engine, and the truck settles with a smelly sigh. "You're doing the right thing," he says. "Go on."

The main office is a grand white-stone affair, with double doors flanked by sidelight windows. Entering a long room with a dark wood counter, she pulls her shawl closer around her, lacing her fingers through the eyelet openings. She left a summer evening outside. In here, autumn has already laid down its first chill hand.

She makes her request to the clerk behind the counter. His eyes flick over her for an instant before he catches himself, reddening with embarrassment. "Yes, ma'am. He's out at the engine house. I'll fetch him for you. Wait right here."

The clerk steps into an office behind him and closes the door. Annie hears the latch slip, and the door drifts open a hand's width.

"There's a woman asking for McCandless." The clerk's tone teeters on incredulous.

Annie can't see who it is that replies, "No kidding? Who is it?"

"She won't say. Says 'he'll know.'"

"I'll be. What's she look like?"

"Not much."

"Huh. Better go get him, I guess."

When he appears from the back of the office, she's suddenly afraid of every outcome she can think of. His duck-cloth jacket, stained like a topographic map. A dented metal lunch box crouches under his arm. She's never seen him this late in the day, with his five-o'clock shadow darkening his jaw. He looks very real to her. She starts to smile.

But it's clear to her from his question-mark look that he wasn't expecting this. He hesitates, lays a hand on the counter, and that's when she understands.

He too has changed his mind.

The smile dies; she drops her chin and moves toward the door, her head filling with a fog of humiliation she can only hope kills her soon.

"Annie!" His voice is muffled by the door. It scrapes open, and he catches her outside. "You got me for a minute." His hand hovers around her face. "You cut your hair. I didn't recognize you."

Her fingers crawl up the back of her neck to the edge of the bob she's still getting used to herself.

"I'm so happy to see you," he says.

She needn't have worried about talking fast. She can only manage one word.

"Yes."

In the years since she last allowed herself inside a man's arms, she's forgotten how right it can feel. She buries her face in the crook of his elbow and closes her eyes. She breathes deeply the smells of coal soot and engine grease and turpentine and smelter smoke, and knows they will be the cologne of her life here. She's a long way from the aromatic wheat rustling beyond the fragrant apple and pear trees. A long way from the starlit river, smelling of snow long into spring. A long way from animals and vegetables. And if she's lucky, a long way from the hospitals she thought would destroy her very sense of smell, the disinfectants that couldn't cover the decay, the reek of human bodies in transition.

She can be done with people moving through the turnstile of her life on a one-way pass.

That's all behind her.

Yes.

Will and Nels ask Annie to meet them in the living room. They stand away from the window, hands in pockets, conversing as they always do, like hand-me-down cellos slightly out of tune. Annie pauses at the sight of them beyond the arched entry. How is it they are not her uncles, when they are a thousand times more dear than any kin? Will reaches out to Annie, drawing her to where his crinkled hand can come to rest on her shoulder. It steadies her, fills her with sudden certainty that she'll never lose her balance again.

Nels takes her hand and lays in her palm a twenty-dollar bill, as worn and warm as his face. "Buy something for your home, the first something that belongs to both of you. And may God richly bless you and your new family."

"How can I thank you? It's I who should have something to give you. Something as meaningful as what you've given me."

"You have," Will says. "You've given us just what we wanted."

Nels smiles and nods.

She throws herself into their arms, holding them tightly and tearfully until Will tickles her under the chin and she laughs; they all laugh.

At the noon hour, when the women's cottage is empty, she closes the oak door at the end of the second-floor hallway and walks away, satchel bumping at her side. Before the week is out, another woman will warm herself under the quilt that grants Lily Stanhope's wish for remembrance and find Annie's note, tucked into the gap between the cupboard and the wall:

What people say you cannot do, you try and find that you can. —Henry David Thoreau

Annie follows the weed-flanked lane out to the road and waits under a trio of whitebark pines for the sound of a Model T.

She met the children at a picnic two weeks ago. It had to be a picnic, she told Phil. *No walls*, she said, *let the children run if that's how their spirits move them*. But they neither ran, nor ate, nor talked. Somehow it wasn't a bad thing. Annie loved them on sight: Kieran stoic, Jeannie hopeful, Molly wary. Their eyes limped through an hour neither pleasant nor unpleasant, after which Annie whispered to Phil, "That's enough for now." From the corner of her eye, she saw Jeannie smile.

"Third floor, west corner," says the clerk, handing Phil a pen to sign the register. Converging from different paths of thought, she and Phil agreed that the hotel was the right thing: Phil suggesting that the trip to the children's home would be too tedious if left to the day they're to retrieve Nora, Annie feeling they owe themselves privacy on their first night together.

The clerk hands Phil a key. "We hope you and Mrs. McCandless will be comfortable." Annie thanks him and sheds the remark without effort, how easy it was, nodding politely to the lie she's agreed to live. Marriage may be a matter of public record, but sidestepping it is a private affair.

The heavy curtains in their room hold off the light of the stars and street. In the darkness Annie prays: if she's good for one wish, it's that her body not betray her, that it do her bidding, shut out qualms and comparisons, and allow her to respond and cleave to this man as she must and as he deserves. *One wish.* If she shivers, will he take it for cold, for desire, for apprehension—or for recoil? He mustn't know that it could be all those things, loosed in a brief but telltale shudder of her faithless body. *One wish.*

The room isn't cold, she wants to want him, and she's tired of being afraid. So she doesn't shiver as his lips explore her face, her fingertips tracing his jaw as he undoes her buttons gently as if she were a child; she doesn't shiver, but simply falls in rhythm with his quickening breathing. She follows his lead, echoing his soft gasps when his hands cradle her breasts, holding her breath as he does when skirt and trousers fall to the floor, and letting go, letting go of so much as their bodies' dormant memories of pleasure begin to resurface.

"I can't see you," she whispers with alarm that surprises her. "Shouldn't I be able to see you?"

"There'll be plenty of time for that," he murmurs.

She needs to see to be able to believe her eyes as well as her heart, telling her that it is indeed opening a book whose ending isn't proscribed. That she'll see in his face all the things she believes he brings to her and takes from her. No failure, no dread, no disequilibrium. No devastating debt of dollar or soul. If she can see this, if she can believe her eyes, she'll believe his promises, his faith in her, the longing they share for their children to be at peace.

"There's time now." She slips from his arms, three steps to

the draperies, parting them enough to let in the light but not the world. The streetlamp a block away pencils in the floor beneath the window. Moonlight must do the rest of the job, compromised by a slow-moving membrane of clouds.

Naked in the shadows by the window, she hears his wordless urgency behind her. An image rises in her: undulating boulevards of corn a head taller than her and cottonwoods dipping in the wind. The image molests her from all around, the corn tassels stroking her neck, the slender tree branches twining about her waist, stalks and boughs waving before her face, but she flings the vision away like the viper it is. *Do not take this from me,* she appeals to whatever trickster of the heart or mind would visit upon her something so cruel. *This is the way it's going to be.* She stands before Phil at the edge of the bed, at the edge of the life they will make together. The light is weak but enough to expose every detail. Her story is carved into her body; best he see it now. Her abdomen, scythed with surgical scars and slackened by birthings of children dead and alive. Her ribs a brittle corset under wan breasts, nipples long ago grown pale. Her navel protrudes slightly, as if issuing a dare.

In one motion he pulls her into bed and under him. His soft moaning against her neck pulses with gratefulness. She could melt into the night with this unaccustomed peace, this unexpected contentment.

With him there will be no soaring highs, no crashing lows. A gray-and-black tin of Dr. Robinson's 333s—PRESS HERE TO OPEN—will see to that. She gropes for the tiny box on the nightstand.

Chest to chest they lie, the hair on his chest brushing her skin, smooth and quiet. Her fingertips disappear into it, probing, she needs to know exactly where he begins, to find his borders so she can cross them.

"Are you in there?" she asks, half joke, half need. His answer swells between her thighs, the whole of him undulating against her with uncomplicated rhythm. Her head floats in his hands, their commingled scents crowding out the baggy feather pillows and unvarnished headboard, the dusty corners of the room and dustier corners of their pasts. His climax overtakes them quickly.

"Yeah," he breathes. "I'm in here."

After a while she asks, "How old are you?"

"About three hundred twenty-one, in dog years." He chuckles and guides her hand to his belly. "But I think I got a few of 'em back tonight."

Annie rouses from a semiconscious bog of suspended thought that can't rightly be called sleep. The gnashing huff of Pa's tractor churns at her back, steam dampening her neck. Confused and terrified, she knows she must move but can't. The tractor plows into the length of her. She braces for bone-splintering catastrophe. Instead the impact is warm and supple. She lets herself sink into it. It's not a tractor; it's Phil.

They're to call for Nora at ten o'clock. Until then, Annie must pass more than two hundred tauntingly elongated minutes until Nora's face will stop the sun in the sky and Annie will lock her arms around her bright golden child and, after the longest year of her life, the world will at last make sense.

Annie lies still, envying Phil's slumber. She tries to move to the edge of the bed, to drop her arm over the side and count the loops in the rug. But it's like perching on the lip of a ditch. The bed insists she submit to its contours. Phil rolls over and Annie tumbles into him. With his back to her, she can't tell if he's awake and doesn't know if she wants him to be. He hooks a foot over her ankles and pulls the blanket tighter to his chest. The blanket falls across the bridge of her nose. She watches it rise and fall. In this manner she fills a full minute of the two hundred. Her face grows moist; she pushes the blanket arm's length away and examines, one by one, the spots and flecks between her wrist and elbow. Eight. And nine on the other arm.

The room grows lighter. She's seeing Phil's back for the first time, splattered with faded freckles, reminding her of the sheet under his work the day they met. She closes her eyes and pictures Nora draped over his back, her arms around his shoulders, his arms hooked under her knees at his waist, her feet swinging free. He'll carry Nora up the bleachers at the ballpark, play horsey-goes-off-to-bed, give her a piggyback ride to town to let her see the world at grown-up eye level. Annie will laugh and say, as her pa did, "Things look different up there, don't they?"

And she'll be grateful and happy and Nora will be happy and Annie will never, ever think about—

Phil stirs, runs a hand through his hair. His watch on the dresser chews the time like cud, too loud, too slow. Annie takes his hand in hers and wraps it around his waist, her arm over his. She doesn't want him to wake yet, not when there are one hundred eighty-three minutes to be endured. It will be a parallel ordeal for Nora. Although apart, Annie decides, they'll do it together.

She closes her eyes again. Nora is awake now. She'll leave her dormitory for the last time, skipping between the rows of beds. In the lavatory she'll step to the farthest of a dozen basins, each no larger than a curled-up cat, with cat's-eye rings of stain circling the drain. She'll push up the sleeves of her chocolate-colored sweater and slap her face with ice-cold water, forgetting in her excitement to turn on the hot-water tap. Her eyes will fly open wide and blue as the sky, and she'll laugh at herself. And Annie, behind dark eyes still closed, hopes Nora will teach her to do the same.

"Hungry?"

Phil's simple question prods her gut, but how could she be hungry? Nora won't be hungry either. She'll jab patterns in her hotcake with her fork. She'll nudge the stewed prunes around her bowl, pretending they're toads. She'll sip her milk like it's medicine.

Annie opens her eyes and blinks herself back into the dimpled bed. "What do you like for breakfast?" she asks Phil, disturbed that she doesn't know. Tomorrow she'll begin to learn such things. Now she swings herself from the bed and plants herself at the washbasin. Last night's lovers are today's parents.

One hundred sixty-three minutes.

In the dining room, Annie adds enough cream to her coffee to make Phil laugh and moo. The cup sits square in front of her, fending off any suggestion of food. Phil eats a bacon-and-potato omelet with endearing appetite. The waitress refills his cup. "In town for the show at the opera house? *Parsifal*, ain't it?" she asks in a voice plump as Sunday chicken and dumplings.

"My cousin saw it in Fargo," Phil says in that indefatigably affable way of his. "Said it was as long as some jail sentences. No, we're here to pick up our daughter at the home."

"Oh!" crows the waitress. "You're adopting one of those dear little nippers, God bless you. My brother's the groundskeeper there, since it opened in eighteen-and-ninety-two, and that's half his life. Knows every brick and nail in every building, every inch of those tunnels that run under the place. Told us about every kid who managed to break out using those spiral-chute fire escapes." Her chubby finger twirls a cylinder from shoulder to knee. "He's seen hunnerds of adoptions. Always hopes for happily ever after. Now, honey, let me bring you a Danish," she croons to Annie. "New mothers need to keep up their strength."

"No, please," Annie demurs. "I couldn't possibly."

One hundred thirty-four minutes.

"We're not adopting," Phil steps in smoothly. "Our daughter has been at the home while her mother here was ill. But as you can see now, she's sound as an angel's drum. And we'd love a Danish. Anything but lemon. Thank you."

"Oh, a reunion!" The waitress's grin spreads broad enough to make her chin disappear. "God bless you twice." She bustles off.

"I hope it's cherry." Phil taps a fist on the table. "Does Nora like Danish?"

What does Nora like? Annie stares past Phil, through the lobby that leads to the street that will take her to the road that will end with Nora in her arms. They've been apart for a year, a quarter of Nora's life. What has she shed of her previous self? Until now it hasn't entered Annie's thoughts that Nora may be something other than happy to see her. What of anger? Fear? The comfortable familiarity of what has been home for a whole year? How could she have blithely assumed that Nora will accept Phil, that she'll take to his children and they to her? Why has she staked Nora's future on the word of a man so little known to her? Why has she not thought of these things until now?

Annie jumps as the waitress sets down a plate of Danish in the center of the table. Phil slips a half dollar into her apron pocket and she backs away, gushing thanks. When she disappears into the kitchen, Annie says to Phil, "I don't know what Nora thinks of Danish."

One hundred twenty-seven minutes.

The two cherry Danish, shiny red centers tucked into crinkled pastry rounds, stare clown-eyed from the white plate, daring, coaxing Annie to laugh or cry at the absurdity, the agony of having to mark time in increments of how many bites it takes a man she barely knows to finish a couple of breakfast confections.

One hundred nineteen minutes. Nora will be given chores to pass the time. She'll carry towels to the washroom. Feed the dogs. Set out napkins for lunch, less one. *How long?* she'll ask. Won't she? *How long till Mama comes?*

"You," Phil observes, "are the only person I've ever seen pace the floor while seated."

Annie smiles weakly. He pushes his chair back and wanders out of the room. Hunting up a newspaper, she supposes. Reliable time killers, newspapers. Less so, though, now that she skips over anything related to agriculture and gets right to politics, labor strife, fires, and train wrecks. If she can draw her reading out to one paragraph a minute, the blessed newspaper might see her through the next insufferable hour.

"Let's go." Phil eases her chair away from the table.

"No newspaper?"

"Newspaper?"

"I thought you went to find a newspaper."

"I went to find a phone," he says. "I called the home and explained that you were not going to survive the wait. We're leaving as soon as you pack your bag."

She stands so abruptly he has to grab her elbows to steady her. Before God and a passing waitress tickled pink as dawn, Annie kisses his face, over and over. She may think she doesn't know him, but he knows her.

When they turn off the road, they can see the main house and the long drive snaking through thinly scattered pines. It rises white and gothic like a dowager duchess amid humble brick subjects, the low-slung stables and gatehouse, dormitories square and solid as shipping crates. Two turrets rise along opposite sides of the house, each with a single window at the top. Their shades stop halfway to the sill, giving them the look of narrowed black eyes.

At the top of a graying tongue of porch stairs, a child strains to break free of the starchily dressed woman holding her with kind but firm hands. Any young girl might be dressed in a drop-waist dress of dark red checks and ruffled anklets peeking over canvas oxfords tied with wide ribbons. But only Nora could be wearing a chocolate-colored sweater with the sheen of brave resilience.

"Phil." Annie grabs his hand on the steering wheel. "I need to——"

"I'll wait here," he says, cutting the engine.

Annie steps down from the car. The distance to the ground seems unending. Nora wrenches free of the woman on the porch and flies down the stairs. "Mama!" she screams, rosy knees churning and palomino waves capering about her cheeks and chin and collar. "Mama!"

In the pause between heartbeats, Annie sheds the fetters of the months that stood between them, her fierce-won mother self and her daughter, this miracle of perseverance. The dead weight of the lost year rushes to the sky and bursts over her head in a chrysanthemum firework, winking into nothingness.

"Nora!" Her knees find the ground. The small blond tornado slams into her. "Oh, Nora." Back and forth she rocks her daughter, all hot cheeks and tears of pure bliss. "Never again, sweetheart. Never, never again."

"Mama, you look so beautiful." Nora's peony lips collide full on Annie's own. "I knew you would come."

A woman wearing a dark blue suit steps to the top of the porch. "Mrs. Fielding, if you'll come inside, we can sign the release papers."

"No, Mama! Not back in there. I want to go!" Nora's arms tighten around Annie's neck to where she must pry a breathing space. "Shhhh," she says, tugging little fingers away. "I'll turn as purple as my dress." Nora's trust is a wondrous thing. *I want to go,* although she hasn't the slightest idea where.

The woman smiles. "We'll bring a clipboard."

Half a dozen women, some in uniforms, some in day dresses, gather on the porch to say goodbye. Annie doesn't know who they are, doesn't need to know. She folds the release papers in careful thirds and tucks them into her waistband. The woman in the dark suit glances at Phil standing by the car, then at Annie with a *who's this?* arch of the brow.

"Thank you so very much for taking care of my baby," Annie says.

"We all love her to pieces, Mrs. Fielding. Best of luck to you. We'll miss you, Nora dear."

With Nora welded to her like a glowing sconce, Annie turns from the knot of well-wishers and descends the steps. The car and the man who will take them away from here forever are a few yards away. Nora lays her head at the base of Annie's throat, hair curling soft and pale as hay. Annie breathes the scent of a child's happiness tinged with innocence lost too soon. "Don't look back," she whispers to the top of Nora's head, and Nora burrows closer still. The last sounds from the porch fade away: "There's something we don't see enough." "Can hardly believe they're related to look at them!"

The sun encases them. Were Annie alone, she would give in to the thankfulness that overwhelms her, allow it to knock the knees from under her and let flow a river of joyful tears. Nora is hers, wholly and irrevocably hers. And for the forty-three paces between the queenly house and the lowly Model T, they are the only two people in the world.

"They said you wouldn't come," Nora says.

"They were mistaken."

The doors of the Model T stand open in welcome. Nora's eyes widen at the sight of Phil. Later, when they're in bed, Annie will tell him that he has the kindest smile that ever graced a face.

28

Annie finds a bone, brittle as chalk, behind the stove.

"Daddy got us a puppy," Jeannie tries to explain. "He pooed under the table, and when we put him outside, he ran away."

It's the most words any of the children have spoken to Annie in the weeks since she arrived with a pebbled leather satchel and an exuberant four-year-old, since the day she stepped into a dejected kitchen with a naked curtain rod sagging across the window. Kieran said only, "They caught on fire."

A hundred poignant signs expose a household that's been struggling for some time. A few store-bought canned goods cower in a tall cupboard. Unused baking pans cradle dormant utensils, trussed together by thin cobwebs. Clearly the dining table hasn't seen a cloth lately, strewn as it is with pale rings left by coffee cups and milk glasses. *A cloud of bubbles,* Annie thinks, running her fingers over them. She finds a stack of tablecloths, their fold lines permanent from disuse, in a cabinet shoved to the end of the back porch. Under the cloths, a silver photo frame, facedown. Annie doesn't lift it, doesn't open the other drawers.

At first she stays close to home. Phil was right: it's good to have a home again. But soon she ventures out, a little farther each day, until she's traversed every block of Copper Creek. The town teems with diversity, every imaginable human condition. She draws less attention than she feared. Everyone seems relieved that Phil McCandless has a new wife, and her simple answers satisfy the polite questions. "How did you meet?" she's asked, and in her reply, "At the hospital," folks assume employment, not commitment. To questions of where she came from, Annie replies, "Iowa, and you?" Everyone here is from somewhere else.

Annie and Nora explore, Nora skipping ahead, examining every puddle, pebble, and crack in the sidewalk. "This way, Mama. Look at this building. The windows are pieces of colored glass." Annie explains that it's a church. But Nora has already moved on. "There's Mrs. Conover's store! May I go in and say hello?" Annie hands her a nickel along with instructions that she mustn't let Mrs. Conover give her a soda bun without paying for it.

Dozens of these stores speckle the town, most run by widows or women otherwise alone, struggling to keep the family together. They toil killing hours. They live on the brink. Annie plays a grim game of roulette with herself, spreading her meager business around, moving through neighborhoods of tiny homes crammed close together like stale loaves of bread. She buys things she's never had to buy from someone else before—canned goods, produce, eggs, chicken. One store has a slot machine in the back. Customers gripe that it rarely pays.

"Oh, it pays," the owner confides to Annie. "It pays the bills."

Annie finds herself staring at Phil one evening, reading the newspaper in his comfortable old horsehair chair. He doesn't look up, just asks, "What is it, dear?"

"This town is rife with women like me, and you, alone with children. You could have . . . Long before I came along."

He lowers the paper and regards her in his mild, Phil way.

"No, I couldn't have."

The children need time. They float ghostlike through the house, answering her questions, remarks, and requests with "yes, ma'am" and "no, ma'am." They tiptoe through their chores, avoid Annie and Phil's bedroom, and put themselves to bed early.

Notes come from the school on a regular basis: *Kieran has forgotten his multiplication tables. Molly refuses to read out loud.* Annie presents herself to the principal. The children are being mocked and berated, she tells him. He nods in a patronizing way. "We know the children lost their mother, but it's been several years. We have seen no incidences of undue provocation."

"Children aren't going to call a classmate's mother a slut within your hearing," Annie snaps. She knows there's little chance of changing a sentiment so many of the townsfolk seem to share, but there's nothing to lose in trying. "Ignore it if that's the best you can do, but see to it that I don't receive any more scornful notes from teachers wondering why the McCandless children's school-work sometimes falls off a cliff."

Bit by bit, Nora's perpetual high spirits buoy her new siblings. "Oh, this house is grand!" she exclaimed upon first sight, running from room to room. Jeannie's and Molly's eyes widened, for the house was as grand as a cracker tin and about as dark inside. But Nora has never lived in a house. A hearth right in the front room that she can sit upon any time she chooses? A dining room table for only the six of them? An icebox for them alone, and she's allowed to open it and have an apple whenever she wants? "Oh my!" she exclaimed. "What a darling tiny bathroom—just one sink, one commode, and one tub, and a door that closes!" Nora began her life as part of the McCandless family by redefining luxury in a manner none of them had ever considered.

The girls—twins who don't look or act alike—fascinate Nora. Jeannie, a copy of Phil, with her easygoing demeanor, ash-blond hair, and bracken-colored eyes. Molly, with her saucier manner and cocoa-colored hair that seems unable to decide from day to day whether to crimp or swing straight. The twins are three years older than Nora and in school, which makes them royalty in her eyes.

Jeannie is the first to thaw, and Annie and Phil are the last to know, illuminated one evening by a single incandescent question from Nora, whispered to Jeannie during supper: "Can I sleep with you?"

"Sure," Jeannie says agreeably, stacking carrot coins on her fork. "You already do."

Nora looks stricken. With one tine of her fork she begins separating grains of rice, lining them up against the blue rim of her plate.

"What do you mean?" Annie asks, but the children focus intently on their plates. Phil puts his fork down with that answer-when-you're-spoken-to speech on his lips, but Annie stops him by lifting a forefinger from the table. Molly asks boldly if she can have jelly on her rice. Kieran announces that his idol, the Brown's George Sisler, ended the season with the league high of fifty-one steals.

"You have your own room, dear," Annie says to Nora. Annie and Phil agreed, the sewing room was a perfect Nora-sized cocoon. "Molly and Jeannie's room isn't big enough for three."

Nora's feet swinging under her chair pick up speed, catching Annie in the calf. "Sorry, Mama," Nora blurts. "I'm tired. May I be excused?"

The hand of conscience upon her shoulder is a night visitor long familiar to Annie. Hours after the house has fallen still, Annie wakes to the replay in her head of a handful of girlish words. *Can I sleep with you? Sure, you already do.*

Annie shrugs into her bathrobe, pulling the belt tight. At the door of the twins' bedroom, she waits and listens before turning the knob as quietly as she can. Curled against the wall, Nora shivers in a tight ball at the foot of Jeannie's bed. Her whimper, "Mamaaa," when Annie scoops her up wakes Jeannie.

"Don't be mad," Jeannie says, sitting up.

"She has her own room," Annie replies. "She mustn't be in here disturbing you and Molly."

"She isn't disturbing us." In the second bed, Molly hasn't stirred. Nora burrows into Annie's chest, a fist under her chin. Jeannie reaches up and pats her shoulder. "Nora told us about the orphans' home. She slept in a dormitory. She's never slept in a room by herself. She says it's lonely and cold and too quiet and scary."

Annie gathers both girls in her arms and marvels at her own foolishness. That a child's wisdom exceeds her own will keep her awake for hours.

And in the morning, Phil, without a moment's deliberation, declares that the wall between the two rooms is not load-bearing. Three days later, down it comes, crumbling as surely as Nora knocked down the wall between the two fractured families.

But Kieran remains out of reach.

When he appears at the bedroom door on a flat, gray afternoon, Annie knows it's a turning point. Sliding clean shirts into a dresser drawer, she meets his eyes, behind her, in the vanity mirror.

"Hello, Kieran."

His eyes dart around the room. "I wanted to . . ." He can't finish the sentence.

Annie turns and faces him. "Come on in and we'll talk."

"My father doesn't allow us in this room."

"I understand. Some parents keep their bedrooms private, but this is my room too, and I'm making an exception today."

Kieran doesn't move. His dark eyes churn. "You're not my parent. What are you?" His strange question comes with an air of defiance that doesn't sit square on him. "My dad said you were coming to live with us. How long? Are you another housekeeper? The housekeepers don't sleep in my dad's room."

"I'm not another housekeeper. How many have there been?"

"Twenty. Thirty. A hundred. They hear things about my mother and they leave." His voice rises. "Do you know where she is? I hear things in town. That she's living sinfully. That she's never coming back."

Annie burns with outrage. What wicked tongues would repeat such monstrous talk within earshot of him? Please let there be a special place in hell for such types.

"Neither I nor anyone else here knows for sure where she is or if that's true," she says gently. "I do know that people who gossip viciously in front of children have no call to be pointing a finger at others. A skunk smells his own first."

He plunges on. "I heard the principal call you Mrs. McCandless. My sisters and I, we were wondering why we weren't invited to your and Dad's wedding. If you don't like us enough to—"

"Kieran, stop right there. I wouldn't be here if I didn't like you immensely." This child, she decides, deserves the truth. "You weren't invited to our wedding because we didn't have one."

He gazes at her until his eyes look to drop under the weight of his lids. His head falls against the wall with a sigh. "I hate my name."

Is that dark smudge by his ear a trickle of dried blood? "Oh, honey. Did something happen at school today?"

He fingers his ear. "I looked up my name. Kieran. It's Gaelic for 'small and dark.'" He draws a quivering breath. "I'm the smallest in my class. Kids say rotten things about my mother. If I fight back, I get pounded. What if I never outgrow my dimwit name?" His face clenches with the effort of damming his tears.

"Kieran, come over here by the mirror with me." He comes, hesitantly. "Look here. You're eleven and you're already up to my brow. By the time you get to high school, you will be looking down at me. I'll have to wear a sweater all the year round because I'll be chilly from standing in your shadow. But today you're exactly as you're supposed to be. Why do you think you're the fastest streak on the baseball team?"

As she hoped, his head comes up and his whole face snaps to attention.

"Dad tells me you always beat the throw to first. Don't be surprised when Coach puts you in as a pinch runner, or a pinch hitter. What's your RBI percentage? You know, I must go over to the high school tomorrow and stake my seat in the bleachers. It's only three years until you play for them, and then I'll be spending a lot of time there."

"Really?" His face asks many questions. *Really, you know how to talk my favorite subject, baseball? Really, I will grow tall? Really, I'll play on the high school team? Really, you'll be here in three years to see it?*

"Really. I'm the one who will stay small and dark. We should trade names." She nudges him with her elbow, and he manages a laugh.

"I wouldn't like that, ma'am. Ann— I don't know what to call you."

"You'll know. Give it time." She pulls him over to sit on the bed with her. "Kieran. We both know that I'm not your mother. No one can be that but her. But other people can care about you, protect you, try to do what's best for you. It's okay to be confused. But what you do need to know is that I'm here for you, for keeps. I will not leave, not for anything anyone says about your mother, or your father, or even about me. We're a family now."

After a deep breath, which he holds until his fingers uncurl, he says, "I'm hungry."

In the kitchen, she puts a dish of graham crackers and a glass of milk in front of him. He breaks the cracker squares into rectangles and drops one into the milk. It disintegrates into a sodden mess. Annie waits. He still has something to say.

"My mother must have hated us to leave us like that. Jeannie and Molly and I, we don't know what we did that was so bad. What if we do it again?"

He's reaching for her heart and she hands it over before the next beat has faded.

My mother must have hated me to leave like that. Those are Cynthia's eyes, her long-ago-lost Cynthia, looking at her through Kieran's face.

Cynthia's mother hated herself, never her baby.

For half her life, Annie has borne the punishment of knowing her daughter only through her brother's occasional letters, which stopped years ago. The girl grew up in able hands. She didn't suffer for the loss of a mother she never knew.

Did she?

Annie can never know for sure, and that is why she now stands in a kitchen in Copper Creek, Montana, surgeon and nurse, weaver and seamstress, healer of four abandoned children.

Annie pulls a chair from the table and sits as close to him as she dares. "Your mother doesn't hate you. I swear to you, it's nothing you did. There were things in her life that became too much for her. Sometimes in church you hear the pastor say that God doesn't give us more than we can handle. Maybe God doesn't, but sometimes life does. I believe that's what happened to Nora's father. But he loves her tremendously. I believe your mother loves you, too. She just wasn't able to stay here with you."

He reaches for another cracker, raises his hand over the glass of milk, and crushes the cracker in his fist.

"Why is Nora always happy?"

"Nora had no family but me. She can't miss what she never had, but she loves having it now. For her it's that simple. For you, more complicated. That's why I said you don't have to know how you feel about it yet. Take as long as you need. I'll still be here."

His face reflects tiredness that shouldn't come to someone twice his age. Enough questions for today. She clears away the glass of milk clogged with swollen crackers and replaces it with a fresh one. He grabs the glass and drains it, wolfing crackers between gulps. Color returns to his cheeks as he stands up and brushes off his shirt.

"Thanks." He heads out of the kitchen but stops long enough to try out the unaccustomed words: "Thank you, Annie."

The maroon velvet chair in their bedroom has seen better days. Running her hand over the piping worn shiny, Annie tells Phil that Kieran doesn't like his name, and why.

"Little and dark? Good grief. I had no idea what the name meant. We named him after my great-grandfather. You'd think he might appreciate being distinguished from all those Johns and Jameses."

"I wouldn't think that, but that's coming from a family who got carried away in that department." She's learned that Phil's a sucker for family stories, that she can soften a sore piece of news with a well-told tale. Her father's uncle and aunt, she tells him while he unbuttons his soiled work shirt and pants, believed all girls should be named Mary, and they inflicted that on their five daughters. Then they compounded the fright by giving them virtuous middle names. She ticks them off on her fingers. "Mary Faith, Mary Constance, Mary Patientia, Mary Arete, and, taking utter leave of their senses at the end, Mary Mindwell. The legend," she relates, "is that Mindwell did not. Mind well. As an adult she went by Mamie, keeping enough of the two *M*s to aggravate her parents while she enjoyed a long career in burlesque in Chicago."

Phil peers at her, his shirt and mouth hanging open. "You're kidding this time, right? No? Lord, and I thought I was devout." He steps over his shirt on the floor on the way to the bathroom. Every night he does this, strips off his work clothes and leaves them where they lie.

She gathers his clothes off the floor, hoping this is the worst habit he ever reveals. Sitting on the edge of the bed, she considers how she'll phrase what she needs to say.

"You look thoughtful." He shrugs into a clean shirt, buttoning the cuffs without looking at them.

"Well," she begins, then stops and smiles. "My grandfather used to say, that's a deep subject."

"Another story?"

"Not tonight. Phil, what Kieran wanted to say is that I'm not his mother." Phil frowns but she puts up her hand. "Let me finish. I told him that's something we both know, but what he needs to know is that, unlike his mother or the many housekeepers, I'm here to stay. For better or worse, he won't wake up some morning and find me gone." What an extraordinary vow she's made. She has married Phil's children even as she has not married their father.

"Is that what he wanted to hear? It's certainly what I want to hear."

"It got more complicated when he asked me why he and his sisters hadn't been allowed to come to our wedding."

"And?"

"I told him we didn't have a wedding."

"And?"

"That's when he told me he hated his name." Phil starts to speak again, and again she puts up her hand. "I have something I want to say. I will never leave your children. We both know the agony of losing children, and we've also seen what losing a mother can do to a child. Your children have given me the gift of their trust, and I will not see them devastated again. I will never leave them," she repeats, sealing her own conviction. "If something goes wrong between you and me, you'll have to fight me for them. Even if they are your own and even if we never marry."

"What a terrible thing to say." He comes across the room and lays a finger under her chin. "What a terrible and wonderful thing to say. But you won't ever be held to the test."

"You never know." She gets to her feet. "As you once pointed out, we have seen some of the worst life has to offer."

"I do know. And I have something I want to say to you." He slips an arm around her waist and presses his face to the back of her neck. "Nora's father is a fool."

"Don't." Fat tears spring but don't spill. "He's many things, but he isn't a fool."

"Then we agree to disagree." This time it's he who puts a hand up, to her lips. "Shhhh. Swallow those," he says to her brimming eyes. "That part is over."

29

She's fallen down a well. It's a deeper subject than her grand-father ever let on. She can see the light above, but the well is filling with groundwater, and though she pushes with all her might against the slimy walls, she can't get a hold to climb out. The bucket rope has snapped, and its frayed end waves high above her: *Goodbye, Annie, sorry* . . . The water climbs over her chin and creeps into her ears, canceling out all sound save the hammering of her heart. She's been close to death many times, but not this way, and not when she's had something vital to live for. With her last bit of strength she tries to heave herself above this freezing, suffocating—

She starts awake, the cold and damp springing from her own pores. There's no black water, no rope, no well. Across the hall, her daughter sleeps in a royal blue flannel nightgown. A gibbous moon glints behind the curtains. All is as it should be with her world. Isn't it? She clutches her knees, trying to recover her breath. Beside her, Phil stirs but doesn't wake, throws an arm across her, drawing her back to their bed. This is how it is with Phil. He just knows. In a few hours they'll begin another day of placid routine. The children will go to school, Phil will go to work, and Annie will go through the motions of homemaking. She and Phil don't ask each other for much. What little they need seems to happen without asking.

They are safe.

Late October sun teases the front window, low and tepid. Nora sings, "Let's sit in the sunbeams, Mama," and Annie can't think of a solitary thing she has to do that's more important. On the sofa in front of the hearth, Nora reaches her arms to the sun. "In the home, I used to pretend that the sunbeams were you, coming to hug me," she says. "The grown-ups hardly ever hugged us, and we missed our parents. But no one was mean. Unless you count Miss Bunneigh. She always got my name wrong. I told her, a hundred times: my name is Nora Marielle Fielding. She would call me Nori-elle, or Mary Nell, or Nellie Belle. One time when she asked me to carry the butter plates to the table, I said to myself, 'Yes, Miss Rabbit.' But she heard me and did I get scolded. I don't see why. A bunny is a rabbit, right?"

Annie ruffles her daughter's hair. "I think you knew what you were doing."

Annie can't know all that Nora had to cope with at the children's home, but she gets these glimpses. How deeply it moves her, that the Nora they took from her at age three comes to her a year later a wise old soul with a gift for asking questions that cut to the core.

"Daddy isn't my first papa, is he?"

"No, he isn't. But he's your daddy now."

"Is my first papa dead?"

Annie closes her eyes. *Please, no.* "Baby, I don't know. Since we don't know, we can believe he isn't."

"Do you think he loved me?"

"Oh yes. I know. He loves you very much. With all his heart."

"Is it okay if I love him? I want to, even if I don't know him."

"It's very okay. He gave you life. In giving you life he gave me the best thing in my life. It doesn't take anything away from Daddy if you love your first papa."

"Then I do." Nora nestles into her mother's arms. "It's like you're not Kieran and Jeannie and Molly's first mama, but you're their mother now."

"Yes, it's just like that."

"Mama, did you know they tried to make me go away with another family? A man and a lady came to meet me. They told me that you had a sad sickness and couldn't take care of me. But I told them that you would come for me before the orange moon. And I was right."

"Yes, you were. But tell me, how did you know?"

"Sometimes at night, I would push my pillow away and put my ear right on the bed. I would listen real hard and I could hear your voice. I remembered how when I don't know what to do you always tell me, 'Think, Nora.' So I thinked. What I thinked was that you would never let someone else have me. If you were sick, you would get well and then you would come get me. When they tried to talk to me about another family, I said, 'Stop it very much!' Mama, I always wondered how far those tunnels went. I knew if I started running, I would make it back to you. I'm a fast runner, and—owww, Mama, you're squeezing me too hard."

"I'm sorry, baby." Annie blinks down on her tears before Nora can see. Unbearable, how close she came to losing this daughter too—to her illness, to her own husband, to nameless strangers.

She tries not to question what price she's paid for this life of safety she felt her daughter deserved. Phil has drawn a protective blanket over them; it warms and mends even as it covers and mutes things she must leave behind. They are not building or creating anything new. They are sustaining, maintaining, trying to heal what they already have. When Phil reaches for her in the night, she reaches for the tin in the nightstand. Their couplings are gentle and satisfying, but once in a while is enough. It has to be enough, because there's one thing about which Annie is adamant: there will be no more pregnancies.

Nora giggles as Annie relaxes her hold. "Did your mama ever squeeze you that hard?"

"I didn't have a mother," Annie replies, the most honest response she can muster.

And when Nora winds her arms around Annie's neck and cries, "Oh, that's terrible! I'm so glad I have one," every horrendous thing Annie has lived through to get to this moment again becomes worth it, twice over.

Nora is indeed a fast runner. She's had to be, to outdistance the unfair amount of adversity she's faced in her short life. It's all she knew until recently. So Annie douses her thoughts and dares her daughter, "How about a race up to the school? We can walk home with Jeannie and Molly, and bake brownies while Kieran's on his paper route."

It's no race because Nora is out the door and halfway up the block before Annie can stand and smooth her clothes. The door slams behind her; she raises her hand to call, "Wait, Nora!" but what comes out is, "Run, Nora!" The least Annie can do is encourage her daughter to use her speed to dash headlong into their new, safe life.

"Will you carve us a jack-o'-lantern?"

The question comes from Jeannie but prompts a chorus of babble from the other children. "Yes, please!" "Can we each have our own?" "Our dad tried to do one but it wasn't very good." "Knock it off, Molly, that's not nice." "It's true. It was supposed to be a monster but it looked like a clown." "Oh, like you could do better."

Nora's small voice cuts through the others. "What's a jack-o'-lantern?"

That stops the bickering but not the babble. "Oh, Nora, it's fun!" exclaims Jeannie. "You cut the top off a pumpkin and scoop out the guts. Then you carve a face in the pumpkin and put a candle in it on Halloween night."

"The face has to be horrible scary," says Kieran.

"That's not true," Jeannie scolds. "It can be a goofy face if she wants."

"Yeah," chimes in Molly. "You don't make the rules, Kieran. It can be anything."

"Stop it, stop it," Annie laughs. "You're confusing Nora."

"Nora, we're sorry." Jeannie grabs her hand. "You know what pumpkins are, don't you?"

"They're for making pies."

"That's right," Annie says. "But before it can be a pie, it has to be grown in a garden. I lived on farms for more than thirty years. One of the things we always grew was sugar pumpkins. They're about the size of a cabbage, and that's where pumpkin pie begins."

"I love pie. Can we have a pie?" This from Jeannie.

"I want a jack-o'-lantern," Molly states firmly.

"We can have both." Annie feels like a referee. "But I have to warn you that I've never carved a jack-o'-lantern before. If you laugh or make fun of it, it may be my first and last time."

Again the babble. "No laughing, we promise." "When can we have the pie? I'm starving just thinking about it." "I want the nastiest jack-o'-lantern in town, Mom. I want it to scare the stuffing out of that lunkhead Frank Hurder. Frank Furter, it should be." "Molly, you're mean." "Easy for you, Kieran. It's not your hair he's pulling every darn day."

The children are starved for more than pie; they crave

normalcy. Annie knew it the day her name ceased being ma'am and became Mom.

After school, they cover the porch with newspaper. An hour later it's saturated with pumpkin pulp and seeds. Kieran and Molly produce frightful bogeys, while Jeannie isn't sure what hers is. After turning it this way and that, she decides it is Scrooge's Ghost of Halloween Present. "Jeannie loves *A Christmas Carol*," Molly explains to Annie. "She has a crush on Bob Cratchit." "Do not!" screams Jeannie.

Nora wants her pumpkin to be an orange kitty. They carve triangles for the eyes; then Annie sinks hairpins into the cutouts to attach as ears on the top of the pumpkin. Nora rubs the pumpkin behind one ear and whispers, "Poos."

"Next year," Annie announces, "we'll grow our own pumpkins. Right over there along the fence."

"Golly," Jeannie breathes. "We've never had a garden."

"Pumpkins practically grow themselves," Annie assures her. "You put them in the ground, keep them watered, and off they go. They put out huge green leaves"—she indicates with her hands spread wide—"and curly tendrils. You can each have your own. We'll have a contest. See who can grow the biggest one."

"Nora would probably win," Jeannie says kindly.

"What's it like to live on a farm?" Kieran asks.

Nora jumps to her feet. "Mama doesn't like to talk about that," she states in a manner that closes discussion. The McCandless children stare.

"That's enough for today." Annie gathers up their knives and spoons. They spread the seeds out to dry. They fold up the gooey newspapers and leave a fresh stack for Annie. She'll carve her pumpkin tomorrow while the kids are at school, although she hasn't the foggiest idea what it might be.

The children lug their jack-o'-lanterns to the front porch. "Mom knows everything about pumpkins," Jeannie declares to Nora.

"Mama knows about lots of things."

The tip of Annie's knife plays over the curve of the pumpkin, waiting for a surge of imagination. It's childish for a going-on-forty-year-old woman to be carving a jack-o'-lantern. She doesn't need more bogeys in her life. Besides, there are about fifty-seven more important things that need doing, including those pies the kids are so excited about.

Don't make rules. It can be anything.

Her knife sinks in to the hilt. She pulls it out and it dives in again at a forty-five-degree angle to the first cut. Again. And again.

She pushes on the cut shape with her thumb and it pops backward into the hollow of the pumpkin—a small star. She cuts another, and another, and another. A shower of stars. Below them she pulls the knife along in a curve, forming an arc. This she also pushes into the hollow. When she reaches in to remove it, she finds it won't leave her hand. A bright orange waxing crescent. The next thing she knows, the children are clattering up the porch and her lap is steeped in brown sludge. Her hands are powerful. They have crushed the moon to pap.

Phil is impressed.

"You outdid yourself on the jack-o'-lanterns. If that was your first effort, I don't dare imagine what you'll turn out next year."

"Thanks, but let's not worry about making room for the Venus de Milo."

"You don't know how to accept a compliment, do you? And the kids told me you talked about growing their own pumpkins. What's that about? I distinctly remember telling you that your gardening days were over. You don't have to do it for the kids."

"If you could have seen their faces. They had such fun. Growing pumpkins is easy."

He drops his shirt on the floor and crosses the room to her. "I wasn't wrong about you. You've given us our lives back." He lowers her to the bed, moving her clothing out of the way. "I have to do this, and you have to let me," he says, only half teasing.

"You're so demanding," she says, only half teasing.

Yule Night is a week away but for Annie, the days of Advent slip from the calendar into the cesspit of her growing anxiety. The constant retreats to the bathroom, sometimes forcing herself to wait a complete hour. Staring into the toilet bowl, water clear as gin below her parted thighs. Digging her fingers into her belly, eating handfuls of aspirin. Guzzling an evil-smelling potion of penny-royal and blue and black cohosh. For the sixth time today, lifting her dress reveals nothing but disdainfully white undergarments.

"Damnation!" she snaps, slamming the toilet lid and the medicine cabinet in concert.

"Why the tizz?"

Her arms jerk to her chest; her pulse jumps off a cliff. When did he come in, and does he know he's the last person she wants to see?

"I hope this isn't about Christmas," he says. "It's not that important to me."

"It's not about Christmas." She pushes him aside and storms to the bedroom.

"Then what? Is it one of the kids?"

"'Is it one of the kids?'" she mimics. "'Is it one of the kids?' Yes, it's one of the kids. One we haven't met yet."

"What are you saying?"

"I've missed."

"Oh my goodness. That's wonderful."

She shakes her head so violently she must put her hands up to stop it lest her brains come loose. "No, it isn't. It's not wonderful, Phil. It is *not wonderful*."

"Honey, it is by me. Another child is welcome here."

"It isn't the child! It's the pregnancy. Please, please don't play stupid. You met me in the state hospital. You know why I was there. I can't do this. I can't go through it again. It is *not wonderful*."

"Annie, I'm trying hard not to be insulted by your attitude. I'm not concerned in the slightest. Forewarned is forearmed." He reaches for her with a naïve look of delight that claws her bowels. "If we know what to expect, we can't be blindsided. It's wonderful."

She sinks to the floor and pulls her knees up close. "Insulted?" Her voice drops. "I was wrong about you. You will never under-stand." With that, she shuts her eyes and shuts down.

The worst part of it is the month of strain between them and the look on his face when she tells him she was wrong; she was only late. The wadded-up pads in the trash write the ending of a chapter in what is now her life, stranded somewhere between happy and sad, safely afloat, both shores in sight but out of reach.

30

For three years now, home has been a warm room in the Edmonton boardinghouse where Adam drops his laundry and picks up his mail once a month when he comes in from the road. The Hudson Bay Company thrived for two centuries before he came along; he's a small cog in a big wheel now, and the anonymity suits him. He pushes his bosses to send him ever farther north, and they do, places that have never been pierced by a tractor or train whistle, where he can remove himself from time and pretend those things don't exist, aren't part of his story.

The northern lights spew a fountain of shimmering green and pink across the chill sky outside his window. Barren tree branches reach toward the street, their pale fingers sparkling with the first heavy frost of autumn. It cannot be happenstance that this cold front has swept in on the day the mail brought him something that makes him return to the headquarters building during the witching hour, when most of the staff have left but the doors are not yet locked for the night. The few diehards dotting the labyrinth of unkempt desks don't even look up when he passes through. In a far corner he finds a telephone and places the call that will cost a few dollars and all his pride.

The agent is brusque but effective. His account comes at Adam like a barrel jolting its way downhill. Annie and Nora live in Copper Creek, Montana, going by the name McCandless. The agent describes a small woman with a coal-black bob and a towheaded girl leaving a nondescript house in a workaday neighborhood. The woman matched the image in the photograph Adam had provided, a couple smiling in front of a vegetable display at a country fair.

"Guy's a railroad maintenance worker," the agent finishes. "Straight up as far as we can tell. Three older kids plus your daughter. Couldn't find a marriage record for him and your wife, or record of divorce for your marriage or his. You want us to get photos?"

The numbskull didn't take a photo? Adam watches a crow strut across the narrow ledge outside the window. Bad omen. Trickster.

"No." *Leave them alone now.*

The agent gives him a long minute to change his mind.

"That you in the picture at the fair?"

"Yes."

"Your girl looks like you," the agent says before ringing off.

The beer parlor's mahogany bar stretches into oblivion. Even soused, Adam knows it's a trick with mirrors, but the booze is making his eyes lazy and it isn't worth working harder to see where it might end. He tries counting the tiles on the floor but loses interest when a brass cuspidor interrupts his count. It's only a diversion, anyway, to tune out the conversation around him. A couple of HBC chaps elbowed him over to join their merry band, and he wasn't swift enough with a dodge. "Let the Yank in, men. We'll make a Canuck outta him yet." The bartender shot him a sympathetic wink and refilled his glass.

Adam tips back on two legs of his chair. His eyelids drop lower in direct proportion. In conversation more squawk than talk, the subject of women volleys around the all-or-nothing group. The quieter men have the kind of wives the squawkers envy, though the squawkers would sooner chew glass than admit it. They bray long and loud about the hardships visited upon them by women, the devil's own sidekicks in skirts.

"What about you?" a faceless voice caws at him. "Mr. Silent over there. You hitched?"

It's futile to ignore them. He's already tried.

"I was married." *I am married.*

"Hooo," rises the cry. "Was? How'd you get outta that?"

How much can he down in one pull, and how long can he draw it out? Where was it, maybe the Prairie Dog, the time he cold-cocked the slob who, draped over his chums, crowed that after three drinks, there are no ugly women? No respect. No respect at all.

"She had plumbing trouble." The last word comes out on the crest of a belch, acrid enough that he turns his own face from it.

"Aww, so what?" *So what? So what?* echoes off mirrors. "They all do! 'Monthlies,' hooooo! More like dailies! Drive a man nuts. Hooooo!"

He eyes the top of his head in the mirror over the bar. Good. It's still there. "Lots of pregnancies. Lots of trouble."

"Hooooo. Live ammo, folks. How many kids?"

"No kids." Too long the explanation.

The hoots drop a few decibels.

"Yeah. Puerperal trouble." *Pu-er-per-al.* A word most everyone in this room will die without ever hearing. Is it three syllables or four? Can't remember. "She'd unhinge. Stay awake for two weeks. Two. Weeks." He holds up two fingers, centering his nose between them. "Then she shot up my stash. Lined up the bottles so she'd only have to waste one bullet."

"Oh, damn, man. That's fightin' grounds. Did you thrash her good?"

"No." He smiles, for reasons no one will understand, as it should be. "I's proud of her. She's a crack shot. Taught her myself."

Their protests rumble over him. "A man don't put up with that shit. C'mon."

"Lots of misfires. Lots of trouble." The chair teeters back another centimeter. It doesn't seem possible, to be floating and leaden at the same time.

"Not enough! Didja turn the barrel on her on the way out? Gawww, good riddance."

Speaking of putting up with shit. His glass is empty. How on earth can they still be talking?

"She was the only woman I ever took my pants all the way off for."

From behind him, someone nudges his vacant glass aside with a full one, a kindness quickly squelched by the bawling of a grizzled miner with skin the consistency of oatmeal. "Awww, so what? Tha's your pecker talkin'! Hell, man, where I come from, what she done would be a capital offense." His screeching laugh opens up half his face.

With his last shred of restraint, Adam silently, laboriously, counts to five, the number of rotten molars leering from the man's mouth, before replying.

"Seen enough of the cemetery, Sourdough. Already had a daughter up there." He hopes the shock factor will end the exchange. But no, the lout stirs the air with a dirty paw, stoking the crowd. A dribble of whiskey slinks through his mangy beard.

"Hawww. Coulda saved space. Plant 'em together!"

Two chairs over from Adam, one of his colleagues—Jim? Joe? Jehoshaphat?—glances at him, then turns to the miner and tries to slide his glass away. "That's enough, Dusty. Lay offa him"—but the miner is too impressed with his own wit.

"Goin' deep, folks, goin' deep!" The man pulls a crumpled cigarette paper from his shirt pocket and digs into his tobacco pouch but drops it as he wipes the mirth from his eyes. With a florid digging motion, he bends forward to pick it up.

Adam learned something that night. He learned how fast he could get out of a chair and how far up a man's *cavitas nasi* he could propel his foot if sufficiently provoked. *That's Latin for that big empty space in your head, how about that?* He barely feels the contact.

Bedlam. Screaming. Bellowing. Glasses crashing. Chair upending. Bodies colliding. Adam watches it all in slow motion.

"Ye kicked his face in," observes a bag of skin and clothes planted at the bar, winching a quavering glass to flaccid lips with both hands. "That there's a gusher."

I've seen worse, Adam thinks. *In my own home and without the caterwauling.*

Someone shoves him toward the door—"Get moving, Yank"—and in the background he makes out a slurred "gonna regret this."

Outside, he manages to put one foot in front of the other and cover some distance. Gonna regret this? Doubtful. Guy asked for it. And the law? If they deported every boor who got in a barroom brawl, the country would soon be nigh empty. All things considered, Adam thinks himself quite the upstanding citizen, when not being incited by riffraff.

He passes under the mustard glow of a grimy streetlamp. A patina of blood bathes the front of his boot. He plunges it into a snowdrift. A few handfuls scrubs most of it away.

He walks on, picking up his pace.

Regrets?

Where once he strove to keep her out of the reach of other men, now she lies each night with one. How does it feel to her? Does she quake in his arms, as she did with him? Does she love him?

Does she ever wonder what became of her husband, the father of her daughter? She ended up with the better father, the better man, didn't she?

He can't stop the train of thought that punts him into sobriety. Beer and bile erupt from his gut; he heaves the mordant remnants of the evening into the street. Folded at the waist, hanging over the curb, he imagines he looks like any other halfpenny drunk staggering out of a twopenny bar.

But regrets? What would be the point? Carrying around that kind of millstone, at his age? He's nearing fifty this year, an age when people start to catalogue their regrets. His simply lie at the foot of his bed, mute and limp. Like a shot doe.

But he knows more than he knew when the sun came up today. She's not married to this man. She's still married to Adam Fielding. He could reclaim her. Retrieve what's his. He could take a stand, for his daughter, his marriage, his family.

But she left him. *She* left *him*. And he simply let her.

The aurora borealis undulates overhead in shape-shifting curvature reminiscent of her, arching toward him, then bending away in mourning. He let her leave, and because of that, he must for the rest of his life be unselfish; though his need for her, for their daughter, is never far from the surface, he must keep it a carefully watched simmer, never allowed to boil over. That would make things worse for his daughter, who's old enough to know he's never been there for her, old enough to love the man who cares for her. *Your girl looks like you.* The most and best father he can be is to leave her be. Now he understands how Annie punished herself, how she grieved for Cynthia, how she measured herself and came up short.

The iced gravel underfoot glistens its cold sweat. In the grainy shaft of a streetlamp that's probably played confidant to number-less drunks before him, with the blood of a stranger speckling his trousers, Adam searches to his core. Does he have regrets?

It's time, Adam thinks, *to hear it out loud.*

"Yes," he says to the streetlamp. "I do."

Part Three

*From the mountains we do not discern our native
hills; but from our native hills we look out easily to the
far blue mountains. . . .
I see the very peak . . . but how much I do not
see, that is between me and it! How much I overlook!
In this way we see stars.*

—"Mountains in the Distance," from the journal of
Henry David Thoreau, September 27, 1852

31

The yellow postmaster's note drops through the mail slot on a balmy May morning just before Nora's twelfth birthday. Annie almost misses it, stuck between the electric-company bill and an invitation to a McCandless cousin's wedding. The postmaster requests that Annie pick up a package in person. She isn't expecting anything, but Phil sometimes mail-orders tools or books.

"Have you seen Dad?" Annie asks Jeannie.

"He took his pencils up to the caves. He goes there to draw sometimes."

Jeannie's information lifts Annie's dark brow. He has a hidden artistic side? This is unexpected, and delightful. She's seen no evidence of his work, no sketchbook, no portfolio, no finished work or work in progress.

Jeannie leaves to walk their elderly neighbor's dog, leaving Annie to ponder. Why wouldn't he share this with her?

Perhaps there's too much they don't share, Annie thinks as she goes to straighten their bedroom. Everything they need to know seems to be right there on the surface. She reaches across the bed and tugs the sheet and chenille spread smooth, an effort almost unnecessary. Neither she nor Phil moves much in their sleep. Sometimes of a morning, the bed looks as if someone has but paused upon it.

Phil must have his reasons for keeping his drawings from her. Perhaps he lacks confidence in his work. She'll have to change that. She'll ask him to teach her. She can see herself sitting with him on a rock up by the caves, bending over his arm while he sketches and says, *We'll start at the beginning, a stick figure named Annie. . . .*

When he slips in the back door, she sees under his arm a large folder that would not have drawn her attention. She hurries to greet him, radiating enthusiasm.

"Jeannie told me you'd gone to draw. I had no idea you did this—what a marvelous thing. May I see?"

"No." He seems fixed to the spot. "I never show anyone. It's less than amateur."

She laughs at his hand-in-the-candy-jar face. "Not even me? At least tell me what you're drawing. The mountains? Birds? Flowers?"

"My grandmother. From Switzerland." He starts to move around her, but she lays a hand under his elbow. "I was trying to imagine her as a young woman."

"What a splendid thing. Just a peek?"

She doesn't mean to pressure him. She wants only to support him. He works hard to support all of them. Long hours, double shifts, no complaints. She tries to convey her appreciation by being as acquiescent as possible. Discovering that there are mysterious parts of him, unrevealed, arouses her. She likes the feel of it. She hopes it shows on her face, because it's underlaid with contrition. The pull of ardor, that spark—it's something she can't often muster.

He stares at her for a moment. She can't miss the apprehension in his hand as he opens the flap of the envelope and slides a piece of paper halfway out, taking a step back as he does.

His pencil has turned the woman's face away; her eyes follow the ridge where the mountains cut into the sky. She stands coatless, a hand at the base of her throat, the other wrapped around her waist. Layers of delicate strokes from the broad side of the pencil spread a shadow across the woman's face. In the distance, a snake makes for the hills; an osprey dips over the ridge.

The skin along Annie's arms prickles. She understands this woman, far from where she started out, in a foreign landscape that may never feel like home.

"She's lovely, Phil. I feel like I know her. I can see who Molly takes after. Goodness. What other talents are you hiding from me?"

He smiles but doesn't answer.

Everything about his stance and tone is telling her to stop, but she can't. "Where in Switzerland was she from? I had a German grandmother. We think she came from somewhere near Freiburg, not far from Basel, but we couldn't pin her down on that."

"Same for our family. I . . . never knew the name of the town. But here's something I know. I'm famished. What's for supper?"

"What would you like, my reluctant Rembrandt?"

"What have you got?" He reaches for her waist. Her belly meets his and her hands slide under his belt. The drawing falls to the floor, forgotten.

For a sweet half hour, they disarrange the carefully straightened bed. When it quiets under them, he pushes her hair back from her forehead and says, "Wanna get married?"

"It's Saturday."

"We could do it on Monday. What do you say?"

"I say it might be some spectacle, walking into the courthouse and making public record of righting a lie the whole town has believed for some years now."

"We'll go to Lewiston. Or Spokane."

"Dear man, no five-dollar piece of paper is going to make me feel more married to you."

Jeannie's voice sounds in the alley, calling to a neighbor. *Hello! Beautiful day, isn't it?* Phil springs up and grabs for his trousers. Kicking into them, his foot catches the edge of a basket just under the bed. In it is a Stonington shawl in progress. She's completed the second flange, the exact halfway point.

"What's this?" He fingers the delicate piece.

"A shawl. I still have yarn from Pearson's. I'm going to sell it and—"

"You're going to what?" His voice has an unsettling ring.

"Sell it. For a pretty price. I told you, this is what I was starting to do when you—"

"Yes, I know." He lets the lacy web sift between his fingers. "But it's different seeing it close up. This isn't your usual mitten or sock—"

"Yes. That's why—"

"I can't let you do this."

"*Let* me?"

"The only person I want to see in this shawl is you. I don't want to run into some society dame wearing this and know that you traded it for skates for the kids, or draperies—"

"What's wrong with that? We need those things, and a nest egg besides wouldn't—"

"I provide those things." His eyes harden into thunderclouds. "What I don't provide, we don't need."

He wins their duel of unfinished sentences. A dozen retorts

leap to her lips, but she bites down on them, eyes filling with her determination to say nothing more as he strides from the room, her skin still warm from his embrace. The back door rattles, Jeannie blowing in with "Oh, bye, Dad." The galumphing of his boots is the last she hears of him until after midnight, when voices in the alley awaken her. Moving to the window and nudging the curtain aside a finger's width, she makes out two figures, one stooped and shambling, the other upright and uniformed.

". . . a good woman you've got, Mr. McCandless. Now get on in there," the officer says. She meets Phil in the kitchen. From the look and smell of him, he's passed the hours at Michalek's speakeasy.

She says nothing while his hands flop about in his pockets. His green eyes have shriveled to wrinkly peas. She dares his God to be forbearing enough to grant that the kids won't wake, won't have to see their father in this state of mildewed dignity. After a minute he lowers his head and exhales, long and reedy, like the air leaking from the punctured tire they had to replace last week. "Finish the shawl, Annie. Before you sell it, enter it in the fair. I'm sure you'll win big."

"Oh, honey." She holds her breath against the skunk stench of his booze-logged displeasure and, summoning conviction she hopes will persuade them both, whispers, "I've already won big."

In the morning, his contrition irks rather than appeases her. He leaves for church with the children, same as always. She scrapes breakfast plates, same as always. She feels entitled to her ill temper, but prolonging the disaccord can only hurt the children. Still, she needs a shot of defiance to settle the matter with herself. "Pick up your own damn mail," she mutters, and a small yellow note from the postmaster follows today's waffle crumbs and yesterday's newspaper into the trash bin.

The forces of nature pock the hills above the cemetery with caves that beckon the young and small, drawn to the dark cool that nurtures many needs. Protection, adventure, solitude. Annie and Phil's children explored the rocky recesses tirelessly when they were younger. A particular cave, Annie knows from a hundred field reports, cuts clean through the hills, an exhilarating quest for one nimble enough to slither through on one's belly. She's cleaned enough skinned knees, elbows, ankles, and foreheads to feel as if she's been through the passage herself.

She stands at a gash in the rock, an entrance narrow and tall and chill of breath. Is this the cave? Three wind-warped scrub trees lean in skew-whiff stances of eternal boredom. Annie bends to peer into the opening. Is this it? The place where a child can crawl through a mountain and come out on the other side?

"Yes, it is," says Phil, squeezing her fingers, sweaty from their hand-in-hand climb up the last steep yards of the slope. "I can't believe we never brought you up here." He lets go her hand to open his pencil pouch and sketch pad. "Sit on that rock and look directly at me, please."

"Gosh, no, Phil. I wanted you to teach me, not sketch me."

"We don't always get what we want, do we?" he says, pencil already working. "Sit, please. I want you to see you the way I see you. Aren't you curious?"

Who has time to be curious when a family of six commands more than the hours allotted to the day? One rainy afternoon she calculates the logistics of it. In a year's time she prepares 6,500 meals, washes 4,400 socks, makes two hundred trips to the market, swabs and sweeps three acres of floor, knits her way through two miles of yarn.

Tinker, tailor, laundress, cook. Housekeeper, bookkeeper, timekeeper, peacekeeper. Judge, jury, preacher, teacher. Year after year, she's listened to the children's whoops and woes, their squabbles and squarings, their jokes and jibes. She's wiped away tears, soup sloshes, muddy prints. She's listened to their school recitations, their singing with the radio, their fears and dreams and prayers.

They've grown while her back is turned. She knits incessantly. The basket in the front room overflows; someone always needs a sweater or socks. Phil was right about the Stonington shawl, albeit for the wrong reason. The shawl business was a stirring aspiration, but she has no room for it in this demanding life. It would take her a year to finish the one she's started. Each week her mop nudges it farther under the bed, until it's reached the darkest corner of a room that's dark for most of the time she spends in it. Out of sight, not worth the fight.

Three weeks after the half shawl last saw light, another yellow postcard drops through the mail slot. *Second notice! Please claim your package immediately.* Contrite but not curious, Annie puts aside her morning's work and walks the mile to the post office.

The postmaster hands her a stout manila envelope. She nearly drops it.

Mrs. Analiese Fielding McCandless, General Delivery, Copper Creek, Montana, USA.

That postmark. Edmonton, Alberta, Canada.

"Didn't know you had family in Canada, Mrs. McCandless."

"Enjoy your day, Mr. Bensonhill." She nods on her way out. That subtle crowbar edge to his voice. His wife would flay him for not digging harder, and that ensures that the package will remain a confidence between her and the only other person in Copper Creek to have seen it.

On the sidewalk, the decisions she faces overwhelm her. Must she open this envelope? With its official typed label from a courthouse in Edmonton, it can mean but one thing.

Where to go to open it? Not home, not the park, not the coffee shop. Blind footsteps have brought her to the town cemetery. She finds a bench. The envelope waits in her lap.

She can't do it. Inside the envelope she'll find official papers telling her that Adam is dead. He must have left something to Nora. Why does she have to know? The postmark swims before her eyes. She hopes that however the end came, it wasn't painful. A dozen awful images crowd her head: he's clutching his chest, hurtling through a windshield, coughing rivers of blood, trapped by flame. Putting his shotgun in his mouth. What will she say to Nora?

Whatever his final wishes, she decides, she will carry them out to the letter. She slides her finger under the flap of the envelope and pulls out a sheaf of papers. *Dominion of Canada, Department of the Secretary of State, Naturalization Branch.*

She holds her breath as she rifles the pages. *Certificate of Naturalization, Adam Weatherston Fielding.* File numbers, dates, signatures. A page with his familiar, forceful handwriting: *I swear by Almighty God that I will be faithful and bear true allegiance to His Majesty King George the Fifth. . . .*

Bewilderment crowds out her relief that he isn't dead. He's become a Canadian citizen; why has he sent her this information?

They've been apart more years than they were together. She's made another life for herself, and what should she have assumed but that he'd done the same?

She scours more pages, until—oh dear God. Again his handwriting stares up at her:

> I respectfully submit . . . My name is . . . I was born on . . .

> I am married. My wife's name is Analiese Fielding. She was born in Iowa, USA, and now resides in Copper Creek, Montana. I have one child under the age of 21. Her name is Nora Marielle Fielding. She was born in Montana, USA. She resides at Copper Creek, Montana.

Annie shuffles feverishly through the rest of the papers. The last page is the showstopper: a form letter from the Department of State, Naturalization Branch, advising her that Canadian law entitles her to derivative citizenship via her husband's, should she join him in residence within two years.

What now, what now? The papers spill from her lap. She crawls around in the grass, scrabbling in vain for a personal note. What in heaven's name is happening?

She eases herself onto the bench, an inch at a time, because it feels as if every bone in her body is breaking at once. She can't think. She has to think. What is he trying to do?

I am married.

He knows where she is. He knows she isn't legally married to anyone but him. But of course he knows—he knows how to dig, oh, he knows how to do that.

He never got over losing his daughter. Daughters. He's offering her an extraordinary opening: *Come back to me.* He is too proud, or too afraid, to ask her directly.

I am married.

She could go. She could take her daughter to the father who pines for her, who has no other child, the man to whom she is still married. They could forgive and forget and rekindle and resurrect. They are older, sadder, wiser now. *Come back to me. Come back to life.*

She reassembles the papers and slides them back into the envelope, then walks home on feet she can't feel. She takes to her bed before supper, deaf to Phil's concern. When he comes to bed hours later, she lies at the edge, feigning sleep when he slides his arms around her and pulls her close.

In the morning, she tells him she's feeling better, thank you, and kisses him goodbye with more emphasis than usual. "Wow," he says. "I'll take that."

"Goodbye, Daddy," Nora calls. "Don't forget our gin rummy game tonight. You're gonna lose!"

He calls back, "I wouldn't miss it, and don't spend the day thinking up ways to cheat." The rest of the children, the ones Annie swore she would never leave, laugh and hoot that Nora doesn't need to cheat to beat him. Out the door, they scatter to school, to work. The house settles into hush.

I will never leave your children.

Only then does Annie let herself cry, a cry for the ages from one who thought she had long ago cried all a person could cry and not die of it, crying so hard it takes six matches for her to strike a spark to the corner of the envelope in the fireplace, then holding her hand as close as she dares to the blue flame that leaps to fill the firebox.

32

The three officers of the Ladies Auxiliary of Samaritan General Hospital sit before a tea tray of mismatched cups in Annie's living room. Three sets of knees confront her, their somber dresses of gray feedcloth and loden wool matching the February sky. "This wretched depression," the president of the group begins, "is in its sixth year. A desperate number of people in the county are in need of public aid."

"Indeed," Annie agrees, as if she doesn't see it, smell it, and speak to it every Sunday when she appears at the back door of the town's poorest church with a pan of Scotch hot pot while Phil and Nora attend mass across town. Annie holds charity most authentic when it's inconspicuous. "Please feel free to come straight to the point. Do you need more shawls and slippers? You'd like me to oversee a knitting group?"

The president leans forward, stockings making comical zipper noises as her knees rub. "The auxiliary proposes to plow the south side of the hospital grounds and put in a vegetable garden. We've come to you for obvious reasons." When Annie sits back, the woman adds, "Eulalia here says . . . well, your exquisite daughter Nora told her that you can make a fence post sprout. Most of us, to be frank, have found gardening in Copper Creek a tough go."

"For obvious reasons," Annie says. "Conditions we can't change. The altitude. The lack of rain. Pollutants in the soil and water."

The secretary, wife of a copper executive, waves a coral-varnished finger and scolds, "We don't know that for sure."

The president of the auxiliary leans forward, a triangle of white hankie saluting from the breast pocket of her dress as she shushes her colleague with a hand to the shoulder. "Please, Mrs. McCandless. You are the voice of authority on this."

"Based on one remark from my daughter? She's sixteen and—"

"Not given to exaggeration. Mr. McCandless confirmed that you have forgotten more on the subject than we will ever know."

"A productive garden demands more than hiring a tractor to break ground," Annie says. "Planning, planting, thinning, irrigating, harvesting, cold storage, preservation, inventory, distribution. Crop rotation, pest control, soil amendment. It's dirty, smelly, backbreaking work, and lots of it. At least seven months, nonstop. Are your committee members prepared to take that on?"

Mrs. Copper Boss crosses her ankles, silk pumps humming, thumb flicking the inside of a jade cocktail ring. The third woman, Eulalia, is a member of Phil's church, probably the one who suggested this visit. The woman's hands stay in her lap as she says, "Annie, many are in need of your expertise."

Annie, who can already smell the soil under her fingernails, hasn't forgotten enough. She can't come up with a reason to say no.

A week later she tells a gathering of the Ladies Auxiliary, "We'll keep it simple, a dozen crops at most. We have less than an acre to work with, but if it's managed diligently, the output may surprise you."

Her pencil flies over a large pad of paper propped on an easel. "Timing is important. We want to start as early in the season as possible and go up to the first fall frost. We'll start the upper quadrant with things that can tolerate a light frost. Irish potatoes, spinach, cabbage. Meanwhile, anyone who has space in their house can start tomatoes or cauliflower. Show of hands, please. Eulalia, will you take names?"

Her pencil races on. "Second group can go in when the ground is cold but the frost danger is over. Carrots and beets, with lettuce along the edge, as we will be replenishing it every four weeks. We'll have to shelter the string beans if we get a late run of cool weather. Save your boxes and newspapers." She gestures to the group to write it down. "Last group goes in after the ground has warmed. Squash, melons, tomatoes. Beans and beets turn every six to nine weeks, so we'll have two plantings, maybe three. We'll stagger them every three weeks to get a supply line going."

The women of the Ladies Auxiliary sit mute. Some have known Annie more than ten years and not once seen her so much as pick up a trowel. Annie continues, "We'll need as much soft water as we can muster, and that means rain barrels. Sheep manure is the best fertilizer. Who will volunteer to find us a source?"

"Mom, I feel terrible watching you do all this and knowing you don't want to. I made an offhand remark. I didn't dream they would pick it up as the eleventh commandment."

Mid-May, midmorning. Annie should be at the garden now, to oversee the installation of the water barrels and set up gravity-drip soaker lines. Instead she's standing at the sink in her kitchen with arms crossed at the waist, wondering why she bothers wondering why about anything anymore.

"Nora dearest, sometimes we're called upon to answer a need greater than our want." Annie picks up a plate from the kitchen table and tips her untouched breakfast into the garbage pail. "That's all this is." She twists the faucet too hard, and cold water splatters off the plate and soaks the pushed-up cuff of her sweater. "And I know you meant it only as an affectionate overstatement."

"Indeed no." From the aluminum pot on the stove, Nora pours coffee in a thick white cup and tucks it into Annie's hands, wrapping her mother's palms and fingers around it.

"No? Then what?"

Nora tips a tablespoon of cream into the cup. "Have you ever tried to make a fence post sprout? Then you don't know that you can't. My mother always says so. Look, if you don't want to go, I will. Tell me what to tell them, and I'll say you aren't feeling up to snuff today."

"That is true. Estella's there today, and I feel ill at the thought of listening to her prattle about her daughter's wedding."

"Is this the one who's getting married next New Year's Day?"

"Yes. I may vomit if I hear one more simper about 'what a symbolic day for fresh beginnings.'" No sooner have the words left her mouth than she clamps her jaw. She's never dodged the subject of Adam, but neither has she volunteered information. Nora knows only what she's asked about her first papa. She knows about an indigo gown worn on a long-ago January 1. She knows a New Year's Day wedding didn't bring her parents a long and happy life together. She doesn't know how hard her mother has worked to banish the memory of it, and how in vain the effort has been.

"Mom," Nora says, picking up the hospital garden planning notebook. "Remember the history paper I wrote last year about Teddy Roosevelt? He said we should do the best we can with what we've got, whatever the situation we find ourselves in. You did that. This may be the first time I've ever heard you complain about anything. I'll drop your instructions with whoever's at the garden today. It's Saturday. Go do something you want to do."

The phone jangles in the hall and Nora goes to answer it. The depth of Nora's wisdom humbles Annie yet again. She picks up her cream wool shawl from the chair, wondering for the first time in forever what "something you want to do" might be.

With the afternoon sun at its height, Annie is content to sit in the shade of the entrance to the hillside cave that once delighted her children. She herself feels as if she's crawled through mountains without the luxury of a cave passage. Nora told her to do something she wanted to do, and here she is. Above it all.

Nora Marielle. Nora is her treasure, her miracle, her lifesaver. But living with Nora means she's never allowed to be done with Adam. Like the smudge from a dirty eraser, his words and presence are gone but the mark of his existence remains. It could be him, the way Nora presses her fingers into her forehead when she's frustrated, or the effortless skill with which she can sell a request Annie wants to refuse. Annie went faint when she first confronted Nora about the auxiliary's insistence that she take charge of the garden project. Nora's biting retort—"Who else? Those ladies couldn't breed flies on manure"—sounded familiar.

The sun slumps into the hills, stirring chill air up and over the ridge. Annie tosses a pebble down the hill and watches it skitter and bounce out of sight. She casts her thoughts out on the wind, that it might carry them to someone far away, that he might know of her immeasurable gratitude for the gift of Nora.

Today has been a day for wondering, but a rare day, for only rarely does she allow herself to wonder if he ever thinks of her.

An osprey dives over the ridge, a missile of power and confidence until a rogue current in the wind bumps it off course. It tumbles, all but touching her as it swoops by. The sickle edge of its wing carves a crescent on her heart, exposing what she knows and can no longer deny knowing.

He thinks of her. He does.

At times, he thinks of nothing else.

33

Adam has no desire to own property again. It isn't practical, given his long, unbroken weeks on the road. So why does the yellow house draw him? Why doesn't he take any of the dozen shorter routes to reach the streetcar, the grocer, the pharmacy, the saloon, the newsstand?

One call to the realty office. Desperate American seller. Lost everything in the crash, then inherited the house. Can't pay the taxes. Will take rock-bottom price if it's cash.

"I don't know," Adam tells the real estate agent, "if I want to take such drastic advantage of another's misfortune." *Having been there myself.*

The agent says, "Suit yourself, Mr. Fielding. If you don't, someone will. It's a honey. All that mahogany millwork. And the—"

"I'll let you know." Adam starts to hang up, but the agent lays on the pitch even thicker.

"You can get anything delivered from right there in the neighborhood. Coal, mail, laundry, ice, groceries. That cozy porch, you can sit there and let the world come to you."

Sit on the porch. The agent must be in cahoots with his doctor.

"You're north of sixty now, Adam," the man said the last time Adam saw him. "Birthdays, not latitude. Your heart is showing signs of protest. It's time to give some thought to a life that allows you to sleep in your own bed."

"This is what I do."

"And I've enjoyed your stories over the years. I've seen more frostbite than Santa Claus, but you're the only one who froze his hindquarters plugging a hole in a canoe hurtling down the Mackenzie River. It's a younger man's job, my friend."

"It's what I do."

He buys the yellow house. He doesn't need three bedrooms, doesn't need the flat, sun-soaked yard. Doesn't need to be wielding a hoe again, letting it drop under its own weight into the soil. Or maybe he does. In buying a yellow house from a broken man who never lived in it, might Adam somehow unbreak himself?

The hoe exemplifies the paradox of his life, its underscore of arrogance, his forever thinking he can create something better by breaking things. Breaking wild horses, breaking wild prairie sod, breaking new trade routes into wild, forbidding territories.

Breaking his vows to Annie.

He leans on the hoe and looks at the house. He's broken his vow to himself, never again to settle. And there are still things to break. He could break his silence. He could ask his daughter to come to him, to meet her father. He could find her with one call to the Copper Creek Library, one look in the city directory and if Nora's not living with Annie *McCandless*, one call to the county clerk for a marriage record. The window under the eaves at the back of the house glints in the slanting sun. The wide bedroom is the only room on the upper floor. Nora would be comfortable, with its view of her father's garden. The stories would tumble out of both of them, dotted with rich, replenishing pauses of quiet when they would go to the kitchen and make coffee and—

And what? Indulge his selfish desires and fantasies at the cost of opening old wounds and straining her loyalties? Ignore the part of him that refuses to conjure the face and voice and manner of the man his daughter thinks of as her father? He dare not ignite his jealous heart, the source of so much of his sorrow. *I always knew you would dig for it.* His digging has never brought him happiness, and he has no reason to think his revealing himself to Nora would bring her happiness. Might it not devastate Annie, too? In the end, he cannot do that.

So the hoe drops and another cycle of life begins again. He's been away from it longer than he did it. But he moves with a deep-rooted rhythm, and it all comes back.

The growing season is brief but the days linger late. The cabbages swell and glisten from the 4:00 a.m. dawn to the 11:00 p.m.

twilight. The carrots wave their lacy tops in a languid chorus line. The potatoes nap in the warm soil and the squash grow into somber gnomes of outlandish proportions. Even the magpies stay away.

Market gardens dot vacant lots throughout the city. His plot is unremarkable. Except that, he overhears, the whole neighborhood wonders how he keeps it up when he's away from home for weeks at a time. And a man alone can't possibly make use of all those vegetables. They're waiting for him to come selling, but it doesn't happen.

The orphanage sends their deepest thanks. *Mr. Fielding, you're a godsend.*

He's pacing off the north side yard for a flower plat when the postman hands him an envelope addressed in his sister's hand. He knows what it means.

Father is dead, she wrote. *Even if you don't care, I thought you should know.*

The rest of the letter can wait. He props it on a shelf in the shed. Does he care? He knows it appears he doesn't because he's never crossed the borders, real or imagined, that separate them. He's never traveled the distance to embrace his mother, to allow her to hold his face in her hands trembling with pining and age. To reach out in peace to his father. To the siblings who long ago explained him away to their children.

In his mind's eye, they arrange themselves as for a camera. Jonas and Julia, a couple grown old together without ever questioning that it might be otherwise. Their children standing behind them, their grandchildren—some of them—at their feet. Together, they form a portrait of all that life has denied Adam. His brother with his vivacious wife and matching daughter. His sisters, comfortable paeans to familial duty fulfilled. Adam isn't in the portrait because to step before that lens would be to behold his brother living a life snatched from him, to see the joy in his mother's face undercut by the grief inflicted by his years of self-exile. And most unbearable of all, to be mocked by the fact of Jonas, a man five times granted the gift of fatherhood. Five times, at least as many as paternity scorned Adam.

He needs his full weight to bear on the spade as it bites into ground long undisturbed. Grape-hued worms thrash in the unwelcome light hitting the first overturned shovelful.

The daughter who lived is grown. *Your girl looks like you.* Perhaps she's already married. Perhaps he's a grandfather. He tries to picture her black-haired mother. Does she wonder if he ever thinks of her?

At times, he thinks of nothing else.

He thinks of all the nevers, now that he knows *never* to be the most contemptible word in the English language. He'll never see her or speak to her again, so there's much she'll never know. She never knew how highly he valued her feisty ways, even as he fought them. She's never known how tiresome he's found a lifetime of other women when he compares them to her.

He never told her he loved her. He never let himself admit it.

At the bottom of his jacket pocket, he rolls between stiffened fingers a piece of trash he's hauled around for more than a quarter of a century, a creased penny thimble from another life in another country. Kept it, never wondering why—*doesn't matter, so small, so weightless it almost doesn't exist anyway.* FR DR OODS G O COFFEEN'S.

He realizes now that it carries the weight of a failure at the only thing that might have been a meaningful reason for his existence. And it has taken up space that might have let someone else in.

His father is dead. Does he care? He too is someone's father, and soon enough he'll cross that inevitable western gate himself. Will anyone care?

When he hangs his spade in the shed, his sister's letter remains on the ledge. He leaves the house, heading west. On this most pleasant of late summer evenings, he walks a meandering route across the grand grounds of the Alberta legislature and onto the High Level bridge. Below, the North Saskatchewan River rushes by, dark drops sparkling here and there. The bridge is too high and the sun too low for him to see any reflection in the water, to read his own face to try to figure out whether he should do it. One flick would consign the thimble to the custody of the river, where it might bob along for a thousand miles until it reaches the splendor of Lake Winnipeg. Heady fate for an ancient, useless thimble. Over and over he walks it between his fingers. Would it ride the river to Manitoba? Or might it get tossed along for a while, buffeted and abused, then claimed by the mud, as it was when he rescued it as a newlywed, but this time disappearing forever while the mighty river thunders overhead for time eternal?

He snaps his head from these foolish thoughts, unable to imagine why the fate of a mangled piece of metal should matter in the slightest. Enough already. He should drop it over the side, catch the streetcar, and be home in fifteen minutes. But he can't do it, and as the last streaks of the prairie sunset slip below the horizon, he knows why.

Once he lets it go, he can't change his mind.

34

She knew when she made the appointment. The bleeding and the pain, not portents of good health. The house she returns to is the same one she left just two hours ago, but it has aged, caught up with her. She moves through the rooms, sees the tableau of her life and Phil's now that the children are grown and gone, and she feels the need to change something, to purge and reorder.

A corner closet in their bedroom is stuffed chockablock with family flotsam he can't part with. She opens the door, half expecting the contents to cascade forth and bury her. First glance tells her it's mostly junk. A good place for a purge.

The musty smell makes her queasy, and she warns herself to be careful. Vermin, dead or alive, aren't out of the question. A box, split at three corners, holds sheet music from the girls' piano lessons, "Jeanie with the Light Brown Hair" and "Molly Malone," curling at the edges. A wicker creel crumbling around a welter of lures and flies. Phil's grandfather's battered canteen. Kieran's first skates, dry and cracked as a map of the moon.

She piles several armloads outside as trash, then gets a stool to tackle the upper shelf. It's stacked with boxes of old Christmas cards. Good grief, did Phil save every little thing that crossed their threshold? Even on the stool she has to stretch to reach the rear of the shelf, and even then she can't see what she's doing. As her hand moves along the wall, it suddenly hits empty air. She tries to lean in closer, groping. It's an alcove, wide enough for her hand if she folds in her thumb over her pinkie.

Her fingertips brush against a box in the cubbyhole. More cards? Jeepers, there are enough here for a bonfire. She strains to hook a finger over the edge and pull it toward her, and when she does, she pulls too hard. The box slides to the edge of the shelf and plunges over, spilling its contents across the rug.

These pink vellum letters are not for her eyes. Branded with Oregon postmarks, addressed to Phillip McCandless in care of a post office box fifteen miles down the rail line.

They date almost to the beginning of her time with Phil. An arm's length from the bed they've shared for decades, Analiese Rushton Fielding McCandless, who has never asked about her husbands' pasts, faces off against a pile of letters that can only be damning.

> April 23, 1926: . . . am grateful, but if she were truly a wonderful mother she would want them to be with their real mother, and you to be with your real wife. Our children would adjust. You've only been her little girl's stepfather for a few years; they would adjust. I do wonder why she won't give you more children. Or do you not do that for thinking of me?

> June 17, 1928: . . . heartened to know that you still love me. You have, however, convinced me that you will not reconsider. I weep in frustrated disagreement with your view that you are putting the children first, at acceptable sacrifice to yourself. But so be it. I have decided I might as well accept Samuel's proposal. He is a kind, hardworking man, although being a farmer's wife isn't . . .

> November 12, 1931: Stephen is starting to ask questions. He would like a photograph of his father. Better yet, present yourself. You have plenty of cousins here, excuse enough for a visit in anyone's book.

> February 25, 1933: Such a long silence, my darling. I'm sure you're right in that once would not be enough. Believe me, I'm properly ashamed that I can't help thinking, "and what of it?"

January 4, 1939: Come soon if you want to see Stephen before he goes into the Army. I'll miss him terribly, as he's been a tremendous help since my husband died.

The scrape of the kitchen door opening means she has only a moment to compose herself before Phil appears. In the mirror behind him she sees what he sees, a woman who takes up little space, seated prettily on the floor with her slender legs in their wide trousers tucked to the side.

"Where exactly is Amity, Oregon?" How academic her voice sounds. An everyday geography lesson. "Such a sweet name. And you were asked to visit. How nice."

He grips the foot rail of their bed, face turning as gray as his flannel shirt. He can't be expected to speak in such a state of shock. But she doesn't have all day. In fact, as the doctor informed her, she doesn't have much time at all.

"Bleeding after menopause almost always means a cancer of the uterus," the doctor said in his cracked-bell baritone. "I wish you had come in sooner. We can operate to stop the bleeding and do a course of radiotherapy. But the disease has likely spread. I'm sorry."

"No need for sorry," she told him. Why, if she had a dollar for every time a doctor told her "I'm sorry," she could buy her own hospital. It seemed logical and inevitable. Why wouldn't the organ that's always been the source of intractable grief now deliver the final betrayal?

She might be an eel now, the way Phil is looking down at her and the splay of seditious letters.

"Say something, dear," she prompts.

"I don't know that there's anything I can say."

"How convenient. C'mon, you can cough up a few sentences."

His face masks over, transfiguring someone she thought she knew. "Very well," he says. "If I have to say something, I'd say that this is none of your fucking business."

"Oh, isn't that apt?" More than twenty years with this man, and today she's learning all kinds of new and gruesome things. "And here I thought you'd gone home in thirty-four to bury your mother."

"Don't try to go moral on me, Annie. I've spent all these years watching my step, expecting any day to trip over the piece of your heart that still belongs to him."

Not this again. Jealousy, the tie that binds and blinds. Life can be so wearying. Now that she knows the hourglass is running out, her patience and forbearing may be the first casualties of her final illness.

Her eye catches a spot toward the ceiling where the wallpaper curls away like a beckoning finger. Her knees shake for only a second getting up from the floor; then she drags the chair from the vanity to the wall, climbs up, and tugs the corner of the paper, enough to get a fistful. Most of the sheet follows her as she jumps from the chair. It rends the air more loudly than she would have imagined. She regards the naked expanse through narrowed eyes before picking up the chair and swinging with all her might at the wall. *Two outs, two strikes, bottom of the ninth.* A burst of lath and plaster rains down.

"Tear the house apart, Phil. Bust the walls to the studs. Peel back the roof; dig up the cellar. Excavate the yard. Bring me one shred of evidence of anything I ever did that will fit into even a corner of the shadow of what you've done."

How calm she feels as she shoves the bent vanity chair into the avalanche of rubble, kicking up a cloud of white dust. "I got locked up for this sort of conduct, you know. Perhaps I'm still insane. Or perhaps the men in my life make me so. Or is this my punishment for never officially marrying you?"

His defenses are already faltering. "I know this sounds weak, but I honestly believe this took nothing away from you. I'm here, aren't I? I love you. Do you hear me? I love you."

Someone this guilty shouldn't be able to look her in the eye as he is. "Sorry, Phil," she says evenly. "There's no putting lipstick on this pig."

The room snickers at them, the sound of tiny splinters of debris trickling from the gash in the wall. His words start as a trickle too, but soon split the dike.

"The letters began a few years after you came to live with me. She turned up in Oregon, without her brother Jack and without an explanation. Her feelings of guilt were monumental. I've sat a lifetime in church where they preach that everyone who repents deserves a second chance. I lived more than ten years with her; we brought four children into the world. I found I couldn't turn off those feelings and close my eyes to her suffering." He lowers himself into the maroon chair, fingering the piping on the arm.

"But I was not willing to undo what you and I had so painstakingly put together. You made it clear from the beginning that you would not give up the children, no matter what happened between us. They had made a life with you, and Nora with me. I never expected to hear from Diana again. It shocked and frightened me. I thought she might do herself harm, and wouldn't that have made things even worse? I'd brought her here, to a place she hated enough to abandon her children to escape. I've tortured myself all these years with how the kids might someday judge me for it."

He heaves himself out of the chair, skirts the pile of letters on the floor, and throws open the window. The heartbeat of the neighborhood rushes in: dogs barking at birds with laughable bravado, children playing Simon Says in the alley, a Bromo Seltzer jingle gasping from the ancient radio on the neighbor's kitchen sill. Annie envies the dogs, the children, and the hucksters, who needn't be alone in a room with betrayal. Thousands of times she's been alone in this room with him, the days, months, years playing like a flip book in her head, ending with this day that threatens to wipe out all others.

"I had to live with loving two women," he says. "Years and years trying to think, what is right here? What I came back to every time was that she gave birth to my children. But you are the one they think of as their mother."

"Thank you," Annie says to her clasped hands.

"You are their mother," he repeats fervently. "So I did the weak thing. Tried to play both sides. I convinced myself that it wasn't infidelity; it was penance I had to pay, for my role in the life of someone who wreaked horrible havoc she could never repair." He stops for breath, his jaw working with the effort of confession. "That job fell to you. You did it beautifully."

The mantel clock in the living room strikes one o'clock, and the lone chime hangs in the air.

Annie tilts her head and regards him with no emotion. "You needed a housekeeper. And a bedmate. You got what you needed."

"What if I did?" His green eyes burn. "As long as it's all coming out, let's be completely honest. You've always played the latter role a little half-heartedly. I used to wonder if that's just the way you are, but somehow I don't think so. You had a way of making sure I knew that you couldn't work up any passion for me.

The way you hug the edge of the bed, I've often wondered why you don't just sleep on the floor."

She starts to say, *Count on one hand the times I ever said no to you. About that or anything else.*

The words don't come, but it's as if he hears her thoughts. He suddenly sways as if someone has taken a club to the back of his knees, and for a moment she thinks he may collapse.

"It's too late to be questioning long-ago motives and actions," he presses. "In this town, children with only a father ended up in the church orphanage. Ninety percent of the kids in there weren't orphans. Why do I have to stand here and ask you if that sounds familiar?"

"Why do I have to sit here and listen to this? You hung on to—"

"I hung on, all right. By the skin of my teeth. With a ten-year-old son looking after his little sisters, dishing out bread and milk for supper when I had to work evenings. Buying time was as crucial to me as being able to buy food." His anger has ebbed again, and now he just looks old. *He wants absolution,* Annie thinks. Confession, forgiveness. She uncurls her clenched fingers. Even his God isn't all-forgiving. How is it that she should be?

"What is so awful about what we have together?" he asks. "If it was more about the children than us, so what? We played the cards we drew. It's been more than good enough in my book. You had the notion that you and Nora could make it alone, and maybe you could have. It was your determination and resilience that drew me to you in the first place. I did press my case with you most sincerely, but I did not hold a gun to your head. You can sit there in judgment of me today and decide that our life together has been nothing but a tumbleweed bouquet of lies and that I've been a faithless partner, but I will still stand by the job I did as Nora's father. I have always loved that girl as my own. And I will say it again. I do love you. But I think I've given up the right to ask you to believe me."

"You need to ask yourself if you believe it, Phillip."

The silence between them swells like a blister. When he does speak, it is one more agonizing admission.

"I guess we are never free of the ones with whom we create life."

How many more times today is she going to get her feet kicked out from under her? In a handful of words, he's spoken the greatest truth of their years together. He speaks of being beholden, but she feels instead release.

Never free of the ones with whom we create life, but she could tell him: *some make the effort, though it near kills us.* His secret is out, right there, splayed across the floor. And he's not the only one to ever get a letter from a bygone life. *You are entitled to derivative citizenship through your husband, should you join him in residence.* She moves to the window, flattens a shoulder against the casing.

She could pour the gasoline of her own secret over his and watch yet more of Annie and Phil, long-standing Copper Creek couple, go up in smoke. But then it wouldn't be a secret anymore, wouldn't be hers.

Annie slams the window shut and lets her eye rove around the room. The wall will have to be mended. Or she could move her things into another room and be done with this one. She cares little about the objects that fill the space. Their gaunt brass bed. A wobbly walnut highboy. Her vanity, the mirror in need of resilvering. The maroon velvet chair he won't part with. "It's special. Been in the family a while," he told her when she moved in.

He never said it belonged to his mother, or his grandmother.

It's special, all right. How many women can say they've slept decades with the same man, all the while with a voyeur in the room. A smoldering hatred for the chair stirs in her. It's irrational to hate a chair. But better she channel her hatred into the chair than slip into hating the man.

"Hers?" She tilts her head toward it.

His head hangs like a spent rose. "Wedding gift." He picks it up and strides out of the room. The back door bangs. Through the window she sees him boot the rickety gate and leave the chair in the alley. By morning it will have vanished.

The gate bangs again, and the door. Minutes tick by and he doesn't reappear. Perhaps he's gathering himself for whatever comes next. Perhaps he's not coming back.

He has no idea. But she can't see postponing it.

When he does return, she's seated on the bed and tells him calmly and without preamble, "I'm sick."

"Oh, so am I," he cries. "I never dreamed this would happen."

"No, I mean I'm really sick. I've seen the doctor this morning. The bleeding and the pelvic pain are cancer."

The words are out; she's only vaguely aware of his response. How his face crumples, how he falls to his knees and buries his face in her lap, sobbing, "My best friend . . . not ready for this . . . me who should be punished, not you."

"No one is being punished," she sighs. "All life comes to an end, and this is the way this one is ending."

"How can you be so calm? How . . . how long?"

"I didn't ask."

"How could you not ask?"

"At the moment, I guess I don't care. It will be the way it's going to be."

"I care! We still need you."

"Maybe you haven't noticed. The kids have wonderful families of their own. My work is done."

"No! The grandkids adore you. They'll be bereft without you."

"Grandchildren lose their grandparents. It's the way of the world." She stands up slowly. His head against her thighs seems so fragile. "I'm done talking about this now." His hands slide down the length of her as she moves away, stepping over the fan of letters covered in plaster shards, leaving him with the detritus of their afternoon.

In the kitchen, the percolator groans and strains to spit coffee through the bulb. She pours a cup but doesn't lift it, just listens to the sad music her spoon makes clinking around and around. They will not grow old together. The best is not yet to be.

From the bedroom come the sounds of restitution, broom and dustpan, vacuum cleaner, footsteps, clang of the trash-can lid. From the living room, the scrape of the fireplace screen, the thud of something hitting the grate, the spitting of a match followed by quiet hissing and faint smoky drift through the house.

Phil comes into the kitchen.

"Annie, I can't take this silence."

"Phil, I can't take more talk."

"I need to know if—"

"Then know it." She forces herself to put her arms around his waist and rest her head on his chest. It's not as difficult as she thought it would be. His embrace envelops her and carries the conviction of all that cannot be done away with between them. "Forgive yourself, and I'll do the same. But no more talk."

After a while he says, "Let's go to the movies. I need to be with you and you won't have to talk. How about it?"

The movies. Sure. Let's go to the movies, where three dimes buys you happily ever after.

35

The current of four weeks flows by. When she turns the page on her calendar, a shaft of late-summer light teases an 8 into an hourglass. The next calendar she buys will be her last. Lying sly among the march of days will be the one, a day passed blithely and forgettably for six decades. She feels more curious than afraid. At times it seems harder on Phil than on her. He comes near, drawn to her like a candle flame, only to pull back at the briefest touch, her warm skin, tepid affection, cool composure. Twice she hears him crying in fleeting bursts behind closed doors.

She cannot leave him. She cannot hate him. He gave her peace and safety that lasted more than a third of her life. Now her strength and stamina must be methodically rationed for what she alone needs. It doesn't come easily. When, if ever, has she put herself first? She begins to allow herself small luxuries, like this hour of afternoon rest in her bedroom.

The doorbell pings, followed by four knocks: one heavy, one sharp, two heavy, spelling out the visitor's initials in Morse code. After a count of ten, Nora will let herself into the house.

Annie hoists herself to a sitting position, grabbing the book on her nightstand and laying it open in her lap. She didn't tell the children about her surgery until it was over. To Nora she tried to shrug it off as "just another scar among many," but Nora knows a weak denial of an overwhelming truth when she sees one.

Annie smooths the bedspread and her hair and calls to Nora, her voice strong as she waves her in with "I'm just reading." She pats the bed for Nora to come sit.

"How are you today?" Nora leans to hug Annie, the bulk of her near-term pregnancy a warm knoll between them.

"The radiotherapy makes me tired. How are you? You're at that swallowed-a-beach-ball stage."

"The doctor says probably next week."

"Splendid." She held her breath nearly to the point of injury through Nora's first two pregnancies, both blessedly problem-free.

Nora runs a finger over the freshly painted wall. "Where's the maroon chair?"

Annie leans back and closes her eyes. So much for putting up a good show. "It reached the end of its useful life."

Nora climbs onto the bed, as she did hundreds of times as a child.

"Something has happened between you and Daddy, hasn't it?"

"A marriage is coming to its natural end." Annie speaks without opening her eyes. "One is going and one is staying, neither by choice, and that does tint things a bit, yes."

"Mom. It's more than that. I know it."

"What could be more than death?"

"There's something else."

"You know, your Jonathan is a wonderful husband and father, everything I could have wanted for you. But you will not make me privy to every detail of your marriage. You will not."

In the puddle of light falling on the bed, Annie sees herself and her daughter, two women who have meant everything to each other, contemplating a boundary they've never considered before. When Nora leans to push her shoes off, a wave of her palomino mane falls across her eyes. She tucks it behind her ear and looks into Annie's eyes.

"I want to know about my father."

"I can't imagine anything you couldn't ask him yourself that he wouldn't be able to answer better than I."

"Not Daddy. Adam Fielding. Adam W. Fielding. Somersworth, New Hampshire." Annie can almost see the words hanging in the air between them.

"Well." *Here's a deep subject.* Annie smiles. "It sounds like you're capable of coming up with your own information."

"I went to the courthouse and asked for my birth record. I remember being a Fielding, barely. How old was I when you married Daddy, when I took his name? Four?"

"It was never a secret, Nora. But I saw nothing to be gained by bringing it up in conversation, given our circumstances."

"Mom, all my life I've yearned to ask you about Adam

Fielding. I look like him, don't I? What else do you see of him in me? If I don't ask now, it will be too late." She leans closer and takes her mother's hand, sending a jolt to Annie's heart. "I saw on my birth record that I was the second child of that marriage. I want to name this baby after my sister or brother. I want to know what happened to him or her, and I want to *know my father.*"

"Oh, honey." Annie leans forward to gather her daughter in her arms. "Why not give the baby a name all its own?"

"Please stop dodging. Please. This one time, I'm going to dig until I get what I want."

Annie laughs, folding her knees and pulling them in, cornered. Nora is tenacious, and she learned from the best. "You want to know about your father. At the end of our first conversation, which was a doozy, he said, 'Analiese, you are something.' I returned the compliment. That's your legacy. You are really something too."

Their daughter waits.

"Nora, I have loved you more than life itself." She had to say that first. Then she closes her eyes again and speaks the name that has crossed her thoughts every day for decades but never, until now, her lips.

"Julia. Julia Ellen."

Baby Julian made his entrance before another sun had cleared the eastern horizon. Five days later, he sits in the crook of Annie's arm, regarding her with eyes too sage for a newborn. He stirs a calm in her. He seems to say, *I'll take it from here.*

"Tuesday's child is full of grace," Annie croons to the warm spot on the top of his head. "That's you." His blond fuzz fills her head with the nameless, timeless scent of life just beginning. "Your grandfather was a Tuesday's child. I always thought he must have been born on the stroke of midnight. He was more of a Monday's child, a little short on grace, but oh, if anything, fair of face."

Tears stand in Nora's eyes as Annie hands the baby back to her.

"I'm a Thursday's child," Annie says. "Thursday's child has far to go. Didn't I, though?"

And farther yet, it seems. The afternoon is brittle, cold, and dry. After she sees Nora to the door, Annie sits in the old horsehair chair, the sun through the front window filling her lap. Her grandson's new life bids her reconsider her own, what she's held back at each juncture, and what it has cost her. She makes a decision, rooted in what she views as fairness to those she loved best, and still within her power and her right to grant herself. Finally, she can love herself enough to do it.

The next day, in a phone booth at the back of a near-empty café at the edge of town, she feeds quarters into the slot. "Caswell, Montana, please," she says as casually as she can muster, the sound thundering off the dark walls and glass door. That night, she writes a letter that begins without salutation. *If in your heart . . .*

How will the letter be received, if it be received at all? It goes out on wings of slim faith, the only kind she's ever known.

She waits three weeks, then tells Phil she's going home. She won't stay long. She will be back.

"Iowa, after all these years? Why?" His voice quavers with bewilderment, anxiety. It's so far for her to go alone.

"Not Iowa," she says.

Going on forty years ago, she came to Caswell alone, a letter of invitation in her pocket. This time it is she who has issued the invitation, and the reply—accept or decline, with or without regrets—will not come through the mail, nor in words at all. Eight weeks have passed since Phil's secret spilled across their bedroom floor. The decision. The letter. The measured waiting.

The train crawls up to the shoe-box depot. Her heart speeds in dull uneasiness that she'll be recognized, silently called out by faces crosshatched with uncomfortable surprise. But she is the only one to alight. No one is around to notice when she steps onto the platform and stands, for those first few minutes, so still as to blend in with a becalmed midafternoon sky, the wide brim of her black felt hat hiding loosely finger-waved hair the color of night fog. Sun filters through the leaf-shaped cutouts at the edge of the hat, dappling her face like the warm fingerprints of a child.

As she moves to the edge of the platform, a young man, all lean muscle and bronzed face with no expression, materializes from the doorway of the depot and steps in front of her.

"Mrs. McCandless?"

Her breath catches in her throat. She tips her head forward, the brim of her hat shadowing her eyes. He doesn't look like the law. What quarrel could the law still have with her? Her thoughts race painfully. Perhaps she isn't the only one with unfinished business here. By some horrid stretch of ill fate, could she still be held responsible for long-held debts . . . or grudges?

And who knew she would be arriving now? Phil, but would he be so devious as to set up such an interception? The young man before her is brawny enough to muscle her onto a return train. Only two other people know she is here. But surely they wouldn't betray her—unless a heart has turned against her. It wouldn't be a first in this forsaken town, would it?

"I'm Isaak Hartmann," says the young man. "I'm sorry I startled you."

A messenger. The man is a messenger. But from whom?

"Mrs. Eulenberg sent me."

A rill of nausea parses through Annie. She clenches her teeth and swallows hard enough to force it out her ears.

"Has she changed her mind?" Annie whispers.

The youth looks puzzled. "I don't take your meaning, ma'am. I'm Mrs. Eulenberg's hired man. She says I'm to ask no questions, and to drop you a quarter mile past the turnoff to her place." He smiles, but only with his eyes. "And that none of this happened."

Through the window of Margrethe's old Chevy Master, Annie sees that time has been no kinder to the town than to her. Caswell has atrophied to a forlorn core of last-ones-standing against the insurmountable elements. A few blocks, and the town fades behind them.

The young man stops the car at the appointed place, and Annie waits by the side of the road until the sedan chugs from sight. Dear Margrethe. How foolish Annie was to think she could prance off that two-mile walk as she did thirty years ago. The ache in her bones sometimes ebbs, but never leaves completely. The surgery and the radiotherapy are buying her some time, but they cost dearly in vigor. The two-mile walk might have taken her hours.

What else about this dubious quest has she not thought through?

She walks slowly, deliberately. The byway narrows and winds past a dilapidated poultry house and the sunken remnants of an underground storage cache, ridge poles poking through the remaining roof boards. To her left sits an emaciated house few would know was once yellow, now reminiscent of aged bridal veiling, hemmed in by swaths of wild roses rambling below boarded-over windows. From the road, Annie fixes on the south corner of the porch, there, where she stood and clung to the sight of Adam melting away into the sunlight of their last morning together. To stand in that spot again would cleave her in two. She'll do it anyway, but not just yet. The yellow house isn't why she came. At the end of the road lies the object of her journey.

Still standing! Squatting ramshackle in the foot-tall grass, the little homestead sags, overgrown, weather-beaten but not defeated. Anyone who saw what Annie sees when she pushes the door open would think the crumbling shack empty. In her eyes it is anything but.

Like a well, the house fills from an unseen spring, waters bearing both virus and healing, tragedy and ecstasy. Annie's hand trails behind her as she moves through the shack, calling up memory through touch. The brick hearth where Cal's fancy stove once stood, the ladder to the loft. The window once kissed in sultry red, bearded now in decades of dust. Remembrance swells in front of her and overflows, out the red window, across a view untouched by time. The fields, the path to the river, the fruit trees. The wind sifting through the sieve of cottonwood branches, the meadowlark, the river, its odd-colored waters burbling autumn-quietly along. Look at it, all of it: it could be thirty years ago.

Her eye paces off a handful of yards between the shack and the fields. The spot draws her; she can feel it through her soles. Coming up the path between the wheat and the cottonwoods, the river ruffling alongside, that first sight of him, all sinew and hay-blondness and crystal-blue intensity.

You must be Cal's sister.
Charmed, I'm sure.

She spreads her hands across the yoke of her skirt, eyes tracking the road, a sonnet of expectation pulsing in her chest. Any minute now she should hear a truck growling over those ancient ruts.

The sound that reaches her isn't a truck, but a footfall. It's a small sound, but it carries under the big sky; she can hear it long before she can see who it might be. Now she can smile, because the truth is, he never liked that truck.

To see him again! How unchanged he is and yet how aged.

He walks, still straight enough, except where a satchel as battered as her own draws one shoulder lower. A cigarette dangles from his mouth; he takes a deep pull without touching it, exhales a bluish cloud, then tosses it, still glowing, into the road ahead, grinding it out without looking at it.

His fedora hides his hair; under it, his brows drift white like day-old snow. His binocular eyes cast a sharp arc, taking everything in, slowing his pace. Like she did, he pauses at the once-yellow house. Then he turns toward the shack. In the instant before he would see her in the doorway, she shrinks back.

To watch him in surreptitious silence like this is wicked and unfair, but she must.

Now he moves more slowly, toward the woods, leaving his satchel by the road. Beside a large moss-covered rock, he squats, balancing on the balls of his feet, placing his left hand over it. A moment later he brings his other hand to his face, fingers braced against his forehead, covering his features.

Annie can't imagine why a rock in the woods would pull him down so, or why it pulls her, too. Suddenly burning under her coat, she pushes the buttons through their slots until it hangs open, a shy invitation. She takes a step toward the door.

But he rises abruptly and strides to the old toolshed; it too still stands, though listing at an angle that flouts gravity. He emerges with a shovel. At the road's edge, he removes his overcoat and suit jacket, folds them in fours, and lays them atop his satchel. He moves a few paces beyond the moss-covered rock and leans the shovel against a thigh that seems slight beneath the gray trousers. When he folds his shirtsleeves back, two folds, this far, just so, creasing the edges, Annie fears she might faint.

He digs into ground softened by recent rain, but he is old and the work is hard. What is he doing? Annie clutches the neck of her blouse, feeling that her watching game has turned sinister but finding herself unable to move. The digging intrigued her for the first few shovelfuls, but now she's frightened. He stops every third or fourth spade, recovering his breath, sometimes gazing into the hole, sometimes gazing away to the river as if he can't believe it's still there. His finger traces light circles over his chest, as if he can't believe his heart is still there too.

He labors on, stooping lower as the hole deepens, while she

screams silent abuse at herself. He isn't well; she must stop him. When he pauses to undo his tie and open his collar, she moves the door aside. It acquiesces noisily, and she stands against the frame.

What words, what words? As he nears, he draws her as he always did. She moves, hands clenched in pockets, to close the distance, until the buttons of her coat all but touch him. The smell of train and time and Chesterfields can't mask the essence of him; it fills her head as it did the day he backed her against the doorway of the shack. *Tell me how you knew my horse was missing something.*

She can only stare at his chest, the layers of fabric over his heart, the crisp shirt, the smooth striped vest. She can't help it: she leans in to him, her forehead resting against him. His hand goes to the back of her head, a gentle caress for a few moments, then pressing her to him.

Adam. She mouths the syllables soundlessly, as if she must practice before giving voice to the name she hasn't uttered for nearly half a lifetime. Unnamable emotions pile atop one another until she must defend herself by feeling nothing.

When she raises her head, their eyes unite—oh, the indescribable melding of the knowing, the not knowing. "They say you see something when you look into a horse's eyes," she whispers. "What do you see?"

He draws her left hand from her pocket and raises it to his lips. His touch electrifies.

"Something missing."

A silver thimble speaks for both of them, warm and lustrous from its berth in her coat pocket. She hands it to him, and without hesitation he places it on the third finger of her left hand. From his own pocket comes another thimble, homely, deformed, and well traveled, but it too has come full circle: FR DR OODS G O COFFEEN'S. He places it in her palm and her fingers close around.

With her thimbled hand in both of his, he leads her into the trees, past the mossy stone. Their eyes meet as he picks up the shovel and again sinks the blade into the ground. His barely there smile colors his face with a quiet something she would have to coin a new word to describe.

He squares the corners as he deepens the opening in the earth. She bends to move the mossy stone out of his way, but he stays her hand without a sound. Down and down he digs. By and by the spade thunks against metal. Grabbing a long leather lead, hand over hand, he guides from the earth a trunk as brown as the cradle where it has obviously lain for many years, deep enough and sealed tight enough to withstand the floods. A blow from the shovel placed just right shatters a padlock worthy of a jail cell. He still packs quite a wallop for an old man.

She wouldn't be human if she didn't feel a surge of anticipation when he lifts the lid and painstakingly peels away layers and layers of protective packing. When did he acquire this kind of patience? How meticulously this treasure, whatever it is, has been cared for. He brings it into the light, and the only two people who have ever laid eyes upon it do so again. A shower of stars across a dark sapphire sky. Beneath the stars, a jubilant chrome-orange waxing crescent moon. Beneath the moon, a faded green river cut by faint triplet arcs of off-white, curving through the night.

Here they are, two as one, Thursday's child, whose journey has ended, and Tuesday's child, who has found his grace. She fits under his chin with room to spare. They have nothing between them. The distance between heaven and earth dissolves under *The River by Starlight*.

He knocks the boards off the bedroom window of their once-yellow house with a crowbar from the shed. They lie together on a bed of hay and army surplus blankets left by Margrethe in the otherwise empty house. Time has softened their bodies even as life has chiseled away at them. The years have folded his edges in. The pleating of the corners of his eyes, the shallow, desert-sand wrinkling of the pale skin of his arms. His lips move along the palliated scars of her belly, sealing them at last. They always belonged to him.

When, too soon, pink light strafes the bank of the river, he gathers her to him as a delicate spoon and says, "I couldn't stand not knowing where you were."

"I don't want to know how you found me. Please don't tell me."

"You might have answered me."

"Silence was the only *no* you would have accepted. I could not take Nora from the man she knew as her father. He never treated her as less than his own."

"And you? How has he treated you? As his own?"

What is she to say? That there is enough faithlessness to go around and it all seems to negate itself?

"Your silence. Your loyalty," he continues. "He must have done something to betray it. Or you wouldn't be here."

"I have never spoken of you to him. I won't speak of him to you."

"He's betrayed you, and you're protecting him."

Still possessive, still digging. She sighs. He hasn't changed, but neither has she. The truth but not the whole truth will have to serve; it can do neither of them good to share the god-awful truth. "He could say the same of you. Shall we fight, Adam? To the bitter end? That would be bitter indeed."

The sparrow tracks around his eyes dampen. "So now we come to it, Annie. Why now?"

It's hard to say the words again, to another man who cares for her; *cancer* and *uterus* circle in the air above them and clash. It's hard to watch him wince, to listen to him rasp, "Not fair!"

She lays her hand over the arm around her waist and sighs, "What ever has been fair? And you?" she asks. "I saw you digging. How is your health?"

"Fair," he says. He waves a hand vaguely. "Heart. Inflammation. It will kill me sooner or later if something else doesn't finish the job first. Death by our most vulnerable organs. Is that fair?"

"My fair one," she says, slipping her fingers into the soft hair along his temple, "I can't answer that."

After a while he asks, "Have you been happy?"

"I've been content. And happy to have been that." She pushes her head back into the hollow of his shoulder. And though her life-long conviction warns her not to, she overrides it long enough to force out one question. "What's under the mossy rock?"

"Our first child. Our almost-child," he says. She turns in his arms, hers flying around his neck, her face pressing against his. "Having to leave this all again is going to be harder than I could have imagined," he whispers. The wetness seeps between their cheeks. Annie releases her hold and wipes his cheek with her sleeve.

"I didn't know if you'd come," she says. "But I hoped. I brought you something." She reaches into her satchel next to the bed and hands him a book.

"Thoreau," he says. He turns the pages slowly. "'June 15, 1852. 'The River by Starlight.'"

"And this." Annie turns to the entry for September 27, 1852.

From the mountains we do not discern our native hills;
but from our native hills we look out easily to the far
blue mountains. . . . I see the very peak . . . but how
much I do not see, that is between me and it! How much
I overlook! In this way we see stars.

She closes the book gently. "We saw stars together many
times. Didn't we?"

He rolls onto his back and holds the book to his chest. "You
never said goodbye, you realize that? I came home and you were
gone. You left the back door open. I understand now. . . . I lived on
that all these years." He closes his eyes. "I don't want to leave you."

"And you never will." She kisses the hollow behind his ear.
"Where I'm going . . . I will find a way to let you know."

The lights in the Eulenberg house across the fields go off one
by one as the sun rises higher.

"Will we see them before we go?" Adam asks.

"No." They curl into spoons again, the chanting of the river
filling her head. "I knew you had sold to them. I called Margrethe
to ask if they still owned the place, and if we might sneak in and
out. She understood. She sends her love."

Adam pulls her closer. "Her last words to me were, 'I still pray
you will find your way back to Annie.'"

"Then a good woman's prayer has been answered."

"Will you take the quilt to Nora?" he whispers. "It's all I've
ever wanted for it."

"No," she says. "Not me." She reaches for her coat and takes
a small, heavy envelope from the pocket. Inside is a cabinet photo
of a young woman looking over her shoulder, her pale blond waves
caught up in a gorgeous mantilla-style tortoiseshell comb. On the
back, an address. "To look at her is to know she's yours, and you
are hers. The comb. You chose it, or perhaps it chose you. She says
she feels your touch, through the comb, as I always did." She lays
her cheek against his, hoping to draw from him something she can
carry within when she goes. "I don't have much time. She will let
you know. We have spoken of it."

"Oh God. What did you say?"

"That we charged hell with a bucket of cold water and got
separated in the fray."

"I can't imagine how she judges me." He touches one finger to Nora's cheek. "I'm scared. More than I can ever recall."

"No need to vex yourself with what we can't know yet." His heart beats faster, slower, faster again where she leans against him. What a terrible double-edged wait he faces. Knowing what is near and inevitable and dreaded. Knowing that beyond it lies the thing he most wants and most fears. "Tell her what you know. You can't make a mistake. Trust that."

Full circle, as blond as the light rising through the trees, this final sun they will see with each other, this consummation of all things that matter. With the cabinet photo between them, at long last they hold their child in their arms together. Their most cherished dream will live on, carrying and passing on the best of themselves.

No need for him to try, as he is now, to undam all that was never said. Of all the ways they loved each other without ever uttering the word, of the bottomless sorrow and regret that will never release him, and of the soul-crushing brew of jealousy and gratitude he feels for "your man," whose name he can't bring himself to speak.

"Shhhh," she says. "I know. *I know.*"

"Please let me say these things. No one in this world has ever awed me more than you. You have always been the most generous person I will ever know. Here you are, sharing Nora with me despite my failing you, and her, and myself."

"So you had nothing to do with raising her. But everything to do with her being alive," Annie says. "Is that not important enough? You'll have to go to her believing that."

The sun will see them down opposite paths today, for the last time, but it is not the end. She can look directly at the swelling light and it doesn't hurt her eyes. With a sense of wonder that there are still things she can learn in this life, she asks, "Can you see behind the sun?" and he answers only, "Analiese," repeating it twice, three, four times. She understands: he hasn't spoken her name since they parted, and never will again. When he speaks to Nora, Annie will be "your mother," or perhaps he'll even lapse into "my wife."

She can see behind the sun. Soon enough, a river of stars will light their way. In the predawn pall of a buff sandstone church in a

Montana mining town, the flicker of one candle will be enough to prevail over the darkness. A young woman with pale blond waves held in a tortoiseshell comb will lift folded hands to her heart and offer a prayer to the memory of Analiese Fielding, and for the joy of knowing that her parents have seen their way safely home.

The River by Starlight
Questions for Group Discussion

1. Annie remembers her pa's Civil War wound leaving him feeling forever that he was "missing something." Later, Annie remarks that Adam's horse is "missing something." How does this theme of "missing something" manifest itself throughout Annie's and Adam's lives?

2. Annie takes a long time making a decision about Adam's proposal and, later, Phil's. What is the tipping point for each choice? Are they both sound decisions?

3. Consider the gender double standards throughout the story. What behaviors does Adam get away with that have grave consequences when Annie does the same thing?

4. Annie is adamant that she does not want to know the details of Adam's past, or Phil's. Is this wise? Who, if anyone, benefits from her insistence that the past remain private?

5. Contrast Adam's expectations of Annie ("I want enough output from you to export") with Phil's ("What I don't provide we don't need"). In what ways do their expectations confirm or contradict Annie's understanding of "partnership"?

6. What choices does Annie make to keep her children safe? Are all these choices sacrifices? Are any of them mistakes?

7. When Nora knows that Annie is dying, she says, "I want to know about my father." What—and how much—do you think Annie tells her?

8. In the final moments of their time together, Adam asks if Annie has been happy. She replies that she has been "content. And happy to have been that." What answer do you think Adam wanted? How does Annie's answer make you feel?

9. Why, at the end, does Nora offer her prayer to the memory of Analiese Fielding rather than Analiese McCandless?

10. Discuss the theme of abandonment. How is each character affected by feelings of having been abandoned—and of having abandoned others? Annie and Adam each harbor feelings of abandonment about the other, though their perspectives change over the course of their years apart. Does their reunion in Caswell resolve these feelings?

Author's Note

Those who read initial drafts of this book invariably asked, "Were Annie and Adam real?" And I would respond, "Do you think they were?" before answering the question. An early edit of the book, seven years before publication, came back marked up with numerous notations of "Absurd!" next to things that had in fact happened, because, yes—Annie and Adam were real. When I relayed this back to the editor, the comments of "Absurd!" changed to "Remarkable!"

The research for this book took me far beyond what made it onto the page. The numbers do and don't tell the story. Fourteen research trips, writing residencies, and solitary retreats. More than forty libraries and archives. More than a mile—maybe two—of microfilm newspaper accounts and records from more than a dozen states and provinces. Amassing my own collection of more than eighty books and thousands of pages of records and narratives. Always, the need to know just one more thing, and one more and one more, spurred me on. Still, elusive gaps remained. At some point I had to stop researching and tell the story from what I knew or sensed, what I accepted or interpreted, from the aggregation of facts and from the ethereal perspective that came with walking in Annie's and Adam's very footsteps across Montana, North Dakota, and Alberta.

So while the framework of the story is true, *The River by Starlight* is a work of fiction. Some of the characters are based on real people, although most are composites, with their personalities and actions largely invented. Other characters were wholly invented by me. Some locations are composites; some are real.

What mattered most to me was bringing forth the themes of the story: giving voice to women of that era who faced mental health issues with few or no resources, and illuminating in starkest terms what it could cost them. As the story unfolded, the issue of gender double standards seemed to magnify. Even today, women battle stigma, societal rejection, loss of parental rights, and financial devastation along with their mental illnesses, and even today, women are held to a different standard than men for the very same actions.

As I wrote, however, something unexpected happened. I began to see that there was more, much more, to Adam's perspective, and that his too was a story virtually never told: the yearning to be a father, strong enough to drive him to unthinkable actions; the grief that engulfed him when the dream of home and family was crushed. How confounded, fearful, and helpless must husbands of women with postpartum psychosis have felt? The uncomfortable questioning if it was in any percentage their fault. Stings of conscience, of shame, for being unequal to the challenge, enough to want out, enough that love became an unaffordable luxury, though the cost would be lifelong regret.

So as much as Annie and Adam's story is based in truth, it was left to me to fill in a great deal, and it became a tale of what might have been, or could have been, or perhaps should have been.

From the time I first considered writing Annie's story to the day *The River by Starlight* was published, more than twelve years passed. In that time, I had the assistance and guidance of a small army of people, at every stage, for countless details. They provided facts, insights, encouragement. They welcomed me to their institutions and businesses. They arranged access to people and places I would not otherwise have had; they gave me documents, artifacts, and photos I would not otherwise have been able to obtain. They invited me into their homes, even into their families. My coldest fear is that if I begin to name names, I'll leave someone out. So to all of you, with all the appreciation, admiration, and affection I hope I expressed at the time our paths crossed: You know who you are, and I am beholden.

I did have muses. Brittney Corrigan-McElroy and Wendy Cook walked this long, long road with me, reading and editing revisions beyond number with supernatural patience and gusto, year after year. I'm glad they know my heart, because no adequate words of thanks exist.

Abundant thanks to my visionary publisher, Brooke Warner, and the She Writes Press and SparkPoint Studios teams, to my remarkable rainmaker publicist Caitlin Hamilton Summie, and to Karen Sherman for her masterful editing and compassionate coaching, without which the book would not have risen to its highest and best self.

I thank my sons, Connor and Bryce, for their calm confidence that I could and would finish the book. Last and best, I thank my husband Mark, who deemed the book "a member of the family" and unfalteringly supported what he called my "grand adventure." In that, he gets the final word, because the multifarious and some-times mercurial meaning of family and its power to shape us is indeed what the grand adventure was and always will be about.

About the Author

An internationally renowned author, Ellen Notbohm's work has informed and delighted millions in more than twenty languages and on every continent. In addition to her award-winning books on autism, her work has spanned a diversity of subjects including history, genealogy, education, baseball, writing, and community affairs. A lifelong resident of Oregon, Ellen is an avid genealogist, knitter, beachcomber, and thrift store hound who has never knowingly walked by a used bookstore without going in and dropping coin. *The River by Starlight* is her first novel.

Author photo © Andie Petkus Photography

Selected Titles from She Writes Press

She Writes Press is an independent publishing company founded to serve women writers everywhere. Visit us at www.shewritespress.com.

The Vintner's Daughter by Kristen Harnisch. $16.95, 978-163152-929-0. Set against the sweeping canvas of French and California vineyard life in the late 1890s, this is the compelling tale of one woman's struggle to reclaim her family's Loire Valley vineyard—and her life.

The Rooms Are Filled by Jessica Null Vealitzek. $16.95, 978-1-938314-58-2. The coming-of-age story of two outcasts—a nine-year-old boy who just lost his father, and a closeted young woman—brought together by circumstance.

Lum by Libby Ware. $16.95, 978-1-63152-003-7. In Depression-era Appalachia, an intersex woman without a home of her own plays the role of maiden aunt to her relatives—until an unexpected series of events gives her the opportunity to change her fate.

Eliza Waite by Ashley Sweeney. $16.95, 978-1-63152-058-7. When Eliza Waite chooses to leave a stagnant life in rural Washington State and join the masses traveling north to Alaska in 1898 during the tumultuous Klondike Gold Rush, she encounters challenges and successes in both business and love.

The End of Miracles by Monica Starkman. $16.95, 978-1-63152-054-9. When a pregnancy following years of infertility ends in late miscarriage, Margo Kerber sinks into a depression—one that leads her, when she encounters a briefly unattended baby, to commit an unthinkable crime.

A Cup of Redemption by Carole Bumpus. $16.95, 978-1-938314-90-2. Three women, each with their own secrets and shames, seek to make peace with their pasts and carve out new identities for themselves.